The critics on Lawrence Block

'Scudder is one of the most appealing series characters around' *LA Times*

'Bull's-eye dialogue and laser-image description . . . any search for false notes will prove futile . . . [Block's] eye for detail is as sharp as ever, and characters almost real enough to touch abound' *New York Times Book Review*

'Fast-paced, insightful, and so suspenseful it zings like a high-tension wire' Stephen King

'Outstanding . . . excellent . . . smoothly paced, deftly plotted, brightly phrased study of perversity'
Chicago Tribune

'One of the very best writers now working the beat'
Wall Street Journal

'Cries out to be read at night . . . First class . . . Tough and sharp . . . It would be hard to find a better mystery'
People

'Absolutely riveting . . . Block is terrific'
Washington Post

'What he does best – writing popular fiction that always respects his readers' desire to be entertained but never insults their intelligence' *GQ*

'There with the best . . . The real McCoy with a shocking twist and stylish too' *Observer*

Lawrence Block is a Grandmaster of the Mystery Writers of America and has won a total of fourteen awards for his fiction, including one Edgar award and two Shamus awards for best novel for titles in the Matt Scudder series. He is also the creator of other great detectives such as Bernie Rhodenbarr, Evan Tanner and Chip Harrison and has written dozens of award-winning short stories. Lawrence Block lives in New York City.

ALSO BY LAWRENCE BLOCK

The Sins of the Fathers
Time to Murder and Create
In the Midst of Death
A Stab in the Dark
Eight Million Ways to Die
When the Sacred Ginmill Closes
Out on the Cutting Edge
A Ticket to the Boneyard
A Dance at the Slaughterhouse
A Walk Among the Tombstones
The Devil Knows You're Dead
Even the Wicked
Hit Man
Everybody Dies

A LONG LINE OF DEAD MEN
A MATT SCUDDER NOVEL

Lawrence Block

ORION

An Orion Paperback

First published in Great Britain by Orion in 1995
This paperback edition published in 1999 by
Orion Books Ltd,
Orion House, 5 Upper St Martin's Lane,
London WC2H 9EA

Typeset at The Spartan Press Ltd,
Lymington, Hants
Printed and bound in Great Britain by
Clays Ltd, St Ives plc

I that in heill wes and gladnes,
Am trublit now with gret seiknes,
And feblit with infermitie;
    Timor mortis conturbat me.

Our plesance here is all vain glory,
This fals world is but transitory,
The flesche is brukle, the Feynd is slee;
    Timor mortis conturbat me.

The stait of man does change and vary,
Now sound, now seik, now blith, now sary,
Now dansand mery, now like to dee;
    Timor mortis conturbat me.

No stait in Erd here standis sicker;
As with the wynd wavis the wicker,
Wavis this warldis vanitie;
    Timor mortis conturbat me.

On to the dead gois all Estatis,
Princis, prelotis, and Potestatis,
Baith rich and pur of all degree;
    Timor mortis conturbat me.

He sparis no lord for his piscence,
Na clerk for his intelligence;
His awfull straik may no man flee;
    Timor mortis conturbat me.

Sen he hes all my brether tane,
He will nocht lat me lif alane,
On force I mun his next prey be;
    Timor mortis conturbat me.

WILLIAM DUNBAR
Lament for the Makers

Look at the mourners:
Bloody great hypocrites!
Isn't it grand, boys, to be bloody well dead?
Let's not have a sniffle
Let's have a bloody good cry!
And always remember the longer you live
The sooner you'll bloody well die!
– an Irish Lullaby

ONE

It must have been around nine o'clock when the old man stood up and tapped his spoon against the bowl of his water glass. Conversations died around him. He waited until he had full silence, then took another long moment to scan the room. He took a small sip of water from the glass he'd been tapping, set it on the table in front of him, and placed his hands palm-down on either side of the glass.

Standing as he did, with his angular frame tilted forward, his thin beak of a nose jutting out, his white hair swept straight back and combed down flat, his pale blue eyes magnified by thick lenses, he put Lewis Hildebrand in mind of a figure carved on the prow of a Viking ship. Some great idealized bird of prey, scanning the horizon, seeing for miles and miles, for years and years.

'Gentlemen,' he said. 'Friends.' He paused, and again worked the room's four tables with his eyes. 'My brothers,' he said.

He let the phrase echo, then leavened the solemnity with a quick smile. 'But how could we be brothers? You range in age from twenty-two to thirty-three, while I have somehow contrived to be eighty-five years old. I could be the grandfather of the oldest man here. But tonight you join me as part of something that stretches across years, across centuries. And we shall indeed leave this room as brothers.'

Did he pause for a sip of water? Let's suppose that he did. And then he reached into a pocket of his suit jacket and drew out a piece of paper.

I

'I have something to read to you,' he announced. 'It won't take long. It's a list of names. Thirty names.' He cleared his throat, then tilted his head to peer at his list through the lower portion of his bifocal lenses.

'Douglas Atwood,' he said. 'Raymond Andrew White. Lyman Baldridge. John Peter Garrity. Paul Goldenberg. John Mercer . . .'

I've made up the names. There's no record of the list, nor did Lewis Hildebrand recall any of the names the old man intoned. It was his impression that most of them were English or Scotch-Irish, with a couple of Jews, a few Irish, a handful that would have been Dutch or German. The names were not in alphabetical order, nor was there any evident scheme to them; he was to learn later that the old man had read their names in the order of their death. The first name read – not Douglas Atwood, although I've called him that – was the first man to die.

Listening to the old man, hearing the names echo against the room's wood-paneled walls like clods of earth falling on a coffin lid, Lewis Hildebrand had found himself moved almost to tears. He felt as though the earth had opened at his feet and he was gazing into an infinite void. There was a pause of some length after the reading of the final name, and it seemed to him that time itself had stopped, that the stillness would stretch on forever.

The old man broke it. He took a Zippo lighter from his breast pocket, flipped its cap, spun its wheel. He lit a corner of the sheet of paper and held it by its opposite end while it burned. When the flame had largely consumed the paper, he laid what remained in an ashtray and waited until it was ashes.

'You will not hear those names again,' he told them. 'They are gone now, gone to wherever the dead go. Their chapter has closed. Ours has just begun.'

He was still holding the Zippo, and he held it up, lit it, and snapped it shut. 'This is the fourth day of May,' he said, 'in the year 1961. When I first sat with the thirty men whose names I've read to you, it was the third of May and the year was 1899. The Spanish-American War had ended just ten months ago. I myself was twenty-three years old, just a year older than the youngest of you. I had not fought in the war, although there were men in the room who had. And there was one man who had served with Zachary Taylor in the war with Mexico. He was seventy-eight years old, if I remember correctly, and I sat and listened to him read the names of thirty men of whom I'd never heard. And I watched him burn those names, but of course he did so by putting a wooden match to the list. There were no Zippo lighters that day. And that gentleman – I could tell you his name but I won't, I spoke it for the last time a few minutes ago – that gentleman was twenty or twenty-five when he saw another old man set another list of names afire, and that would have been when? The early 1840s, I would suppose. Did they have wooden matches then? I don't believe they did. There would have been a fire on the hearth, and I suppose the fellow – and I couldn't tell you *his* name if I wanted to – I suppose he dropped the list into the fire.

'I don't know the date of that meeting, or where it took place. My first meeting, as I said, was in 1899, and there were thirty-one of us in a private dining room on the second floor of John Durlach's restaurant on Union Square. It's long gone, and so's the building that housed it; the site's occupied now by Klein's Department Store. When Durlach's closed we tried a different restaurant

3

each year until we settled on Ben Zeller's steak house. We were there for years, and then there was a change in ownership twenty years ago and we weren't happy. We came here to Cunningham's and we've been here ever since. Last year there were two of us. This year there are thirty-one.'

And where was Matthew Scudder on the fourth day of May in the Year of Our Lord 1961?

I might have been at Cunningham's. Not in one of the private dining rooms with the old man and his thirty new brothers, but standing at the bar or seated in the main dining room, or at a table in the smaller grill room that Vince Mahaffey liked. I'd have been twenty-two, with less than two weeks until my twenty-third birthday. Six months had passed since I cast my first vote. (They hadn't yet lowered the voting age to eighteen.) I voted for Kennedy. So, apparently, did a great many tombstones and empty lots in Cook County, Illinois, and he won by a nose.

I was still single, although I had already met the girl I would soon marry, and eventually divorce. I wasn't long out of the Police Academy, and they'd assigned me to a Brooklyn precinct and teamed me up with Mahaffey, figuring I'd learn something from him. He taught me plenty, some of it stuff they didn't much want me to know.

Cunningham's was Mahaffey's kind of place, with a lot of dark hand-rubbed wood and red leather and polished brass, tobacco smoke hanging in the air and hard booze in most of the glasses. There was a decent variety of beef and seafood dishes on the menu, but I think I must have had the same meal every time I went there – a shrimp cocktail, a thick sirloin, a baked potato with sour cream. Pie for dessert, pecan or apple, and a cup of coffee strong

4

enough to skate on. And booze, of course. A martini to start, ice-cold and bone-dry and straight up with a twist, and a brandy after to settle the stomach. And then a little whiskey to clear the head.

Mahaffey taught me how to eat well on a patrolman's salary. 'When a dollar bill floats down from the skies and happens to land in your outstretched hand,' he said, 'close your fingers around it, and praise the Lord.' A fair amount of dollars rained down on us, and we had a lot of good meals together. More of them would have been at Cunningham's but for its location. It was in Chelsea, at the corner of Seventh Avenue and Twenty-third Street, and we were across the river in Brooklyn, just five minutes away from Peter Luger's. You could have the same meal there, in pretty much the same atmosphere.

You still can, but Cunningham's is gone. Back in the early seventies they served their last steak. Somebody bought the building and knocked it down to put up a twenty-two-story apartment house. For a few years after I made detective I was stationed at the Sixth Precinct in Greenwich Village, about a mile from Cunningham's. I guess I got there once or twice a month during those years. But by the time they closed the place I had turned in my gold shield and moved to a small hotel room on West Fifty-seventh Street. I spent most of my time at Jimmy Armstrong's saloon around the corner. I had my meals there, met my friends there, transacted business at my regular table at the back, and did my share of serious drinking. So I never even noticed when Cunningham's Steak House, est. 1918, closed the doors and turned off the lights. Sometime after the fact I guess somebody must have told me, and I suppose the news called for a drink. Almost everything did, those days.

But let's get back to Cunningham's, and back to the first

5

Thursday in May of 1961. The old man – but why keep calling him that? His name was Homer Champney, and he was telling them about beginnings.

'We are a club of thirty-one,' he said. 'I've told you that my membership dates back to the last year of the last century, and that the man who spoke at my first meeting was born eight years after the War of 1812. And who spoke at *his* first meeting? And when did the first group of thirty-one assemble and vow to convene annually until only one of their number was left alive?

'I don't know. No one knows. There are vague references to clubs of thirty-one in various arcane histories down through the centuries. My own research suggests that the first club of thirty-one was an offshoot of Free-masonry over four hundred years ago, but it is arguable on the basis of a section in the Code of Hammurabi that a club of thirty-one had been established in ancient Babylonia, and that another, or perhaps a branch of the same one, existed among the Essene Jews at the time of Christ. One source indicates that Mozart was a member of such a club, and similar rumors have surfaced involving Benjamin Franklin, Sir Isaac Newton, and Dr Samuel Johnson. There's no way of knowing how many clubs have sprung up over the years, and how many chains have maintained their continuity across the generations.

'The structure is simple enough. Thirty-one men of honorable character pledge themselves to assemble an-nually on the first Thursday in May. They take food and drink, they report on the changes the year has brought to their lives, and they note with reverence the passing of those members claimed by death. Each year we read the names of the dead.

'When there is one man left of the thirty-one, he does as I have done. He finds thirty ideal candidates for membership and brings them all together on an appointed

6

evening. He reads, as I have read to you, the names of his thirty departed brothers. He burns the list of names, closing one chapter, opening another.

'And so we go on, my brothers. We go on.'

According to Lewis Hildebrand, the most memorable thing about Homer Champney was his intensity. He had retired years before that night in '61, had sold the small manufacturing firm he'd founded and was evidently quite comfortably fixed. But he had started out in sales, and Hildebrand had no trouble believing he'd been a successful salesman. Something made you hang on every word he spoke, and the longer he talked the more fervent he became, and the more you wanted to hear what he had to say.

'You are not well acquainted with one another,' he told them. 'Perhaps you knew one or two of the people in this room before tonight. There might even be as many as three or four you count as friends. Prior friendships aside, it is unlikely that much of your lifelong social circle will be found in this room. Because this organization, this structure, is not concerned with friendship in the usual sense. It is not about social interaction or mutual advantage. We are not here to trade stock tips or sell each other insurance. We are closely yoked, my brothers, but we walk a very narrow path toward an extremely specific goal. We mark one another's progress on the long march to the grave.

'The demands of membership are small. There are no monthly meetings to attend, no committees on which to serve. There's no membership card to carry, no dues to pay beyond your proportionate share of the cost of the annual dinner. Your only commitment, and I ask that you be utterly committed to it, is your annual attendance on the first Thursday in May.

'There will be years when you may not wish to show

up, when attendance seems inconvenient in the extreme. I urge you to regard this one commitment as unalterable. Some of you will have moved away from New York, and may find the prospect of an annual return burdensome. And there may be times when you think of the club itself as silly, as something you have outgrown, as a part of your life you would prefer to cast aside.

'Do not do it! The club of thirty-one plays a very small part in any member's life. It takes up but one night a year. And yet it gives our lives a focus that other men never know. My young brothers, you are links in a chain that reaches back unbroken to the founding of this republic, and you are part of a tradition with its roots in ancient Babylon. Every man in this room, every man ever born, spends his life approaching his death. Every day he takes another step in death's direction. It is a hard road to walk alone, a much easier road to walk in good company.

'And, if your path is the longest and you should turn out to be the last to finish, you have one further obligation. It will be up to you to find thirty young men, thirty fine men of promise, and bring them together as I have brought you together, to forge one more link in the chain.'

Repeating Champney's words three decades later, Lewis Hildebrand seemed a little embarrassed by them. He said that they probably sounded silly, but not when you heard Homer Champney say them.

The old man's energy was contagious, he said. You caught his fever, but it wasn't just a matter of getting swept up in his enthusiasm. Later on, when you'd had a chance to cool off, you still bought what he'd sold you. Because he'd somehow made you understand something you never would have seen otherwise.

★

'There's one further part of the evening's program,' Champney told them. 'We'll go around the room. Each man in turn will stand up and tell us four things about himself. His name, his present age, the most interesting fact he can tell about himself, and how he feels now, right now, about embarking on this great journey with his thirty fellows.

'I'll begin, although I've probably covered all four points already. Let me see. My name is Homer Gray Champney. I'm eighty-five years old. The most interesting thing I can think of about me, aside from my being the surviving member of the club's last chapter, is that I attended the Pan-American Exposition in Buffalo in 1901 and shook the hand of President William McKinley less than an hour before he was assassinated by that anarchist, and what was his name? Czolgosz, of course, Leon Czolgosz. Who could forget that poor misguided wretch?

'And how do I feel about what we're doing tonight? Well, boys, I'm excited. I'm passing the torch and I know I'm placing it in good and capable hands. Ever since the last man of the old group died, ever since I got the word, I've had the most awful fear of dying before I could carry on my mission. So it's a great load off my mind, and a feeling of, oh, of a great beginning.

'But I'm running off at the mouth. Four sentences, really, is all that's required, name, age, fact, and feeling. We'll start at this table, I think, with you, Ken, and we'll just go around . . .'

'I'm Kendall McGarry, I'm twenty-four, and the most interesting fact about me is that an ancestor of mine signed the Declaration of Independence. I don't know how I feel about joining the club. Excited, I guess, and also that it's a big step, although I don't know why it should be. I mean, it's just one night a year . . .'

'John Youngdahl, twenty-seven. The most interesting . . . well, just about the *only* fact about me I can think of these days is I'm getting married a week from Sunday. That's got my head so scrambled I can't tell you how I feel about anything, but I have to say I'm glad to be here, and to be a part of all this . . .'

'I'm Bob Berk. That's B-e-r-k, not B-u-r-k-e, so I'm Jewish, not Irish, and I don't know why I seem to feel compelled to mention that. Maybe *that's* the most interesting thing about me. Not that I'm Jewish, but that it's the first thing out of my mouth. Oh, I'm twenty-five, and how do I feel? Like you all belong here and I don't, but that's how I always feel, and I'm probably not the only person here who feels that way, right? Or maybe I am, I don't know . . .'

'Brian O'Hara, and that's with an apostrophe and a capital *H*, so I'm Irish, not Japanese . . .'

'I'm Lewis Hildebrand. I'm twenty-five. I don't know if it's interesting, but I'm one-eighth Cherokee. As for how I feel, I can hardly say how I feel. I have the sense of being a part of something much larger than myself, something that started before me and will extend beyond my lifetime . . .'

'I'm Gordon Walser, age thirty. I'm an account executive at Stilwell Reade and Young, but if that's the most interesting thing about me I'm in trouble . . . Well, here's something hardly anybody knows about me. I was born with a sixth finger on each hand. I had surgery when I was six months old. You can see the scar on the left hand but not on the right . . .'

'I'm James Severance . . . I don't know what's interesting about me. Maybe the most interesting thing is that I'm here with all of you right now. I don't know what I'm doing here, but it sort of feels like a turning point . . .'

'My name's Bob Ripley, and I've heard all the Believe It or Not jokes . . . One thought I had before I got here tonight is that it's morbid to have a club of people who are just waiting to die. But that's not how it feels at all. I agree with Lew, I have the sense that I've become a part of something important . . .'

' . . . know it's superstitious, but the thought keeps coming to me that forcing ourselves to be aware of the inevitability of death will just make it come along sooner . . .'

' . . . a car accident the night of high school graduation. There were six of us in my best friend's Chevy Impala and everybody else was killed. I got a broken collarbone and a couple of superficial cuts. That's the most interesting thing about me, and it's also how I feel about tonight. See, that was eight years ago, and I've had death on my mind ever since . . .'

' . . . I think the only way to describe how I feel is to say that the only other time I felt anything like this was the night my baby daughter was born . . .'

Thirty men, ranging in age from twenty-two to thirty-three. All of them white, all of them living in or around New York City. They'd all had some college, and most had graduated. More than half were married. More than a third had children. One or two were divorced.

Now, thirty-two years later, more than half of them were dead.

TWO

By the time I met Lewis Hildebrand, thirty-two years and six weeks after he became a member of the club of thirty-one, he had lost a lot of hair in front and thickened considerably through the middle. His blond hair, parted on the side and slicked back, was silver at the temples. He had a broad, intelligent face, large hands, a firm but unaggressive grip. His suit, blue with a chalk stripe, must have cost a thousand dollars. His wristwatch was a twenty-dollar Timex.

He had called me late the previous afternoon at my hotel room. I still had the room, although for a little over a year I'd been living with Elaine in an apartment directly across the street. The hotel room was supposed to be my office, although it was by no means a convenient place to meet clients. But I'd lived alone in it for a good many years. I seemed to be reluctant to let go of it.

He told me his name and said he'd got mine from Irwin Meisner. 'I'd like to talk to you,' he said. 'Do you suppose we could meet for lunch? And is tomorrow too soon?'

'Tomorrow's fine,' I said, 'but if it's something extremely urgent I could make time this evening.'

'It's not that urgent. I'm not sure it's urgent at all. But it's very much on my mind, and I don't want to put it off.' He might have been talking about his annual physical, or an appointment with his dentist. 'Do you know the Addison Club? On East Sixty-seventh? And shall we say twelve-thirty?'

The Addison Club, named for Joseph Addison, the

eighteenth-century essayist, occupies a five-story lime-stone townhouse on the south side of Sixty-seventh Street between Park and Lexington avenues. Hildebrand had stationed himself within earshot of the reception desk, and when I gave my name to the uniformed attendant he came over and introduced himself. In the first-floor dining room, he rejected the first table we were offered and chose one in the far corner.

'San Giorgio on the rocks with a twist,' he told the waiter. To me he said, 'Do you like San Giorgio? I always have it here because not many restaurants stock it. Do you know it? It's basically an Italian dry vermouth with some unusual herbs steeped in it. It's very light. I'm afraid the days of the lunchtime martinis are over for me.'

'I'll have to try it sometime,' I said. 'Today, though, I think I'll have a Perrier.'

He apologized in advance for the food. 'It's a nice room, isn't it? And of course they don't hurry you, and with the tables so far apart and half of them empty, well, I thought we might be glad of the privacy. The kitchen's not too bad if you stay with the basics. I usually have a mixed grill.'

'That sounds good.'

'And a green salad?'

'Fine.'

He wrote out the order and handed the card to the waiter. 'Private clubs,' he said. 'An endangered species. The Addison is presumably a club for authors and journalists, but the membership for years now has run largely to people in advertising and publishing. These days I think they'll pretty much take you if you've got a pulse and a checkbook and no major felony convictions. I joined about fifteen years ago when my wife and I moved up to Stamford, Connecticut. There were a lot of nights when I would work late and miss the last train and have to stay over. Hotels cost a fortune, and I always felt like a shady character checking in without luggage. They have rooms on the top floor here, very reasonable and available at short notice. I'd been thinking about joining anyway, and that gave me an incentive.'

'So you live in Connecticut?'

He shook his head. 'We moved back five years ago when our youngest boy finished college. Well, dropped out of it, I should say. We're living half a dozen blocks from here, and I can walk to work on a day like today. It's beautiful out, isn't it?'

'Yes.'

'Well, New York in June. I've never been to Paris in April, but I understand it's apt to be wet and dreary. May's a lot nicer there, but the song works better with April in it. You need the extra syllable. But New York in June, you can see why they'd write songs about it.'

When the waiter brought our food Hildebrand asked me if I'd like a beer with it. I said I was fine. He said, 'I'll have one of the nonalcoholic beers. I forget which ones you stock. Do you have O'Doul's?'

They did, and he said he'd have one, and looked at me expectantly. I shook my head. The nonalcoholic beers and wines all have at least a trace of alcohol. Whether it's enough to affect a sober alcoholic is an open question, but the people I've known in AA who insisted they could drink Moussy or O'Doul's or Sharp's with impunity all wound up picking up something stronger sooner or later.

Anyway, what the hell would I want with a beer with no kick to it?

We talked about his work – he was a partner in a small public-relations firm – and about the pleasures of living in the city again after a stretch in the suburbs. If I'd met him at his office we'd have gotten right down to business, but instead we were following the traditional rules of a business lunch, holding the business portion until we'd finished with the food.

When the coffee came he patted his breast pocket and gave a snort of ironic amusement. 'Now that's funny,' he said. 'Did you see what I just did?'

'You were reaching for a cigarette.'

'That's exactly what I was doing, and I quit the goddamn things more than twelve years ago. Were you ever a smoker?'

'Not really.'

'Not really?'

'I never had the habit,' I explained. 'Maybe once a year I would buy a pack of cigarettes and smoke five or six of them one right after the other. Then I would throw the pack away and not have another cigarette for another year.'

'My God,' he said. 'I never heard of anyone who could smoke tobacco without getting hooked on it. I guess you just don't have an addictive personality.' I let that one pass. 'Quitting was the hardest thing I ever did in my life. Sometimes I think it's the only hard thing I ever did. I still have dreams where I've taken up the habit again. Do you still do that? Have yourself a little cigarette binge once a year?'

'Oh, no. It's been more than ten years since I had a cigarette.'

'Well, all I can say is I'm glad there's not an open pack on the table. Matt' — we were Matt and Lew by now — 'let me ask you something. Have you ever heard of a club of thirty-one?'

'A club of thirty-one,' I said. 'I don't suppose that would have anything to do with this club.'

'No.'

'I've heard of the restaurant, of course. Twenty-one. I don't think—'

'It's not a specific club, like the Harvard Club or the Addison. Or a restaurant like Twenty-one. It's a particular kind of club. Oh, let me explain.'

The explanation was lengthy and thorough. Once he got started, he reported on that evening in 1961 in detail. He was a good storyteller; he let me see the private dining room, the four round tables (eight men each at three of them, six plus Champney at the fourth). And I could see and hear the old man, could feel the passion that animated him and caught hold of his audience.

I said I'd never heard of an organization anything like what he'd described.

'I guess you didn't hang out much with Mozart and Ben Franklin,' he said, with a quick grin. 'Or with the Essenes and the Babylonians. I was thinking about that the other night, trying to decide how much of it I believe. I've never really researched the subject beyond an occasional desultory hour in a library. And I never came across an organization anything like ours.'

'And no one you've mentioned it to has been familiar with anything similar?'

He frowned. 'I haven't mentioned it much,' he said. 'To tell you the truth, this is the first detailed conversation I've ever had on the subject with someone who wasn't a member himself. There are any number of people who know I get together with a group of fellows once a year for dinner and drinks, but I've never talked about the group's links to the past. Or the deathwatch aspect of the whole thing.' He looked at me. 'I've never told my wife or my children. My best friend, we've been close for over twenty years, and he has no idea what the club is about. He thinks it's like a fraternity reunion.'

'Did the old man tell everybody to keep it a secret?'

'Not in so many words. It's hardly a secret society, if that's what you mean. But I left Cunningham's that night with the distinct feeling that this thing I'd become a part of ought to be kept private. And that conviction deepened over the years, incidentally. It was understood early on that you could say anything in that room with the certain knowledge that it would not be repeated. I've told those fellows things I haven't mentioned to anyone else in the world. Not that I'm a man with a lot of secrets to tell or not to tell, but I would say I'm an essentially private person and I guess I withhold a good deal of myself from the people in my life. For Christ's sake, I'm fifty-seven years old. You must be close to that yourself, aren't you?'

'I'm fifty-five.'

'Then you know what I'm talking about. Guys our age grew up knowing we were supposed to keep our inner-most thoughts to ourselves. All the pop psychology in the world doesn't change that. But once a year I sit around a couple of tables with a bunch of men who are still virtual strangers to me, and more often than not I wind up opening up about something I hadn't planned on mentioning.' He lowered his eyes, picked up the saltcellar, turned it in his hands. 'I had an affair a few years back. Not a quick jump on a business trip, there have been a few of those over the years, but a real love affair. It went on for almost three years.'

'And no one knew?'

'You see what I'm getting at, don't you? No, nobody ever knew. I didn't get caught and I never told anybody. If she confided in anyone, and I assume she must have, well, we didn't have friends in common so it's not material. The point is that I talked about that affair on the first Thursday in May. More than once, too.' He set the saltcellar down forcefully. 'I told *her* about the club. She thought it was morbid, she hated the whole idea of it. What she did like, though, was the fact that she was the only person I'd ever told. She liked that part a lot.'

He fell silent, and I sipped my coffee and waited him out. At length he said, 'I haven't seen her in five years. Well, hell, I haven't had a cigarette in twelve, and I damn well wanted one for a minute there, didn't I? Sometimes I don't think anybody ever gets over anything.'

'Sometimes I think you're right.'

'Matt, would it bother you if I had a brandy?'

'Why should it bother me?'

'Well, it's none of my business, but it's hard not to draw an inference. It was Irwin Meisner who recommended you. I've known Irwin for years. I knew him when he drank and I know how he stopped. When I asked him how he happened to know you he said something vague, and on the basis of that I wasn't surprised when you didn't order a drink. So—'

'It would bother me if *I* had a brandy,' I told him. 'It won't bother me if you have one.'

'Then I think I will,' he said, and caught the waiter's eye. After the man had taken the order and gone off to fill it, Hildebrand picked up the saltcellar again, put it down again, and drew a quick breath. 'The club of thirty-one,' he said. 'I think somebody's trying to rush things.'

'To rush things?'

'To kill the members. All of us. One by one.'

THREE

'We got together last month,' he said. 'At Keens Chop-house on West Thirty-sixth Street. That's where we've been holding our dinners ever since Cunningham's closed in the early seventies. They give us the same room every year. It's on the second floor, and it looks like a private library. The walls are lined with bookshelves and portraits of somebody's ancestors. There's a fireplace, and they lay a fire for us, not that that's what you necessarily want in May. It's nice for atmosphere, though.

'We've been going there for twenty years. Keens almost went under, you know, just when we were beginning to settle in there. That would have been tragic, the place is a New York institution. But they survived. They're still there, and, well, so are we.' He paused, considered. 'Some of us,' he said.

His glass of Courvoisier was on the table in front of him. He still hadn't taken a sip. From time to time he would reach for the small snifter, letting his hand cup the bowl, taking the stem between his thumb and forefingers, moving the glass a few inches this way or that.

He said, 'At last month's dinner, it was announced that two of our members had died in the preceding twelve months. Frank DiGiulio had suffered a fatal heart attack in September, and then in February Alan Watson was stabbed to death on his way home from work. So we've had two deaths in the past year. Does that seem significant to you?'

'Well . . .'

'Of course not. We're of an age when death happens. What significance could one possibly attach to two deaths within a twelve-month period?' He took the glass by its stem, gave it a quarter-turn clockwise. 'Consider this, then. In the past seven years, nine of us have died.'

'That seems a little high.'

'And that's in the past seven years. Earlier, we'd already lost eight men. Matt, there are only fourteen of us left.'

Homer Champney had told them he'd probably be the first to go. 'And that's as it should be, boys. That's the natural order of things. But I hope I'll be with you for a little while, at least. To get to know you, and to see you all off to a good start.'

As it turned out, the old man lasted well into his ninety-fourth year. He never missed the annual dinner, remaining physically fit and mentally alert to the very end.

Nor was he the first of their number to die. The group's first two anniversaries were unmarked by death, but in 1964 they spoke the name and marked the passing of Philip Kalish, killed with his wife and infant daughter three months earlier in a car crash on the Long Island Expressway.

Two years later James Severance was killed in Vietnam. He'd missed the previous year's dinner, his reserve unit having been recalled to active duty, and members had joked that an Asian war was a pretty lame excuse for breaking such a solemn commitment. The following May, when they read his name along with Phil Kalish's, you could almost hear last year's jokes echoing hollowly against the paneled walls.

In March of '69, less than two months before the annual dinner, Homer Champney died in his sleep. 'If there comes a day when you don't see me by nine in the morning,' he'd instructed the staff at his residential hotel, 'ring my suite, and if I don't pick up then come check on me.' The desk clerk made the call and had a bellman take over the desk while he went up to Champney's rooms himself. When he found what he'd feared, he called the old man's nephew.

That nephew in turn made the calls his uncle had instructed him to make. On the list were the twenty-eight surviving members of the club of thirty-one. Champney was leaving nothing to chance. He wanted to make sure everyone knew he was gone.

The funeral was at Campbell's, and it was the first club funeral Lewis Hildebrand had attended. The overall turnout was small. Champney had outlived his contemporaries, and his nephew – a great-nephew, actually, some fifty years Champney's junior – was his only surviving relative in the New York area. Besides Hildebrand, the contingent of mourners included half a dozen other members of the thirty-one.

Afterward, he joined several of them for a drink. Bill Ludgate, a printing salesman, said, 'Well, this is the first of these I've been to, and it's going to be the last. In a couple of weeks we'll be all together at Cunningham's, and Homer'll have his name read with the others, and I guess we'll talk about him. And that's enough. I don't think we should go to members' funerals. I don't think it's our place.'

'I felt I wanted to be here today,' someone said.

'We all did or we wouldn't be here. But I talked to Frank DiGiulio the other day and he said he wasn't coming, that he didn't think it was appropriate. And now I've decided I agree with him. You know, back when this thing first got rolling, there were a few members I used to see socially. A lunch now and then, or drinks after work, or even getting together with the wives for dinner and a movie. But I stopped doing that, and when I spoke to Frank I realized it was the first conversation I'd had with any of the group since dinner last May.'

'Don't you like us anymore, Bill?'

'I like you all just fine,' he said, 'but I find myself inclined to keep things separate. Hell, I haven't even been to Cunningham's since the last get-together. I don't know how many times someone'll suggest it for lunch or dinner, and I always make sure we wind up someplace else instead. "Oh, I'd rather not," I told a fellow just last week. "I had a bad meal last time I was there. The place isn't what it used to be."'

'Jesus, Billy,' somebody said, 'have a heart, huh? You're gonna put them out of business.'

'Well, I'd hate to see that happen,' he said, 'but do you see what I mean? Once a year's enough for me. I like having thirty guys that I only see once a year, in a place I only go to once a year.'

'That's twenty-seven guys now, twenty-eight including yourself.'

'So it is,' he said gravely. 'So it is. But you see my point, don't you? I'm not telling the rest of you what to do, and I love you one and all, but I'm not coming to your funerals.'

'That's okay, Billy,' Bob Ripley said. 'We'll come to yours.'

'Thirty men in 1961, ranging in age from twenty-two to thirty-three with a median age of twenty-six. Thirty-two years later, how many would you expect to find alive?'

'I don't know.'

'Neither did I,' Hildebrand said. 'After the dinner last month I went home with a headache and tossed and turned all night. I woke up knowing something was very wrong. You've got a group of men in their late fifties and early sixties, you're going to have some losses. Death is going to start making inroads.

'But it seemed to me we were way over the probabilities. My mind kept coming up with different explanations, and I decided the first thing to do was find out if my sense of things was accurate. So I called up a fellow I know who's always trying to sell me more life insurance and told him I had an actuarial problem for him. I ran the numbers for him and asked him what percentage of deaths you'd expect over that span of time in a group like that. He said he'd make a couple of calls and get back to me. Take a guess, Matt. How many deaths would you expect in a group of thirty?'

'I don't know. Eight or ten?'

'Four or five. There ought to be twenty-five of us left and instead we're down to fourteen. What does that say to you?'

'I'm not sure,' I said, 'but it certainly gets my attention. The first thing I'd do is ask your friend another question.'

'That's just what I did. Tell me your question.'

'I'd ask him to gauge the significance of a sample with three or four times the expected number of deaths.'

He nodded. 'That was my question, and he had to call somebody to find out. The answer that came back to me was that sixteen deaths out of thirty was remarkable, but it wasn't significant. Do you know what he meant by that?'

'No.'

'According to him, the sample's too small for *any* result to be significant. We could have one hundred percent surviving or one hundred percent dying and it wouldn't really signify anything. Now if we had the same percentage in a substantially larger group, then it would mean something from an actuarial standpoint. See, actuaries

24

like large numbers. The bigger the group, the more they can read into the statistics. If we had 140,000 survivors in a group of 300, that would have some significance. 1,400 out of 3,000 – that would be even more significant. 140,000 out of 300,000 – that would begin to suggest that the sample was composed of people who lived in Chernobyl, or whose mothers took DES during pregnancy. It would really set the sirens wailing.'

'I see.'

'I've had some experience in direct-mail advertising. We tested everything. You have to. If we had a list of half a million names, and we did a test mailing to a thousand of those names, we knew we'd get the same response ratio within a point or two from the entire list. But we knew better than to send out a test mailing to thirty names, because the results wouldn't mean anything.'

'Where does that leave you?'

'It leaves me impressed with the percentages, and never mind the size of the sample. I can't get past the fact that statistically we should have suffered four or five deaths and instead we took a hit three or four times as heavy. What do you make of it, Matt?'

I gave it some thought. 'I don't know anything about statistics,' I said.

'No, but you're an ex-cop and a detective. You must have instincts.'

'I suppose I do.'

'What do they tell you?'

'To look for special circumstances. You mentioned one man who died in Vietnam. Were there any other combat deaths?'

'No, just Jim Severance.'

'How about AIDS?'

He shook his head. 'We had two gay members,

25

although I don't believe anybody knew they were gay when the chapter was founded. I wonder if that would have made a difference. In 1961? Yes, I'm sure it would have, and when we stood up and recounted the most interesting fact about ourselves at that first meeting, that particular fact went unmentioned. But later on both of the fellows saw fit to tell the group about their sexuality. I don't know when those revelations burst upon us, but we were still meeting at Cunningham's then, I remember that much, so it was quite a while ago. In any event, neither of them died of AIDS. Lowell Hunter very well may, in the course of time. He's told us that he's HIV-positive, but as of our meeting last month he was still completely asymptomatic. And Carl Uhl died in 1981, before anybody even heard the word "AIDS." I gather the disease existed then, but I certainly hadn't heard a thing about it. In any case, Carl was murdered.'

'Oh?'

'They found him in his apartment in Chelsea. He lived just around the corner from Cunningham's, but of course Cunningham's was long gone by the time Carl was killed. I gather it was a sex killing, some sort of sadomasochistic game gone out of control. He was tied up and wearing handcuffs and a leather hood, and he'd been eviscerated and subjected to sexual mutilation. It's a hell of a world we live in, isn't it?'

'Yes.'

'After I spoke to my insurance man, I spent a few nights sitting up late and trying to concoct explanations. The first, of course, is sheer chance. There might be long odds against such a high number of deaths, but any gambler will tell you that long shots come in all the time. In the long run you'll go broke betting on them, but what is it they say? In the long run we're all dead, which, when you stop and think of it, is one of the club's underlying principles.' He picked up his glass, but he still didn't drink the damn thing. 'Where was I?'

'Sheer chance.'

'Yes. No way to rule it out, but I set it aside and looked for other explanations. One that occurred to me was that the group was composed of men with a strong predisposition toward early death. It seemed at least arguable that natural selection might have operated to steer such persons into our club. A person genetically destined for an early grave might be aware of his fate on some unconscious level, and might thus be more likely than the next fellow to accept an invitation to join a group preoccupied with death. I don't know whether or not I believe in fate, it probably depends when you ask me, but I certainly believe in genetic predisposition. So that's one possibility.'

'Tell me some of the others.'

'Well, another one that came to me is a little more mind-over-matter. It strikes me as possible that the club itself could have the effect of increasing its members' chances of dying young.'

'How?'

'By focusing our attention on our own mortality to an unnatural degree. I'd hate to argue that a man can prolong his life by systematically denying his own mortality, but it's still possible that we can hasten the day by sitting around waiting for it, and getting together once a year to find out who caught the bus. I'm sure there's a part of me that longs for death, just as there's another part that wants to live forever. Maybe our meetings strengthen the death wish at the expense of the life urge. The mind-body connection is sufficiently established these days that even the doctors are grudgingly aware of it. People are vulnerable to illness because of their mental state, they become accident–prone, they make dangerous decisions. It could be a factor.'

'I suppose it could.' I wanted more coffee, and I'd barely raised my head to look around for the waiter when he hurried over to fill my cup. I said, 'Homer Champney sounds like a fellow with a pretty strong life urge.'

'He was a remarkable man. He had more energy and zest for living well into his nineties than most men ever have. And don't forget he was of a generation that didn't live as long as we do today, or stay as active. A man our age was supposed to be ready for a rocking chair, assuming he still had a heartbeat.'

'What about the others in his chapter?'

'They died,' he said ruefully, 'and that's all I've ever known about them. I don't remember any of their names. I only heard them the one time, when Homer read the list and burned the paper it was written on. He made a real point of never mentioning any of their names again. As far as he was concerned, the chapter was closed, period. I don't know how long they lived or how they died.' He laughed shortly. 'For all I know, they never even existed.'

'What do you mean?'

'It's a thought I haven't entertained in years, but it came to me late one night and I've never entirely forgotten it. Suppose there never was a chapter before ours. Suppose Homer picked those thirty names out of the phone book. Suppose he made up the whole kit and caboodle, including the man who'd fought in the Mexican War, along with the legends about Mozart and Isaac Newton and the Hanging Gardens of Babylon. Suppose he was just a nut with a gift of gab who thought it would be interesting to eat beef once a year with a group of young fellows while he waited for the man with the scythe.'

'You don't really believe that.'

'No, of course not. But what's interesting is that there's no real way to disprove it. If Homer had any written records of the previous chapter, I'm sure he destroyed them after our first meeting. If any of his chapter brothers left anything on paper, I suppose what their heirs didn't throw out is moldering in some attic somewhere. But how would anyone know where to look?'

'Anyway,' I said, 'it doesn't really matter, does it?'

'No,' he said. 'Because if there's a destiny operating, genetic or otherwise, I don't suppose there's anything to be done about it. And if our membership in the club is killing us by poisoning our psyches in some insidious fashion, well, it's probably too late to look for the antidote. And if Homer was a sly old duffer and ours is the first club of thirty-one in human history, well, so what? I'll still turn up at Keens the first Thursday in May, and if I turn out to be the last man alive, I'll make it my business to pick out thirty honorable men and keep the old flame burning.' He snorted. 'I could say that it gets harder every year to find thirty honorable men, but I don't know that it's true. I have a feeling it was never easy.'

I said, 'You think the members are being murdered.'

'Yes.'

'Because the actual deaths have been so greatly in excess of probability.'

'That's part of it. That's what got me looking for an explanation.'

'And?'

'I sat down and made a list of our deceased members and the various ways they died. Some of them very obviously had not been murdered, their deaths could only have been the result of natural causes. Phil Kalish, for example, killed in a head-on on the LIE. The other driver was drunk, he'd managed to get on the wrong side of the divider and was speeding eastbound in the westbound lane. If he'd lived he might have been prosecuted for vehicular homicide, but it doesn't sound like something some devious mass murderer could have arranged.'

'No.'

'And some Viet Cong or North Vietnamese soldier killed Jim Severance. Death in combat isn't something you usually think of as a natural cause, but I wouldn't call it murder, either.' His fingers just touched the bowl of the snifter, then withdrew. 'There were some natural deaths that couldn't have been anything else. Roger Bookspan developed testicular cancer that had metastasized by the time they caught it. They tried a bone-marrow transplant but he didn't survive the procedure.' His face darkened at the memory. 'He was only thirty-seven, the poor son of a bitch. Married, two kids under five, a first novel written and accepted for publication, and all of a sudden he was gone.'

'That must have been a while ago.'

'Close to twenty years. One of our early deaths. More recently, there were a couple of heart attacks. I mentioned Frank DiGiulio, and then two years ago Victor Falch dropped dead on the golf course. He was sixty years old, forty pounds overweight, and diabetic, so I don't suppose you'd call that suspicious circumstances.'

'No.'

'On the other hand, several of our members have been murdered, and there have been other deaths that could conceivably have been murder, although the authorities didn't classify them as such. I mentioned Alan Watson, stabbed in a mugging.'

'And the fellow in Chelsea who was killed by a sexual partner,' I said, and scanned my memory for the name. 'Carl Uhl?'

'That's right. And then of course there was Boyd Shipton.'

'Boyd Shipton the painter?'

'Yes.'

'He was a member of your club?'

He nodded. 'At our initial meeting he said that the most interesting fact he could tell us about himself was that he'd painted a wall of his apartment to look like exposed brick. He was a trainee on Wall Street at the time, and he made it sound as though painting was just a pastime for him. Later, after he'd quit his job and made his first gallery connection, he admitted he'd been afraid to let on just how important it was to him.'

'He became very successful.'

'Extremely successful, with an oceanfront house in East Hampton and a state-of-the-art loft in Tribeca. You know, I've often wondered what became of that faux-brick wall Boyd painted. He slapped a couple of coats of flat white wall paint on it before he moved, so that the landlord wouldn't have a fit. Well, whoever's living there now has an original Boyd Shipton trompe-l'oeil mural under God knows how many layers of Dutch Boy latex. I suppose it could be restored, if anyone knew where to look for it.'

'I remember when he was killed,' I said. 'Five years ago, wasn't it?'

'Six in October. He and his wife had come into the city for a friend's opening and went out to dinner afterward. When they returned to their loft downtown they evidently walked in on a burglary in progress.'

'The wife was raped, as I recall.'

'Raped and strangled, and Boyd was beaten to death. And the case was never solved.'

'So you've had three murders.'

'Four. In 1989 Tom Cloonan was shot to death at the

wheel of his cab. He was a writer, he published quite a few short stories over the years and had a play or two produced Off-Off-Broadway, but he couldn't make a living at it. He'd make up the difference working for a moving company or renovating apartments for an un-licensed contractor. And sometimes he drove a cab, and that's what he was doing when he died.'

'And they never cleared that case, either?'

'I believe the cops made an arrest. I don't think the case ever went to trial.'

It wouldn't be hard to find out. I said, 'Thirty men, and four of them have been the victims of homicides. I think that's more remarkable than the fact that sixteen of you have died.'

'I was thinking that myself, Matt. You know, when I was a kid growing up, I don't think my parents were acquainted with a single person who'd been murdered. And I didn't grow up in some storybook town in South Dakota, either. I grew up in Queens, first in Richmond Hill and then we moved to Woodhaven.' He frowned. 'I'm wrong, because we did know someone who was murdered, although I couldn't tell you his name. He owned a liquor store on Jamaica Avenue and he was shot and killed during a holdup. I remember how upset my parents were.'

'There were probably others,' I suggested. 'You're less aware of that sort of thing when you're a kid, and parents tend to shield you from it. Oh, there's no question that the homicide rate's higher than when we were kids, but people have been killing each other since Cain and Abel. You know, in the middle of the last century there was a sprawling tenement complex in Five Points called the Old Brewery, and when they finally tore it down the workmen hauled sack after sack of human bones out of the basement. According to informed estimates, that one building averaged a murder a night for years.'

'In one building?'

'Well, it was a pretty good-sized building,' I said. 'And it couldn't have been a very nice neighborhood.'

FOUR

In addition to the homicides, Lew told me, there were cases of suicide and accidental death, some of which might have been murder in disguise. He had a pair of lists, which he took from his inside breast pocket and unfolded for me. One bore in alphabetical order the names of the club's fourteen surviving members, along with their addresses and phone numbers. The other was a list of the deceased – all seventeen of them, including Homer Champney. They were listed in the order they'd died, with the presumptive cause of death noted for each man.

I read through both lists, drank some coffee, and looked across the table at him. I said, 'I'm not sure what sort of role you have in mind for me. If you just wanted a consultation, I'll say this much. Your club's been hit with an awfully high death rate, and it certainly seems to me that a disproportionate number have resulted from causes other than illness. Any of the suicides could have been faked, along with most of the accidents. Even some of the deaths that look natural might be disguised homicide. This one fellow who choked to death on his own vomit, well, there's a way to make that happen.'

'How, for God's sake?'

'The victim has to be unconscious. You jam a pillow or towel over his face and hold it there while you induce vomiting. There's an emetic you can give by subcutaneous injection, but something might show up in an autopsy if anyone had the wit to look for it. A knee in the pit of the stomach is almost as effective. The victim vomits and there's no place for it to go, so he automatically aspirates it into the lungs. It's an easy way to knock off a drunk, you just wait until he's passed out and sleeping it off. And drunks are apt to die choking on their vomit, so it's a very plausible kind of accidental death.'

'It sounds absolutely diabolical.'

'I guess. Back in the mid-sixties there was a United States senator who died like that, and there were strong rumors that he'd been assassinated, either by the Cubans or the CIA, depending on who was telling the story. But this was in the wake of the Kennedy assassination, when every public death brought rumors of murder and conspiracy. If a politically prominent person died of Alzheimer's, you'd hear that the Illuminati had been putting aluminum salts in his cornflakes.'

'I remember.' He drew a deep breath. 'I figured there might have been some elaborate way Eddie Szabo's death might have been brought about. But I had no idea it could have been managed that simply.'

'And it also could have been just what it looks like.'

'An accident.'

'Yes.'

'But on balance you think I have reason to be concerned.'

'I think it calls for investigation.'

'Would you be willing to undertake that investigation?'

I was expecting the question and I had my answer ready. 'If this is what it's beginning to look like,' I said, 'you're dealing with a serial murderer with a remarkable degree of patience and organization. This isn't some drifter on a cross-country spree, snatching truck-stop hookers at random and strewing their corpses along I-80. He's picking specific targets and taking his time knocking them off. He's probably killed eight people, and maybe more.

35

'All of which calls for a full-scale investigation, and I'm just one guy. If this were an NYPD investigation, they'd have a whole roomful of detectives working on it.'

'Do you think I should take this to the police?'

'In an ideal universe, yes. In the real world, I think they'd just shine you on. The way the bureaucracy works, no cop would be all that eager to open this can of worms. You're looking at a whole crazy quilt of conflicting jurisdictions, and some possible homicides dating back twenty years. If I were a cop and this landed on my desk, I'd have every reason to drop it in a file folder and lose track of it.' I took a sip of coffee. 'If you really wanted to get the police moving on this, the best way would be through the media.'

'How do you mean?'

'Just tell some eager reporter the same thing you told me. It's got plenty of news value all by itself, and a whole lot more when you toss a couple of prominent names in the hopper. Boyd Shipton, for one. And your survivors list shows a Raymond Gruliow on Commerce Street. I assume that's the lawyer.'

'The defense attorney, yes.'

'"The controversial defense attorney" is how the press generally phrases it. If you went around telling cops Hard-Way Ray was on somebody's hit list, nine out of ten of them would try to find the guy just so they could buy him a drink and wish him good luck. But if you told a reporter, you'd get a ton of coverage.'

He frowned. 'The idea of publicity,' he said, 'is one I find very disturbing.'

'So I'd imagine.'

'If what I suspect is true, if there's a murderer stalking us and thinning our ranks, then I would do whatever's required to stop him. I'd go on *Oprah*, if it came to that.'

'I don't think it will.'

'But if I'm just overreacting to a statistical coincidence, well, it would be a shame to destroy the club's anonymity unnecessarily. And the attention we'd get as individuals would be most unwelcome, too.'

'For most of you,' I said. 'Ray Gruliow probably thinks "unwelcome attention" is a contradiction in terms. Still, you've got a tough call to make. The fastest way to get a full-scale investigation under way is to sit down with a reporter and tell him the same story you just told me. My guess is you'd have national media coverage within twenty-four hours and a police task force assigned inside of forty-eight. With dead men in several states, plus the serial-killer element, you might even see the FBI come in on it if the publicity heats up enough.'

'It's beginning to sound like a circus.'

'Well, if you hired me you'd get a much lower profile. I don't even have a PI license, let alone influence in high places. Any investigation I might mount would have to proceed at a relatively slow pace, and I don't know how much of a factor time might turn out to be. Have you discussed this with any of your fellow members?'

'I haven't said a word to anybody.'

'Really? That's a surprise. I would have thought . . . Oh.'

He gave a long slow nod. 'The club's not a true secret society, but we've certainly kept it a secret from the world. Nobody else knows we exist.' He took hold of the glass of brandy. 'So if there's a killer,' he said evenly, 'it would almost have to be one of us.'

FIVE

'God, it's such a guy thing,' Elaine said. 'Thirty-one grown men sitting around wooden tables eating meat and checking for chest pains. You can just about smell the testosterone, can't you?'

'I'm beginning to understand why they didn't tell their wives about it.'

'I'm not putting it down,' she insisted. 'I'm just pointing out how intrinsically masculine the whole thing is. Keeping it all a secret, only seeing each other once a year, talking solemnly about Important Subjects. Can you imagine the same club composed of women?'

'It would drive the restaurant crazy,' I said. 'Thirty-one separate checks.'

'One check, but we'll make sure it gets split fairly. "Let's see, Mary Beth had the apple pie à la mode, so she owes an extra dollar, and Rosalie, you had the Roquefort dressing, which is an additional seventy-five cents." Why do they do that, anyway?'

'Split checks item by item? I've often wondered.'

'No, charge extra for a tablespoon of Roquefort. When you're paying twenty or thirty dollars for a meal it ought to include whatever salad dressing you want. Why are you looking at me like that?'

'Because I find you fascinating.'

'After all these years?'

'It's probably abnormal,' I said, 'but I can't help it.'

It had been late afternoon by the time I left the Addison Club. I walked home and took a shower, then sat down and went over my notes. She'd called around six to say she wouldn't be getting home for dinner. 'I've got an artist coming at seven to show me his slides,' she said, 'and I've got my class tonight, unless you want me to skip it.'

'Don't do that.'

'There's some leftover Chinese in the fridge, but you'd probably rather go out. Don't throw out the leftovers, I'll have them when I get home.'

'I've got a better idea,' I said. 'I want to get to a meeting. You go to your class, and meet me afterward at Paris Green.'

'Deal.'

I went to the 8:30 meeting at St Paul's, then walked down Ninth Avenue and got to Paris Green around a quarter after ten. Elaine was on a stool at the bar, chatting with Gary and nursing a tall glass of cranberry juice and seltzer. I went to collect her and he laid a hand on my arm.

'Thank God you're here,' he said archly. 'That's her third one of those, and you know how she gets.'

Bryce gave us a window table, and over dinner she told me about the artist who'd come around earlier, a West Indian black who was the superintendent of a small apartment house in Murray Hill and a self-taught painter.

'He does these village scenes in oil on masonite,' she said, 'and they have a nice folk-art look to them, but they left me underwhelmed. Maybe I've seen too much of that kind of thing. Or maybe *he* has, because that's the feeling I got, that his source of inspiration wasn't his own childhood memories as much as it was the work of other artists he's been exposed to.' She made a face. 'But that's New York, isn't it? He's never taken a class or sold a painting, but he knows to bring slides. Who ever heard of a folk artist with slides? I bet you don't get that crap in Appalachia.'

'Don't be so sure.'

'You're probably right. Anyway, I told him I'd keep his name on file. In other words, don't call us. I don't know, maybe he's the long-lost bastard son of Grandma Moses and Howard Finster, and I just blew the chance of a lifetime. But I have to go with my instincts, don't you think?'

They had served her well over the years. When we met I was a cop with a brand-new gold shield in my pocket and a wife and two sons in Syosset, and she was a young call girl, bright and funny and beautiful. We made each other happy for a few years, and then I drank my way out of my marriage and the police department and we pretty much lost track of each other. She went on doing what she'd been doing, saving her money and investing in real estate, keeping fit at the health club, stretching her mind in night school.

A couple of years ago circumstances threw us together again, and what we'd had was still there, stronger than ever and richer for the years we'd lived through. At first she went on seeing clients and we both pretended that was okay, but of course it wasn't, and eventually I bit the bullet and said so and she admitted she'd already put herself out of business.

We kept inching closer and closer to marriage. Last April she'd sold her old place on East Fiftieth and picked out an apartment in the Parc Vendôme and we'd moved in together. It was her money that bought the place and I'd refused to let her put my name on the deed.

I paid the monthly maintenance on the apartment and picked up the checks when we went out to dinner. She covered the household expenses. Eventually we would put all our money together, but we hadn't gotten around to that yet.

Eventually we would get married, too, and I wasn't sure why it was taking us so long. We kept not quite setting a date. We kept letting it slide.

Meanwhile, she had opened a gallery. First she'd gone to work at one on Madison Avenue with the intention of learning the business. She had an argument with the woman who ran the place and quit after two months, then got a similar job downtown on Spring Street. She didn't much care for the artwork in either establishment; the photo-realists at the uptown gallery struck her as sterile, while she saw the commercial canvases at the SoHo gallery as clichéd and cloying, a high-ticket equivalent of Holiday Inn seascapes and bullfighters.

More to the point, she found the business itself unpleasant, the snobbery, the petty jealousies, the relentless courting of investors and corporate collectors. 'I thought I quit prostitution,' she said one night, 'and here I am pimping for a bunch of bad painters. I don't get it.' She went in the following morning and gave notice.

What she wanted, she decided, was a sort of cross between a gallery and a curiosity shop. She'd stock it with things she liked, and she'd try to sell them to people who were looking for something to hang on the wall, or place on the coffee table. She had a good eye, everyone told her that, and she'd taken more courses over the years at Hunter and NYU and the New School than your average art historian, so why shouldn't she take her best shot?

It turned out to be easy to get started. There were a lot of vacant storefronts in the neighborhood that season, and she checked them all out and charmed the owner of a building on Ninth and Fifty-fifth into giving her a good lease at a reasonable rent. Over the years she'd packed a locker in an Eleventh Avenue warehouse with things she'd bought and tired of; the two of us went through it and filled the back of a borrowed station wagon with prints and canvases, and that gave her enough stock to open.

Toward the end of her first month of operation she paid a second visit to the Matisse show at the Museum of Modern Art and came back wide-eyed. 'It's an exalting experience,' she said, 'even more than the first time, and I was completely blown away, but you know what? I realized something. Some of those early paintings, the portraits and still lifes. If you take them entirely out of context, and if you forget that they happened to be painted by a genius, you'd think you were looking at something out of a thrift shop.'

'I see what you mean,' I said, 'but isn't that a little like looking at a Jackson Pollock and saying, "My kid could do this"?'

'No,' she said. 'Because I'm not knocking Matisse. I'm putting in a word for the anonymous unheralded amateur.'

'What do you mean?'

'I mean context is everything,' she said.

The next day she beeped TJ and hired him to mind the store while she hit every thrift shop she could get to. By the end of the week she had covered most of Manhattan, sorting through hundreds and hundreds of paintings and buying almost thirty, at an average price of $8.75. She lined them up and asked me what I thought. I told her I didn't think Matisse had anything to worry about.

'I think they're great,' she insisted. 'They're not necessarily good, but they're great.'

She picked out her six favorites and had them framed in simple gallery-style black frames. She sold two the first week, one for $300 and one for $450. 'See?' she said, triumphant. 'Stuff 'em in a bin at the Salvation Army at ten bucks apiece and they're thrift-shop art that nobody looks at twice. Treat them with respect and price them at three to five hundred and they're folk art, and people think they're a steal. I had a woman in just before closing who fell in love with the desert sunset. "But this looks like paint-by-number," she said. "That's just what it is," I told her. "It was the artist's favorite medium. He worked only with paint-by-number." What do you bet she comes back tomorrow and buys it?'

It was getting on for midnight when we left Paris Green and walked home on Ninth Avenue. There was rain forecast but you never would have known it. The air was cool and dry, and there was a breeze off the Hudson.

'Hildebrand gave me a check,' I told her. 'I'll deposit it in the morning.'

'Unless you want to use the ATM.'

'No, I want to go straight home,' I said. 'I'm a little tired. And I want to go over my notes some more before I go to sleep.'

'Do you really think—'

'—that somebody's been knocking them off like clay pigeons? I'm not supposed to know yet. I was hired to find out, not to make up my mind in advance.'

'So you're keeping an open mind.'

'Not entirely,' I admitted. 'It's hard for me to get away from the numbers. There have been too many deaths. There has to be an explanation. All I have to do is find it.'

We stood at a corner, waiting for the light to change. She said, 'Why would anyone want to do something like that?'

'I don't know.'

'If they were all in college together, and they raped

some girl at a drunken fraternity party, and now her brother's getting revenge.'

'That's pretty good,' I said.

'Or it's her son, and his mother died in childbirth, so he wants vengeance, but he also has to find out which of the men is his father. How does that sound?'

'Like a Movie of the Week.'

'I guess the killer would have to be one of the survivors, huh?'

'Well, I don't think it's one of the victims.'

'I mean as opposed to—'

'—somebody from outside,' I said. 'That's Hildebrand's fear, of course. That's why he's had to keep his suspicions to himself. He would have liked to voice his concern to a fellow member, but suppose he picked the wrong one to confide in? According to him, nobody on the outside even knows that the club exists.'

'You seem dubious.'

'Well, they've been doing this for thirty-two years. Do you really think nobody let something slip in all that time?' I shrugged. 'Still, the fourteen surviving members would have to be the chief suspects.'

'But why on earth would one of them want to kill the others?'

'I don't know.'

'I mean, if you got sick of the whole thing, couldn't you just quit? Didn't anybody ever resign, incidentally?'

'After two or three years, Homer Champney read the group a letter from one of the members who'd written to explain that he no longer wanted to participate. He'd relocated in California and didn't see the point in flying three thousand miles each way for a steak dinner. He had written to suggest that they might want to replace him. They all agreed with Champney that it was against the spirit of the thing to take in any replacement members, and somebody — Hildebrand thinks it would have been Champney — was going to write a letter designed to draw him back into the fold.'

'What happened?'

'I guess the letter got written, and it seems to have worked. A year later the would-be dropout was back at the dinner table.'

'Just in time for some fatted calf,' she said. 'Well, there you go. They wouldn't let him leave, so he was quietly smoldering with resentment. He's been getting back at them ever since, killing them off one man at a time.'

'By God,' I said. 'I think you've cracked the case wide open.'

'No, huh?'

'I forget the guy's name, but I've got it written down. He never did miss another meeting, and if he had a resentment he kept it hidden remarkably well. Wayne Fletcher, that was his name. Hildebrand says Fletcher used to joke about the time he tried to quit, that it would have been easier to resign from the Mafia.'

'Used to?'

'He died eight or nine years ago, if I remember correctly. I don't remember the circumstances, but it's in my notes. It's hard to keep it all straight. So many men, and so many of them dead.'

'It's so sad,' she said. 'Don't you think it's sad?'

'Yes.'

'Even if nobody's killing anybody, even if all the deaths are perfectly natural, there's something absolutely heartbreaking about the idea of this group just dwindling away. I suppose it's life, but that makes life a pretty sad business.'

'Well,' I said, 'who ever said it wasn't?'

On the way past the desk we traded greetings with the

concierge. We had our individual names on the mailbox and the building's directory, but as far as the staff was concerned we were Mr and Mrs Scudder.

ELAINE MARDELL, her shop sign says.

Upstairs, she made coffee while I went over my notes. Wayne Fletcher had died six years ago, not eight or nine, of complications arising from coronary-bypass surgery. I told Elaine as much when she came into the living room with her tea and my coffee.

'It may have been borderline malpractice,' I said, 'according to Hildebrand, but it's a real stretch to call it murder.'

'That's something. The poor man didn't sign his own death warrant when he let himself be talked into rejoining the group.'

'Unless someone visited him in the hospital,' I went on, 'and tampered with his IV.'

'I didn't even think of that,' she said. 'Honey, are you going to be able to check out all of this on your own? It sounds as though you'll have to go in a dozen different directions at once. And how much help can TJ be?'

TJ is a black teenager with no fixed address beyond his beeper number. 'He's resourceful,' I reminded Elaine.

'So he says,' she said, 'and so he is, but somehow I can't see him interviewing middle-aged businessmen at the Addison Club.'

'He can do some legwork for me. As far as the rest of it goes, I won't have to go over all seventeen deaths with a magnifying glass and a pair of tweezers. All I have to do is find out for certain if there's a pattern of serial murder operating, and be able to support that argument with enough evidence so I can turn it over to the cops and be sure they'll give it their undivided attention. If I can bring that off, the case will get the benefit of a full-scale official investigation without starting out as a media circus.'

'God, once the press gets hold of it—'

'I know.'

'Can you imagine what they'd do with it on *Inside Edition* or *Hard Copy*? The club would come off sounding like a cult of moon worshipers.'

'I know.'

'And Boyd Shipton was a member. That wouldn't exactly discourage their interest.'

'No, he'd still be news. And he wasn't the only prominent member, either. Ray Gruliow is guaranteed front-page news. And Avery Davis is a member.'

'The real estate developer?'

'Uh-huh. And two of the dead men were writers, and one of them had some plays produced.' I looked at my notes. 'Gerard Billings,' I said.

'He was a playwright?'

'No, that was Tom Cloonan. Billings is a broadcaster, he does the weather report on Channel Nine.'

'Oh, Gerry Billings, with the bow ties. Gosh, maybe you can get his autograph.'

'I'm just saying he's in the public eye.'

'A mote in the public eye,' she said, 'but I see what you mean.' She fell silent, and I went back to sifting my notes. After a few minutes she said, 'Why?'

'Huh?'

'It just struck me. All these deaths over all those years. It's not like a disgruntled postal employee showing up on the job with an AK-47. Whoever is doing this must have a reason.'

'You'd think so.'

'Is there money in it?'

'So far there's twenty-five hundred in it for me. If

Hildebrand's check is good, and if I can remember to deposit it.'

'I meant for the killer.'

'I figured you did. Well, if he gets a good agent maybe he'll do all right when they make the miniseries. But if he gets away with it there won't be a miniseries, so where does that leave him?'

'High and dry. Don't you get something for being the last man alive?'

'You get to start the next chapter,' I said. 'You get the right to read the names of the dead.'

'You're sure they don't all leave their money to each other?'

'Positive.'

'They don't each kick in a thousand dollars to start things off, and the money got invested in a small upstate corporation that changed its name to Xerox? No, huh?'

'I'm afraid not.'

'And the whole club isn't some kind of a tom-tom?'

'Huh?'

'Wrong word,' she said. 'A tom-tom's a drum. Dammit, what's the word I want?'

'Where are you going?'

'To look it up in the dictionary.'

'How can you look it up,' I wondered, 'if you don't know what it is?'

She didn't answer, and I drank the rest of my coffee and went back to my notes. 'Ha!' she said, a few minutes later, and I looked up. 'Tontine,' she said. 'That's the word. It's an eponym.'

'Is that a fact.'

She gave me a look. 'That means it was named for somebody. Lorenzo Tonti, to be specific. He was a Neapolitan banker who thought it up back in the seventeenth century.'

'Thought what up?'

'The tontine, although I don't suppose he called it that. It was a sort of a cross between life insurance and a lottery. You signed up a batch of subscribers and they each put up a sum of money into a common fund.'

'And it was winner take all?'

'Not necessarily. Sometimes it was set up so that the funds were distributed when the survivors were down to five or ten percent of the original number. Others, smaller ones, stayed locked up until there was only one person left alive. People would be enrolled by their parents in early childhood, and if the investments did well they could wind up looking at a fortune. But they couldn't collect it unless they outlived the other participants.'

'You got all this from the dictionary?'

'I got the word from the dictionary,' she said, 'so I'd know what to look up in the encyclopedia. I knew the word, I just couldn't think of it. Fifteen or twenty years ago I spent a weekend at an inn in the Berkshires. There was this historical novel on the subject, I think it was even called *The Tontine*, and somebody had left a copy there and I picked it up. I was only a third of the way through it when it was time to leave, so I stuck it in my bag.'

'I think God'll forgive you for that.'

'He's already punished me. I read it all the way through, and do you know what it said on the bottom of the last page?'

' "Then she awoke and found it had all been a horrible dream." '

'Worse than that. It said, "End of Volume One." '

'And you were never able to find Volume Two.'

'Never. Not that I made searching for it my life's work. But I would have liked to know how it all came out. There were times over the years when that's what kept me from jumping out the window. I'm not talking about the book, I'm talking about life. Wanting to know how it all comes out.'

I said, 'You really look beautiful tonight.'

'Why, thank you,' she said. 'What brought that on?'

'I was just struck by it. Watching the play of emotions on your face. You're a beautiful woman, but sometimes it all shows – the strength, the softness, everything.'

'You old bear,' she said, and sat down on the couch next to me. 'Keep saying sweet things like that and I've got a pretty good idea how tonight's going to turn out.'

'So have I.'

'Oh? Give me a kiss, then, and we'll see if you're right.'

Afterward, as we were lying side by side, she said, 'You know, when I was saying earlier that the club was a real guy thing, I wasn't just making war-between-the-sexes jokes. It's very much a male province, getting together to work out a relationship with mortality. You boys like to look at the big picture.'

'And girls just want to have fun?'

'And pick out drapes,' she said, 'and exchange recipes, and talk about men.'

'And shoes.'

'Well, shoes are important. You're an old bear. What do you know about shoes?'

'Precious little.'

'Exactly.' She yawned. 'I'm making it sound as though women's concerns are trivial, and I don't think that for a minute. But I do believe we take shorter views. Can you think of a single female philosopher? Because I can't.'

'I wonder why that is.'

'It's probably biological, or anthropological, anyway.

When you guys finished hunting and gathering, you could sit around the campfire and think long thoughts. Women didn't have time for that. We had to be more centered on home and hearth.' She yawned again. 'I could formulate a theory,' she said, 'but I'm one of those practical broads, and I'm going to sleep. You work it out, okay?'

I don't know that I worked anything out, but a few minutes later I said, 'What about Hannah Arendt? And Susan Sontag? Wouldn't you call them philosophers?'

I didn't get an answer. Ms Practicality was sleeping.

SIX

In the morning I deposited Lewis Hildebrand's check and walked over to the main library at Fifth and Forty-second. A young woman with the unfocused energy of a marijuana smoker got me set up at a table and showed me how to thread the microfiche rolls into the scanner. It took me a couple of tries to get the hang of it, but before long I was all caught up in it, lost in yesterday's news.

The next thing I knew it was almost 2:30. I bought a stuffed pita from one sidewalk vendor and an iced tea from another and sat on a bench in Bryant Park, just behind the library. For several years the little park had flourished as the epicenter of the midtown drug trade. It got so no one went into it but the dealers and their customers, and it had degenerated into a nasty and dangerous eyesore.

Just over a year ago it had been born again, with a couple of million dollars spent to recreate it. An architect's heroic vision had been brought to life, and now the park was a showplace, and an absolute oasis in that part of town. The junkies were gone, the dealers were gone, the lawn was lush and green, and beds of red and yellow tulips made you forget where you were.

The city's falling apart. The water mains keep bursting, the subways break down, the streets are cratered with potholes. Much of the population is housed in rotting tenements, scheduled for demolition sixty years ago and still standing. The housing projects that went up after the war are crumbling themselves now, in worse shape than the hovels they were built to replace. Living here, it's very easy to find yourself seeing the decline as a one-way street, a road with no turning.

But that's only half of it. If the city dies a little every day, so is it ever being reborn. You can see the signs everywhere. There's the subway station at Broadway and Eighty-sixth, its tile walls bright with the paintings of schoolchildren. There's the wedge-shaped garden in Sheridan Square, the pocket parks blooming all over town.

And there are the trees. When I was a kid you had to go to Central Park if you wanted to stand under a tree. Now half the streets in town are lined with them. The city plants some and property owners and block associations plant the rest. Trees don't have an easy time of it here. It's like raising kids in the Middle Ages, you have to plant half a dozen trees to raise one. They die for lack of water, or get snapped off at the base by careless truckers, or choke to death in the polluted air. Not all of them, though. Some of them survive.

It was a treat to sit on a bench in that little bandbox of a park and think that maybe my town wasn't such a bad place after all. I've never been too good at looking on the bright side. Mostly I tend to notice the rot, the collapse, the urban entropy. It's my nature, I guess. Some of us see the glass half full. I see it three-fourths empty, and some days it's all I can do to keep my hands off it.

I went back to the library after lunch and put in another three hours, and that was my routine for the rest of the week, long sessions looking up old newspaper stories interrupted by lunches in the park. At first I concentrated on those members who had unquestionably been murdered, Boyd Shipton, Carl Uhl, Alan Watson, and Tom Cloonan. Then I went looking for any sort of coverage of the thirteen others who had died, and then I started in on the living.

I took the weekend off. Saturday afternoon I spelled Elaine while she scouted out thrift shops in Chelsea and a flea market in a school yard on Greenwich Avenue. I made a couple of small sales, and in the middle of the afternoon Ray Galindez dropped by with two containers of coffee, and we sat and talked for a while. He's a police artist with an uncanny ability to depict people he's never seen, and Elaine has some of his sketches hanging, along with a notice of his availability for portraits from memory. He had done a remarkable drawing of Elaine's father, working with her over several sessions; that had been my gift to her one Christmas, and it was not on view at the gallery, but stood in a gilt frame on top of her dresser.

Saturday night we saw a play at one of the little houses way west on Forty-second Street. Sunday afternoon I watched three baseball games at once, flipping from channel to channel, working the remote like a kid playing a video game, and to about as much purpose. Sunday night I had my usual Chinese meal with Jim Faber, my AA sponsor. Afterward we went to the Big Book meeting at St Clare's Hospital. During the sharing, one fellow said, 'I'll tell you what it means to be an alcoholic. If I went into a bar and there was a sign that said "All You Can Drink – One Dollar," I'd say, "Great – give me two dollars' worth."'

Monday I was back at the library.

Monday night I stopped by my hotel and picked up a message from Wally at Reliable, the agency that has some work for me now and then. I called in the next morning. They wanted me to give them a couple of days, scouting out witnesses in a product-liability case. I said I'd do it.

The job I was doing for Hildebrand wasn't that urgent that I couldn't fit in other assignments along the way.

The plaintiff in the product-liability case contended that his deck chair had collapsed, with painful results and dire long-term consequences. We were working for the company that had manufactured the chair. 'The chair's a piece of crap,' Wally told me, 'but that don't mean the guy's on the up-and-up. An' he's got this personal-injury lawyer, Anthony Cerutti, scumbag goes around reporting damaged sidewalks on Thursday, putting the city on notice so his clients can trip over them on Friday and bring suit. Our client would love to stick this one straight up Cerutti's ass, so whyntcha see what you can do.'

The injured party had driven a UPS truck before the accident and hadn't worked since. I found out that he never left his house much before two in the afternoon, so I arranged my own schedule accordingly, putting in a few hours in the library each morning, then catching the F train to the Parsons Boulevard stop. I generally managed to be nursing a Coke in McAnn's Hillside Tavern when our man paused at the door, shifted both clear plastic canes to his left hand, drew the door open with his right, then hobbled in with a cane in each hand.

'Hey, Charlie,' the bartender told him each and every time. 'You know somethin'? I think you're walkin' better.'

I would slip out for a while and find people to talk to, and before I headed for home I would stop back at McAnn's for another Coke. After a couple of days of this I told Wally I was pretty certain Charlie wasn't working anywhere, on or off the books.

'Shit,' he said. 'You think he's legit?'

'No, I think the limp's bogus. Let me put in another day or two.'

The following Monday I showed up around noon at

Reliable's offices in the Flatiron Building. 'I had a hunch,' I told Wally. 'Saturday night I took Elaine to Jackson Heights for curry, and afterward we went looking for Charlie.'

'You took her to McAnn's Hillside? That must have been a rare treat for her.'

'Charlie wasn't there,' I said, 'but the bartender thought he might be at Wallbanger's. "A bunch of 'em went over there," he said. "They got that Velcro shit."'

'What Velcro shit?'

'The kind where they've got a patch of it on the wall, and you attach some to yourself, and you take a running leap at the wall. The object is to wind up sticking to the wall, generally upside down.'

'Jesus Christ,' he said. 'Why, for God's sake?'

'That's not the question you're supposed to ask.'

'It's not?' He thought about it, and his face lit up. He looked like a kid confronting a gaily wrapped birthday present. 'Oh, boy,' he said. 'This is the son of a bitch never takes a step without both canes, right? Did he do it, Matt? Did he wrap up in fucking Velcro an' take a flying leap at a rolling doughnut? Tell me he did it.'

'He came in second.'

'Come on.'

'They were egging him on,' I said. '"C'mon, Charlie boy, you gotta try it!" He kept telling them to be serious, he couldn't even walk, how could he go stick himself on the wall. Finally somebody brought over a glass with four or five ounces of clear liquor in it. Vodka, I suppose, or maybe Aquavit. They told him it was holy water straight from Lourdes. "Drink it down and you're cured, Charlie. Miracle time." He said, well, maybe, as long as we all understood it was just a temporary cure. A five-minute cure, like Cinderella, and then we're all pumpkins again.'

'Pumpkins, for chrissake.'

'He's a tall, skinny guy,' I said, 'with a potbelly from the beer. According to the paperwork he's thirty-eight, but looking at him you'd say early thirties. The way the thing works, you run up, hit the mark, and take off. On his approach he looked as though he could have been a hurdler in high school, the way he moved those long legs. He only missed winning by two or three inches, and they tried to talk him into taking another turn, but he wouldn't have any part of it. "Are you kidding, man? I'm a cripple. Now, listen, all of you. Nobody ever saw this, right? It never happened."'

'Ah, Matty, you're beautiful. You actually saw this, right? And what about Elaine? Can she give a deposition, or testify in court if it comes to that?'

I dropped an envelope on his desk.

'What the hell is this?' He opened it. 'I don't believe this.'

'I'd have been here earlier,' I said, 'but I stopped at the one-hour photo place first. The light wasn't great, and it was no time to start popping flashbulbs, so it's no prizewinner. But—'

'I call it a prizewinner,' Wally said. 'If I'm the judge, I give it First Fucking Prize, and while you're at it you can throw in the Jean Hersholt Humanitarian Award. That's him, by Christ. Upside down, and stuck to the wall like he's fucking pinned there. Well, scratch one lawsuit. What a stupid son of a bitch.'

'He figured he was safe. He knew everybody in the joint except me and Elaine, and he'd gotten used to seeing me at McAnn's.'

'I still can't believe you got a picture. I'm surprised you even had a camera along, never mind you got a chance to use it.' He held the photo to the light. 'This isn't so bad,' he said. 'When I take pictures of my grandkids I have the

57

light positioned just right, I pose 'em, and the shots don't come out any better than this. The kids always manage to move just as I'm clicking the shutter.'

'You should try Velcro.'

'Now you're talking. Glue the little bastards to the wall.' He dropped the photo on his desk. 'Well, that's one in the eye for Phony Tony. He can call his client, tell him to see if he can get his job back at UPS, because his days as a professional invalid are over. Good job, Matt.'

'I think I should get a bonus.'

He thought about it. 'You know,' he said, 'you fucking well ought to. That's up to the client, but I can certainly recommend it. This isn't just a case of digging up some eyewitness, some neighbor lady with a resentment who's willing to swear she saw him walk down to the corner without the canes. This is the kind of thing where all you really have to do is show Tony Cerutti what you've got and he drops the case like a hot rock.'

'Imagine what Cerutti would pay for the picture.'

'Now let's not even get into that,' he said. 'What did you have in mind?'

'That's up to the client,' I said. 'He can figure out what it's worth. But along with it I want a letter to me personally expressing appreciation for the work that I did.'

He nodded. 'Yeah, that won't be any problem. And it's a good thing to have in the files when you get your own ticket, isn't it? In fact it's more important than the money.'

'Probably,' I said. 'But that doesn't mean I don't want the money.'

'Well, why shouldn't you have it all? The commendation, the bonus, and the satisfaction of nailing the bastard.'

'He's not a bad guy.'

'Who, Charlie?'

'He probably really did hurt himself when the chair collapsed under him. And when he told his drinking buddies about it they all told him he should sue, and somebody steered him to Cerutti. Cerutti sent him to his pet doctors for evaluations and hydrotherapy, and taught him never to go out without crutches, or at least a couple of canes. Of course he's had to give up his job, but it's a worthwhile investment if it gets him a big settlement. But at this point he's been out of work for two months, and he's getting a gut on him because his only exercise is walking funny to McAnn's and back, and now he's not getting a settlement after all, and who knows if UPS'll even take him back?'

'You sound like you feel sorry for him.'

'Well, I just finished knocking him on his ass,' I said. 'I can afford a little sympathy.'

I told Wally I wanted something else, not from the client but from him. I wanted credit reports from TRW on fourteen men. I'd pay for them, I said, but I wanted them at cost. He assured me that would be no problem, and I gave him the list of survivors.

He said, 'Ray Gruliow? I think his credit's pretty good. And Avery Davis could write out a check and buy the building we're in, if it's the same Avery Davis, and it must be if he lives at 888 Fifth. In fact I think he *did* own the Flatiron for a while, didn't he? No, wait a minute, that was the one who went off the terrace two years ago. What the hell was his name?'

'Harmon Ruttenstein.'

'That's the guy. Talk about everything to live for, but you never know, do you?'

'I guess not.'

Three, possibly four, of the club members had killed

themselves. Nedrick Bayliss had shot himself to death while on a business trip to Atlanta. Hal Gabriel hanged himself in his apartment on West End Avenue. Fred Karp, working late at the office, went out a window. Ian Heller jumped or fell from a crowded subway platform.

You never know, do you?

A series of phone calls got me through to one of the transit cops who'd been there to pull Ian Heller's body from beneath the wheels. There was a long silence when I told him I wanted to talk to him about a death that had occurred almost fifteen years earlier. 'You know,' he said, 'I keep my notebooks, and I can probably sort it out somewhat, but you can't expect me to remember too clearly after all these years. I remember my first, they say you always do. But I been on the job close to nineteen years, so I already seen a lot by the time this guy bought it. So don't expect too much.'

I met him at Pete's Tavern on Irving Place. His name was Arthur Matuszak and he told me to call him Artie. 'You were NYPD,' he said. 'Right?'

'That's right.'

'Got your twenty and put your papers in, huh?'

'I didn't hang around long enough for that.'

'Yeah, I almost hung it up myself a couple of times. But then I didn't, and the time goes by before you know it. It's nineteen years in September for me, and I swear I don't know where they went. I been on a desk the past two years, administrative work, and it's a lot easier on you, but I have to say I miss the tunnels. You're switched on every single minute down there, you know what I mean?'

'Sure.'

'You can't help wondering if it would have been different above-ground. The NYPD instead of the Transit Police. There's not a lot of glamor in the tunnels.

How often do you get a Bernie Goetz, does something colorful enough to stay on the front page more than a day or two? He was one in a million.' He sighed. 'It's been nineteen years of con artists and drunks and chain snatchers and nut jobs. And, yeah, a whole lot of jumped-or-fells. I told you I remembered the first one.'

'Yes.'

'It was a woman, just a girl, really, and she lost half of one leg below the knee and part of her other foot. She was a jumper, no question, admitted it right off. I visited her in the hospital and she looked me right in the eye and said she'd get it right the next time. I don't know if she ever did. For a while every time we had a jumped-or-fell, whether I caught the case or not, I was looking for it to be her. It could be a man lying there, six-four, three hundred pounds, and I'm still expecting to see her face on him when we roll him over. But if she ever did it she must have saved it for somebody else's tour of duty.'

'Considerate of her.'

'Yeah, right. Matt, I went over my notes, and I remember your guy. Ian Robinson Heller, killed by the southbound Number One train coming into the IRT station at Broadway and Fiftieth at approximately 5:45 on a Saturday afternoon. Date was the fifteenth of October 1988. Which happens to be my father-in-law's birthday, only he's been dead for ten years and we been divorced for six, so I don't suppose I have to remember all that, do I? Heller was on his way home from work. It was his usual train. He worked two blocks from the station and he normally rode that train to Times Square and caught the express to Brooklyn, which is where he lived. The point is it was natural for him to be there. I gather you're looking to determine whether it was suicide or accidental death.'

'Or homicide,' I said.

He cocked his head. 'Well, you can't rule it out,' he said, after a moment's reflection. 'It was rush hour, the platform was packed with commuters heading for home, and he was at the edge of the platform with the train coming. Maybe he stopped for a drink after work, maybe he was loaded up on antihistamines and it affected his sense of balance. Maybe somebody backed up into him accidentally.'

'Or maybe he jumped.'

'Right, and how can you ever say? Sometimes they plan it. Sometimes they survive and you find out later they never planned it, never even thought about it, that the impulse just swept over them and took 'em right over the edge. Maybe that's how it was with Heller. Or maybe somebody got next to him and timed it just right and gave him a shove or a body block, sent him flying. Again, planned or unplanned, I'll tell you something, I think there's a fucking ton of that goes on.'

'People killed that way?'

'You bet your ass.' He stood up, pushed through the crowd at the bar, and brought back a fresh gin and tonic for himself and another Coke for me. I tried to pay for the round but he waved me off. 'Please,' he said, 'I'm enjoying myself. You know who drank here? O. Henry. You know, the writer. They're very proud of the fact, they don't let you forget it, but I have to say I love drinking in places like this that are older than God. You know McSorley's down in the East Village? "We were here before you were born," that's their motto. Nowadays their crowd is all college kids, Christ, the World *Trade* Center was there before they were born.'

'And still is.'

'Yeah, and no thanks to our Arab brothers.' We talked

about the recent bombing, and then he said, 'About people getting tossed in front of trains, yeah, I do think it happens a lot. People acting on an impulse, they're stoned on something, or they're just nuts, they don't need drugs to go crazy. Easiest way in the world to kill someone and get away with it.'

'But it would be a hard way to murder someone specific, wouldn't it?'

'You mean like somebody you got a reason to kill?' He thought about it. 'You could tail him into the subway, but suppose he stays away from the edge of the platform? Crowded station, you'd have a few dozen people crammed between him and the tracks. Unless you and him were friends.'

'What do you mean?'

'What was his name again? Ian? "Hey, Ian, good to see you. How's it goin', old buddy?" And you throw your arm around him, and you walk this way and you walk that way, and you just manage to be standing right at the edge of the platform when the train's coming. If he thinks you're his friend, he won't draw away, he won't get suspicious, and the next thing he knows he's under the wheels. You think that's what happened?'

'No idea.'

'Fifteen years later and somebody's starting to wonder? Let me know how it comes out, huh? *If* it comes out.' I said I would. 'What I do, I take the subway all the time. I'll be honest with you, I love the subway, I think it's a wonderful and exciting urban rail system. But I am very careful down there. I see a guy who don't look right, I don't let myself be between him and the edge. I got to walk past somebody and it's gonna put me close to the edge of the platform, I wait until I can step past him on the other side. I want to take a chance, I'll go in a deli, buy a lottery ticket. I'll go by OTB, put two bucks on a horse. I love it down in the tunnels, but I don't take chances down there.' He shook his head. 'Not me. I seen too much.'

SEVEN

Hal Gabriel had lived on West End Avenue at Ninety-second Street. At the Two-four station house on West One Hundredth I sat across a desk from a young police officer named Michael Selig. He was still in his twenties and already losing his hair, and he had the anxious look of the prematurely bald. 'This all ought to be on computer,' he said of Gabriel's file. 'We're working our way back, getting our old files copied, but it takes forever.'

Gabriel, forty-six, married but separated from his wife, had been found hanging in his eighth-floor apartment on a weekday afternoon in October 1981. He had evidently stood on a chair, looped a leather belt around his neck, wedged the tongue of the belt between the top of his closet door and the doorjamb, and kicked the chair over.

'High blood alcohol,' Selig said.

'No note.'

'They don't always leave a note, do they? Especially when they get drunk and start feeling sorry for themselves. Look at this – he estimates death as having occurred five to seven days before discovery of the body. Must have been ripe, huh?'

'That's why they broke in.'

'Didn't have to, it says here the super had a key. Woman across the hall noticed the smell.'

She'd also told the investigating officers that Gabriel had seemed despondent since his wife's departure several years earlier, that his only visitors had been delivery boys from the liquor store and the Chinese restaurant. He'd worked up until two months of his death, managing a film lab in the West Forties, but had been out of work since then.

'Most likely drank himself out of the job,' Selig offered.

His wife, apprised of his death, said she hadn't seen Gabriel since they'd signed their separation agreement in June of 1980. She described her late husband as a sad and lonely man, and seemed saddened herself if not terribly surprised by his death.

Fred Karp had left a note. He'd tapped it out on his computer screen, printed out two copies, left one on his desk and tucked the other, neatly folded, into his shirt pocket. *I'm sorry*, it read. *I can't take it anymore. Please forgive me.* Then he'd opened the window of his fifteenth-floor office and stepped out.

That's tough to do in the newer buildings, where you generally can't open the windows. Often they aren't windows at all, just glass walls. At an AA meeting I once heard an architect talk about how he'd had to reassure office workers who had a phobic response to glass walls. He used to run full speed and crash headlong into the wall to demonstrate its solidity. 'People got the point,' he said, 'but I felt pretty stupid the time I broke my collarbone.'

You could open the windows in Karp's building. It was a twenty-two-story prewar office building on Lexington Avenue, just a couple of blocks north of Grand Central Station and the Chrysler Building. Karp was an importer, dealing primarily in goods from Singapore and Indonesia. He'd sent his secretary home at five, called his wife to tell her he'd be working late. A deli on Third Avenue delivered two sandwiches and a container of coffee around seven. At ten after nine he went out the window, and it was easy to pinpoint the time of death because there were people on the street who saw him land. One of them collapsed, and was treated by paramedics at the scene.

This had happened just three years ago, and the police officer I spoke to was still attached to the Seventeenth Precinct and had no difficulty remembering the incident. 'Hell of a mess,' he said, 'and a hell of a way to do it. Suppose you change your mind halfway down. "Hey. I take it back! I was only kidding!" Yeah, right, lots of luck.'

There was no question in his mind that it was suicide. There was the note, on Karp's desk and in his pocket and right up there on the still-glowing screen of the computer monitor. And there were no injuries inconsistent with a fall from a great height, although he agreed that the fall itself would have erased evidence of an earlier blow to the head, or indeed of anything less obvious than a gunshot wound.

I said, 'I wish the note was handwritten. Who on earth types out a suicide note on a computer?'

'It's a new world,' he said. 'You get used to a computer, you want to use it for everything. Pay your bills, balance your checkbook, keep your appointments straight. Here's a guy ran his whole business by computer. He wants to get the note right, he can tinker with it, phrase it just the way he wants it. Then he can print out all the copies he wants with one keystroke, plus he can save it on his hard drive.' He was around thirty, part of the computer generation himself, and he was eager to tell me how the computers in the station house speeded up the paperwork and took a lot of the unpleasantness out of it. 'Computers are great,' he said. 'But they spoil you. The trouble with the rest of life is there's no UNDO key.'

I went to Karp's office, now occupied by an attorney specializing in patents, a man about my age with a

drinker's complexion and the sour smell of failure cling-
ing to him. He'd had the office for less than two years and
knew nothing of its history. He let me look out his
window, although I don't know what either of us
thought I might see out there. I didn't tell him a previous
tenant had taken a dive from that very window. I didn't
want to give him any ideas.

Karp's widow, Felicia, lived in Forest Hills and taught
math in a middle school in South Ozone Park. I phoned
her at home around dinnertime and she said, 'I can't
believe the investigation's been reopened. Does this have
something to do with the insurance?'

I told her it was in connection with another matter,
and that I was trying to rule out the possibility that her
husband's death had not been suicide.

'I never thought it was,' she said forcefully. 'But what
else could it be? Listen, do you want to come to the
house? I have two hours of tutoring to do tonight, but I
could meet you tomorrow. Say four-thirty?'

She was waiting for me in the upper flat of a
semidetached two-family house on Stafford Avenue,
just a few blocks from where they used to play the tennis
tournaments. She was a tall, angular woman with straight
dark hair and a strong jawline. She had coffee made and
we sat at her kitchen table. There was one of those black
cat clocks on the wall, with the eyes rolling from side to
side and the tail swinging like a pendulum. She said, 'Isn't
it ridiculous? The kids gave it to me for my birthday a
couple of years ago, and I have to admit it's grown on
me. Let's talk about Fred.'

'All right.'

'It never made sense to me that he would kill himself.
They said he was having problems with his business.
Well, he was in that business for over twenty years, and
you always have problems. He never had trouble making

68

a living. And we had two incomes, and we were never extravagant. Look where we live.'

'It's a nice house.'

'It's okay, and the neighborhood's decent, but it's not Sutton Place. The point is my husband wasn't under any great financial pressure. Look, after his death I ran the business myself long enough to straighten things out and get a few dollars for the stock and goodwill. The business was in fine shape. Day-to-day chaos, yes, but nothing unusual. Certainly nothing to kill yourself over.'

'It's hard to know what goes on inside another person.'

'I realize that. But why are you here, Mr Scudder? You didn't schlepp all the way out here to talk me into accepting my husband's suicide.'

I asked her if she knew anything about a club her husband had belonged to. She said, 'What club? He was in the men's club at the temple but he wasn't very active. His work took too much of his time. He joined Rotary but that was at least ten years ago and I don't think he maintained his membership. That can't be what you're referring to.'

'This was a club of fellows who had dinner once a year,' I said. 'In the spring, at a restaurant in Manhattan.'

'Oh, that,' she said. 'What threw me off was your using the word "club". I don't think it was that formal, just a bunch of fellows who were friends in college and wanted to stay in touch over the years.'

'Is that how he described the group?'

'I don't know that he ever "described" it as such. That was certainly the impression I had. Why?'

'I understand it was a little more formal than that.'

'It's possible. I know he never missed a dinner. One year we had tickets donated at the school, the Manhattan Light Opera, and Fred told me I'd have to find someone else to go with me. And he loved Gilbert and Sullivan, but he regarded his annual dinner as sacrosanct. What does the dinner have to do with his death? He died in December. The dinner was always sometime in April or May.'

'The first Thursday in May.'

'That's right, it was a set day every year. I'd forgotten. So?'

Was there any reason not to tell her? I said, 'There have been a lot of deaths in the group over the years, more than you'd expect. Several of them were suicides.'

'How many?'

'Three or four.'

'Well, which is it? Three or four?'

'Three definite, one possible.'

'I see. I'm sorry, I didn't mean to snap. Do you want more coffee?' I said I was fine. 'Three or four suicides out of how many members?'

'Thirty-one.'

'There's a suicide virus, I've heard it called. There'll be some perfectly nice middle-class high school in Ohio or Wisconsin, and they'll have an absolute rash of suicides. But that's teenagers, not middle-aged men. Were these suicides all grouped together?'

'They were spaced over a period of several years.'

'Well, ten to fifteen percent, that's a high suicide rate, but it doesn't seem . . .' Her words trailed off and I watched her eyes. I could almost see the wheels turning as her mind sorted the data. She was not a pretty woman by any means but she had a good, quick mind and there was something quite attractive about her intelligence.

She said, 'You mentioned a high death rate overall. How many deaths in all?'

'Seventeen.'

'Of thirty-one.'

'Yes.'

'And they're all Fred's age? They must be if they were all in college together.'

'Approximately the same age, yes.'

'You think someone's killing them.'

'I'm investigating the possibility. I don't know what I think.'

'Of course you do.'

I shook my head. 'It's a little too early for me to have an opinion.'

'But you think it's possible.'

'Yes.'

She turned to look at the cat clock. 'Of course I'd rather believe that,' she said. 'I've never completely come to terms with his suicide. But it's awful to think of someone, God, *killing* him. How was it done, I wonder? I suppose the killer would have knocked him out, then written the suicide note on the computer and opened the window and, and, and . . .' She made a visible effort and got hold of herself. 'If he was unconscious when it happened,' she said, 'he wouldn't have suffered greatly.'

'No.'

'But I have,' she said softly, and was silent for a long moment. Then she looked up at me and said, 'Why would anybody want to kill a bunch of fellows who went to Brooklyn College together thirty-five years ago? A group of Jewish guys in their fifties. Why?'

'Only a few of them were Jewish.'

'Oh?'

'And they weren't in college together.'

'Are you sure? Fred said—'

I told her a little about the club. She wanted to know who the other members were, and I found a page in my notebook where I'd listed all thirty-one members, living and dead, in alphabetical order. She said, 'Well, here's a

71

name that pops out. Philip Kalish. *He* was Jewish, and Fred knew him in college, if it's the same Phil Kalish. But he died, didn't he? A long time ago.'

'In an auto accident,' I said. 'He was the first of the group to die.'

'Raymond Gruliow. There's another name I recognize, if it's the same Raymond Gruliow, and it would almost have to be, wouldn't it? The lawyer?'

'Yes.'

'If Adolf Hitler came back to earth,' she said, 'which God forbid, and if he needed a lawyer, he'd call Raymond Gruliow. And Gruliow would defend him.' She shook her head. 'I have to admit I thought he was a hero during the Vietnam War when his clients were draft resisters and radicals. Now they're all black anti-Semites and Arab terrorists and I want to send him a letter bomb. Fred didn't know Raymond Gruliow.'

'He had dinner with him once a year.'

'And never said a word? When Gruliow was running his mouth on the eleven o'clock news, wouldn't he at least once have said, "He's a friend of mine" or "Hey, I know the guy"? Wouldn't that be the natural thing to do?'

'I guess they kept it private.'

She frowned. 'This club wasn't a sex thing, was it?'

'No.'

'Because I'd find that very hard to believe. I know the most unlikely people keep turning out to be gay, but I can't believe this was—'

'No.'

'Or some sort of Boys' Night Out, with too much to drink and some girl jumping out of a cake. It doesn't sound like Fred.'

'I don't think it was like that at all.'

'Boyd Shipton. The painter?' I nodded. 'Now I know

he was murdered several years ago, or am I confusing him with somebody else?'

I agreed that Shipton had been murdered, and told her that several other members had also been the victims of homicide. She asked which ones they were and I pointed out the names.

'No, I don't know any of them,' she said. 'Why would anyone want to kill these men? I don't understand.'

Heading back to Manhattan, I wondered what I'd accomplished. I hadn't learned very much, and I'd left Felicia Karp wondering what sort of secret life her husband had led. If she could draw any comfort from the thought that he hadn't killed himself after all, it was very likely offset by the disquieting probability that he'd been murdered.

Maybe that was what led me to leave Nedrick Bayliss's widow undisturbed. A series of telephone calls to Atlanta, where he'd died in a room at the downtown Marriott of a single gunshot wound to the head, left me feeling I knew as much as I had to know about him and his death. He'd been a stock analyst, employed by a Wall Street firm, commuting to work from a home in Hastings-on-Hudson. His area of specialization was the textiles industry, and he'd gone to Atlanta to meet with officers of a company he was interested in.

Again, no note, and no indication how he'd come by the unregistered revolver found at his side. 'I don't know how it is up there,' an Atlanta police officer told me, 'but it's not the hardest thing in the world to find somebody who'll sell you a gun in this town.' I told him it wasn't that hard in New York, either.

Instead of a note there was a sheet of hotel stationery in the middle of the desk, with a pen uncapped next to it, as if he'd tried to write something and couldn't think of the right way to say it. Having given up on it, he called the desk instead and told the clerk they'd better send a bellman to room 1102. 'I'm about to take my life,' he announced, and hung up the phone.

The clerk wasn't sure whether he was in the middle of a tragedy or a practical joke. He rang Bayliss's room and no one answered the phone. He was trying to think what to do when someone else called to report a gunshot.

It certainly looked like a suicide. Bayliss was slumped in a chair, a bullet in the temple, the gun on the floor right where you'd expect to find it. Nothing to suggest he hadn't been alone when he did it. He hadn't locked his door with the chain, but he'd have wanted to make it easy for them to get in. He was considerate, after all; he'd proved that when he called the desk to let them know what he was about to do.

How hard would it have been to stage it?

You get Ned Bayliss to let you into his room. Finding a pretext shouldn't be any harder than finding an unregistered gun. Then, when he's sitting down, say, looking at some papers you've handed him, and you're crouching next to him to point out something, you reach into your jacket pocket and come out with the gun and before he knows what's happening you've got the muzzle to his temple and you're giving the trigger a squeeze.

Then you wipe your prints from the gun, press it into his hand, and let it drop to the carpet. You arrange the hotel letterhead and the pen on the desk, pick up the phone, and announce your impending death. Back in your own room, you make another call to report a gunshot.

Easy enough.

A paraffin test would very likely suggest that the dead man had not fired a gun recently, but how much lab work would the police allot to an open-and-shut suicide?

The officer I talked to couldn't find any record of a test, but said that didn't prove anything. After all, he said, it all happened eighteen years ago, so it was a wonder that he'd been able to lay his hands on the file.

I could have called his widow.

I took the trouble to trace her, which wasn't difficult, given that she hadn't been trying to disappear. She had remarried, divorced, and been married a third time, and now she was living in Niles, Michigan, and I suppose I could have called her and asked her if her first husband, Ned Bayliss, had been despondent before his fateful trip to Atlanta. Was he drinking a lot, ma'am? Did he have any kind of a drug history?

I decided to let her be.

I'd called Atlanta from my room in the Northwestern, and when I hung up the phone for the day something kept me right there in the little room. I pulled a chair over to the window and looked out at the city.

I don't know how long I sat there. I started off thinking about the case I was working on, the club of thirty-one. I thought how their ranks had thinned over the past three decades, and before I knew it I was thinking of my own life over the same span of years, and the awful toll those years had taken. I thought of the people I'd lost, some to death, some because our lives had slipped off in different directions. My ex-wife, Anita, long since remarried. The last time I'd spoken to her was to offer condolences for her mother's death. The last time I'd seen her – I couldn't remember the last time I'd seen her.

My sons, Michael and Andrew, both of them grown, both of them strangers to me. Michael was living in northern California, a sales rep for a company that supplied components to manufacturers of computers. In the four years since he graduated from college I'd spoken to him ten times at the outside. Two years ago he got married to a girl named June, and he'd sent me their wedding picture. She is Chinese, very short and slender, her expression in the photograph utterly serious. Mike started putting on weight in college, and now he looks like a bluff, hearty salesman, fat and jolly, posed incongruously next to this inscrutable daughter of the Orient.

'We'll have to get together,' he says when we speak on the phone. 'Next time I get to New York I'll let you know. We'll have dinner, maybe catch a Knicks game.'

'Maybe I could get out to the Coast,' I suggested the last time I talked to him. There was just the slightest pause, and then he was quick to assure me that would be great, really great, but right now wasn't a good time. A very busy time at work these days, and he was traveling a lot, and—

He and June live in a condominium near San Jose. I have spoken to her on the phone, this daughter-in-law whom I have never met. Soon I suppose they'll start a family, and then I'll have grandchildren I've never met.

And Andy? The last time I heard from him he was in Seattle, and talking about heading on up to Vancouver. It sounded as though he was calling from a bar, and his voice was thickened with drink. He doesn't call often, and when he does it's always from someplace new, and he always sounds as though he's been drinking. 'I'm having fun,' he told me. 'One of these days I guess I'll settle down, but in the meantime I'm gathering no moss.'

Fifty-five years old, and what moss had I gathered? What had I done with those years? And what had they done to me?

And how many did I have left? And, when they'd slipped away like the rest, what would I have to show for them? What did anybody ever have to show for the years that were gone?

There's a liquor store right across the street. From where I sat I could see the customers enter and leave. As I watched them, it came to me that I could look up the store's number in the phone book and have them send up a bottle.

That was as far as I allowed the thought to go. Sometimes I'll let myself consider what type of liquor I'd order, and what brand. This time I shook the thought off early on and breathed deeply several times, willing myself to let it go.

Then I reached for the phone and dialed a number I didn't have to look up.

It rang twice, three times. I had my finger poised to break the connection, not wanting to talk to a machine, but then she picked up.

'This is Matt,' I said.

She said, 'That's funny. I was just this minute thinking of you.'

'And I of you. Would you like company?'

'Would I?' She took a moment to consider the question. 'Yes,' she said. 'Yes, I would.'

EIGHT

When I first moved to my hotel, Jimmy Armstrong had a saloon right around the corner on Ninth Avenue, and that was where I spent most of my waking hours. After I got sober Jimmy lost his lease and reopened a long block west, at the corner of Tenth and Fifty-seventh. In AA they tell you to avoid the people and places and things that might make you want to drink, and for several years I stayed away from Jimmy's joint. These days I get there now and then. Elaine likes the place on Sunday afternoons, when they have chamber music, and it's always been a good choice for a late supper.

I walked west on Fifty-seventh, but instead of paying a call on Jimmy I went to the high-rise apartment building diagonally across the street. The doorman had been told I was coming; when I gave him my name he said I was expected and pointed to the elevator. I rode up to the twenty-eighth floor and her door opened even as I knocked on it.

'I really was,' she said. 'Thinking of you just before you called. You look tired. Are you all right?'

'I'm fine.'

'It's probably the humidity. This is going to be some summer if it's like this in June. I just put the air on. This place cools off pretty quickly.'

'How are you, Lisa?'

She turned aside. 'I'm all right,' she said. 'Do you want some coffee? Or would you rather have something cold? There's Pepsi, there's iced tea . . .'

'No, thanks.'

She spun around to face me. She said, 'I'm glad you're here, but I don't think I want to do anything. Is that all right?'

'Of course.'

'We could sit and talk.'

'Whatever you say.'

She walked to the window. Her apartment faces west, and there are no tall buildings to block her view. I moved up behind her and watched a couple of sailboats on the Hudson.

She was wearing perfume, the musky scent she always wore.

She said, 'Oh, who am I kidding?'

She turned to face me once again. I circled her waist and linked my hands, and she leaned back and looked up at me. Her forehead was shining and there were beads of sweat on her upper lip. 'Oh!' she said, as if something had startled her, and I drew her close and kissed her, and at first she trembled in my arms and then she threw her own arms around me and we clung together. I felt her body against me, I felt her breasts, I felt the heat of her loins.

I kissed her mouth. I kissed her throat and breathed in her scent.

'Oh!' she cried.

We went to the bedroom and got our clothes off, interrupting the process to kiss, to clutch each other. We fell together onto the bed. 'Oh,' she said. 'Oh, oh, oh . . .'

Her name was Lisa Holtzmann, and it would not be inaccurate to describe her as young enough to be my daughter, although she had in fact been born almost ten years before my elder son. When I first met her she'd been married to a lawyer named Glenn Holtzmann, and pregnant with his child. She lost the baby early in the third trimester, and not long after that she'd lost her husband; he'd been shot to death while using a pay phone just a couple of blocks away on Eleventh Avenue.

I'd wound up with two clients, one of them the dead man's widow, the other the brother of the man accused of shooting him. I don't know that I did either of them a world of good. The alleged killer, one of the neighborhood street crazies, wound up getting stabbed to death on Rikers Island by someone no saner than himself. The widow Holtzmann wound up in bed with me.

That it happened does not strike me as extraordinary. Traditionally, widows have been regarded as vulnerable to seduction, and as more than ordinarily seductive themselves. My role in Lisa's personal drama, the knight in tarnished armor riding to her rescue, did nothing to hinder our falling into bed together. While I was deeply in love with and committed to Elaine, and by no means uncomfortable with that commitment, there is something in the male chromosomal makeup that renders a new woman alluring simply because she is new.

There had been no other women for me since Elaine and I had found each other again, but I suppose it was inevitable that there would be someone sooner or later. The surprise was that the affair wouldn't quit. It was like the Energizer rabbit. It kept going and going and going . . .

You didn't need a doctorate in psychology to figure out what was going on. I was obviously a father figure to her, and only the least bit more available than the genuine article. For several years back home in White Bear Lake, Minnesota, he had come to her bed at night. He had thrilled her with his fingers and his mouth, teaching her to gasp out her pleasure like a lady, softly, so the sounds would not carry beyond her bedroom door. He taught her, too, to please him, and by the time she went off to college she had become skilled beyond her years.

And still a virgin. 'He would never put it in,' she said, 'because he told me that would be a sin.'

While she and I had not drawn any such line, in other respects our relationship echoed what she'd had with Daddy. Although she had originally made the first overtures, giving me to understand that she was available to me, since then she had initiated nothing. She never called my home or office. I always called, asking if she felt like company, and she always told me to come over.

We were never together outside her apartment. We never walked down the street side by side, or had a cup of coffee together. One night Elaine and I stopped at Armstrong's after a concert at Lincoln Center, and Elaine spotted Lisa in the crowd at the bar. It was Elaine who had introduced me to Lisa and her husband; the two women had met at a class at Hunter College. 'Isn't that Lisa Holtzmann?' she'd said, nodding toward the bar. I looked and agreed that it was, but neither of us suggested going over and saying hello.

In her apartment, in her bed, I could shut out the world. It was as if those rooms on the twenty-eighth floor existed somehow outside of space and time. I would shuck off my life like a pair of boots and leave it at the door.

I suppose it wasn't much of a stretch to say she was like a drug or a drink to me. I'd thought fleetingly of calling the liquor store, reached for the phone, and called her instead. The connection wasn't usually that clearly wrought. I would find myself thinking of her, and wanting to be with her. Sometimes I resisted the impulse. Sometimes I didn't.

I rarely went to her more than once a month, and during the winter there'd been a stretch of almost three months when I'd never even reached for the phone. Shortly after the first of the year I thought of her and thought, *Well, that's over,* feeling a curious mixture of sadness and relief. Early in February I called and went over there, and we were right back where we'd started.

Afterward we watched the sunset. It must have been around nine. The sunsets were coming later every day now, with less than a week to go until Midsummer Eve.

She said, 'I've been working a lot. I got a great assignment, six covers from a paperback western series.'

'Good for you.'

'The hardest part is reading the books. They're what they call adult westerns. Do you know what those are?'

'I could probably guess.'

'You probably could. The hero doesn't say, "Shucks, ma'am." '

'What does he say?'

'In the one I just finished he said, Why don't you get shed of that petticoat so I can eat that sweet little pussy of yours.'

'How the West was won.'

'It's shocking,' she said, 'because you think you're reading Hopalong Cassidy, and the next thing you know somebody's getting fisted behind the corral. The hero's name is Cole Hardwick. That's pretty straightforward, don't you think?'

'One gets the point.'

'I'm doing a different western scene for each cover. The two constants are guns and cleavage. Oh, and Cole Hardwick's weathered face in the foreground, so you'll know right away it's another book in the series.' She extended a hand, ran her forefinger along my jaw. 'I almost used this face,' she said.

'Oh?'

'I started sketching, and what came out began to look curiously familiar. It was a great temptation to leave it. I wonder if you'd ever have seen one of the books, and if you'd have recognized yourself.'

'I don't know.'

'Anyway, I decided you're not right for it. You're too urban, too streetwise.'

'Too old.'

'No, Hardwick's pretty grizzled himself. Look, there goes the sun. Will I ever get tired of sunsets? I hope not.'

The show was even richer once the sun was down. A whole rainbow of colors stained the Jersey skyline.

She said, 'I've been seeing somebody.'

'Somebody nice, I hope.'

'He seems nice. He's an art director for an in-flight magazine. I showed him my book and he didn't have any work for me, but he called me the next day and took me to dinner. He's nice-looking and fun to be with and he likes me.'

'That's great.'

'We've had four dates. Tomorrow we're going to have an early dinner and see *Eleven Months of Winter* at Play-wrights Horizon. And then I suppose I'll sleep with him.'

'You haven't yet?'

'No. A couple of, you know, lingering kisses.' She clasped her hands in her lap and looked down at them. 'When you called, my first thought was to tell you not to come over today. And then I said I didn't want to do anything, and how long did that last? Half a minute?'

'Something like that.'

'I wonder what it is with us.'

'I've wondered myself.'

'What happens if I start sleeping with Peter? What will I say when you call?'

'I don't know.'

' "Come on over," I'll say. And afterward I'll feel like a whore.'

I didn't say anything.

'I can't see myself sleeping with two men at once. I don't mean literally at the same time, I mean—'

'I know what you mean.'

'Having a relationship with Peter, and still going to bed with you. I can't see myself doing that. But I can't imagine saying no to you, either.'

'Daddy stuff?'

'Oh, I suppose so. When you kissed me there was a split second when I could taste liquor on your breath. Of course that was just memory. He never came to my room without liquor on his breath. Did I tell you he was in treatment?'

'No.'

'Well, Minnesota. Land of ten thousand lakes and twenty thousand alcoholism-treatment centers. The doctor was concerned that his liver was enlarged and sent him for treatment. My mother says he's not drinking anything now but a little beer with meals. I don't suppose that will last.'

'It never does.'

'Maybe his liver'll blow up and he'll die. Sometimes I wish that would happen. Does that shock you?'

'No.'

'And other times I want to pray for him. That he'll stop drinking and, and, I don't know what. Get better, I guess. Be the father I always wanted. But maybe he already *is* the father I always wanted. Maybe he was all along.'

'Maybe.'

'Anyway, I don't know how to pray. Do you pray?'

'Once in a while. Not very often, though.'

'How do you do it?'

'Mostly I ask for strength.'

'Strength?'

'To do something,' I said, 'or to get through something. That kind of strength.'

'And do you get it?'

'Yes,' I said. 'I generally do.'

I showered before I left her place, then got to the basement of St Paul's in time for the last half hour of the meeting. I raised my hand and said that I'd thought of drinking earlier. 'I was looking out the window at the liquor store across the street,' I said, 'and I thought how easy it would be to call them up and tell them to send over a bottle. I've been sober a few years now, and I don't get thoughts like that very often, but I'm still an alcoholic, and I've stayed sober this long by not drinking and by coming here and talking about it. And I'm glad I'm sober, and I'm glad I'm here tonight.'

Afterward I joined a few of the others at the Flame. I ate a hamburger and drank a glass of iced coffee. I got home a little before eleven.

'You look a little wilted,' Elaine said. 'Thank God for air-conditioning, huh? Joe Durkin called, he wants you to call him in the morning. And you had a couple of other messages. I wrote them down. I hope your day was more exciting than mine.'

'Things were pretty slow?'

'Well, who wants to go gallery-hopping in this weather? But I think I have a commission for Ray Galindez. A woman in her seventies, a Buchenwald survivor. Her whole family died over there, and of course she doesn't have any pictures. She came over after the war with the clothes on her back and nothing else. She wants Ray to draw them all – her parents, her grandparents, her little sister. She lost everybody, Matt.'

'Can she afford it?'

'She could buy my whole store out of petty cash. She married another camp survivor and they opened a candy store. Her sons went into business together, they have a metal-casting business in Passaic. She has six grand-children, three doctors and two lawyers.'

'And one black sheep?'

'The black sheep is at Harvard picking up an MBA before she moves back to Passaic and starts running the factory. That's if she doesn't get sidetracked and decide to become the CEO of General Motors.'

'You got the whole story, huh?'

'Complete with pictures. Money's no problem. Her only worry is that she won't be able to remember what they look like. 'I close my eyes and try to see them, and I don't see nothing.' I told her to sit down with the artist and see what happens. She got a little teary at the thought. I tried to comfort her and I started to remember what an emotional experience it was when Ray did the sketch of my father. You should have seen us, honey. Two old broads with our arms around each other, crying about nothing.'

'You're really something.'

'Me?'

'I think you're wonderful.'

'I'm just another former whore,' she said, 'with a former heart of gold.'

NINE

Joe Durkin said, 'Tell me something, because I find myself wondering. Just how did I get to be your rabbi?'

'I suppose you went to yeshiva,' I said, 'and studied long and hard.'

'You know,' he said, 'that's the kind of rabbi I should have been. Wear one of those little beanies, stroke my beard anytime I'm stuck for an answer. I wonder if it's too late for a career change.'

'I think you have to be Jewish.'

'I figured there was a catch. It sounded too good to be true.' He leaned all the way back in his chair with his hands clasped behind his neck. 'Seriously, though,' he said, 'how was I chosen to be your friend in high places? Your personal tapeworm, deep in the bowels of the NYPD bureaucracy.'

'Tapeworm,' I said. 'Jesus.'

He grinned. 'You like that? I thought you would. My other choice was your cat's-paw, pulling your chestnuts out of the fire. I think I like the tapeworm better.'

We were in the squad room at Midtown North. The desk next to Joe's was empty. Two desks away, a heavyset black detective named Bellamy was interrogating a skinny Hispanic kid with a wispy goatee on his sharp chin. The kid had a cigarette going and Bellamy kept waving at the smoke, trying to keep it from drifting in his face.

'Four homicide investigations,' Durkin said. 'Earliest one's twelve years ago, most recent's this past February. Four men and a woman killed in different ways in widely separated parts of the city over a twelve-year period. What, I asked myself, could these cases possibly have in common? You want to know what I came up with?'

'What?'

'All of the victims are dead. Still dead, like General Franco. You remember that from *Saturday Night Live*?'

'Vaguely.'

' "This just in from Madrid – Generalissimo Francisco Franco is still dead." ' He made a show of shuffling the papers on his desk. 'Here we go. Carl Uhl, killed by a lover in his West Twenty-second Street apartment. Victim was gay, apartment bore evidence of an S-and-M lifestyle, victim was secured with handcuffs and leather restraints, blah blah blah, multiple stab wounds, genital and pectoral mutilation. You need all this?'

'No,' I said. 'I know most of it, except for the details, and I can look at the notes later. What I want to know—'

'You want to know if the file's still open, right? The answer's yes. The guys from the One-oh picked up a couple of Uhl's acquaintances but their stories checked out. Every once in a while they collar a perp who's been doing gay men this way, picking up tricks in the leather bars on West Street and giving them more excitement than they wanted, and they trot out all their open files with a similar MO and try them on for size. So far Carl Uhl's still an orphan. Why? What do you know that the One-oh doesn't?'

'Not a thing,' I said. 'Is that how the killer got to Uhl? He picked him up on West Street?'

'Nobody knows. Maybe he came down the chimney carrying his bag of tricks. As far as finding out who he is, that's not gonna happen. Unless he gets picked up for doing it again, and he won't, because you know what? Odds are he's dead.'

'How do you figure that?'

'How do I figure it? I figure that twelve years ago he was engaging in high-risk sexual behavior at a time when AIDS was spreading through the bathhouses and back-room bars, but before anybody knew what it was, let alone gave the first thought to precautions. Guy who did Uhl, he probably killed fifty times as many people by giving them the virus as he ever did with his little knife, and when he was done spreading it around he went and died of it himself.'

'Did he leave semen behind?'

'No, he took it home in a doggie bag.' He picked up the report and scanned it. 'Semen traces on victim's abdomen, it says here. Probably Uhl's. His blood type, anyway. Of course this was before DNA testing. Forensics has come a long way, my friend.'

'It certainly has.'

'And that's why nobody gets away with murder anymore. Where'd that question come from, did he leave semen behind? What have you got?'

'Nothing,' I said. 'I just wondered if there was any concrete evidence that they'd had sexual relations.'

'Well, it doesn't sound as though they were talking about the weather. With these leather boys, though, what they call sex might not be what you and I would call sex. One case I had, these two boys had a relationship, and how they worked it, the one would come over to the other's apartment and be told to strip naked and clean the toilet. Not with his tongue or anything, just grab a can of Comet and a roll of paper towels and clean the toilet. Meanwhile the other one sat in the living room watching *Oprah*. Then he'd inspect the toilet and give the guy who cleaned it some verbal abuse and send him packing. It'd be like you or I having the cleaning lady come, an' when she's done instead of paying her you tell her she's a stupid cunt and to get the hell out.'

'I wouldn't dare,' I said. 'It was bad enough the time I asked her to do the windows.'

'As far as Uhl's concerned,' he said, '*somebody* had sex, because the semen on Uhl's belly didn't just grow there. Either it's his semen because he had a good time before his friend got serious with the knife, or it was the killer's and he had the same blood type. Does it make a difference?'

'Not to me,' I allowed.

'Then can we move on? Six years later, 1987, and we've got Boyd and Diana Shipton murdered in their loft downtown on Hubert Street. Two theories on that one. One's they walked in on a burglary in progress.'

'That was my impression from the news coverage.'

'Well, there were things the press wasn't told. The brutality of the crime suggested a more personal motive.'

'He was beaten to death, she was raped and strangled.'

'He was beaten, but not just to death. His head was mashed to a pulp, the skull fractured beyond restoration, the face completely unrecognizable.'

'But it was definitely him.'

'Yeah, they had fingerprint ID, but what prompts a question like that?'

'Nothing in particular. When somebody tells me a corpse's face is completely unrecognizable, the first question that comes to mind—'

'Yeah, I see what you mean. But there's no question it was him. As to the wife, she was garroted with a strip of wire. Her head turned purple and swelled up like a volleyball. As for the rape, well, I don't know if you'd call it that, but it was certainly a violation. She had a fireplace poker thrust up her vagina and well into the abdomen.'

'Jesus.'

'She was already dead when it took place, if that makes

a difference. The whole bit with the poker was withheld from the press for obvious reasons, but even if they had it they couldn't have printed it. Though nowadays I'm not so sure anymore.'

'Nowadays they'll print anything.'

'Did the news stories say that some of the paintings were vandalized? What they didn't let out was that they'd been defaced with satanic symbols. The consensus of some experts—' he rolled his eyes '—is that these were not the work of authentic satanists. I suppose an authentic satanist would have done something horrible to the Shiptons, whereas these fake satanists were just out to have some innocent fun.'

'How many killers?'

'Best guess seems to be two or three.'

'Could one person have done it unassisted?'

'You can't rule it out,' he said. 'The cops in East Hampton had somebody they liked for it, a local contractor who had been having an affair with Mrs Shipton, or else it was the other way around, Boyd was dicking the guy's wife. It could have been done by one person acting alone, lying in wait. One blow to the skull knocks Boyd out, then he gets the wire around her neck and kills her, then he pulps Boyd's head, and finally he does his stupid pet trick with the fireplace poker.'

'Do they still like the contractor?'

'No, his alibi was solid, you couldn't knock it down. There was a ton of theories. The guy was a prominent artist, the wife was a former ballet dancer, they had pots of money, the loft downtown, the beach house in East Hampton, they hung out with a moneyed and talented crowd. What does that suggest to you?'

'I don't know. Cocaine?'

'A big play in the media and a ton of cops assigned, both here and out on the island, that's what I was getting at. Cocaine? I suppose they had a toot now and then, but if there was a major drug element in the case I never heard about it, and the guy I talked to yesterday didn't mention it. Why?'

'No reason. I know there hasn't been an arrest, but do they think they know who did it?'

He shook his head. 'Not a clue,' he said. 'Well, plenty of clues, but none of them led anywhere. Why? What does your snitch say?'

'What snitch?'

'Your snitch, whoever's got you barking up four different trees. Who does he like for the Shiptons?'

'I don't have a snitch, Joe.'

He looked at me. Two desks away, Bellamy picked a burning cigarette from the ashtray and stubbed it out. 'Hey,' the kid with the goatee said. 'I wasn't done with that, man.' Bellamy told the kid he was lucky he hadn't ground it out on his forehead.

Durkin said, 'All right, we'll let it pass for now. Next up is four years ago, 1989, Thomas P. Cloonan. Nice decent Irish fellow, driving a cab, trying to put food on his table. Nobody tied him up, nobody jerked him off, and nobody shoved a poker up his ass. I'll tell you, I'm surprised a guy like yourself's got any interest in him at all.'

According to his log sheet, Tom Cloonan had picked up the last fare of his life at 10:35 on a Tuesday night. He'd just dropped a fare at the Sherry-Netherland hotel, and he made his pickup a few blocks downtown, across the street from St Patrick's Cathedral. The destination he entered on the sheet was Columbia Presbyterian Medical Center, up in Washington Heights.

It was impossible to know if he got there. At approximately 12:15, acting on information received through an anonymous phone tip, a radio car from the Thirty-fourth Precinct found Cloonan's taxi parked next to a fire hydrant on Audubon Avenue at 174th Street. Cloonan, fifty-four, was slumped behind the wheel with bullet wounds in the head and neck. He was pronounced dead at the scene by paramedics.

'Two shots fired at close range, weapon was a nine-mil, and death was instantaneous or close to it. Wallet was missing, coin changer was missing, murder weapon was not left at the scene – no surprise there – and the only question is did the shooter ride all the way up from Saint Paddy's with him or did he drop his long-haul at Columbia Presbyterian and make another pickup right on the spot that he never had a chance to log in? And the answer is who cares, because the case is closed and the shooter's doing twenty-to-life in Attica.'

The surprise must have showed in my face, because he answered my next question before I could ask it.

'He didn't go away for Cloonan,' he said. 'What happened, there was a rash of these in '90 and '91, gypsy cab drivers shot in Harlem or the Bronx, some Third World part of the city. There was a task force formed consisting of cops from five different precincts in the Bronx and upper Manhattan, and they set out a string of decoys and came up with Eldoniah Mims. A Norwegian kid, obviously.'

'Well, they've always been a race of troublemakers.'

'I know, them and the fucking Estonians. They had Mims flatfooted for half a dozen killings, and they took the most rock-solid case to trial, one where they had physical and eyewitness evidence. The plea they offered him, he could cop to six counts of second-degree murder, and in return they'd let him serve the sentences concurrently.'

'Very generous.'

'So he had to turn it down, and the case they brought was a Manhattan killing, so you didn't get one of those Bronx juries determined to avenge three hundred years of racist oppression. The judge and jury both did the right thing, and Eldoniah's got to do twenty upstate before he's eligible for parole, and if he ever gets out they can try him for some of the other cabbies he killed, the useless little son of a bitch.'

'Could they try him for Cloonan?'

'He'd be way down at the bottom of the list. You know, you get someone dead to rights like that, you want to close whatever files you can.'

'But you don't know that he did it.'

'I don't know zip, my friend, because all of this happened up in Washington Heights and the fucking Bronx, so what do I know? What I *hear*, which isn't the same thing, is nobody's all that sure Mims did Cloonan, but what's it hurt to let him take the weight until somebody better comes along?'

'You said gypsy cabs,' I said. 'If Cloonan was picking up on Fifth Avenue, wouldn't he have been driving a metered taxi?'

He nodded. 'He was in a Yellow and the rest were gypsies. He was also shot with a nine-mil and the others with twenty-twos. Not all the same gun, different guns, but all the same caliber.'

'Sounds as though they were reaching some to hang it on Mims.'

'Oh, I don't know,' he said. 'Anyway, there were similarities. They were all driving cabs and they all wound up dead.'

'Of course Mims said he didn't do it.'

'Mims said he didn't do anything. If Mims had gone to confession, all he'd have been able to come up with was impure thoughts and taking the Lord's name in vain.

Matt, it's like muggings and burglaries. The typical mutt, by the time you land on him he's gotten away with it fifty times running. So you clear fifty could-bes and tie them to his ass. It averages out, and if you don't do it your clearance rate looks like shit.'

'I know how it works.'

'Of course you do.'

'I just thought homicide was different.'

'It is,' he said, 'and nobody plays as loose with it as with break-ins and chain snatchings. This case here, Eldoniah flat-out did five out of six of those cabbies, no question, no argument. Cloonan he probably didn't do, and if somebody else ever comes along and looks better for it, well, nobody uptown's gonna argue against reopening the file.' He picked up a pencil, tapped the eraser three times on the desktop, set it down. 'So if you got anything,' he said casually, 'I'd be happy to pass it on.'

'Why would I have anything?'

'Well, you don't own a car, so I figure you probably take a lot of cabs. Maybe one of the drivers said some-thing.'

'Like what?'

'Like, "Hey, mister, you look like you used to be a cop, an' ain't it a hell of a thing what happened to Tommy Cloonan?"'

'Nobody ever said anything like that to me.'

'No, huh?'

'No,' I said. 'As a matter of fact, I don't take very many cabs at all. If it's too far to walk I'll take the subway.'

'What about the bus?'

'Sometimes I'll take a bus,' I said. 'Sometimes I'll stay home. Where are we going with this conversation, do you happen to know?'

'Alan Watson should have taken a cab. He worked down at the World Trade Center and generally took the

E train home to Forest Hills, but when he worked late he'd take an express bus because he didn't like the longer walk late at night, or standing around on subway platforms. So he rode on the bus in air-conditioned comfort, had a slice of pizza on Austin Street, and was a block away from his house on Beechknoll Place when somebody stuck a knife in him.'

'What did he do, resist a mugger?'

'Sounds like it, doesn't it? Guy I talked to said it doesn't really add up that way. Incidentally, he had more questions than answers for me. Watson was an affluent commodities broker, two kids in college, owned a nice home in a solid neighborhood. They want to solve this one, and the case is only four months old so they're not ready to give up on it. So why was I taking an interest, and what did I know that he didn't?'

'What did you tell him?'

'I don't remember, something about we had a case with a similar MO. According to him, forensic evidence suggests Watson's killer surprised him from behind and got him in a choke hold.'

'Muggers will do that.'

'And then he promptly stabbed the poor bastard. Blade about four-and-a-half inches long, or anyway that's as far as he stuck it in. Stabbed him once, got the heart first shot, and death would have been instantaneous or close to it. Watson's wallet was gone, so either it was robbery or it was supposed to look like it.'

'I don't suppose anybody saw it happen.'

He shook his head. 'He wasn't down long, though. Rent-a-cop from a private security patrol found him, called it in right away.'

'Why do you stab a guy if you've already got him in a choke hold?'

'They've been asking themselves the same question in

Forest Hills. That's why my guy got very interested when I talked about a similar MO, and I had to let him down easy, say our perp was a slasher, not a stabber, no choke hold, di dah di dah di dah. Incidentally, why are people surprised when occasionally a cop lies in court? We lie all day long, it's part of the fucking job description. You didn't lie, you'd never get any work done.'

'I know. It's the same thing working private. In fact it's worse, you've got no power to threaten or intimidate because you've got no legal authorization. So you have to con everybody.'

'All in the name of truth and justice.'

'And in the service of a higher good. Don't forget that.'

'Never.'

'What's their thinking, Joe? Ordinary street crime?'

'That's their best guess,' he said, 'but they're not married to it. It's hard to find anybody with a reason to kill Watson. He was married to the same woman for twenty-five years, and if either of them had anything going on the side nobody knows anything about it. Both of them well-liked, both of them active in the community. About a year ago he got phone threats from a client who blamed Watson for a beating he took. That's a financial beating, not two mutts holding you up in an alley while their buddy works on your rib cage.'

'The client checked out?'

'The client moved to fucking Denver. Anyway, what kind of a grudge killing is that, a quick knife in the heart and make it look like robbery for profit? You want to get even with somebody, either you whip out a gun and make a little noise or you tear into him with a baseball bat, break his bones, and beat his fucking brains out. Something wrong?'

'Remind me never to get you mad at me.'

'Why, did I sound like I was really getting into it there?' He grinned. 'I'm ten days off cigarettes.'

'I noticed the ashtray was gone.'

'That snitch of Bellamy's, I wanted to tell him to blow some of that smoke in my direction. Not this time, though. This time I'm not sneaking drags on other people's cigarettes, or checking ashtrays for a butt long enough to relight. This time I get it right.'

'Good for you.'

'But there's moments when I could kill the whole world.'

'Well, I'd better stay on your good side,' I said, and drew an unsealed envelope from my hip pocket and slipped it among the papers on his desk. He glanced around, lifted the flap, and counted the contents without removing the bills from the envelope.

There were two bills, hundreds.

'Couple of suits,' he said.

'If that's low—'

'No, it's fine,' he said. 'What did I do, use the phone on the city's time? I'm happy. But it's not enough, Matt.'

'What do you mean?'

'What do I mean? I want to know what it's about. You're looking for information on four homicides over a twelve-year stretch, all of them unsolved—'

'Cloonan was solved.'

He gave me a look. 'I stuck my neck out,' he said, 'and I can use the suits, but I want to know what's going on. If you've got something that can break these cases, you can't just sit on it.'

'I don't have anything, Joe.'

'What case are you working? Who's your client?'

'You know,' I said, 'one reason a person goes to somebody like me is to keep things confidential.'

'What I figure,' he said, watching me carefully, 'is AA.'

'Huh?'

'Wouldn't be the first time you got a client who knew you from your AA meetings. There's things you have to do when you get sober, right?'

'All you have to do is not drink.'

'Yeah, but isn't there a whole program? Almost like going to confession, but instead of a couple of Hail Marys you make restitution, set things straight.'

'"Cleaning up the wreckage of the past,"' I said, quoting one of the immortal phrases from the literature. 'Say, Joe, if you think you're interested, I'll be happy to take you to a meeting sometime.'

'Fuck you, okay?'

'Well, if you just wanted to see what it was like.'

'I repeat, fuck you. And quit changing the subject.'

'You're the one who brought up AA. I never realized you had a problem, but—'

'Jesus, why do I tolerate you? What I was starting to say, I figure you know somebody from AA who's got guilty knowledge of some crimes, including the four homicides we've been talking about. I wouldn't want to think you're gonna sit on something that ought to be brought out and looked at. Whoever did the gay fellow, Uhl, is probably dead himself by now, and Cloonan's file's closed for the time being, but the boys in the One-oh would love to catch a break in the Shipton case, and Watson, Jesus, the body's barely cold, that's still an active investigation. If you know anything, it should get channeled to the right people.'

'I don't.'

'There's probably a way to keep your client out of it, at least in the early stages.'

'I realize that.'

He looked at me. 'Your client didn't do all four guys himself, did he?'

'No.'

'You answered that one awfully quickly.'

'Well, I knew you were going to ask it. And the answer didn't require a whole lot of thought.'

'I guess not. Matt—'

I had to give him something. Without planning to, I said, 'They knew each other.'

'They? Meaning your client and who? Wait a minute. The *vics* knew each other?'

'That's right.'

'What did they all do, wipe out some Vietnamese village together and some slope's looking to get even?'

'They were part of a group.'

'A group? What kind of a group?'

'Like a fraternity,' I said. 'They got together once in a while to have dinner and compare notes.'

' "Bet my note's bigger than your note." Let's see, you got a commodities broker, a famous artist, a cabdriver, and a faggot. That's a hell of a fraternity. Wait a minute, was this a gay thing?'

'No.'

'You sure of that? Shipton and his wife ran in a kind of a kinky crowd. Wouldn't surprise me to hear he swung from both sides of the plate.'

'It wouldn't surprise me to hear it about anybody,' I said, 'but this wasn't about sex. I can't go into details without clearing it with my client, but there's nothing out of the ordinary about the group. The only thing unusual is that four of them have been murdered.'

'How big's the group?'

'Around thirty.'

'Thirty men and four of 'em murdered, Jesus, that's high even for New York.' His eyes narrowed. 'Same killer?'

'No reason to think that.'

'Yeah, but you think it yourself, don't you? You asked if a single killer could've done the Shiptons.'

'Never forget a thing, do you?'

'Not if I can help it. You got a suspect? A motive? Anything?'

'Nothing.'

'I won't say level with me, Matt, but don't hold out the moon and the stars on me, will you?'

'I'm not holding out anything concrete.'

'Yeah, and what the hell does that mean? What's the opposite of concrete?'

'Asphalt,' I suggested. 'Plaster of Paris.'

'Twelve years between Uhl and Watson,' he said, 'you're talking about a killer who likes to take his time. The other twenty-six guys, time he gets around to them they'll be too old to care. You know what he's like, this guy? He's prostate cancer. By the time he kills you you're already dead of something else.'

TEN

There was a message from Wally Donn at the hotel desk. 'I'll be here for the next hour,' he said when I called. 'I've got those credit reports for you, and something else you'll like.'

First I called TJ on his beeper. He must have been close to a phone; he called me back in well under five minutes. 'Who wants TJ?' he demanded.

'No one with any sense,' I said. 'How come you have to ask? If you don't recognize my voice, you still ought to know the number by now.'

''Course I do, Boo. "Who wants TJ" just be a trademark. Part of my rap, like.'

'Well, I can see where a fellow like you would need a trademark,' I said. 'Something to set you apart from the faceless masses.'

'If we was on one of them video phones,' he said, 'you could see me rollin' my eyes.'

'I'm sorry to miss that. You want to meet me? I might have some work.'

'Say where and when.'

I named a coffee shop on Twenty-third Street half a block from the Flatiron Building. 'Let's shoot for a quarter to twelve,' I said, 'but I might be a few minutes late.'

'Not me,' he said. 'We meetin' in a restaurant, I'm gonna be there on time.'

'The client,' Wally said, 'turned out to be a cheap fuck.'

'Not unheard of.'

'Christ, no. The world is full of cheap fucks. How it went, I told him what a job you did, how you ought to be down for a bonus. I said we as an agency didn't expect anything over and above our standard fees, which we don't, but that when a guy working per diem comes through like you did he ought to see something extra for his troubles.

'So he asked me what was reasonable. You know what went through my mind? The old expression, a picture is worth a thousand words. So okay, figure a buck a word, and I said a thousand dollars struck me as a reasonable amount. Which it did.'

'Thanks, Wally.'

'Well, it wasn't coming out of my pocket, so I could afford the gesture. And what's a thousand dollars to this fuck anyway, five hours of his lawyer's time? If that. So here's his check. Five hundred dollars.'

'Did he say he thought a thousand was too high?'

'He didn't say shit. He just went and cut a check for half of the recommended figure. Oh, and here's the letter of commendation, thanks for your efforts on our behalf, et cetera, et cetera. Look it over, see if it's all right.'

I scanned a glowing testimonial on the client's letter-head. 'This is great,' I said.

'He's got a pretty nice prose style, wouldn't you say?'

'You wrote it?'

'Dictated it,' he said. 'How else are you going to get this sort of thing the way you want it? At least the son of a bitch wrote it down word for word. He could have figured words are money and kept half of them for himself.' He shook his head. 'You know, I think he was just going to give me half of whatever I said. If I asked for two grand I'd have got one, and if I'd asked for five hundred I'd have got two and a half. I thought about sending this back to him, telling him to pay the whole shot or forget it. I'll still do that if you say so.'

I shook my head. 'The five's fine. Let it go.'

'Anyway,' he said, 'it evens out. I got those credit reports for you, fourteen of them, and our company rate as Class B subscribers is thirty-five bucks a pop. Which totals out at four-ninety.'

'Suppose I give you the check back,' I said, 'and we call it a wash.'

He shook his head. 'You don't want to do that, kiddo. Keep the check and take the reports and sustain yourself with the knowledge that being a cheap fuck never pays. The reports aren't costing you a cent, Matt. I billed them to the client.'

'How did you manage that?'

'We did a ton of shit on his behalf, and five hundred dollars' worth of credit reports won't seem out of line to anybody. Hey, fuck him, you know? What's he ask me my advice for if he's gonna take my figure and cut it in fucking half? You see what cheapness does, Matt? It's costing him the same thousand dollars and he's got us hating his guts.'

'Not me,' I said. 'I love everybody.'

I was a couple of minutes early for my lunch with TJ, but he was already seated at a window table, working on a pair of cheeseburgers and a plate of onion rings. I told him about Eldoniah Mims, doing twenty-to-life upstate.

He said, 'Sounds like he be in the right place, Ace. Killin' folks for chump change, dude like that got no cause to be walkin' around.'

I explained that they may have hung one more killing on Mims than he had in fact committed.

'He carrying any extra weight for it?'

'No.'

'So what's it matter?'

The waitress came over and I ordered the spinach pie and a small Greek salad. When she moved off he said, 'You spy the way she was scopin' us out? Like she wondering what fool put you and me at the same table. Then she realize we together, so she got to figure out why. Runs all the numbers through her mind, like you're a john and I'm a hustler, you're a cop and I'm some lowlife you're 'bout to bust.'

I was wearing pleated gray slacks and a white shirt with the sleeves rolled up and the collar unbuttoned. TJ wore a shiny rayon vest striped vertically in black and scarlet, and nothing but brown skin under it. His pants were knee-length baggy black shorts. 'I'm a cop on the take,' I offered, 'and you're a millionaire drug trafficker prepared to pay me off.'

'You talkin',' he said. 'The Excalibur's parked at the curb, Herb.' He took a drink and wiped milk from his upper lip. 'Say this Mims — what's his first name? El something.'

'Eldoniah.'

'Eldoniah. That from the Bible?'

'I don't know.'

' "I swear I don't know *how* those people come up with those names." ' He's a good mimic, and the line came out in a fairly accurate version of Long Island Lockjaw. In his own voice — or one of his voices, anyway — he said, 'You clear Mims for this one killing, he still doin' the same twenty he doin' now.'

I told him I wasn't interested in clearing Mims, who was clearly where he belonged. My food came, and while I ate I explained about the club of thirty-one.

He said, 'Somebody be killing them.'

'It looks that way.'

'Who you figure doin' it, one of them or some other dude?'

'No way to tell.'

'Have to be somebody with a reason, an' it ought to be more of a reason than killing a cabdriver for his coin bank.' He finished his milk, wiped his mouth again. He said, 'I been workin' some for Elaine. Mostly mindin' the store.'

'She mentioned it.'

'Kind of cool to watch people come in and take a look at me. Like they 'spect I'll grab something and go bookin' on out the door, an' then they catch on that I'm in charge.'

'There are black people running stores all over the city,' I said. 'The antique store two doors up the street from Elaine is run by a black woman.'

'Yeah, an' there's black receptionists in the big office buildings, and black folks at department-store information desks, all of 'em right out where you can see them. Thing is, they don't be lookin' like they just got in off the Deuce. They dressed for success, Bess.'

'Has Elaine said anything?'

He shook his head. 'She cool with it. But what I might do is keep some straight clothes on a hanger in her back room.'

We talked about that some, and then he said, 'I guess I could take a ride uptown, see what the brothers and sisters know about my uncle Eldoniah. Thing is, folks just be talkin' different types of trash. Dude's on the street, all he'll tell you is how bad he is, like he dusted six cops and robbed the Bank of England. Same dude's in prison, it's always for something he didn't do.'

'I know,' I said. 'The prisons are all overcrowded, and none of those guys ever did what they went away for.'

'I'll go up to the Bronx, see if anybody knows anything. All this is four years ago, that what you said?'

'It's been almost that long since Cloonan was killed. The murder Mims was tried for came later on, and the trial was postponed a couple of times. He's only been working on his twenty for the past year and a half.'

'Makes it a little easier,' he said. 'Least there's a chance somebody'll remember who he was.'

I got the check. While I was leaving the tip he said, 'I was just thinking. These dudes in the club? How it's suspicious that half of 'em's dead after thirty years. Is that right, thirty years?'

'More like thirty-two.'

'Thirty-two years,' he said. 'You couldn't start a club like that on the Deuce. Never mind no thirty-two years. 'Fore you knew it, you wouldn't have nobody left to have a meeting with. The ones that wasn't dead themselves, they most likely be locked up for killin' the other ones.' He took a black Raiders cap from the back pocket of his shorts, tucked his hair into it, checked his reflection in the mirror. He said, 'Group of dudes I knew four, five years ago, half of 'em's dead. Didn't take thirty-two years, neither. Dyin' must be easy, when I think of all the dudes caught on real quick how to do it.'

'Try to be a slow learner,' I said.

'Oh, I tryin',' he said. 'I doin' the best I can.'

ELEVEN

I treated myself to the afternoon, catching a movie on Twenty-third Street, then walking downtown to the Village. I passed the apartment building that had risen where Cunningham's had once stood, and the brown-stone a block away where Carl Uhl had been murdered. I got down to Perry Street in time for the four o'clock meeting and stood in the rear with a cup of coffee from the pastry shop around the corner.

The speaker told what a friend alcohol had been, and how it had turned on him. 'Toward the end,' he said, 'it just didn't work anymore. Nothing worked. Nothing relaxed me, not even seizures.'

While I waited for a bus on Hudson Street, a florist's display caught my eye. I had them wrap a dozen Dutch iris, rode the bus to Fifty-fourth, and walked over to Elaine's shop.

'These are beautiful,' she said. 'What brought this on?'

'They were going to be diamonds,' I said, 'but the client got cheap about the bonus.'

'What bonus?'

'For the picture we took at Wallbanger's.'

'Oh, God,' she said. 'What a crazy evening that was. I wonder how many bars like that there are in the city, with grown men and women sticking themselves to the wall.'

'I know one on Washington Street,' I told her, 'where they stick each other to the wall, but they don't use Velcro.'

'What do they use, Krazy Glue?'

'Manacles, leg irons.'

'Oh, I think I know the place you mean. But didn't they have to close?'

'They reopened again under another name.'

'Is it boys only these days? Or is it still boys and girls?'

'Boys and girls. Why?'

'I don't know,' she said. 'One isn't obliged to participate, is one?'

'One doesn't even have to walk in the door.'

'I mean you can just observe, right?'

'Why you ask, kemo sabe?'

'I don't know. Maybe I'm interested.'

'Oh?'

'Well, look how much fun we had at the Velcro Derby out in Queens. It might be even more of a hoot to watch people get kinky.'

'Maybe.'

'It would finally give me a chance to wear that leather outfit that I had no business buying.'

'Ah, that's why you want to go,' I said. 'It's not sex at all, it's to make a fashion statement. You're right, though, it's the perfect costume for the well-dressed dominatrix. But what would I wear?'

'Knowing you, probably your gray glen-plaid suit. As a matter of fact you'd look really hot in a pair of jeans and a black T-shirt.'

'I don't own a black T-shirt.'

'I'll get you one. I'd get you a black tanktop if I thought you'd wear it, but would you?'

'No.'

'That's what I thought. Let me put these in water, and then I'll close up and you can walk me home. Unless the flowers were for the apartment?'

'No, I thought they'd look nice here.'

'You're right, and I've even got an empty vase the

right size. There, don't they look pretty? We'll stop at the Korean and pick up something for a salad, and I'll fix us some pasta and a salad and we'll eat at the kitchen table. How does that sound?'

I said it sounded fine.

After dinner I opened the envelope I'd been carrying around all day and got out the printouts of the TRW reports, along with the letter of commendation Wally had dictated to the client. Elaine went into the other room to watch *Jeopardy* and I had a look at what just about anybody with a couple of bucks to spend could find out about the financial standing and bill-paying habits of the fourteen living members of the club of thirty-one.

I had gone through most of the stack when Elaine brought me a cup of coffee and the news that none of the three contestants had known that Benjamin Harrison was the grandson of William Henry Harrison.

'Neither did I,' I admitted. 'What was the category, Guys Named Harrison?'

'Presidents.'

'Oh, William Henry Harrison. Tippecanoe?' She nodded. 'And Tyler, too. It all comes back to me. He died, didn't he?'

'No shit, Sherlock. He was elected president in 1840, so what do you want from him? What's this?' She took the client's letter from me and read it through. 'This is great,' she said. 'Wally dictated it?'

'So he says.'

'It's perfect, don't you think? You should make it a point to get one of these whenever you've got a client who tells you what a great job you did for him.'

'I suppose.'

'Your enthusiasm is contagious.'

'I guess I should have it framed and hang it on my

office wall,' I said, 'if I ever get a real office. And I could tuck a copy in the portfolio I show to prospective clients.'

'If you ever put together a portfolio.'

'Right.'

'But you don't know if you want all that.'

The coffee was too hot to drink. I blew on the surface to cool it. I said, 'It's about time I got off my ass, don't you think? It's been twenty years since I turned in my gold shield.'

'You were bottoming out with your drinking,' she said. 'Remember?'

'Vividly.'

'And then you were getting sober.'

'And now I've been dry so long I'm a fire hazard, as I've heard it said, and what the hell have I done with my life?' I tapped the sheaf of credit reports. 'Here's a group of guys my age,' I said, 'and they've got families and careers, they own their own homes, and most of them could retire tomorrow if they wanted to. What have I got to put up against that?'

'Well, for one thing,' she said, 'you're alive. More than half of those men are dead.'

'I'm talking about the living ones. Anyway, nobody's been trying to kill me.'

'Oh? I can think of one fellow who really put his mind to it for a while there. If you forget what he looks like, look in the mirror.'

'I get the point.'

'And,' she said, 'give yourself a little credit, will you? From the day you left the department you've made a living.'

'Some living.'

'Were you ever on welfare? Did you ever miss a meal or sleep in the park? Did you break into parked cars and steal radios? I don't remember seeing you on the street with a paper cup, asking for spare change. Did I miss something?'

'I got by,' I said.

'You made a living,' she said, 'doing the work you're best at, and you didn't chase after it, either. You let it come to you.'

'The Zen detective,' I said.

'And now you're fifty-five years old,' she said, 'and you think you ought to be more of a man of substance. You got along for twenty years without a PI license, but now you think you need one. Your clients somehow found their way to you when you worked out of your hotel room, but now you think you need an office. Look, if you want those things, that's terrific. You can rent office space in a good building and get stationery and promotional brochures printed and go after the law firms and the corporate clients. If that's what you want, I'll back you up all the way. I'll run the office for you, if you'd like that.'

'You've got a shop to take care of.'

'I can hire an assistant. Every day I get people asking if I can use help, and some of them are better qualified to run the place than I am. Or I could close the place.'

'Don't be ridiculous.'

'What's ridiculous? It's a hobby, something to keep me from going crazy.'

'When I walked over there this afternoon,' I said, 'I stood in front of the window and I was in awe of what you've done.'

'Come on.'

'I mean it. You've made something out of nothing. You took an empty storefront and all the artworks you've collected over the years, and you've added things nobody else saw the beauty in until you pointed it out to them.'

'My thrift-shop masterpieces.'

'And Ray's stuff, for God's sake. He was nothing but a cop with a useful skill until you made him realize he was an artist.'

'That's exactly what he is.'

'And you put it all together,' I said. 'You've made it work. I don't know how the hell you did it.'

'Well, I've been having fun with it,' she admitted. 'But I don't know if it'll ever make a profit. Fortunately it doesn't have to.'

'Because you're a rich lady.'

She owns rental properties in Queens, all of it managed for her by a company that does that sort of thing. Every month she gets a check.

She said, 'That's part of it, isn't it?'

'What's part of what?'

'I have some money saved,' she said. 'And you don't.'

'Both of those statements are true.'

'And we're living in an apartment I paid for.'

'Also true.'

'Which means you ought to have a more substantial career so we can be on an even footing.'

'You figure that's it?'

'I don't know. Is it?'

I thought about it. 'It's probably a factor,' I said. 'But what it does is make me take a good look at myself, and I see a guy who hasn't accomplished a hell of a lot.'

'You've got some former clients who would disagree with that, you know. They might not be able to give you an endorsement on a fancy company letterhead, but they amount to a lot more than helping some manufacturer of schlock patio furniture avoid a lawsuit. Look at the difference you've made in people's lives.'

'But I haven't done much for my own self, have I.' I brandished the stack of credit reports. 'I was reading these,' I said, 'and imagining what the wonderful people at TRW would have to say about me.'

'You pay your bills.'

'Yes, but—'

'Do you want the license and the office and all the rest of it? It's up to you, honey. It really is.'

'Well, it's ridiculous not to have the license,' I said. 'There have been times when it's cost me work not to have it.'

'And the respectable office, and a string of operatives and security personnel under you?'

'I don't know.'

'I don't think you want it,' she said. 'I think you feel you ought to want it, but you don't, and that's what upsets you. But it's your call.'

I went back to the stack of credit reports. It was slow going, because I didn't know what I was looking for. My hope was that I would recognize it when I saw it.

Douglas Pomeroy. Robert Ripley. William Ludgate. Lowell Hunter. Avery Davis. Brian O'Hara. John Gerard Billings. Robert Berk. Kendall McGarry. John Young-dahl. Richard Bazerian. Gordon Walser. Raymond Gruliow. Lewis Hildebrand.

I knew what a few of them looked like. I'd seen Gerry Billings on television, talking about cold fronts and the threat of rain. In my library research I'd come upon news photos of Gordon Walser (with two partners, celebrating the opening of their own ad agency) and Rick Bazerian (with two punked-out rock stars who'd just signed with his record label). And of course I'd been seeing Avery Davis's picture in the paper for years.

I'd been in the same room with Ray Gruliow a couple of times over the years, although we'd never been introduced. And I knew Lewis Hildebrand, my client.

But it seemed to me as though I could picture all of them readily enough, including the ones whose faces were wholly unfamiliar to me. As I read their names and reviewed their credit histories, images kept popping into my mind. I saw them walking behind power mowers over suburban lawns, I saw them dressed in suits, I watched them bend over to scoop up small children and hold them aloft. I pictured them on the golf course, then saw them having a drink in the clubhouse after they'd showered and changed, drinking whiskey and soda, say, in a tall frosted glass.

I could see them, in their well-tailored suits, leaving their houses at dawn, coming home at dusk. I could see them standing on platforms with their newspapers, waiting for the Long Island Rail Road or Metro North. I could see them striding purposefully along a midtown sidewalk, carrying brassbound attaché cases, on their way to meetings.

I could picture them at the opera or the ballet, their wives finely dressed and bejeweled, themselves at once resplendent and slightly self-conscious in evening clothes. I could imagine them on cruise ships, in national parks, at backyard barbecues.

It was silly, because I didn't even know what they looked like. But I could see them.

'I'll give it another day or two,' I told Elaine, 'and then I'm going to call Lewis Hildebrand and tell him it's just a statistical anomaly. His group's running a high death rate and an unusual number of homicides, but that doesn't mean somebody's knocking them off one by one.'

'You got all that from a batch of credit reports?'

'What I got,' I said, 'is a picture of fourteen very orderly lives. I'm not saying these men don't have a dark side. The odds are a couple of them drink too much, or gamble for high stakes, or do something they wouldn't want their neighbors to know about. Maybe this one slaps his wife around, maybe that one can't keep it in his pants. But there's a degree of stability in every one of their lives that just doesn't fit a serial murderer.'

'If he's been doing it for this long,' she said, 'he's unusually disciplined.'

'And patient, and well organized. No question about it. But there'd be chaos in his life. He'd be holding things together, but not without a lot of backing and filling, a lot of fresh starts and makeovers. I'd expect to see a lot of job changes, a lot of geographics. It's almost inconceivable that he'd have stayed married to the same person for a substantial period of time, for example.'

'And have they all managed that?'

'No, there have been quite a few divorces. But the ones who've divorced show a consistent pattern of career stability. There's nobody in the whole group who looks at all like the kind of loose cannon he'd almost have to be, in order to do the damage he's done.'

'So it's not somebody in the group.'

'And who could it be outside the group? Nobody else knows these people exist. I told you I went out and saw Fred Karp's widow. She was married to him for something like twenty-five years. She knew he had dinner with some old friends once a year, but she thought they were fraternity brothers of his from Brooklyn College. And she didn't know the names of any of them.'

'She also told you she didn't think he could have killed himself.'

'Well, the survivors always tell you that about suicides. If you go up in a tower and shoot twenty people, the neighbors tell the press you were a nice quiet boy. If you kill yourself, they say you had everything to live for.'

'Then you think he did kill himself?'

'I think it's beginning to look that way.'

'I thought you said the suicides could have been faked.'

'Most suicides could have been faked,' I said. 'There are exceptions, like the poor son of a bitch who shot himself on live TV with the camera rolling.'

'I'm glad I missed that one.'

'But even if most suicides could have been faked,' I went on, 'that doesn't mean they are. Most of them are just what they look like. So are most accidents.'

'You think the Warren Commission got it right?'

'Jesus, where did that come from?'

'Left field. I just wondered. Do you?'

'I think they're a lot closer to the truth than Oliver Stone. Why? You think I'm too quick to believe what I want to believe?'

'I didn't say that.'

'Well, it's a possibility, whether you said it or not. It seems to me I've been working hard to prove that somebody really is knocking them off, and that I'm coming reluctantly to the conclusion that the true villain of the piece is our old friend Coincidence. But maybe that's what I wanted to conclude all along. I don't know.'

'It just seems to me,' she said, 'that you're attaching an awful lot of significance to a good credit rating.'

'It's not just that I'd be inclined to okay these guys for Master-Card. The whole lifestyle that goes with it, the whole—'

'I know. You look at the TRW reports and all you see is one big Norman Rockwell painting. They're the American Dream, aren't they?'

'I suppose so.'

'And you feel excluded because you can't have that life, and even more excluded because you don't even want it. That's a big part of it, Matt, isn't it?'

The telephone rang.

'Saved by the bell,' she said, grinning, and reached to answer it. 'Hello? May I ask who's calling? Just a moment, I'll see if he can come to the phone.' She covered the mouthpiece with her hand. 'Raymond Gruliow,' she said.

'Oh?'

I took the phone from her and said hello. He said, 'Mr Scudder, this is Ray Gruliow. I think we ought to get together, don't you?'

The voice was his, all right, rich and rasping, an instrument that he wielded like a rapier. I'd heard it last on the television news, when he was lecturing a gang of reporters on the insidious effect of institutionalized racism on his client, Warren Madison. Madison, as I recalled, had been so victimized by racism that he dealt dope, robbed and murdered other dope dealers, and shot six of the cops who showed up at his mother's house to arrest him.

'Maybe we should,' I said.

'I've got a court appearance scheduled in the morning. How's the later part of the afternoon? Say, four o'clock?'

'Four is fine.'

'Do you want to come over to my house? I'm on Commerce Street, if you know where that is.'

'I know Commerce Street.'

'Oh, of course you would. You were at the Sixth Precinct, weren't you? My house is number forty-nine, right across the street from the Cherry Lane Theater.'

'I'll find it,' I said. 'Four o'clock? I'll see you then.'

'I look forward to it,' he said.

'Four o'clock tomorrow,' I told Elaine, 'and he looks forward to it. I wonder what the hell he wants.'

'Maybe it's unrelated to what you're working on. Maybe he wants to hire you as an investigator.'

'Oh, sure,' I said. 'He heard what a bang-up job I did nailing the Velcro Vaulter and he wants to sign me up for his team.'

'Maybe he wants to confess.'

'That's it,' I said. 'Hard-Way Ray Gruliow, with his house on Commerce Street and his twenty-grand lecture fees. He's been killing his old friends for the past twenty years, and he wants my help in turning himself in.'

TWELVE

Commerce Street is only two blocks long. It angles south-west from Seventh Avenue a block below Bleecker, and runs along parallel to Barrow Street. The first block is all of a piece, with both sides lined with brick three-story Federal townhouses. Most are residential, but a few have commercial tenants on the first floor. One window shows a lawyer's shingle, with a second matching shingle hanging just below the first. I ALSO DABBLE IN ANTIQUES, it announces, and there are antiques and collectibles in the window. The building two doors down houses a macrobiotic restaurant, its menu listing dishes of tofu and seitan and seaweed. Whatever else they dabble in remains unstated.

The second block of Commerce Street, on the other side of Bedford, is more of a jumble architecturally. Buildings of different heights and shapes and styles are jammed together like straphangers in a rush-hour subway car. The street, as if confused by this sudden change of character, veers abruptly to the right and runs into Barrow Street, where it calls it quits.

The Cherry Lane Theater is in the middle of the block, just before the street's sudden change of direction. Raymond Gruliow's townhouse, four stories tall and two windows wide, stood on the other side of the street, buttressed by a shorter and wider building on either side. I climbed a half-flight of steps. There was a heavy brass door knocker in the shape of a lion's head, and I had my hand on it when I saw the recessed button for the doorbell. I pushed that instead, and if a bell or buzzer rang within, no sound came through the heavy wooden door. I was ready to try the knocker when the door opened inward. Gruliow had answered it himself.

He was a tall man, around six-three, and rail thin. His hair, once black, was an iron gray now, and he'd let it grow; it cascaded over his collar and lay in ringlets on his shoulders. The years had worked on his features like a caricaturist's pen, lengthening the nose, accenting the bony ridge of brow, hollowing the cheeks, giving a forward thrust to the jaw. He looked searchingly at me, and then his face lit up with a smile, as if he were genuinely glad to see me, as if someone had played a cosmic joke on the world and the two of us were in on it.

'Matthew Scudder,' he said. 'Welcome, welcome. I'm Ray Gruliow.'

He led me inside, apologizing for the condition of the house. It looked all right to me, if marked by a comfortable level of disorder – books overflowing the built-in cabinets and piled on the floor, a stack of magazines alongside a club chair, a suit jacket folded over the back of a Victorian sofa. He was wearing the pants to the suit, and a white shirt with the collar open and the sleeves rolled up. He had sandals on his feet, Birkenstocks, and they looked odd over the thin black socks that went with the dark pinstriped suit.

'My wife's in Sag Harbor,' he explained. 'I'm going to join her out there tomorrow afternoon, come back in time for court Monday morning. Unless I call her and tell her I've got too much work. And I might just do that. What the hell's the point of running out of town for a weekend, then running right back in again? Is that supposed to be relaxing?'

'Some people do it all the time.'

'Some people go to truck-pulling contests,' he said.

'Some people sell Amway dealerships to their friends. Some people believe the earth is a hollow sphere, with another whole civilization living on the inside edge.' He shrugged eloquently. 'Some people keep getting married. Are you married, Matt?'

'Virtually.'

'"Virtually." I like that. All right to call you Matt?' I said it was.

'And I'm Ray. "Virtually." I suppose that means living together? Well, you're an unlicensed private eye, why shouldn't you be an unlicensed spouse? I assume you were married previously.'

'Once, yes.'

'Children?'

'Two sons.'

'Grown now, I suppose.'

'Yes.'

'I've been married three times,' he said, 'and I've had children with all three of them. I'm sixty-four years old and I have a daughter who was two in March, and she's got a brother who'll turn forty next month. He's damn near old enough to be her grandfather. For Christ's sake, I've got three generations of families.' He shook his head at the wonder of it all. 'I'll be eighty years old,' he said, 'and still paying to put a kid through college.'

'They say it keeps you young.'

'In self-defense,' he said. 'I think it's late enough for a drink. What can I get you?'

'Plain club soda, thanks.'

'Perrier all right?'

I said it was. He fixed the drinks from a sideboard in the dining room, filling two glasses with Perrier, adding Irish whiskey to his. I recognized the shape of the bottle; it was JJ&S, Jameson's premium label. The only other person I know who drinks it is a career criminal who owns a Hell's Kitchen saloon, and he'd have blanched at the thought of diluting it with soda.

In the front room Gruliow gave me my drink, cleared off a chair for me, and sat on the sofa with his long legs out in front of him. 'Matthew Scudder,' he said. 'When I heard your name the other day, it wasn't entirely unfamiliar to me. Actually, I'm surprised our paths haven't crossed over the years.'

'As a matter of fact,' I said, 'they have.'

'Oh? Don't tell me I had you on the stand. I've always said I never forget a hostile witness.'

'I was never called to testify in any of your cases. But I've seen you in the Criminal Courts Building and a couple of restaurants in the area, Ronzini's on Reade Street and a little French place on Park Row that's not there anymore. I don't remember the name.'

'Neither do I, but I know the place you mean.'

'And years ago,' I said, 'you were at the next table at an after-hours way the hell west on Fifty-second Street.'

'Oh, for God's sake,' he said. 'One flight up over an Irish experimental theater, with burned-out buildings on either side and a rubble-strewn lot across the street.'

'That's the one.'

'Three brothers ran it,' he remembered. 'What the hell were their names? I want to say Morrison, but that's not right.'

'Morrissey.'

'Morrissey! They were wild men, red beards halfway down their chests and cold blue eyes hinting at sudden death. According to rumor, they were tied in with the IRA.'

'That was what everybody said.'

'Morrissey's. I haven't so much as thought about the place in years. I don't think I went there more than two or three times all told. And I imagine I was always fairly well lit by the time I got there.'

'Well, there was a time when I was there a lot,' I said, 'and everybody was fairly well lit by the time he got there. People behaved themselves, the brothers saw to that, but you'd never have looked around and thought you were at a Methodist lawn party.'

'That must have been twenty years ago.'

'Close to it.'

'Were you still on the police force?'

'No, but I wasn't long off it. I moved into the neighborhood and drank at the local ginmills, most of them long gone now. On the nights when they were ready to quit before I was, there was always Morrissey's.'

'There was something very liberating about a drink after hours,' he said. 'Lord, I drank more in those days than I do now. Nowadays an extra drink makes me sleepy. Back then it was fuel, I could run all day and night on it.'

'Is that where you learned to drink Irish?'

He shook his head. 'You know the old formula for success? "Dress British, think Yiddish?" Well, it spoils the rhyme, but I'd add "drink Irish" and "eat Italian" to that, and I learned both of those principles right here in the Village. I learned to drink Irish at the White Horse and the Lion's Head and right across the street from here at the Blue Mill. Did you ever get to know the Blue Mill when you were at the Sixth?'

I nodded. 'Food wasn't great.'

'No, terrible. Vegetables out of cans, and dented cans at that, but you could get a steak for half what it cost most places and if you had a sharp knife you could even manage to cut it.' He laughed. 'It was a hell of a good place to sit around with friends and drink until closing time. Now it's calling itself the Grange, and the food's

124

much better, and you can't drop in for a quiet drink because you can't hear yourself think in there. The customers are all my wife's age or younger, and Christ they're a noisy bunch.'

'They seem to like the noise,' I said.

'It must do something for them,' he said, 'but I've never been able to figure out what. All it does for me is give me a headache.'

'I'm the same way.'

'Listen to us,' he said. 'We're a couple of old farts. You're a lot younger than I am. You're fifty-five right?'

'I guess it stands out all over me.'

He looked me in the eye. 'I made it my business to learn a little about you,' he said. 'That can't come as a surprise to you. I imagine you did the same.'

'Your credit rating's good,' I said.

'Well, that's a load off my mind.'

'And you're sixty-four.'

'I mentioned that a few minutes ago, didn't I? Not that it comes under the heading of closely held information.' He leaned back, one arm extended along the back of the sofa. 'I was the second-oldest member of the club of thirty-one. Not counting Homer, that is. That's Homer Champney, he's the man who founded our chapter.'

'So I understand.'

'I was thirty-two then, working for Legal Aid, thinking about joining the Village Independent Democrats and trying to make a place for myself in politics. Trouble was I found the reform Democrats even more odious than the regulars. The old clubhouse hacks were full of crap, but at least they knew it. The reformers were always such sanctimonious little shits. Who knows, if I could have learned to put up with them I might have turned out to be Ed Koch.'

'There's a thought.'

'Frank DiGiulio was about ten months older than me. I barely knew him but I liked him. Face off an old Roman coin. He died, you know.'

'Last September.'

'I saw the obit in the *Times*. That's the first page I read these days.'

'I'm the same way.'

'That's my definition of middle age. It starts the day you pick up the morning paper and turn to the obituaries. When Frank dropped dead, I thought to myself, Well, Gruliow, you're walking point.' He frowned. 'As if it would be my turn next. Instead it was Alan Watson. Decent fellow, very straight, stabbed to death for his watch and wallet. You don't expect that in Forest Hills.'

'They've evidently had more street crime lately. It was a private security guard who found him, and you don't hire a private security force if you don't have to.'

'Sign of the times,' he said. 'They'll have them everywhere soon.' He looked down into his glass of whiskey and soda. 'I had a call from Felicia Karp,' he said. 'I didn't know who she was, and when she told me she was Fred Karp's widow I was still in the dark. Fred Karp? Who the hell was Fred Karp? A lawyer, a mob guy, a radical? Remember, he was a guy I used to see once a year at dinner, and then three years ago I stopped seeing him because he jumped out his office window. So it took me a minute, and then she went on to say that she'd had a visit from a detective, and this chap had told her there was a possibility her husband hadn't killed himself after all, that he'd been murdered. And she'd seen my name on a list of some sort of club, and it was the one name on the list she recognized, so she was calling in the hope that I could shed some light on the matter.'

'And?'

'And I did what I could to conceal my own ignorance, which at the time was all-encompassing, and told her I'd see what I could find out. I made the obvious phone calls, and when I felt I'd learned enough about you I called you up myself.' He smiled engagingly. 'And here you are.'

'And here I am.'

'Who's your client?'

'I can't tell you that.'

'You're not an attorney, you know. It's not privileged information.'

'And we're not in court.'

'No, of course we're not. I have to assume your client is one of the other surviving members. Unless you've been hired by a widow or some other survivor.' He watched my face as he spoke. 'You're not giving anything away,' he said after a moment.

'My client may be willing for you to know who he is. But I'd have to check with him first.'

' "He, him." Hardly a widow, not with those pronouns. Although I think you might be a subtle man, Matt. Are you?'

'Not very.'

'I wonder. Still, it almost has to be a group member, doesn't it? Who else would know the names of all the other members? Although I suppose some of us may have talked openly about the club with our wives.' A smile, this one a little darker at the corners. 'Our first wives,' he said. 'If your first divorce teaches you nothing else, it teaches you discretion.'

'Does it matter who hired me?'

'Probably not. I like to know everything about people – jurors, witnesses, the lawyer on the other side. Preparation's everything, you know. The courtroom theatrics may make me a hot ticket on the lecture circuit, but it's the pretrial prep work that wins the cases. And I like to win cases.'

He asked if I wanted more Perrier. I said I was fine.

He said, 'Well, what's your best guess, Matt? Is someone killing us off? Or is that confidential, too?'

'The club's had a lot of deaths.'

'I don't need a detective to tell me that.'

'Several murders, several suicides, a few accidents that could have been staged. So it looks as though more than coincidence would have to be involved.'

'Yes.'

'But it's impossible. The killer would almost have to be one of you, and there's no motive, no financial incentive, at least none I'm aware of. Or am I missing something?'

'No,' he said. 'There was some talk early on about laying down a case of good Bordeaux for the last man to drink. We decided whoever was left would be too old to enjoy it. Besides, it seemed inappropriate, even frivolous.'

'So the killer would have to be crazy,' I said. 'And not just sudden-impulse crazy, because he'd have been at it for years. He'd have to be long-term crazy, and all fourteen of you look to have been leading sane and stable lives.'

'Ha,' he said. 'I've got two ex-wives who would give you an argument on that point, and I could name a few other people who'd be quick to tell you I'm only eating with one chopstick. Maybe I'm the killer.'

'Are you?'

'How's that again?'

'Are you the killer? Did you kill Watson and Cloonan and the others?'

'My God, what a question. No, of course not.'

'Well, that's a load off my mind.'

'Am I a suspect?'

'I don't have any suspects.'

'But did you seriously think—'

'That you might have done it? No idea. That's why I asked.'

'You think I would have told you?'

'You might have,' I said. 'Stranger things have happened.'

'Jesus.'

'What I was taught to do,' I said, 'was ask all the questions, including the stupid ones. You never know what somebody'll decide to tell you.'

'Interesting. In a trial it's the exact opposite. There's a basic principle, you never ask a question of a witness unless you already know the answer.'

'You'd think it would be hard to learn anything that way.'

'Education,' he said, 'is not the object. I'm going to have another drink. Join me?'

I let him top up my Perrier.

I said, 'I'll tell you this much. I was surprised to see your name on the list of members.'

'Oh?'

'It seemed to me,' I said, 'that it was an unusual group for you to join.'

He snorted. 'I'd say it's an unusual club for anybody to join. An annual celebration of mortality, for God's sake. Why would anybody want to sign on for that?'

'Why did you?'

'It's hard to remember,' he said. 'I was much younger then, obviously. Undefined personally and professionally. If Karp's widow – what was her name, Felicia?'

'Yes.'

'You name a child Felicia and you're just daring the whole world to call her Fellatio, aren't you? If Felicia

Karp had seen my name on a list in 1961, she wouldn't have looked at it twice. Unless she thought Gruliow was a typographical error. I ran into that years ago, you know. People thought it must be Grillo.'

'Now they know the name.'

'Oh, no question. The name, the face, the hair, the voice, the sardonic wit. Everybody knows Hard-Way Ray Gruliow. Well, it's what I wanted. And that's a great curse, you know. "May you get what you want." Hell of a thing to wish on a man.'

'The price of fame,' I said.

'It's not so bad. I get tables in restaurants, I get strangers saying hello to me on the street. There's a coffee shop on Bleecker Street named a sandwich after me. You go in there and order a Ray Gruliow and they'll bring you some godforsaken combination of corned beef and raw onion and I don't know what else.'

His second drink was darker than the first, and he looked to be making it disappear faster.

'Of course it's not all corned beef and onions,' he said. 'Sometimes they break your windows.'

My eyes went to the front window.

'Replaced,' he said. 'That's high-impact plastic. It looks like glass, unless the light hits it just right, but it's not. It's supposed to stop bullets. Not high-velocity rounds, concrete won't stop them, but your run-of-the-mill gunshot ought to be deflected. It was a shotgun last time around, and I'm told shotgun pellets will bounce right off of my new window. Won't even mar the finish.'

'They never caught the guy, did they?'

He cocked his head. 'You don't really think they knocked themselves out trying, do you? I think the shooter was a cop.'

'I think you're probably right.'

'It was right after twelve public-spirited citizens of the Bronx gave Warren Madison judicial absolution for his sins, and that rubbed a lot of cops the wrong way.'

'And a few ordinary citizens, too.'

'Including you, Matt?'

'What I think's not important.'

'Tell me anyhow.'

'Why?'

'Why not?'

'I think Warren Madison is a homicidal son of a bitch who ought to spend the rest of his life in a cell.'

'Then we agree.'

I looked at him.

'Warren,' he said, 'is what some other clients of mine might characterize as a stone killer. I'd call him an utterly remorseless sociopath, and I'd like to see him live out his days as a guest of the state of New York.'

'You defended him.'

'Don't you think he's entitled to a defense?'

'You got him off.'

'Don't you think he's entitled to the best possible defense?'

'You didn't just defend him,' I went on. 'You put the whole police department on trial. You sold the jury a bill of goods about Madison being a snitch for the local Bronx precinct, in return for which they let him deal dope and supplied him with stash confiscated from other dealers. Then they were afraid he would talk, though God knows who he would talk to or why, and they went to his mother's house not to arrest him but to murder him.'

'Quite a scenario, wouldn't you say?'

'It's ridiculous.'

'Don't you think cops use snitches?'

'Of course they do. They wouldn't make half their cases if they didn't.'

'Don't you think they allow snitches to pursue their criminal careers in return for the help they provide?'

'That's part of how it works.'

'Don't you think confiscated dope ever finds its way back onto the street? Don't you think some police officers, cops who've already broken the law, will take extreme measures to cover their asses?'

'In certain cases, but—'

'Do you know for a fact, an irrefutable fact, that those cops didn't go to Warren's mother's house looking to kill him?'

'For a fact?'

'An irrefutable fact.'

'Well, no,' I said. 'I don't.'

'I do,' Gruliow said. 'It was utter bullshit. They never used him as a snitch. They wouldn't use him to wipe their asses, for which I can't say I blame them. But the jury believed it.'

'You did a good job of selling it to them.'

'I'll be happy to take the credit, but it didn't take much selling. Because they wanted to buy it. I had a jury full of black and brown faces, and that ridiculous scenario I cooked up struck them as perfectly plausible. In their world, cops pull shit like that all the time, and lie like hell about it afterward. So why should they believe a word of police testimony? They'd rather believe something else. I gave them an acceptable alternative.'

'And you put Warren Madison on the street.'

He gave me a look, eyebrows raised, mouth on the verge of a smile. I'd seen it before; it was his patented expression of disappointed skepticism, flashed in court at a difficult witness, in the hallways at an uncooperative reporter. 'In the first place,' he said, 'do you seriously think the quality of life in this city is going to be measurably different for the rest of us if Warren Madison or anybody else is on or off its streets?'

'Yes,' I said, 'but a cop has to believe that or it's hard to get to work in the morning.'

'You're not a cop anymore.'

'It's like being raised Catholic,' I said. 'You never get over it. And I do think it makes a difference, not so much in terms of the people Madison's likely to kill but in the message people get when they see him walking around.'

'But they don't.'

'How's that?'

'They don't see him walking around, not unless they're in maximum security at Green Haven. That's where Warren is, and where he's likely to be until you and I are both long past caring. Remember what Torres said when he sentenced the kid for stabbing that Mormon boy in the subway? "Your parole officer hasn't been born yet." You could say that about Warren. He killed those drug dealers, and he was convicted, and he'll be behind bars as long as he lives.'

'You couldn't get him out from under those charges?'

'I never even tried. He had other counsel. And I wouldn't have wanted the case. Killing a drug dealer is murder for profit, and there are plenty of other lawyers who can represent you. Shoot a cop and you're making a political statement. That's when a guy named Gruliow can do you some good.'

'Somehow no one remembers that Madison's serving time.'

'Of course not. All they remember is Hard-Way Ray got him off. And the cops don't care whether he's locked up in Green Haven or out in Hollywood fucking Madonna. Their take on it is the same as yours, that I put the department on trial. I didn't, I put the system on

133

trial, which is what I always do, in one sense or another. Whether it's civil-rights workers or draft resisters or Palestinians or, yes, Warren Madison, I put the system on trial. But not everybody sees it that way.' He pointed at his plastic window. 'Some of them take it personally.'

I said, 'I keep seeing that picture of you and Madison after the trial.'

'Embracing.'

'That's the one.'

'You figured what? Bad taste? Theatrical gesture?'

'Just a memorable image,' I said.

'Ever hear of a criminal lawyer named Earl Rogers? Very flamboyant and successful, represented Clarence Darrow when the great man was brought up on charges of jury tampering. In another case his client was charged with some particularly odious murder. I forget the details, but Rogers won an acquittal.'

'And?'

'And when they read the verdict, the defendant rushed to shake hands with the man who got him off. Rogers wouldn't take his hand. "Get away from me," he cried out right there in the courtroom. "You son of a bitch, you're as guilty as sin!"'

'Jesus.'

'Now that's theatrical,' he said with relish. 'And bad taste, and ethically questionable at the very least. "You're guilty as sin!" They're almost all of them guilty, for God's sake. If you don't want to defend the guilty, find another line of work. But if you do defend them, and if you're lucky enough to win, you can damn well shake their hands.' He grinned. 'Or give 'em a hug, which is more my style than a handshake. And I felt like hugging Warren, I didn't have to fake it. It's goddam exhilarating when they say "Not guilty." It's moving. You want to hug somebody. And I liked Warren.'

'Really?'

He nodded. 'Very charming man,' he said, 'unless he had reason to kill you.'

THIRTEEN

'**I**'m hungry,' he announced around six. He called up a Chinese restaurant. 'Hi, this is Ray Gruliow,' he said, and ordered several dishes, along with a couple of bottles of Tsing-tao, telling them not to forget the fortune cookies this time. 'Because,' he said, 'my friend and I need to know what the future holds.'

He hung up and said, 'You're in the program, right?'

'The program?'

'Don't be coy, huh? You asked me in my own house if I was a fucking serial murderer. I ought to be able to ask you if you're a member of Alcoholics Anonymous.'

'I wasn't being coy. People outside of AA don't generally call it "the program."'

'I went to a few meetings a couple of years ago.'

'Oh?'

'Right here in the neighborhood. The basement of St Luke's, on Hudson, and a little storefront on Perry Street. I don't know if they still have meetings there.'

'They do.'

'Nobody told me, "Gruliow, get your ass out of here, you don't belong." And I heard things I identi-fied with.'

'But you didn't stay.'

He shook his head. 'It was more than I wanted to give up. I looked at the First Step and it said something about life being out of control. I forget how they phrased it.'

' "We admitted we were powerless over alcohol – that it made our lives unmanageable." '

'That's it. Well, I looked at my life, and it wasn't

136

unmanageable. There were nights I drank too much and mornings when I regretted it, but it seemed to me that was a price I could afford to pay. So I made a conscious effort to cut back on my drinking.'

'And it worked?'

He nodded. 'I'm feeling the drinks I had just now. That's why I ordered food. I don't usually have this much to drink before dinner. I've had some stress lately. I think it's only natural to drink more at times of stress, don't you?'

I said that sounded reasonable.

'I wouldn't have brought it up,' he said, 'but I didn't want to order beer for you if you were the nondrinker I understood you to be, nor did I want to appear inhospitable.' He slurred the last word just the least bit, and stopped himself from taking another stab at it. Shifting gears, he said, 'The woman you live with. How old is she?'

'I'll have to ask her.'

'She's not thirty years younger than you, is she?'

'No.'

'Then I guess you're not as much of a damned fool as I am,' he said. 'When the club first met, Michelle was still in diapers. Jesus, she was the age Chatham is now.'

'Chatham's your daughter?'

'Indeed she is. I'm even beginning to get used to her name. Her mother's idea, as you no doubt assumed. A man in his sixties does not name his daughter Chatham. I suggested to Michelle that if she wanted to name the kid after an English prime minister she should give some thought to Disraeli. It goes better with Gruliow than Chatham. Dizzy Gruliow. It has a nice ring, don't you think?'

'But she didn't like it?'

'She didn't get it. She's half my age, for God's sake, but

God help me if I treat her like a child. I have to treat her like an equal. I told her, making a joke of it, that I don't treat anybody like an equal, young or old, male or female. "Yes," she said. "I've noticed." You know something? I don't think I'm going out to Sag Harbor tomorrow. I think the pressures of work are going to prove too great for me.'

We ate in the front room, with the plates balanced on our laps. He found a Coke for me and drank his two bottles of Chinese beer.

He said, 'It's funny. It was Homer's death that shocked me. He was a very old man by the time he died, older than anybody I'd ever known, but I must have expected him to live forever. He wasn't the first to go, you know. He was the third.'

'I know.'

'It was a shock when Phil died, but a car crash, that's the kind of lightning that's always there. It's going to strike somebody sooner or later. Did you grow up in New York?'

'Yes.'

'So did I. In the rest of the country you don't get through high school without having a friend or two die in a wreck. Every prom night you know there's going to be at least one car that doesn't make it around Dead Man's Curve. But kids don't drive in the city, so it's a form of population control we're spared here.'

'We've got others.'

'God, yes. There's always some form of attrition that thins out the ranks of the young males. Historically, war's always played that role, and did a fine job before the dawn of the nuclear age. Still, limited wars and local skirmishes take up the slack. In the ghettos, dope's the medium. Either they overdose on it or they traffic in it and shoot each other.' He snorted. 'But I digress. If I ever write my memoirs that'll be the title. *But I Digress.*'

'You were talking about Kalish's death.'

'It didn't scare me. That's what we're talking about, isn't it? Fear, fear of dying. They say man's the only animal that knows he's going to die. He's also the only animal that drinks.'

'You think there's a connection?'

'I'm not even sure I buy the first part. I've had cats, and I always had the feeling they were as aware of their mortality as I've ever been of mine. The difference is they're fearless. Maybe they don't give a shit.'

'I can't even tell how people feel about things,' I said. 'Let alone cats.'

'I know what you mean. You know why I felt no fear when Phil died? It couldn't be simpler. I didn't own a car.'

'So you couldn't—'

'Die the way he did. Right. I had the same reaction years later when Steve Kostakos crashed his plane. Do I fly a plane? No. So do I have to worry about it? Certainly not.'

'And when James Severance died in Vietnam?'

'You know,' he said, 'that wasn't even a shock. One year he didn't show up for the dinner and we learned he was in the service. The next year we learned he was dead. I think I expected it.'

'Because he was in combat?'

'That must have been part of it. That fucking war. Whenever somebody went over there, you figured he wasn't coming back. It was easy to feel that way about Severance. I don't know how much of this is hindsight, but it seems to me that there was something about him. An aura, an energy, whatever you want to call it. I'm sure there's a New Age way of putting it, but my wife's not here to tell us what it is. Have you ever met anyone and somehow just sensed he was doomed?'

'Yes.'

'You got that feeling with Severance. I don't want to imply I had premonitions of an early grave for him, just that he was . . . well, doomed. I can't think of another word for it.' He tilted his head back, squinting at a memory. 'You said you thought I was an odd choice for that group. I wasn't, not really. I was more like the rest of those guys than you'd imagine now. Most of the court-room armor, a lot of the media image, it all came later. It may have grown naturally out of the person who attended that first dinner in '61, but it wasn't in place then. I was like the rest of the members, older than most but just as earnest, every bit as intent on playing the game of life and getting a decent score. I fit in just fine.' He drained his glass. 'If there was a good choice for odd man out, it was Severance.'

'Why?'

He thought for a moment before speaking. 'You know,' he said, 'I didn't really know the man. I try to picture him now and I can't bring the image into focus. But it seems to me that he was on a different level from the rest of us.'

'How?'

'A lower link on the food chain. But that's just an impression, founded on three meetings three decades ago, and maybe it would have changed if he'd lived long enough to grow into himself and shed some of the emotional puppy fat. He didn't have the chance.' He drew a breath. 'But no, his death held no fear for me. I wasn't slogging through rice paddies getting shot at by little guys in black pajamas. I was busy helping other young men stay out of the army.' He put his glass on the table. 'Then Homer Champney died,' he said, 'and in a sense the party was over.'

'Because you thought he was going to live forever?'

'Hardly that. I knew he was mortal, like everybody else. And I knew he was failing. So I had no reason to be shocked. When a man in his nineties dies in his sleep, it's not a tragedy and it can't come as a great surprise. But you have to understand that he was a remarkably dynamic human being.'

'So I gather.'

'And he was the end of an era, the last of his line. Phil and Jim were accidents, they might as well have been struck by lightning. A bolt from the blue, zap, kerblooey. Once Homer was gone, though, it was our turn in the barrel.'

'Your turn?'

'To do our own dying,' he said.

We talked about coincidence and probability, about natural and unnatural death. 'The easiest thing in the world,' he said, 'would be to hand this off to the media and let them run with it. Of course it would be the end of the club. And it would subject us all to more police and press attention than anyone should have to put up with. If this is all a coincidence, a cosmic thumb in the eye for the actuarial tables, we all get our world turned upside-down for nothing.'

'And if there's a killer out there?'

'You tell me.'

'If he's one of you fourteen,' I said, 'a full-scale investigation might tag him. With enough cops asking questions and cross-checking alibis, he'd have a tough time staying in the dark. There might not be enough evidence to go to trial with, but there's a difference between clearing a case and winning it in court.'

141

'And if he's an outsider?'

'Then it's a little less likely they'd get him. I would think the investigation and the attendant publicity would scare him off, though, and keep him from killing anyone else.'

'For the time being, you mean.'

'Well, yes.'

'But the bastard's in no hurry, is he?' He leaned forward, gesturing expansively with his long-fingered hands. 'My God, the son of a bitch has the patience of a glacier. He's been doing this for decades if he's been doing it at all. Scare him off and what happens? He goes home, pops a tape in the VCR, brews up a pot of coffee, and waits a year or two. The media has the attention span of a fruit fly. Once the story's died down, it's time for him to arrange another accident, or stage a street crime or a suicide.'

'If the cops got on to him,' I said, 'he might be scared off permanently, even if they never had enough to bring charges against him. But if he never even got scooped up in the net, I'd say you're right. He'd just bide his time and start in again.'

'And even if he didn't, he wins.'

'How do you mean?'

'Because the club's over. The newspaper stories would be enough to kill it, don't you think? It's anachronistic enough, fourteen grown men assembling annually to see who's still alive. I don't think we'd be able to find the heart for it after a little attention from our friends in the press.'

He got up and fixed himself a fresh drink, just pouring the whiskey straight into the glass, sipping a little of it on his way back to the couch. The Chinese food had cleared his head. He wasn't slurring words now, or showing any effect of the alcohol.

He said, 'It can't be one of the fourteen. Are we agreed on that?'

'I can't go all the way with you. I'll say it's unlikely.'

'Well, I have an edge. I know them all and you don't.' A rope of gray curls had fallen across his forehead. He brushed it back with his hand and said, 'I think the club ought to convene. And I don't think we can afford to wait until next May. I'm going to make some calls, get as many of us here as I can.'

'Now?'

'No, of course not. Monday? No, I may not be able to reach some of them until Monday. This time of year people get away for the weekend. Tuesday, say Tuesday afternoon. If I have appointments I can clear them. How about you? Can you be here Tuesday afternoon, let's see, say three o'clock?'

'Here?'

'Why not? It's better than my office. Plenty of room for fifteen people, and we'll be lucky to get half that number here on such short notice. But even if you just have five or six of us all here in one room—'

'Yes,' I said. 'It would be useful from my perspective.'

'And from ours,' he said. 'All of us ought to know just what's going on. If we're in danger, if somebody's stalking us, we damn well ought to be aware of it.'

'Is there a phone I can use? Let me see if I can sell this to my client.'

'In the kitchen. On the wall, you'll see it. And Matt? Let me talk to him when you're done.'

'Hildebrand went for it,' I told Elaine. 'He seemed relieved.'

'So you've still got a client.'

'I did as of a couple of hours ago.'

'What did you think of Gruliow?'

143

'I liked him,' I said.

'You didn't expect to.'

'No, I brought the usual cop prejudices into his house with me. But he's a very disarming guy. He's manipulative, and he's got an ego the size of Texas, and his client list adds up to a powerful argument for capital punishment.'

'But you liked him anyhow.'

'Uh-huh. I thought he might turn ugly with drink, but it never happened.'

'Did his drinking bother you?'

'He asked me that himself. I told him my best friend drinks the same brand of whiskey he does, and drinks a lot more of it. And when it comes to killing people, I said, his score is somewhere between Warren Madison and the Black Death.'

'That's a good line,' she said, 'but it doesn't really answer the question.'

'You're right, it doesn't. If I was going to take his inventory—'

'Which of course you're far too spiritually advanced to do.'

'—I'd have to say he's a drunk. I'd say he knows it, too. He controls it, and obviously he can keep it together enough so that his life still works. He gets the big cases and he wins them. Incidentally, I learned something. I always wondered how he made a living representing clients who haven't got any money.'

'And?'

'The money's in the books and lectures. The defense work's almost entirely pro bono. But there's a lot of self-interest operating, because by getting the hot cases he's hyping the book sales and goosing the fees for his public appearances.'

'That's interesting.'

'Isn't it? I asked him if there was anyone he wouldn't represent. Mafia dons, he said. White-collar sharpies, like the Wall Street insider-trading guys and the savings-and-loan swindlers. Not that they were necessarily the worst human beings in the world, but he had no affinity for them. I asked him if he'd represent a Ku Kluxer.'

'What did he say?'

'He said probably not, if it was your basic Dixie segregationist or some White Power type from the Midwest. Then he said it might be interesting defending those skinheads they arrested in Los Angeles, the ones who wanted to start a race war by killing Rodney King and shooting up the AME church. I forget how he got there, but he had them all established as disenfranchised outsiders. "But," he said, "they probably wouldn't want a lawyer named Gruliow." I still haven't answered your question, have I? No, his drinking didn't bother me. He didn't get sloppy or nasty, and once we'd eaten he didn't even show the effects of the booze. On the other hand, I'd been planning to drop in on Mick at Grogan's tonight, and I think I'll put that off until tomorrow or Saturday.'

'Because you've been around enough booze for one day.'

'Right.'

'I never met him myself,' she said thoughtfully, 'but I could have.'

'Oh?'

'He's a big john, or at least he used to be. All that New Left rhetoric, well, he was certainly a staunch supporter of the working girl. You know who had a whole string of dates with him? Connie Cooperman.'

'Of blessed memory.'

'She said he was a real nice guy, fun to be with. Kind of kinky.'

'I thought call girls never talked about their famous clients.'

'That's right, darling. And if you put your tooth under your pillow, the Tooth Fairy will come and leave you a quarter.'

'I think I'd rather keep the tooth.'

'Well, you're just an old bear,' she said. 'Anyway, he liked leather, and he liked to be tied up.'

'We tried that.'

'And you fell asleep.'

'Because I felt safe in your presence. Look, I'm sure it's interesting that Ray Gruliow's a bondage queen, but—'

'Not to mention golden showers.'

'Golden showers?'

'I told you not to mention them. I bet *he*'d take a girl to Marilyn's Chamber.'

'Huh?'

'Formerly the Hell-Fire Club,' she said. 'We were talking about it the other day, remember? That's its new name, Marilyn's Chamber. As in torture chamber, I guess, and as in the former porn star. See Mick tomorrow night and you can take me there on Saturday.'

'You really want to go?'

'Sure, why not? I checked, and it's fifty dollars a couple and there's no pressure to do anything. And the price includes soft drinks, and that's all they serve, so you won't have to be around booze.'

'Just whips and chains.'

'There's a body-piercing exhibition scheduled for Saturday. You're fifty-five years old. Don't you think it's about time you witnessed a body-piercing exhibition?'

'I don't know how I lasted this long without it.'

'I tried on the leather outfit and I think it looks hot.'

'I wouldn't be surprised.'

'But it's the least bit tight. I found out it looks better if I don't wear anything under it.'

'Be awfully warm,' I said. 'In this weather.'

'Well, the club's probably air-conditioned, don't you think?'

'In a basement on Washington Street? I wouldn't count on it.'

'So? If I sweat, I sweat.' She moistened her lips with the tip of her tongue. 'You don't mind a little sweat, do you?'

'No.'

'I think I'll try that outfit on again,' she said, 'and you can tell me what you think.'

She took my hand, drew me willingly to my feet. At the bedroom door she said, 'You had a couple of messages. TJ wants you to beep him when you have a chance. But he didn't say it was urgent, so I suppose it can wait until morning, don't you think?'

'It'll have to,' I said.

FOURTEEN

In the morning I beeped TJ and met him for breakfast across the street at the Morning Star. He was wearing the same shorts and cap, but in place of the vest he wore a denim shirt with the sleeves and collar removed and the three top buttons unbuttoned. I had already ordered and been served when he got there. He dropped into the seat opposite me and told the waiter he wanted a pair of cheeseburgers and a large order of well-done hash browns.

I said, 'No french fries?'

'For breakfast?'

'Forgive me,' I said. 'I lost my head.'

'Yeah, well, you lost it earlier, sendin' me up to the Bronx chasin' down shit happened three years ago. Neighborhoods I had to go, how you gonna find anybody remembers anything? Be like tryin' to find a needle in a crack house. An' if you did, why'd they want to talk about it?'

'Well, it was a long shot,' I said, 'but I thought it might be worth a try. I gather it was a waste of time.'

'Who said, Fred? All I's sayin' is it be impossible. That don't mean I ain't done it.'

'Oh?'

'Went all over the Bronx. Went places the trains don't go. You get off the train, then you has to take a bus.' He shook his head at the wonder of it all. 'Took a while, but I found folks used to know this Eldoniah. Thing is, that weren't the name they called him by.'

'What did they call him?'

'Shy.'

'Shy? He sounded about as retiring as a cobra.'

'Well, he retirin' now, where he's at upstate. The way he be shy, see, the gang he run with, dudes'll look you right in the eye an' pull the trigger, shoot you while they smilin' at you.'

'That's what I heard about Eldoniah.'

'No, see, 'cause he too shy for that. That's why he's so happy the day he discovered cabdrivers. No need to be lookin' 'em in the eye, 'cause all you got to do is shoot 'em in the back of the head.'

'And that's why they call him Shy.'

'Din I just say that?'

'So as far as the street's concerned, he did those cabdrivers.'

He nodded. 'The bust was righteous. But the white dude in the Yellow wasn't one of his.'

'They told you that?'

'Didn't have to. The MO was all wrong.' He grinned at my expression. 'Well, don't that be how you'd say it? I gone be a detective, I might as well get down with the language. What Shy would do, he'd always call a cab from one of them livery services. An' he wouldn't drop it on Audubon Avenue where they found Cloonan, 'cause that be a Spanish neighborhood an' he likely to attract attention there. But just to make sure, I axed people who knew him.'

'And they talked to you?'

'Story I told, I had the word from my mama that Eldoniah Mims was most likely my daddy. She just tol' me this right before she died, Clyde, so I was makin' it my business to see what I could find out about him.'

'How old is Mims? I didn't think he was old enough to have been your father.'

'He ain't, but none of the fools I talked to bothered to

run the 'rithmetic. An' I guess Shy wasn't too shy, 'cause this one friend of his took me 'round an' introduced me to this kid and said we's evidently brothers. Kid was twelve years old an' meaner'n cat shit. I don't 'spect he'll live to be voting age, 'less they save his damn life by lockin' him up for the next six years.' He grinned. 'He glad to see me, though. Likes the idea that he's got an older brother. Someone to pull his coat, teach him the ways of the world.'

'You'll be a good influence on him.'

He rolled his eyes. 'Only way you gone influence him is how Shy influenced those drivers. Shoot him in the back of the head. Anyway, all he told me is what I already figured out. Shy didn't do the dude in the Yellow. But you knew that, too, didn't you?'

'It certainly looked that way.'

He washed down the last bite of cheeseburger with the last swallow of milk, pulled a napkin from the dispenser, and wiped his mouth. 'Somethin' you don't know, though.'

'There's a great deal I don't know.'

'Killer was white.'

'How do you know that?'

'Girl told me.'

'That's damned interesting,' I said. 'I wonder how a rumor like that got all the way to the Bronx.'

'Who said anything about the Bronx? We talkin' Audubon Avenue in Washington Heights where the guy in the Yellow got shot.'

'What were you doing there?'

'Same thing I doin' everywhere, mindin' other folks's business. Did I say it a Spanish neighborhood? I didn't blend in too good.'

'I guess your Spanish is rusty.'

'I best get some of those tapes, learn it in my sleep. But

what good's bein' able to talk Spanish in your sleep?' He shrugged. 'Don't make no sense. What I done, I was this assistant to Melissa Mikawa, does them features on New York One?'

'I know who you mean. You told them you were her assistant?'

'Why not? I wasn't wearin' these clothes, Rose. Got me some long pants, neat little polo shirt, pair of penny loafers. Put on a Brooks Brothers accent to match the clothes. You think I didn't look like some kind of assistant to a TV reporter?'

'What about the hair?'

He whipped off his cap. His hair was a tight cap of curls that rose a scant half-inch from his scalp. 'Got it cut,' he said. 'What you think?'

'It looks good.'

'Looks better with the cap on,' he said. 'Least when I'm on the Deuce it does.' From the red Kangaroo circling his waist he produced a pair of horn-rimmed glasses, put them on. 'I was wearin' these,' he said. 'An' I was carryin' a clipboard. That's even better than the glasses. Man with a clipboard, you know he's there on legitimate business, an' everybody can't hardly wait to tell him the combination to the safe. You know who told me that?'

'Some legendary con artist, I'm sure.'

'Yeah, well, he ain't that slick, 'cause he be payin' for my breakfast this morning.'

'I told you about the clipboard?'

''Bout a year ago. We havin' coffee, you reminiscin', tellin' me stuff. You don't recall? Well, see, I pay attention when Matthew Scudder be talkin'. Even if you don't.'

'What did you tell them on Audubon Avenue? Melissa Mikawa's planning a segment on murdered cabdrivers?'

He nodded. 'I said she doin' a story on that particular case, an' how it was never solved, 'cause what do they know on Audubon Avenue about Shy Mims an' his upstate huntin' lodge? I said how anybody who was aroun' when it went down, anybody who heard or saw anything, might get to be on television. An' they be gettin' to meet Melissa Mikawa. Man, they loves that bitch up in Washington Heights! She Japanese, right?'

'If she isn't,' I said, 'it's a hell of an act she puts on.'

'Well, they actin' like they think she's Rican. Axin' me all this shit, what's she like, has she got a boyfriend. Time I got done makin' up stories about her, I was starting to believe 'em myself. Anyway, I found this one girl, she was right there when Cloonan got killed.'

'What did she see?'

'Saw the Yellow pull up an' park in the bus stop on the corner. Then a little while later she saw this dude get out an' close the door an' walk away.'

'"A little while later." Five minutes? Ten minutes?'

'Man, this was four years ago. An' she still in high school, so how old was she when it went down? An' who remembers how long a cab stands around 'fore some fool gets out of it? She wouldna thought anything of it at all, except later on the police came and drugged a body out of the Yellow.'

'She didn't hear a shot.'

'Says she didn't.'

'He must have used a suppressor. You say she got a look at him?'

'She got a look. Don't know how good a look it was.'

'And she said he was white? Could he have been a white Hispanic?'

'I said was he Spanish, and she said he was white.'

'Like, no, he wasn't Spanish, he was white?'

'Like that, yeah.'

'And he got out of the cab, and—'

'Leaned in, like he was sayin' something to the driver. Like, wait for me. That's why nobody thought nothin' when the Yellow stayed right where it was.'

'Was the meter on?'

'Wasn't on in the first place.'

'He threw the flag before he pulled up to park? They do that sometimes but—'

'What she said,' TJ said, 'and you got to keep in mind this was four years ago—'

'And she was just a kid, I understand that part. What did she say?'

'Dude wasn't a fare.'

'The passenger? The man she saw?'

'He was ridin' in front.'

'You don't mean he was driving, because they found Cloonan behind the wheel.'

'Didn't say drivin', said ridin'. In the passenger seat, 'cept they should be callin' it somethin' else, 'cause you a passenger in a cab, you ride in the back, Jack. But he was ridin' up front with the driver.'

'How far away was she?'

'Two, three doors down the street. She showed me the candystore they was standin' in front of, her an' her friends. 'Splained to me how Melissa Mikawa could do a stand-up interviewin' her in front of the store. Man, *she* coulda been Melissa Mikawa's assistant, all the media trash she was talkin'.'

'What did he look like?'

'White.'

'Tall, short, fat, thin, young, old—'

'Just white. But don't forget—'

'It was four years ago and she was a kid, right. You think I'd get anywhere putting her together with Ray Galindez?'

'So Elaine'll have another picture to hang up in the shop? I can see her gettin' into it, but what comes out might be more imaginin' than rememberin'. She'd swear he had tits an' a tail if it'd get her on New York One.'

'I probably ought to talk to her.'

'Like you a cop? Or like you workin' for Miss Mikawa also?'

'I'll be an assistant news director,' I said. 'How's that?'

He considered, then nodded. 'I'll go get my polo shirt and my khakis,' he said. 'An' my penny loafers. I meant to bring 'em anyway so's I can leave 'em at Elaine's.' He eyed my clothing. 'Maybe you could dress up a little yourself,' he said, 'so we don't start no rumors about New York One's on the skids.'

I put on a blue blazer, and New York One's sartorial reputation stayed unsullied. We rode uptown on the A train and spent forty minutes finding Sombrita Pardo and another half hour getting her story between bites of sausage pizza at a pizza parlor adjacent to the candy store in front of which she'd been standing four years earlier. She was a little dumpling with glossy black hair, olive skin, Indio features, and surprising light brown eyes. Her name meant Little Shadow, she said, which was kind of silly and she used to hate it, but now she was beginning to like it because it was like different.

Her story didn't change. The man who got out of the metered cab was white, and that was as much of a physical description as she could provide. And he'd emerged from the front passenger seat, and she'd had the feeling that he was going to run an errand and return to the cab, but he walked around the corner and disappeared. And then she had to go home, and she forgot about it, and the next day she heard that there was all this commotion, police cars and everything, and it turned out the driver was dead. He'd been shot, or so they said, but couldn't he have just had a heart attack or something? And maybe the friend had gone for help, and—

And just forgot to come back?

Well, she said, maybe, you know, he OD'd, the driver, that is, and the friend decided he didn't want to get involved, so he, like, 911'd it in and went home. Except she knew they found bullets in him, or at least that's what she heard, but you heard lots of things, and how did you know what to believe?

How indeed?

Fifteen or twenty minutes in TJ excused himself to go to the john, at which point Little Shadow grew at once older and younger. She straightened up in her seat and said, 'Be honest with me? I'm not gonna be on TV, am I?'

'I'm afraid not.'

'Are you cops? You could be a cop, but no way Mr T. J. Smith's a police officer. 'Course, I never thought he was Melissa Mikawa's assistant, either.'

'You didn't?'

'He's too young and too street for that. You got to go to college to get a job like that, don't you? He never went to college.'

As I said, older than her years. Then I asked her why, if she saw through his act, she'd been so cooperative. 'Well, he's real cute,' she said, and giggled, and looked about twelve years old.

'I'm an insurance investigator,' I said. 'Mr Smith's a trainee. No need to let him know that you, uh, saw through his act.'

'Oh, I wouldn't,' she said, and sucked the last of her Coke through her straw. 'Insurance? I hope I didn't get anybody in trouble.'

'Certainly not.'

'Or keep someone from getting their money.'

'It's really just a matter of getting the paperwork straightened out,' I said, 'and maybe saving the company a few tax dollars.'

'Oh, well,' she said. 'That's good, isn't it?'

FIFTEEN

We got on the A train and split up at Columbus Circle. TJ was on his way to the shop to show Elaine how he looked in his Young Man of Promise costume. I walked over to Midtown North to look for Durkin. I caught him at his desk, eating a sandwich and drinking bottled iced tea.

'Thomas Cloonan,' I said. 'Playwright, part-time cabdriver, shot and killed four years ago, Audubon Avenue and 174th Street, guy they tagged for it never went to trial—'

'Jesus,' he said. 'What am I, the central figure in a granny-dumping? You figure me for no short-term memory at all?'

'I just wanted to refresh your memory.'

'It hasn't had time to get stale. We just talked about the son of a bitch the other day.'

'What did Cloonan do to become a son of a bitch?'

'Not Cloonan, for chrissake. The shooter.' His eyes narrowed in concentration. 'Mims,' he said. 'How's that for memory, considering it's a case I got no reason to give a shit about?'

'You want to try for the first name?'

'Obadiah.'

'Try Eldoniah.'

'Well, fuck, I came close enough. What about him?'

'The guy who shot Cloonan was white.'

I gave him what I had. It wasn't his case – it wasn't anybody's case at this stage – but he was too much of a cop not to take an interest, sifting data, proposing and discarding theories.

'Front-seat passenger,' he said. 'Who rides up front?'

'In Australia,' I said, 'when you get a cab, you automatically sit in front next to the driver.'

'Because the rear springs are shot?'

'Because there's no class system, and you're all mates. Getting in back would be a snub.'

'Yeah? What's the chances you got an Australian shooting cabbies and robbing them?'

'Well, it makes a refreshing change from Norwegians.'

'All that aside, implication's the shooter's a friend of the driver, right?'

'Known to him, anyway.'

'Front-seat passenger, meter's not running, no entry on the log sheet. He had a pickup in Midtown, long haul up to Columbia Presbyterian. How's the shooter know he's gonna be there?'

' "Tommy, next fare you get anywhere near the neighborhood, drop by the Emerald Grill, I got something to talk about with you." '

He thought about it. 'I don't know. That's about as hard to swallow as the Crocodile Dundee theory.'

'Or it's Cloonan's idea. He's in the neighborhood, so he decides to look up his friend.'

'Who latches on to the opportunity to kill him.' He took a swig of iced tea. 'Raspberry-flavored,' he said. 'All of a sudden there's, I don't know, a dozen, fifteen different flavors of iced tea. I used to think, why do we fill up the shelves with so many different choices? How are we gonna keep up with the fucking Russians if we're dicking around with flavored tea while they're building tanks and going to the moon? So their whole system fell apart and we're working on ten more flavors and doing fine. Which shows what I know about anything.' He took another drink and said, 'How reliable's your witness?'

'On a ten scale,' I said, 'somewhere between zero and one.'

'What I figured. Shooter gave Cloonan two in the back of the head. How do you manage that, you're sitting next to the guy?'

' "Hey, Tom, what's that out the window?" '

'He turns to look, bang bang. Yeah, I suppose. I'd have to see the lab report. Why would he do that, though? So it would look like the shot came from the rear seat?'

'Or just so Cloonan wouldn't see it coming.'

'Makes sense. Try this. Shooter's in the back, cab pulls to the curb, shooter puts a pair in Cloonan. Then he gets out, and then he gets back in, next to the driver this time, and grabs the wallet and the coin changer, whatever else he's after. *Then* he gets out a second time, and that's when Carmen Miranda gets a look at him.'

'It could be.'

'Or try this on. Same opening, two shots from the backseat, and the shooter slips out from the rear on the street side, so nobody talking trash in front of the candy store ever gets a look at him. Maybe he's from the same town in Norway as Obadiah, pardon me, Eldoniah, or maybe he's Hispanic like the neighborhood, and either way he walks around the corner and disappears.'

'And?'

'And then you have this white guy walking down the street, and he wants to get a cab, and who can blame him, a white guy in that neighborhood?'

'It's not a bad neighborhood.'

'Can we just accept the idea that a white guy on that block might just as soon get in a taxi? He sees this cab, and there's a man behind the wheel, and he opens the door to ask if the guy's waiting for a fare.'

'And he sees the driver's dead.'

'Right. And he does what most people would do,

especially out of their own neighborhood, which is get the hell out of there, because who wants to be a witness, and maybe he was up in the Heights buying dope or getting laid, so why get involved?'

'And the witness didn't see him until he was getting out of the cab?'

'Why would she?'

'I don't know,' I said. 'She doesn't see the shooter get out of the cab and she doesn't see the white guy get in.'

'Why should she? She's got other things on her mind.'

'I guess.'

'Basically,' he said, 'you haven't got anything, have you?'

'No.'

'In terms of evidence, I mean.'

'Not even close.'

'But if you're trying to build a case that a single killer did these four people—'

'Five, with Shipton's wife.'

'—then this doesn't slow you down any. I can't recommend you talk to anybody up in the Three-four, though. They got enough open files, they don't have to get cracking on one of the closed ones.'

'I know.'

'Unless you wanted to go on the record. Reopen all those cases at once. If your client'll go for it.'

'My client and some of his friends are meeting in a couple of days to see what they want to do.'

'What, all twenty-six of them?'

'Where'd you get twenty-six?'

'Thirty guys, four of them killed. That leaves twenty-six, right?' He grinned. 'Nothing wrong with this granny's short-term memory.'

'The arithmetic's wrong.'

He looked at me. 'Thirty minus four equals—'

'Fourteen.'

'Huh?'

'There were four murders,' I said, 'and twelve other deaths.'

'What kind of deaths?'

'A few suicides, a few accidents. A few resulting from illness.'

'Jesus Christ, Matt!'

'They weren't all faked,' I said. 'It's hard to make murder look like testicular cancer, or a combat death in Vietnam. But the suicides could have been, and a few of the accidents.'

'What's your guess?'

'Including the four that went into the book as homicides? A guess is all it is, but I'd say twelve.'

'Jesus *Christ*. Over how many years?'

'Hard to say. Thirty-two since the group was formed, but the first deaths didn't happen for a couple of years, and they were probably legitimate, anyway. Say twenty, twenty-five years.'

He pushed his chair back. 'I don't see how I can sit on this.'

'Sit on what?'

'Do you swear this isn't a sex thing?'

'On a Bible, if you've got one handy.'

'You know what I think? I think I ought to take a statement from you.'

'Fine. Type up "No comment" and I'll sign it.'

'You'd hold out?'

'Until I'm instructed otherwise.'

'I don't get it,' he said. 'What's your client more scared of than getting killed?'

'A media circus.'

'What makes you think they'd be that interested?'

'Are you kidding? Some clown targeting a group of

men and taking decades to knock them off? If that won't put reporters in a feeding frenzy—'

'Yeah, you're right. And Boyd Shipton was one of the victims.'

'There are three survivors who are at least as prominent as he is.'

'Seriously? That's some club. And it had a cabdriver in it, and a commodities broker, and what was the gay guy? Interior decorator?'

'Carl Uhl? I think he was a partner in a catering firm.'

'Same thing. Three guys as prominent as Shipton?'

'Household words.'

'Jesus.'

'I don't want to sit on this, Joe, but at the same time—'

'Yeah, sure. You said the fourteen of them are having a meeting?'

'Some of them, anyway.'

'When's that?'

'Tuesday.'

'Today's Friday. What do you do between now and then?'

'Whatever I can,' I said. 'I was thinking about Forest Hills.'

'The guy who got stabbed. The commodities guy, Watson.'

'Right. I was wondering what the private security guard might have seen.'

'He saw a man lying on the ground and he ran over and called it in. If he saw anything else it would be in his statement. Believe me, they would have asked him.'

'Would they have questioned him about what he saw earlier?'

'Earlier?'

'If someone was waiting for Watson, planning to ambush him—'

'Oh, I get you. Maybe they would have, back when they were thinking it might be a client with a resentment. But it wouldn't hurt to ask him again. You want his name?'

'And where he works.'

He reached for the phone, then turned to look at me. 'You seen these AT&T ads about the information highway? They don't say anything about it's a one-way street.'

'I know that, Joe.'

'Just so you know,' he said, and made the call.

SIXTEEN

I caught the Number Seven train and got off at the 103rd Street station in Corona, two stops before Shea Stadium. Two blocks away on Roosevelt Avenue, Queensboro-Corona Protective Services occupied the top floor of a two-story brick building. The store on the ground floor sold children's clothing, and had a lot of stuffed animals in the window.

Most security firms are run by ex-cops, the majority of whom look the part. Martin Banszak, head man at Queensboro-Corona, looked as though he ought to be downstairs selling jumpers for toddlers. He was a small man in his sixties, round-shouldered, balding, with sad blue eyes behind rimless bifocals and a severely trimmed mustache under a button nose.

I carry two styles of business cards. One, a gift from my sponsor, Jim Faber, has nothing on it but my name and phone number. The second, supplied by Reliable, identifies me as an operative of that firm. It was one of the Reliable cards that I gave to Banszak, and it led to a little confusion; the next thing I knew he was explaining that Queensboro-Corona was mostly involved with furnishing uniformed guards and mobile security patrols, that they didn't employ trained operatives of my caliber often, but that if I would fill out one of these forms he'd keep it on file, because they did have need of investigators periodically, so I might get some occasional work from them.

We got that straightened out and I explained who I was and what I wanted.

'James Shorter,' he said. 'May I ask the nature of your interest in Mr Shorter?'

'There was an incident several months ago,' I said. 'He was the first person on the scene of a street crime in Forest Hills, and—'

'Oh, of course,' he said. 'Terrible thing. Hardworking businessman struck down on his way home.'

'I thought your man might have noticed something unusual that night, some unfamiliar presence in the neighborhood.'

'I know the police questioned him at length.'

'I'm sure they did, but—'

'The whole episode was very troubling for Shorter. It may have precipitated the other problem.'

'What problem would that be, Mr Banszak?'

He looked at me through the lower portion of his eyeglasses. 'Tell me something,' he said. 'Has Jim Shorter applied for a position with your firm?'

'With Reliable? Well, I don't think so, but I wouldn't know if he did. I'm not part of management. I just give them a few days now and then.'

'And you're not working for them now?'

'No.'

He thought about it. Then he said, 'He was, as I said, very troubled by that crime. After all, it had occurred on his watch. There was never the slightest implication that he ought to have been able to prevent it. Each of our mobile units has a considerable area to patrol. We aim for maximum deterrent capability through maximum visibility. The criminals see our marked patrol cars, they know the area's under constant surveillance, and they're that much less apt to commit their crimes.'

'Isn't it more a case of their committing them somewhere else?'

'Well, what can any police presence do, public or

private? We can't change human nature. If we can reduce crime in the neighborhoods we're hired to protect, we feel we're doing our job.'

'I understand.'

'Still, I suppose Shorter must have felt some element of responsibility. That's human nature, too. And there was shock as well, coming upon a crime scene, discovering a corpse. There was the stress of multiple police interrogations. I don't say this caused anything, but it may well have precipitated it.'

'Precipitated what, sir?'

For an answer, he bent his elbow and moved his wrist up and down, like a man throwing down shots.

'He drank?'

He sighed. 'If you drink, you're gone. That's a rule here. No exceptions.'

'It's understandable.'

'But I did make an exception,' he said, 'because of the stress he'd been under. I told him I'd give him one more chance. Then there was a second incident and that was that.'

'When was this?'

'I'd have to look it up. I'd guess he didn't last more than a month after that man was killed. Say six weeks at the very outside. When was the fellow killed? End of January?'

'Early February.'

'I'd say he was gone by the middle of March. *Middlemarch*,' he said surprisingly. 'That's a novel. Have you read it?'

'No.'

'Neither have I. It sits on my bookshelf. My mother owned it and died, and now it's mine, along with a couple of hundred other books I haven't read. But the spine of that one always catches my eye. *Middlemarch*.

George Eliot wrote it. I'm sure I'll never read it.' He waved a hand at the futility of it all. 'I have James Shorter's telephone number. Would you like me to call him for you?'

No one answered Shorter's phone. Banszak copied the number for me, along with an address on East Ninety-fourth Street in Manhattan. I grabbed a quick bite at an Italian deli and caught the train back to the city. At the Grand Central stop I switched to the Lexington Avenue express and got off at Eighty-sixth. I tried Shorter from a pay phone and got my quarter back after half a dozen rings.

It was a quarter to five. If Shorter had found a new position, he was probably at work right now, like most of the rest of the city's working force. On the other hand, if he was still in the same line of work there was no guessing his schedule. He could be a uniformed guard at a checkcashing facility in Sunset Park or night watchman at a warehouse in Long Island City. There was no way to tell.

Sometimes I tuck a meeting schedule in my pocket, but it's a bulky affair, listing every AA meeting in the metropolitan area, and more often than not I don't have it with me. I didn't today, so I dropped the quarter in the slot again and dialed New York Intergroup. A volunteer was able to tell me that there was a 5:30 meeting in the basement of a church at First Avenue and Eighty-fourth Street.

I got there early and found out they didn't have coffee – some groups do, some don't. I went to the bodega across the street and ran into two others on the same mission, one of whom I recognized from a lunchtime meeting I go to sometimes at the West Side Y. We trooped back across the street with our coffee and took seats around a couple of refectory tables, and by half-past five a handful of others had straggled in and the meeting got under way.

There were just a dozen of us — it was a new group, and if I'd had my meeting book with me I'd never have found it, because it wasn't listed yet. A woman named Margaret, sober a little over a year, told her story and took most of the hour getting through it. She was about my age, the daughter and granddaughter of alcoholics, and she'd been careful to keep alcohol at bay for years, limiting herself to a single cocktail or glass of wine at social occasions. Then her husband died of an esophageal hemorrhage — she'd married an alcoholic, of course — and in her midforties she turned to drink, and it was as if it had been waiting for her all her life. It embraced her and wouldn't let go, and the progression of her alcoholism was quick and sudden and nasty. In no time at all she'd lost everything but her rent-controlled apartment and the Social Security check that enabled her to pay the rent.

'I was rooting around in garbage cans,' she said. 'I was waking up in strange places, and not always alone. And I was a well brought-up Irish Catholic girl who never slept with anybody but my husband. I remember coming out of a blackout one time, and I won't tell you what I was doing or who I was doing it to, but all I could think was, "Oh, Peggy, the nuns would not be proud of you now!"'

After she was done we passed the basket and went around the room. When it was my turn I found myself talking about how I'd gone looking for a security guard and found he'd been dismissed for drinking. 'I had a strong sense of identification,' I said. 'My own drinking picked up after I left the police force. If I'd kept on drinking any longer than I did I'd have gone after jobs like this man's, and I'd have drunk my way out of them, too. I don't really know anything about him or what his life's like, but thinking about him has given me an idea of what my own life could have been like if I hadn't found this program. I'm just glad to be here, glad to be sober.'

I went out for coffee after the meeting with a couple of the others and we continued informally the sharing we'd done at the meeting. I tried Shorter's number when we arrived at the coffee shop and tried it again fifteen minutes later. I tried it a third time on my way out, which must have been a few minutes after seven. When my quarter came back once again I used it to call Elaine.

There were no messages for me, she said, and the mail had held nothing of interest. I told her what I was up to, and that I might be out most of the evening. 'If he had an answering machine,' I said, 'I'd leave a message on it and call him again in a day or two if I didn't hear from him. But he doesn't, and I'm in the neighborhood, and it's not a neighborhood I get to often.'

'You don't have to explain it to me.'

'I'm explaining it to myself. And it's not as though he's likely to have any answers. Any question I've got, the Forest Hills cops already asked. So how could he have anything for me?'

'Maybe you've got something for him.'

'What do you mean?'

'Nothing really. Well, there's a lecture and slide show at the French church. I might go to that, and if Monica wants to go with me maybe we'll have a Girls' Night Out afterward. You'll be having a late night, won't you?'

'I might.'

'Because you were going to drop in on Mick, weren't

you? Just so you're home in time for Marilyn's Chamber tomorrow night.'

'You still want to go?'

'After the time we had last night?' I could picture the expression on her face. 'Now more than ever. You're pretty hot stuff, Mr Scudder, sir.'

'Now cut that out.'

'"Now cut that out." You know who you sound like? Jack Benny.'

'I was trying to sound like Jack Benny.'

'Well, in that case, it wasn't a very good imitation.'

'You just said—'

'I know what I said. I love you, you old bear. What have you got to say about that?'

North of Eighty-sixth Street, the landscape on the Upper East Side is one of a neighborhood in transition, neither Yorkville nor East Harlem but reminiscent of both. Luxury condos rise across the street from low-income public-housing projects, the walls of both impartially scarred by unreadable graffiti. The upwardly mobile stride along with briefcases and grocery bags from D'Agostino's; others, no less mobile but headed in the opposite direction, shake paper cups of change and drink forty-ounce bottles of malt liquor, or suck on crack pipes that glow like fireflies.

Shorter's building turned out to be a six-story brick tenement on Ninety-fourth between Second and Third. In the vestibule I counted over fifty doorbells, each with a slot beside it for the tenant's name. More than half the slots were empty, and none had Shorter's name on it.

Originally the building would have had four rooms to a floor, but over the years they'd been partitioned and the apartment house turned into a rooming house.

I'd been in and out of hundreds of such places over the years, and if each was different they were still somehow all the same. The cooking smells in the halls and stairwells changed with the ethnic origin of the inhabitants, but the other smells were a constant throughout the city and through the years. The reek of urine, the odor of mice, the unventilated stench of neglect. Now and then a room in one of those rabbit warrens would turn out to be bright and airy, clean and trim, but the buildings themselves were always dark and sorry and sordid.

Something like that would have been my next stop after the hotel. If I hadn't stopped drinking, the day would have come when I couldn't make the rent or talk them into carrying me until I caught a break. Or I'd have reached a point where, money or no, I no longer had the self-esteem to walk past the desk each day, and would have looked for something more in keeping with my station.

I asked a man on his way out of the building if he knew a James Shorter. He didn't even slow down, just shook his head no and kept walking. I asked the same question of a little gray-haired woman who was on her way into the building, walking with a cane and carrying her groceries in one of those mesh bags. She said she didn't know anyone in the building but that they all seemed to be very nice people. Her breath smelled of mint and booze – peppermint schnapps, I suppose, or a beaker of gin with a breath mint for a chaser.

I walked to Second Avenue and tried Shorter's number from a pay phone on the corner. No answer. It struck me that if he wasn't working he might very well be somewhere having a drink, and the neighborhood afforded plenty of opportunities. There were half a dozen taverns on Second within two blocks of Ninety-fourth

Street. I worked my way through them, asking bartenders for James Shorter. Was he in? Had he been in earlier? Nobody knew him, at least not by name, but the bearded fellow behind the stick at O'Bannion's said he'd heard precious few last names over the years, and not that many first names, either. 'He could be one of these lads, for all I know,' he said.

I considered calling out his name. *James Shorter? Is James Shorter here?* But then I'd have had to repeat the process in the saloons I'd already covered, and I didn't feel like it. I'd had enough of their boozy ambience.

And how about the gin joints on First Avenue? Shouldn't I go ask for the elusive Mr Shorter there?

I might have, but first I tried his number again, and this time he answered.

I told him my name, said I'd got his from the police and his address and phone from Mr Banszak at Queensboro-Corona. 'I know you've been over this plenty of times,' I said, 'but I'd appreciate a few minutes of your time. I'm in your neighborhood right now, as it happens, so if I could come by and see you—'

'Oh, let's meet somewhere,' he suggested. 'There's a nice place around the corner on First Avenue, the Blue Canoe. It's a good place to talk. Say ten minutes?'

The Blue Canoe was paneled to look like a log cabin. There were a couple of trophy heads on the wall, a stuffed marlin displayed above the mirrored back bar. The lighting was subdued and indirect, the taped music a mix of jazz and soft rock. The crowd was light and upscale for the neighborhood.

I stood in the doorway for a moment, looked around, then walked directly to a table where a man sat alone with a glass of beer. I said, 'Mr Shorter?' but I already knew that's who he was. I'd waited for him across the

172

street from his rooming house and tagged him to the bar, then gave him time to settle in before making my own entrance.

Old habits die hard, I guess.

We shook hands and I took the seat across from him. I'd formed a mental picture of him – the mind will do that, helpfully conjuring up an image to fit the sense one has of a person. People don't usually wind up looking much like I've pictured them, and he was no exception, being older, darker, and, yes, shorter than I'd had in mind. Late forties, I figured. Five-eight, wiry, with a round face and deep-set eyes. A pug nose, a narrow-lipped mouth. No beard or mustache, but a good two days' worth of stubble darkening his cheeks and chin. Dark hair, black in the dim light of the Blue Canoe, cut short and combed flat on his round skull. He was wearing a T-shirt, and had a lot of dark hair on his forearms and the backs of his wrists.

'It must have been a shock,' I said. 'Finding Watson's body.'

'A shock? Jesus, I'll say.'

The waitress came and I ordered a Coke. Then I took out my notebook and we started going over his story.

There wasn't a lot to get. He'd gone over it repeatedly with detectives from Queens Homicide and the One-one-two, and he'd had close to five months to forget anything he might have left out. No, he hadn't seen anybody suspicious in the neighborhood. No, he hadn't spotted Alan Watson earlier on, heading home from the bus stop. No, he couldn't think of anything, not a damn thing.

'How come you're checking now?' he wondered. 'Do you have a lead?'

'No.'

'Are you from a different precinct or what?'

He'd assumed I was a cop, an assumption I'd been perfectly willing for him to make. But now I told him I was private.

'Oh,' he said. 'But you're not with Q-C, are you?'

'Queensboro-Corona? No, I'm independent.'

'And you're investigating a mugging in Forest Hills? Who hired you, the victim's widow?'

'No.'

'Somebody else?'

'A friend of his.'

'Of Watson's?'

'That's right.'

He caught the waitress's eye and ordered another beer. I didn't much want another Coke but I ordered one anyway. Shorter said, 'I guess people with money see things differently. I was just thinking how if a friend of mine got stabbed on the street, would I hire detectives to find out who did it?' He shrugged, smiled. 'I guess not,' he said.

'I can't really talk about my client.'

'No, I can understand that,' he said. The waitress brought the drinks and he said, 'I guess it's your own policy, then. Not drinking on duty.'

'How's that?'

'Well, like if you were a cop, you wouldn't be drinking on duty. Or private, either, if you worked for somebody like Q-C. But working independent, you can judge for yourself whether you should be having a drink or not having a drink, right? So you're ordering Coke, I figure it has to be your own policy.'

'Is that what you figure?'

'Or maybe you just like Coca-Cola.'

'It's all right, but I can't say I'm crazy about it. See, I don't drink.'

'Oh.'

'But I used to.'

'Yeah?'

'I loved it,' I said. 'Whiskey, mostly, but I probably drank enough beer over the years to float a light cruiser. Do you have a law-enforcement background yourself, Mr Shorter?' He shook his head. 'Well, I do. I was a cop, a detective. I drank myself off the police force.'

'Is that right?'

'I never got in trouble for it,' I said. 'Not directly, but I would have the way I was going. I walked away from it, the job, my wife and kids, my whole life . . .'

I don't see what he could have for me, I'd told Elaine. Maybe you've got something for him, she'd said.

Maybe I did.

The way it works is remarkably simple. A day at a time, you don't drink. You go to meetings and share your experience, strength, and hope with your fellow alcoholics.

And you carry the message.

You do that not by preaching or spreading the gospel but by telling your own story – what it used to be like, what happened, and what it's like now. That's what you do when you lead a meeting, and it's what you do one-on-one.

So I told my story.

When I was done he picked up his glass. He looked at it and put it down again. He said, 'I drank myself out of the job at Q-C. But I guess you know that.'

'It was mentioned.'

'I was kind of shook, finding the body and all. Not the sort of thing I'm used to, you know what I mean?'

'Sure.'

'So I was hitting it a little heavy for a while there. It happens, right?'

175

'It does.'

'General rule, I don't drink that much.'

'They say it's not how much you drink,' I said. 'It's what it does for you.'

'Have to say it does a lot for me,' he said. 'Lets me relax, unwind, get some thinking done. That's some of what it does for me.'

'Uh-huh. How about what it does *to* you?'

'Ha,' he said. 'Now that's something else, isn't it?' He picked the glass up again, put the glass down again. 'I guess you're pretty strong on this AA stuff, huh?'

'It saved my life.'

'You been sober awhile, huh? Two, three years?'

'More like ten.'

'Jesus,' he said. 'No, uh, little vacations along the way?'

'Not so far.'

He nodded, taking it in. 'Ten years,' he said.

'You do it a day at a time,' I told him. 'It tends to add up.'

'You still go to the meetings after all this time? How often do you go?'

'At first I went every day. Sometimes I went to two or three meetings a day during the early years. I'll still go every day when I feel like drinking, or if I'm under a lot of stress. And sometimes I'll let my attendance drop to one or two meetings a week. Most of the time, though, I go to three or four meetings a week.'

'Even after all these years. Where do you find the time?'

'Well, I always had time to drink.'

'Yeah, I guess drinking does pass the time, doesn't it?'

'And it's easy to find meetings that fit into my schedule. That's a nice thing about New York, there are meetings around the clock.'

'Oh, yeah?'

I nodded. 'All over town,' I said. 'There's a group on Houston Street that has a meeting every day at midnight and another at two in the morning. What's ironic is the meeting place was one of the city's most notorious after-hours joints for years. They stayed open late then and they still do today.'

He thought that was pretty funny. I excused myself and went to the john, stopping on the way back to use the phone. I was pretty sure there was a late meeting on East Eighty-second Street, but I wanted to make sure of the time and the exact address. I called Intergroup, and the woman who answered the phone didn't even have to look it up.

Back at our table, Shorter was still looking at the same half-ounce of beer. I told him there was a meeting in the neighborhood at ten o'clock and that I thought I would probably go to it. I hadn't been to a meeting in a couple of days, I told him, which was a lie. I could use a meeting, I said, which was true.

'You want to go, Jim?'

'Me?'

Who else? 'Come on,' I said. 'Keep me company.'

'Gee, I don't know,' he said. 'I just had these beers, and I had one or two earlier.'

'So?'

'Don't you have to be sober?'

'Just so you don't start shouting and throwing chairs,' I said. 'But I don't think you're likely to do that, are you?'

'No, but—'

'It doesn't cost anything,' I said, 'and the coffee and cookies are generally free. And you hear people say really interesting things.' I straightened up. 'But I don't want to talk you into anything. If you're positive you haven't got a problem—'

'I never said that.'

'No, you didn't.'

He got to his feet. 'What the hell,' he said. 'Let's go before I change my mind.'

SEVENTEEN

The meeting was in a brownstone on Eighty-second Street off Second Avenue. An AA group had rented the second floor and held half a dozen meetings there every day, starting at seven in the morning and ending at eleven. In concession to their residential neighbors, there was no applause at the late meeting; one indicated approval or enthusiasm by snapping one's fingers.

The speaker was a construction worker with five years' sobriety, and he told a basic, straightforward drinking story and told it succinctly, wrapping it up in twenty minutes. Then there was a break with announcements and the passing of the basket, and then we continued with a show of hands.

I was glad of that. All he had to do was keep his hands in his lap and he wouldn't have to say anything. No reason he should be put on the spot at his first meeting, the way he would be if they went around the room.

When I first came in, the last thing I wanted was to open my mouth in a roomful of alcoholics. And I kept finding my way to round-robin meetings. *My name is Matt*, I said, time and time again. *I pass.* I'd have a dozen things buzzing around in my head, but none of them made it past my lips. *My name is Matt. Thanks for your qualification. I'll just listen tonight.*

At eleven we went downstairs and out. I suggested a cup of coffee and he said that sounded good. We walked to Eighty-sixth, where there was a diner he liked. I was hungry enough to order a grilled cheese sandwich and an order of onion rings. He just wanted coffee.

He said, 'I almost raised my hand. I was this close.'

'You can, any time you want. But you don't have to.'

'People say anything, don't they? I thought what one person said would relate to what the person before him said, but it doesn't necessarily work that way, does it?'

'You say whatever's on your mind.'

'Around our house, what I always heard was, "Don't tell your business to strangers." I'm used to keeping things to myself.'

'I know what you mean.'

'It really works, huh? You don't drink and you go to meetings and you stay sober?'

'It works for me.'

'Jesus, I guess it does. Ten years.'

'The days add up.'

What about God, he wondered. What about the sign on the wall, the list of the twelve suggested steps. You just don't drink, I told him, and you come to meetings, and you keep an open mind. Did I believe in God? Some of the time, I said. I didn't have to believe in God all the time. The only thing I had to do every minute of every day was not pick up a drink.

He said, 'I shouldn't be keeping you. You've probably got things to do.'

'I'm glad to have the company, Jim.'

'You know, I was thinking. In the meeting, because I would be listening to somebody and my mind would wander. I was thinking about Alan Watson. The guy who got stabbed?'

'And?'

'It seems to me there's something nagging at my memory but I can't get ahold of it.'

'Maybe if we go through that evening step by step,' I said.

'I don't know. Maybe it'll just come to me. You say this friend of his thinks it wasn't just a random mugging?'

'That's what I'm trying to determine.'

'Why, is there someone had a reason to kill him?'

'Not that I know of.'

'Then—'

No reason he couldn't know. 'There have been some other deaths.'

'In the same neighborhood?'

'No,' I said, 'and they didn't happen on the street, either.'

'Then what's the connection?'

'The victims knew each other.'

'Victims? Then they were all murdered, same as Watson?'

'Some were. Some might have been.'

'Might have been?'

'There were suicides that could have been staged,' I said, 'and a couple of accidental deaths that could have been arranged.'

'So you got this group of guys . . . What is it, a club or something?'

'I can't really go into the details.'

'Sure, I understand. What happened, one of the guys hired you? Why didn't they go to the cops?'

'One of the things I have to do,' I said, 'is determine if it's a police matter or not.'

'It would have to be, wouldn't it? If a group of guys are being killed off one after the other—'

'That's what I have to determine.'

'I thought you said—'

'The murders could be unconnected. And the suicides could be genuine suicides.'

'And the accidents could be legit,' he said. 'I get it. Are you making much headway?'

'I can't really—'

'—go into details, right. I'm sorry. I'm just trying to get an idea what it is I should be trying to remember. You know, I just took it for granted it was a mugging, what I guess they'd call a crime of opportunity. I think one of the cops used that phrase, meaning the mugger was out there looking to score a few dollars from somebody, and Mr Watson came along, good neighborhood, looked like he belonged there, suit and tie, obviously a professional man coming home from work, figure he'll have a good watch on his arm and some big bills in his wallet.' He frowned. 'But if somebody was setting out from the jump to murder Watson, how would he do it? Just stake out his house and wait for him to come home?'

'That's one way.'

'Then you'd have somebody lurking in the neighborhood,' he said. 'I don't remember seeing anything like that, but I don't know if it's something I'd notice. Some sleazebag with dirty clothes and a scruffy beard skulking around in the shadows, well, yeah, part of my job was to spot people like that and either roust them myself or call nine-one-one and drop a dime on them. But the guy you're looking for wouldn't operate like that, would he?'

'Probably not.'

'He'd probably be dressed decent,' he said, 'and he'd want to be able to keep an eye on Watson's house, or on the approach to it. And, come to think of it, he'd most likely be in a car, wouldn't he? You think mugger, you picture a guy on foot, but somebody looking to fake a mugging might have his own car, right?'

'It's very possible.'

'Was there a car parked in the neighborhood? Now there were plenty of cars, so the real question is was there anybody sitting in a parked car, and the answer is I would never have noticed something like that. What's the guy look like, the guy you're after?'

'No idea.'

'You don't have a suspect in mind, huh? Or a physical description?' I shook my head. 'So if he had a car—'

'No idea of the make or model or plate number.'

'What I figured, Matt.'

'Or even if he had a car,' I said. 'See, if I knew who did it, I'd be coming at it from another angle entirely.'

'Yeah, I see what you mean.'

We talked a little about the nature of detection, about the ways I'd approached other cases in the past. He didn't have a police background but the time he'd spent doing guard work and street patrol had left him with an interest in the subject, and he asked good questions and caught on quickly. The conversation died down when the waiter came around to refill our cups, and when it resumed the topic shifted to AA and alcoholism and where Jim might decide to go from here.

'I don't know if I'm an alcoholic,' he said earnestly. 'I heard a lot tonight that was interesting, but there's plenty that happened to the speaker that never happened to me. I was never hospitalized, I was never in a detox or a rehab.'

'On the other hand, he never lost a job because of his drinking.'

'Yeah, and I did. No argument there.'

'Look,' I said, 'who knows if it's for you or not? But you're between jobs right now, you were saying how you've got time on your hands, and it's cheaper to kill time in meetings than around the bars. The coffee's free and the conversations are more interesting. It's the same people, you know, in the meetings and in the ginmills. The only difference is the ones in the meetings are sober.

That makes them more fun to be around, and a lot less likely to throw up on your shoes.'

At the meeting we'd just attended, I'd bought a meeting book during the secretary's break, and I went through it now with him, pointing out some meetings in his neighborhood. He asked me which ones I went to, and I told him I went mostly in my neighborhood. 'Every meeting has its own style,' I said. 'If you try different ones you'll find out which one suits you best.'

'Like different bars.'

I gave him my card, one of the minimalist ones with my name and phone number. 'That's my office,' I said, 'but when I'm not there the calls get forwarded automatically to my home. If it's an emergency you can call me any hour, day or night. Otherwise it's not a good idea to call after midnight. If it's after midnight and you get antsy, you can always call Intergroup. The number's in the meeting book, and they've got volunteers taking calls around the clock.'

'You mean just call up and talk to a stranger?'

'It's better than picking up a drink.'

'Jesus,' he said, 'you've given me a lot to think about, you know that? I mean, I didn't see this coming.'

'Neither did I.'

'You called me, I figured what the hell, I'd meet you, drink a glass of beer or two, gab a little, maybe I'd get lucky and you'd spring for the beers. I didn't figure they'd be the last beers I'd ever have in my life.' He laughed. 'I'd known that, maybe I'd've ordered something imported.'

EIGHTEEN

It was well past midnight by the time I got home. Elaine's Girls' Night Out had evidently had an early ending; she was sleeping soundly, and didn't stir when I got in beside her. I was exhausted – it had been a long day – but the time I'd spent with Jim Shorter had energized me, leaving me tired but wired. My mind was all over the place, and I thought I was going to have to get up and read or watch television to unwind. I was bracing myself to do just that when sleep came along and took me by surprise.

Over breakfast I told her how I'd spent the evening. 'I don't know if he'll ever get to another meeting,' I said, 'let alone get sober and stay sober. He says he didn't drink that much and it didn't screw him up that badly, and for all I know he's right. But I'll tell you, it did me good. They say there's nothing like working with a newcomer to reinvigorate your own commitment to the program.'

'Did he have anything helpful on the murder in Forest Hills?'

'Nothing,' I said. 'He had a lot of questions and a couple of theories, but he didn't suggest anything I hadn't thought of myself. As far as Forest Hills is concerned, I think I'm going to have to go out there. What's the forecast? Is it going to rain?'

'Hot and humid.'

'That'll be a change, won't it?'

'More of the same tomorrow. Possibility of rain on Monday.'

'That won't do me any good,' I said. 'I was hoping it would rain today, or at least threaten to.'

'Why?'

'So I could get out of traipsing out to Forest Hills. I ought to see Alan Watson's widow and I'm not looking forward to it.'

'No, but you'll do it,' she said. 'And if it was raining you'd go out there in the rain, knowing you. It'd be the same trip, only you'd get wet. So you're lucky it's only hot and humid.'

'I'm glad you pointed that out to me.'

'So enjoy yourself with the widow. What's the matter? Did I say something wrong?'

'No, of course not. Although I can't say I expect to enjoy it.'

'Whatever, darling. Just so you're back here by eight this evening. We've got a date, remember?'

'You still want to go?'

'Uh-huh. We should get there by ten, and we'll want to have dinner first. Should I cook something for us or do you want to eat someplace downtown?'

I told her not to cook, that there was no end of nice restaurants within a five-minute walk of Marilyn's Chamber. 'Although for fifty bucks a couple,' I said, 'you'd think the bastards could feed us.'

'The body parts are just for show,' she said. 'It's considered bad form to eat them.'

I went across the street to my hotel, collected my mail at the desk, went upstairs, and called the number I had for Alan Watson. It rang ten times, unanswered by human being or machine. I sorted my mail, threw out most of it, wrote checks for the rent and phone bill, checked the number with Queens Information to make sure I had it right, then dialed it again and listened to it ring another eight or ten times.

I broke the connection and called Lewis Hildebrand.

The woman who answered told me he was working and offered to give me his office number. I told her I already had it, and when I dialed Hildebrand answered it himself.

'You're as bad as I am,' he said. 'Working on a Saturday. Though I don't know if I'm working or I just felt like getting out of the house. There's something extremely relaxing about a suite of offices when you're the only person around. It feels as though the whole place belongs to me.'

'Doesn't it?'

'Well, yes, in a manner of speaking. But it's different when I'm the only one here. Late at night, or on a weekend. I had a call from Ray Gruliow.'

'I was there.'

'A second call. As of last night, there are still two members he hasn't been able to reach. Three of the others said they definitely can't make it on Tuesday, and a fourth has a conflict but will try to be there.'

'Assuming he can't work it out, how many is Gruliow expecting?'

'Eight.'

'That's including you and Gruliow?'

'Yes, and you'll be the ninth person present. I believe we'll be expecting you at three-thirty.'

'I thought three o'clock.'

'We'll be getting together at three,' he said. 'The members. The consensus was that we'd have half an hour together to discuss the situation, and then you'll join us.'

'All right,' I said. 'That sounds good. I don't know exactly what role I'll play, but I suppose I'll be reporting on what I've determined and making recommendations as to what I think you ought to do.'

'I would assume so, yes.'

'But you're the man who hired me, so I wanted to give

you a preliminary report.' And I did, going over what I'd learned and what I'd come to suspect, summarizing, running it all down as much for my own benefit as for his.

'It sounds,' he told me, 'as though you've done a great deal.'

'I know it does,' I said. 'It sounds that way to me, too. God knows I've been busy. I haven't kept track of my hours, but it seems to me I've put a lot of time in.'

'If you've done more work than your retainer covers—'

'I don't know if I have or not, and that's something I don't want to worry about now. No, the point is I've done a lot and I've even assembled a fair amount of data, but I'm not sure what it amounts to. Am I any closer to wrapping it up than I was when we sat down to lunch at the Addison Club? I don't know that I am.'

'What would constitute "wrapping it up"?'

'Answering the major questions.'

'Which are?'

'Is someone killing off the members? If so, who is he? And where is he, and how can we nail him for it? I'd say those are the main questions. I'm inclined to answer the first question with a tentative yes, but as far as the other questions are concerned, I'm still completely in the dark.'

'Answering them would constitute bringing the entire case to a conclusion, wouldn't it?'

'I guess it would.'

'So it's hardly surprising they're as yet unanswered. There's another question which I would certainly call a major one, although it's less a matter for investigation than for decision. Is it time for us to go public? Have we gone as far as we can reasonably expect to go with a discreet, low-profile investigation?'

'That's a big question,' I agreed. 'But it's not one for me to answer. I'm glad there'll be eight of you at

Gruliow's house Tuesday. I'd rather there were more. I wish you could all be there.'

'So do I.'

'Because the question of where we go from here is one of the things you'll have to decide,' I said. 'And I guess that's when you'll have to decide it.'

I spent the rest of the day in my room at the North-western. Every hour or so I tried the number in Forest Hills, and each time it went unanswered. I made other phone calls throughout the day, and watched the Yan-kees on the MSG channel. (Elaine asked me once, in all apparent seriousness, why they had named a cable channel after a food additive. Madison Square Garden, I told her. Oh, she said.) Wade Boggs tied it for New York with a rare home run in the top of the ninth. Two innings later, Travis Fryman hit a hard grounder down the third-base line. Boggs bobbled it, then threw it over Mattingly's head. Fryman wound up on second and scored on a shot to left by Cecil Fielder, all of which made them very happy in Detroit.

I turned off the set and the phone rang. It was Jim Shorter.

'I hope I'm not, you know, interrupting anything,' he said. 'But you gave me your card and said to call anytime.'

'I'm glad you did,' I said. 'How's it going?'

'Not so bad. I haven't had a drink yet today.'

'That's great, Jim.'

'Well, it's early. The day's not over yet. Anyway, there's days when I don't drink at all.' And, after a pause, 'I went to a meeting.'

'Good for you.'

'I guess it was good for me. I don't know. I can't see how it could have been bad for me, right?'

'Right. Where'd you go?'

'The same place we went last night. I put a buck in the basket and I had two cups of coffee and a handful of cookies. You can't lose on a deal like that, can you?'

'The price is right.'

He told me about the meeting. The crowd was lighter than last night, he said, but he recognized a couple of the same people. He gave me some highlights from the speaker's story.

'I wanted to raise my hand,' he said.

'You could have.'

'People who'd been sober for less than ninety days were raising their hands and giving their day count and getting a round of applause. I was going to raise my hand and say it was my first day, but I thought, shit, let me wait a few days.'

'Whatever you're comfortable with.'

'Maybe I'll go again tonight,' he said. 'Is it okay to go to more than one in a day?'

'You can go all day long,' I said. 'There's no limit.'

'Are you going? Maybe I could check out a West Side meeting, see if there's a difference.'

'I'd like that,' I said honestly, 'but I've got plans tonight.'

'Another time, then. How's the case coming?'

'Let's say it's a slow day.'

'Well, I won't keep you,' he said. 'Maybe I'll, uh, give you a call tomorrow.'

'Anytime,' I said. 'I mean it.'

I was crossing the lobby on my way home when I remembered I hadn't put Call Forwarding back on. I went upstairs, punched in the code, dialed the apartment across the street, and told Elaine I'd be home in two minutes. 'So why call?' she said. 'Oh, right. Call Forwarding.'

She was already dressed when I got there, wearing the leather outfit she'd modeled for me earlier, along with more perfume and makeup than was her custom. 'What I decided,' she explained, 'is that a dungeon is no place for understatement.'

'You don't think people will be exercising a little restraint?'

'I'll forgive you for that,' she said, 'but only because I love you. You probably want to shower, and your clothes are laid out for you on the bed.'

I showered and shaved and put on the pair of dark slacks she'd laid out for me, then walked into the living room holding the shirt. 'What's this?' I asked.

'It's a guayabera.'

'I can see that. Where did it come from?'

'Yucatán, originally, except I think this particular one was produced in Taiwan. Maybe it's Korea. It says on the label.'

'What I mean is—'

'I bought it for you. Try it on. Let me see. Hey, it looks great.'

'What are all these pockets for? And all this piping.'

'It's the style. Don't you like it?'

'If you'd told me in time,' I said, 'I could have let my sideburns grow and grown a little mustache. Then, with just the right haircut, I could look like a pimp in a 1940s movie.'

'I think you look casual yet commanding. It's a present, incidentally, but you don't have to thank me.'

'Good,' I said.

Marilyn's Chamber was located in the basement of a warehouse on Washington Street. Meat packagers occupied the premises on either side, and across the street. There was no sign to lead you to the club. The green door was unmarked, with a low-wattage red light bulb just above it. It was ten o'clock when we knocked and were admitted by a young man with dark black skin, a shaved head, a sleeveless black jumpsuit, and a black mask. It was a quarter after one when the same young man opened the door and let us out.

There was a cab cruising down Washington Street and I stepped to the curb and hailed it. I gave the driver our address and sat back, and when Elaine started to say something I interrupted her to suggest that we ride home in companionable silence.

'I'd rather talk,' she said.

'I'd rather you didn't.'

'Are you afraid I'll embarrass the driver?'

'No, I'm afraid—'

'Because his name is Manmatha Chatterjee. He's from India, home of the *Kama Sutra*. His people invented fancy fucking.'

'Please.'

'So he's not going to be embarrassed.'

'I am.'

'Besides, if he blushed, who'd know?'

'God damn it . . .'

'I'm whispering,' she said, 'and he can't possibly hear me, you silly old bear, you. I'll stop. I'll behave. I promise.'

She didn't say anything the rest of the way. In our elevator she said, 'May I speak now, master? Or do you suppose the elevator is bugged?'

'I think we're safe.'

'I had a good time. And I wasn't too warm in the leather.'

'You might have been if you kept the top on.'

'I suppose. You looked dashing in your guayabera.'

'Casual yet commanding.'

'I'll say. I'm really glad we went. I'll tell you, it's going to be a while before you see anything like that on television.'

'Let us hope.'

'What I really loved is how ordinary the people looked. I'm not talking about what they were wearing, but the people themselves. You go expecting extras from a Fellini movie and you run into folks who could host a Tupperware party.'

'Some sexual underground.'

'But that makes it more exciting,' she said, 'because it's more real. With the body piercing, everybody was so matter-of-fact. And it all seems so weird, doesn't it? Tribal, primitive.'

'And permanent.'

'Like tattoos, but more than skin deep. But my ears are pierced, and when you come right down to it, what's the difference between an earlobe and a nipple?'

'I give up,' I said. 'What's the difference?'

We were in our apartment now. 'I don't know,' she said, slipping both arms around my waist. 'What's the difference between mashed potatoes and pea soup?'

'Anybody can mash potatoes.'

'I already told you that one, huh?'

'Many times.'

'The old jokes are the best jokes. That was fun, wasn't it? Did you have a good time?'

'Yes.'

'Did it upset you when I took my top off?'

'It surprised me,' I said. 'It didn't upset me.'

'Well, with all those tits in your face, I didn't want you to forget what mine look like.'

'No chance of that. Yours were the prettiest.'

She danced away from me. 'Ha,' she said. 'You're gonna get laid tonight anyway, kiddo. You don't have to lie.'

'Who said I was lying?'

'Let's put it this way – if you were Pinocchio, now would be a good time to sit on your nose.'

'I'll tell you what else surprised me,' I said. 'I thought we agreed we weren't going to participate.'

'So who participated? Oh, you mean the girl–girl stuff? I didn't think that counted.'

'Oh.'

'I sort of got into the spirit of things, I guess. Did it bother you?'

'I don't think "bother" is the right word for it.'

'Did it upset you?'

'I'm not sure "upset" is the right word, either.'

'Got to you, huh?'

'Got to me.'

'Well,' she said, 'that's why we went, isn't it? So it would get to us? You old bear, you. You know what I think I'm going to do? I think I'm going to tie you up. You're not going to fall asleep this time, are you?'

'Probably not,' I said. 'Not for hours.'

NINETEEN

Paris Green does a nice brunch on Sundays, with tables set up outside under green-and-white umbrellas. We slept late and started the day there. Then Elaine took a cab to the Sixth Avenue weekend flea market to resume the hunt for urban folk art. I had a second cup of coffee and walked back home.

Jim Shorter had called in our absence, leaving a message on the machine. I rang him back and arranged to meet him in an hour at a meeting at Amsterdam and Ninety-sixth. Then I called another Jim, my sponsor, Jim Faber, to confirm our dinner date and decide which Chinese restaurant to favor with our presence.

We wound up at Vegetarian Heaven, on Fifty-eighth a few doors west of Eighth. The restaurant is a flight below street level, and the chambered dining room is cavernous, with no end of booths and tables, most of them empty.

'I'm glad we got here,' Jim said. 'I've been meaning to try this place but it looks so tacky from the outside. Do they ever do any business? I hope they're heroin importers and this is just a sideline.'

'Sometimes they get a crowd at lunch. Elaine loves the place because she can order anything on the menu. Most Chinese restaurants have the same four or five vegetable dishes, and she gets tired of them.'

'She could come here forever,' he said, paging through the menu. 'You want to order, since you're familiar with the place?'

'Sure. What are you in the mood for?'

'Food,' he said. 'Good food, and plenty of it.'

While we ate, I talked about how I'd spent the afternoon, and how an unpromising sidetrack in a difficult investigation had turned into an unintended Twelfth Step call.

'It's not like you,' Jim said. 'You've never displayed a whole lot of missionary zeal.'

'Well, I never figured it was my job to sober up the world,' I said. 'Early on I wasn't all that sure if I wanted sobriety for my own self, so the last thing I was going to do was try selling it to somebody else. Then, the longer I stayed away from a drink, the more convinced I became that it was none of my goddamn business whether or not other people drank. Maybe the ones who drink are better off drinking. Who am I to say?'

'Your friend Ballou—'

'My friend Mick Ballou drinks heavily every day of his life, and if he ever walked into a meeting there's nobody who would dream of telling him he was in the wrong place. And I'm sure it's affecting him physically and mentally, even if he's not showing it yet. But he's a grown-up, for Christ's sake. He can make his own decisions.'

'But with this fellow uptown—'

'I guess I identified with him,' I said. 'I looked at his life, or what I figured his life must be, and saw how I could have followed a similar path. Anyway, I didn't set out to drag him to a meeting. I just found myself talking about it, and he seemed interested, and open to suggestion.'

'I think it's good for you. You're not sponsoring anybody else, are you?'

'I'm not sponsoring him.'

'Well, it sounds to me like you are, whether either of you are calling it that or not. I think it'll do you good to be working with a newcomer. Just don't be surprised when he drinks.'

'No.'

'You can't get anybody sober and you can't keep anybody sober. You know that.'

'Sure.'

'And I hope you remember the definition of successful sponsorship.'

'That's when the sponsor stays sober.'

'You're damn right it is. You know, this stuff fools you. You think you're eating meat but you're not. This here is supposed to be what, eel?'

'I think they make it out of soy.'

'There'll come a day,' he said, 'when they make everything out of soy. Chairs, tables, automobiles, hot turkey sandwiches. Everything. But this is supposed to look and taste like eel, and the thing is if it was the genuine article I wouldn't have anything to do with it, because I don't happen to like eel. I think I'm marginally allergic to it.'

'You should have said something when I was ordering it.'

'But if it's fake eel, what's the difference? I'm not allergic to fake eel. As a matter of fact, I like it.'

'Have some more.'

'I intend to. Elaine eats like this all the time, huh? I don't mean this stuff, I mean vegetarian. She doesn't even eat fish, does she?'

'No.'

'I'd miss meat myself. Everything good with you two?'

'Everything's great.'

'You still seeing the other one?'

'Now and then.'

At first I hadn't told him about Lisa, but not for fear of his disapproval. He knows Elaine, and I didn't want to burden him with something I had to keep secret from her, especially if it was something that would end in a couple of weeks. When it didn't, when it went on and on, I talked about it.

'The last time I saw her,' I said, 'I started out wanting a drink. I called her instead.'

'Well, if those were the two choices, I'd say you picked the right one. I don't know that the relationship has much of a future, but I watched a PBS special last night on the greenhouse effect, and you could say the same thing about the human race. She's not likely to try to break up your marriage, is she?'

'I'm not married.'

'You know what I mean.'

I nodded. 'She's just there,' I said. 'She never calls, and when I call she says to come over.'

'Sounds like the answer to a prayer,' he said. 'Do me a favor, will you? Find out if she's got a sister.'

We sat a long time over dinner and arrived a few minutes late for the Big Book meeting at St Clare's. Afterward I walked Jim home, then kept going to Grogan's Open House at Fiftieth and Tenth. Mick Ballou owns the place, although you won't find his name on the license. He has a farm in Sullivan County, a couple of hours from the city, and another man's name is on the deed. He has a couple of apartments around town, too, and drives a Cadillac Brougham, but for the record he doesn't own a thing. When they finally make their RICO case against him, they'll be hard put to find anything to confiscate.

I'd intended to drop by Friday night, but spent the evening on the Upper East Side instead, saving souls for sobriety. Now, two nights later, the saloon was almost empty, with three old men sitting in silence at the bar and two others sharing a table. Burke, behind the bar, told me out of the side of his thin-lipped mouth that the big fellow wasn't expected.

I stayed long enough to drink a Coke and watch a little of the game on ESPN, the Brewers playing the White Sox, with a lot of players on both teams hitting the ball into the seats. But I wasn't paying any real attention, and when my glass was empty I went home.

Wally Donn called first thing in the morning. 'I could use you a couple or three days this week,' he said. 'You up for it?'

'I'm in the middle of something,' I told him.

'Keeping you busy?'

It wasn't, not really. There wasn't much I could do until we had our big meeting at Gruliow's Tuesday afternoon.

I said, 'Suppose I call you Wednesday morning? Or late tomorrow afternoon, if I get the chance. By then I'll have a better idea of how I stand.'

'I really need you today,' he said. 'You call me Wednesday, I might not have anything for you. But call and we'll see.'

I could have gone in that day, for all the work I wound up doing. I made my usual call to Forest Hills and was not all that surprised when nobody answered. I had already decided that Mrs Watson was out of town, and was beginning to wonder what I could possibly ask her if she ever turned up again.

Sometime after lunch I went over to Elaine's shop, intending to spell her, but she wasn't there; TJ, cool and professional in his preppy outfit, was minding the shop for her. I sat around talking with him for half an hour, during which time he sold a pair of bronze bookends to a stoop-shouldered man in a Grateful Dead T-shirt. The man offered thirty dollars, then forty, then said he'd pay the full fifty-dollar sticker price if TJ would forgo the sales tax. TJ stood firm.

'You're tough,' the man said, admiringly. 'Well, I'm probably paying too much, but so what? Ten years from now when I look at them on the shelf, will I even remember what I paid?' He handed over a credit card, and TJ wrote up the sale and did what you have to do with the card as if he'd been doing this sort of thing for years.

'They're really nice,' he said at last, handing over the wrapped bookends. 'All said, I think you got yourself a bargain.'

'I think so, too,' the man said.

Over dinner I gave Elaine a play-by-play description of the transaction. '"All said, I think you got yourself a bargain." Where do you suppose he learned to talk like that?'

'No idea,' she said. 'How come he got full price? I told him he can cut any price ten percent to make a sale.'

'He said he knew the customer would pay the full fifty if he just held firm.'

'Plus the tax?'

'Plus the tax.'

'I guess shilling for the three-card monte dealers teaches you something. I guess if you can buy and sell on Forty-second Street you can buy and sell anywhere.'

'Evidently.'

'But it still amazes me when he turns the language on and off. Is it possible he's actually a middle-class kid and all the street jive's an act?'

'No.'

'That's what I figured. But you never know, do you?'

'Sometimes you know,' I said.

Jim Shorter hadn't called. I tried him after dinner and got no answer. I went over to St Paul's. The woman who spoke had very strong opinions on everything. I left on the break and went over to my hotel room and sat there looking out the window.

I'd taken off Call Forwarding as soon as I came in. I was trying to make this automatic, and to put it on again automatically when I left. I picked up a book and read for a while, then put it down and looked out the window some more. And the phone rang, and it was Shorter.

'Hi,' he said. 'How's it going?'

'Just fine,' I said. 'How about yourself?'

'Well, I didn't drink yet.'

'That's great.'

'And I was at a meeting,' he said, and told me where he'd gone and more of the speaker's story than I needed to know. We talked AA for a few minutes, and then he said, 'And what about your investigation? How's that going?'

'It's sort of stalled.'

'Tomorrow's the big day, isn't it?'

'The big day?'

'You know, when you get together with everybody and find out where you go from here. Do you suppose the killer'll be there?'

'There's a thought. I don't know for sure that there *is* a killer.'

'Hey, Matt, I discovered Watson's body, remember? Somebody sure as hell killed him. I mean, he didn't do that to himself.'

'A single killer,' I said. 'As I said, I don't know for sure that there is one, and if there is I have no reason to believe he's a member of the group.'

'Who else would it be?'

'I don't know.'

'Well, what I think – but where do I get off having an opinion? Forget it, you don't want to hear this.'

'Sure I do, Jim.'

'You sure? Well, I bet it's one of the members. Some guy whose life looks picture-perfect on the surface, but underneath it's a mess. You know what I mean?'

'Yes.'

'Are all of them coming tomorrow?'

'Most of them. A few can't make it.'

'If you were the killer,' he said, 'and if somebody called a meeting like this, would you go? Or would you say you couldn't make it?'

'Impossible to say.'

'I'd go. How could you stay away? You'd want to hear what they were saying, wouldn't you?'

'I suppose so.'

'You better get a good night's sleep,' he said. 'Tomorrow you're going to be in the room with the killer. Do you think you'll be able to sense anything?'

'I doubt it.'

'I don't know,' he said. 'You were a cop a long time. You've got the instincts. That might keep him away.'

'My instincts?'

'Knowing that you're going to be there. Unless, you know, he wants to be face-to-face with his adversary. What do you think?'

'I think you've been watching too much TV.'

He laughed. 'You know what? I think you're right. Where's this going to happen tomorrow? Somebody's office?'

'I really can't say, Jim.'

'But it's in Manhattan, right? Sorry, I'm sticking my nose in, and I don't mean to.'

'It's in the Village, but I don't want to say any more than that.'

'Not important. Speaking of the Village, I was thinking I might go to that midnight meeting on Houston Street. I don't suppose you're up for that tonight, are you?'

'Not tonight.'

'No, you got a busy day tomorrow. I don't know if I want a late night myself. One o'clock by the time the meeting lets out, and then I've got to get all the way uptown. And it might rain. It's threatening. You know what? I think I'll stay home.'

'I don't blame you.'

He laughed. 'It's good talking to you, Matt. Believe me, it helps. Before I called you I was thinking, why the hell can't I have one glass of beer? I mean, who would even feel the effects of one glass of beer?'

'Well—'

'Don't worry,' he said. 'I'm not gonna have it. I don't even want it now. Have a good day tomorrow, huh? And give me a call afterward if you get a chance, will you do that?'

'I'll do that,' I said.

I must have been waiting for his call. Once I'd finished talking to him, I put on Call Forwarding and went home. Ray Gruliow had called in my absence. I called him back.

He said, 'Three-thirty tomorrow. That work for you?'

'Fine.'

'I told the others three o'clock. That'll give us a chance to bring everybody up to speed before you join us.'

There would be eight of them, he said, nine if Bill Ludgate could clear his calendar. And it would be strange seeing them again so soon, not quite two months after the last dinner. Strange to see them away from the usual venue, in a private living room instead of a restaurant.

'Incidentally,' he said, 'I enjoyed our conversation the other night.'

'So did I.'

'We'll have to do it again sometime,' he said. 'After this nonsense is all taken care of. Deal?'

'Deal,' I said.

I hung up and poured myself a cup of coffee. I went and watched television with Elaine, but I couldn't keep my mind on the program.

Depending on Bill Ludgate's ability to cancel his appointments, we'd have eight or nine members at Gruliow's house, five or six absentees. Would the killer be present or absent? Would curiosity draw him? Would fear keep him away?

Maybe it was his house.

Ridiculous to think it could be Gruliow. Hard-Way Ray as diabolical murderer? God knows he was bright enough to work out the details, and resolute enough to carry it out. And there were people who would say he was ruthless enough, and even crazy enough.

I couldn't see it. But I couldn't see it for any of them, and nobody else had a motive. Forget motive – no one else even knew the club existed.

Could I rule out anyone? Hildebrand, I thought. The one thing the killer wouldn't do was bring in a private detective.

Unless—

Well, it was crazy, but why expect sane behavior from someone who was systematically wiping out his lifelong friends? Maybe bringing in a detective would add a little excitement to the game. Maybe it was getting dull, knocking off somebody every year or so. Maybe it was infuriating the way the rest of them refused to realize what was going on. So maybe Lew Hildebrand had decided to even the odds a little by bringing in a detective. But, because he didn't want to make things too hard for himself, he'd had the good sense to hire a detective who wasn't all that bright . . .

Get a good night's sleep, Jim Shorter had urged.

Fat chance.

TWENTY

They assembled, nine of fourteen of thirty-one, at three o'clock on the last Tuesday in June, a hot and hazy day with the burnt reek of ozone soiling the dense air. No one was anxiously early or fashionably late. The first to arrive were Gerard Billings and Kendall McGarry, who came in separate taxis that discharged their passengers simultaneously. The two men rang Gruliow's bell at five minutes before the hour. They had no sooner taken seats than the bell rang again. When Bob Berk arrived at 3:02, apologizing for being late, he was the ninth man. It was five minutes after three when Ray Gruliow got to his feet to open the meeting.

He had done this once before. With Frank DiGiulio's death the previous September, he had become the club's senior member, and had accordingly presided at the annual meeting in May. This was only the second time the gavel had passed in thirty-two years – from Homer Champney to Frank DiGiulio, and now to Gruliow.

What he had not done before, what no one had done, was open a meeting at other than the traditional time and place. He had given some thought to the form this meeting ought to take, and had consulted several of the others on the matter. His conclusion was that it ought to vary as little as possible from the usual form, and he began accordingly by intoning the names of deceased members in the order of their passing, beginning with Philip Michael Kalish and James Severance and Homer Gray Champney, concluding in due course with Francis DiGiulio and Alan Walter Watson.

'I want to thank you for coming,' he said. 'I've talked with each of you about the situation we're facing, and I know some of you have talked to one another. Let me see if I can summarize what we're up against, and then we can go around the room in our usual fashion and get a sense of where we are on this. There's a fellow who'll be joining us at three-thirty, a detective by the name of Scudder. It would be good if we could reach some sort of consensus by the time he gets here . . .'

I got to Commerce Street fifteen minutes early and killed the time wandering the narrow winding streets. It took me back to when I was a new face at the Sixth Precinct, itself housed on Charles Street in those days. I was new to the Village, and excited by what I saw, but I kept getting lost on those eccentric streets. I thought I'd never get the hang of it, but nothing familiarizes you with an area like a tour of duty there. I caught on.

At 3:30 exactly I mounted the steps at Gruliow's house and worked the lion's head door knocker. Gruliow opened the door at once and met me with a smile, one he'd shown me before, the one that suggested that we two shared a secret. 'You're right on time,' he said. 'Come on in. There's a bunch of fellows here who want to meet you.'

The heat notwithstanding, I was glad I'd worn a suit. They were all in dark business suits, except for Lowell Hunter, whose suit was seersucker, and Gerard Billings, the TV weatherman, with his trademark bow tie and a Kelly-green blazer. Gruliow introduced me and I shook hands all around, trying to fix each face in my mind and match it with a name I already knew. I didn't have that many to remember; of the nine, I had already met Gruliow and Hildebrand, and I recognized Billings and Avery Davis. That left Hunter, along with Bob

Berk, Bill Ludgate, Kendall McGarry, and Gordon Walser.

Of the other five, Brian O'Hara was trekking in the Himalayas with his eldest son and wouldn't be back for another ten days. John Youngdahl lived in St Louis; he'd moved there eight years ago, never missed the annual May meeting, but was unable to come in this afternoon on such short notice. Bob Ripley was in Ohio to attend a daughter's college graduation, while Douglas Pomeroy and Rick Bazerian had business appointments they'd been unable to reschedule.

After the introductions we all took our seats and they all waited for me to say something. I looked around at the ring of expectant faces and all I could think of was that I wanted a drink. I took a deep breath and let it out and pushed the thought aside.

I told them I was grateful to them for the meeting. 'I know you've had a little time to discuss the situation,' I said, 'but I thought I might tell you what it looks like from my perspective, which is that of an outsider and a professional investigator.' I talked for fifteen or twenty minutes, discussing the various deaths in turn, speculating on the probable legitimacy of the suicides and accidents. I don't remember exactly what I said, but I didn't trip over my own tongue and I guess I made some sort of sense. From the looks on their faces, they were hanging on every word.

'Where we go from here,' I said, 'is up to you gentlemen. Before I list the alternatives, I'd like to use this conference for another purpose and take advantage of the opportunity to ask you some questions.'

'Like what?' Gruliow wanted to know.

'Your club's had a death rate well in excess of average. That's what prompted Lew to hire me. I wonder how many of you were similarly disturbed at the number of deaths, and if the possibility of murder ever suggested itself to you.'

Kendall McGarry, one of whose ancestors had signed the Declaration of Independence, said he'd had exactly that thought, and that it had come to him a full two years ago. 'But I dismissed it at once as fanciful and preposterous, the sort of premise you'd hang a miniseries on, good enough for television but utterly incredible in real life.'

Bob Berk confessed to a similar fleeting thought. Gordon Walser, who'd announced at the very first meeting that he'd been born with an extra finger on each hand, said that he'd lost both parents and several other family members over the past decade, and that this may have kept him unaware of the club's high death rate. Similarly, Lowell Hunter had lost 'more friends than I could count' to AIDS; the club's death rate, he could assure us, was considerably lower than that of his own social circle.

Gerard Billings said he'd have been bothered more if a higher proportion of the deaths had been the result of illness. 'That's threatening,' he said. 'Cancer, heart attacks, all those little time bombs in your cells and blood vessels. Those are the things that scare you. Suicide, though, that's a choice, and one I've never even considered for myself. A private plane crash, well, I don't fly my own plane, so how's that going to happen to me? As far as murder's concerned, that's like getting struck by lightning. It happens to other people. You stay out of bad neighborhoods, you keep your hands off other men's wives, you don't walk through Central Park at night, and you don't mess around with Jim. You know, the Jim Croce song?' He sang a few bars, his voice trailing off as the others stared at him.

Bill Ludgate said he'd been acutely aware of the high death rate, but that it had never made him suspicious.

He'd just been bothered by the realization that his generation had started to die off, and that he himself might be closer to the end of life than he'd thought. Avery Davis said, 'You know, I took the same thought and went in the opposite direction with it. I figured the fellows who'd passed on had done the dying for us. If they were dead, then my odds of hanging around for a while were that much better. Which is nonsense when you think about it, but it seemed almost logical at the time.'

I asked if any of them had noticed anything suspicious. Any sense that they were being followed or stalked? Any strings of wrong numbers, or callers who rang off without identifying themselves?

No one had anything substantial. Bob Berk, who lived in Upper Montclair, New Jersey, said there had been a lot of clicking and static on his residential phone line for a while, almost as if it were tapped, but that the problem had cleared up several months ago as inexplicably as it had started. Bill Ludgate said his wife had been bothered by someone calling and hanging up without saying anything, and that he'd been on the verge of doing something about it when he happened to learn the identity of the caller; it was a girlfriend of his, trying to reach him at home.

'You dog, you,' Gerry Billings said.

But the affair was over, Ludgate said, and the calls had stopped.

I asked a few more questions. I didn't tell them this, but I was less interested in the information they could give me than in the sense I got of who they were. I knew where they lived, I knew how old they were, I knew what they did for a living and how good a living it brought them, but I wanted some sense of who they were as individuals.

I wasn't sure what I wanted with it.

When they were out of answers and I was out of fresh questions, I reviewed their options. They could go to the police, starting either with Joe Durkin, who knew a little about their situation, or anywhere else in the chain of command. If they weren't happy with the response they received, or if they wanted to ensure a full-scale high-priority investigation from the jump, they could go directly to the media.

Or I could continue my one-man investigation, moving slowly, sifting leads, and waiting for some kind of break. That would keep the spotlight off the club, and keep everybody's name out of the paper, but it might not get anywhere. Still, I'd have certain recommendations to make regarding personal security, and they'd be able to function as auxiliary investigators, keeping in contact and reporting anything irregular or suspicious the minute they noticed it.

'There's no guarantee I'll get anywhere,' I told them. 'But the cops can't give you a guarantee, either. And they'll turn your lives inside out.'

'Because of the media attention, you mean?'

'Even without that. If I were a cop, you know the first thing I'd do? I'd ask each of you to account for your whereabouts on the night in February when Alan Watson was murdered.'

A couple of them reacted visibly; it had not yet struck them that they were suspects. 'Maybe you should anyway,' Avery Davis said. 'All of us and the five men who couldn't make it.' I shook my head. 'Why not?'

'Because I haven't got the resources to check your alibis effectively. Personally, I don't think the police would crack this by checking alibis. My guess is that there'd be a few of you who'd be unable to prove you couldn't have followed Watson home and killed him.

That's no indicator of guilt. As a matter of fact, whoever did kill Watson might very well have an alibi in reserve, and it might be impossible to disprove. But the cops would have to check everything out, because you can't leave a single stone unturned in an official investigation. Especially when the case has a high profile.'

Gruliow said, 'What's your recommendation, Matt?'

'I don't have one. How can I recommend anything? You gentlemen have to make the call. You're the ones with your necks on the block.'

'And if it were your neck?'

'I don't know,' I said. 'It's easy to argue either side. It would seem obvious that the safest course is to go public right away, but I'm not sure that's so. This is a very patient killer. What would he do if the police gave the investigation priority and the newspapers splashed it all over the front page? My guess is he'd crawl in a hole and lay low. He's in no hurry, he hasn't got a train to catch. He can afford to wait a year or two. Then, when everybody's convinced he never existed in the first place, he can select his victim and kill again.'

'For God's sake, why?' Lowell Hunter demanded. 'It's not one of us, is it? It can't be.'

'I can't believe it's anybody in this room,' Bob Berk said.

'And outside of this room? You think it's Ripley or Pomeroy or Brian O'Hara or – who else? John Young-dahl? Rick Bazerian?'

'No.'

'If it's one of us,' Bill Ludgate said, 'that means one of us is crazy. Not a little bit eccentric, not marching to a different drummer, but genuinely nuts. I only see you fellows once a year, but I think you're all relatively sane.'

'Can I quote you on that, Billy?'

'So it has to be someone outside the club,' he

continued, 'but who could possibly want to kill us? Who even knows we exist, for Christ's sake?'

'An ex-wife,' Ray Gruliow said. 'How many of us have been divorced?'

'Why would an ex-wife want to—'

'I don't know. Alienation of affections? Who the hell knows why an ex-wife would do anything? But we're spinning our wheels now, aren't we? We came here to reach a decision, and I think we should do that before we do anything else.' He turned to me. 'Matt,' he said, 'would you mind giving us ten minutes to figure out how we want to handle this? You're welcome to wait upstairs, there's a bedroom where you could stretch out if you want.'

I said I'd just as soon get some fresh air, which turned out to be a particularly inappropriate figure of speech; when I left Gruliow's centrally air-conditioned house, the airless heat hit me with physical force. I stood on the top step for a moment to get my bearings. Across the street, a black limousine was parked in front of the Cherry Lane Theater. The driver was leaning against the fender and smoking a cigarette. For a moment I thought he was staring at me, but his eyes didn't follow me when I came down the stairs, and I realized he was looking at the door to see if anyone else was about to come through it.

'They'll be another fifteen minutes,' I called to him. 'Minimum.'

He shot me a guarded look; he was glad to have the information but didn't think it was appropriate for me to talk to him. Well, fuck you, I thought, and walked down the street to where I could get a look at the back of the limo. ABD-1, the license plate read. I decided the limo belonged to Avery Blanchard Davis, and gave myself credit for having figured something out. It was about time.

It was 4:19 when I walked out of Gruliow's house and just past 4:30 when the front door opened again and Hard-Way Ray stepped out and looked first to his left and then to his right. He didn't see me.

I had walked to Seventh Avenue and picked up an iced coffee at a deli, then perched on the stoop of an apartment house across the street to drink it. Davis's chauffeur had finished his cigarette by then and disappeared behind the limo's tinted glass. No one passed, on foot or on wheels, except for one redheaded kid on a skateboard who zoomed around the corner from Bedford Street, raced on past me and around the bend, and disappeared forever. I finished my coffee and flipped the cup into an uncovered garbage can. Then the door opened across the street and Gruliow came out and looked for me and didn't see me.

I got up, and the movement caught Gruliow's attention. He beckoned and I let a car pass, then walked on across the street. Meanwhile he'd come down the steps to meet me on the sidewalk.

'We'd like you to stay with it,' he said.

'If you're sure.'

'Let's go back inside,' he said, 'so I can tell you officially.'

TWENTY-ONE

'They each put up a thousand dollars,' I told Elaine. 'The ones who'd brought their checkbooks along wrote out checks, and the rest handed over markers.'

'You had to take their markers?'

'Ray Gruliow took their markers,' I said. 'And their checks. He's the one they hired. They engaged him collectively as their legal counsel.'

'What are they going to do, sue the murderer?'

'And Gruliow hired me. He gave me a check drawn on his office account for nine thousand dollars, which represents the checks and markers he received from the others plus a thousand dollars of his own.'

'So you're working for him?'

I shook my head. 'I've been hired by him,' I said, 'to conduct an investigation in his client's interest, his client being the group as a whole. The point of this, according to him, is to get me under the umbrella of attorney–client privilege.'

'What does that mean? You can refuse to answer questions in court?'

'I don't think anybody's concerned about that. No, it means I'm not bound to divulge the results of my investigation to the police, or to repeat anything said to me by my employer, Gruliow, or his clients.'

'Does that really cover you?'

'I don't know. Gruliow seemed to think it does. In any case, if I should feel it was appropriate for me to withhold information from the police, I'd do it irrespective of the legal ramifications. So it can't hurt to have whatever shield attorney-client privilege provides, but I'm going to do the same thing with or without it.'

'My hero,' she said. 'He'll do anything for a client.'

'Not exactly,' I said, 'because I told them I reserved the option of bringing the cops in at any point. My main concern is stopping this guy before there are any more killings.'

'That's their concern, too, isn't it?'

'You'd think so, wouldn't you? I don't know what was said while I was sitting on the stoop across the street, but my impression was that they're more interested in keeping the club of thirty-one off tabloid television than they are in keeping their own names out of the obituary column. If the story ever breaks, that's the end of the club. Don't forget, it was in existence before they were born, and they expect it to survive them all. They're not particularly eager to die for it, but they don't want to have to live without it, either.'

'Guys,' she said.

'Hell, that's not the worst of it,' I said. 'Two of them were wearing identical red-and-black striped ties, and nobody said a word about it. I don't even think they noticed.'

'Shocking,' she said. 'Except I don't believe it. You're making it up, aren't you?'

'Yes, as a matter of fact. How'd you know?'

'Because you wouldn't have noticed either, you bear.'

'I might. I'm a trained observer.'

'Describe their ties.'

'Whose ties?'

'Everybody's ties.'

'Well, Gerry Billings was wearing a bow tie.'

'He always wears a bow tie. What color?'

'Uh—'

'And don't make something up. Do you remember any of their ties?'

'Some were striped,' I said.

'Uh-huh. And some weren't.'

'I had more important things on my mind,' I said, 'than ties.'

'Right,' she said. 'I rest my case.'

Before I took Gruliow's check I talked to them about security. 'What you have to do,' I said, 'is pay attention to things you're in the habit of overlooking, or taking for granted. Is someone following you on the street? Is the same car circling your block over and over, or staked out across the street from your house? Are you getting a rash of suspicious phone calls? Is there a lot of static on your telephone line, or a batch of clicks along with abrupt changes in volume?'

'Paranoia time,' someone said.

'A certain degree of paranoia's part of life in our times,' I said. 'You people have a right to be a little more paranoid than the norm. You've just paid out a thousand dollars a man because someone's trying to kill you. You don't want to make it easy for him.'

'What about hiring bodyguards?'

'My driver's armed,' Avery Davis volunteered, 'and the car's bulletproof. That's not a response to this particular threat. A couple of friends of ours were carjacked — Ed and Rhea Feinbock?'

'I read about that,' Bill Ludgate said.

'Well, I heard about it firsthand, from Ed. The sons of bitches pistol-whipped him. And then I read about other instances, and I bought a limo and hired a pro to drive it. While I was at it, I picked a man with bodyguard experience.'

'Will he leap into the line of fire?' Bob Berk wanted to know. 'Will he take a bullet for you, Avery?'

'I wouldn't think so, not for what I'm paying him.'

I said, 'I don't want to talk anybody out of employing bodyguards, but I don't think the situation warrants it. I think it's more important for you to live defensively than that you hire someone to defend you. You're going to have to keep your guard up all the time.'

'By checking to see if we're being followed?'

'Among other things. Remember how Ian Heller died.'

'Jumped in front of a subway,' someone said.

'Jumped or fell,' I said, 'and let's assume for the moment he was pushed. The cop on the case has spent enough time underground to be very cautious himself on subway platforms. He's wary of ambulatory psychotics, careful not to get between some potential maniac and the edge of the platform. But that kind of caution alone wouldn't have protected Ian Heller.'

'Why not?'

'Suppose it was someone Heller knew. Suppose it was a friend of his.'

'You're saying it was one of us,' Ken McGarry said.

'Not necessarily, although I can't rule it out. You didn't all automatically clear yourselves by writing out a thousand-dollar check. But let's say Heller was in the subway, waiting for a train, and someone approached him.'

'Someone he knew?'

'Someone who knew him,' I said. 'Someone who called him by name. "You're Ian Heller, aren't you? You don't remember me, but we met at So-and-so's party." He'd know enough about Heller to find a pretext for conversation. Heller wouldn't worry about getting shoved in front of a train. If anything, he'd feel more secure than he'd felt a few minutes ago. He wasn't all alone with a group of potentially dangerous strangers. He had a friend with him.'

Gordon Walser said it was diabolical. Lowell Hunter said, 'You know, it reminds me of *The Godfather*. "The attack when it comes will be from someone you trust, someone you would never doubt for a moment. That's who they'll use."'

'That's how he must do it,' I said. 'In a way, Ian Heller was a bad example. His death occurred during rush hour. The platform was crowded, and anybody could have positioned himself properly and given him a well-timed shove. But it could have happened at an off-hour in an empty station, just the way I described it.'

'So we'll stay away from subways,' someone said.

'What you ought to do,' I suggested, 'is think of the killer more as a confidence man than a wild-eyed assassin. Think of him stalking Alan Watson on his way home, then conveniently running into him after Watson stopped for pizza on Austin Street. "Alan, how are you? You walking home? I'm going the same way, I'll keep you company." Even if Watson had never seen the guy before, he'd have to assume he was a neighbor, someone he'd met and forgotten. And they probably had a very pleasant conversation, right up to the time when the guy stuck a knife in Watson's chest.'

'I don't know if I got through to them,' I told Elaine. 'A couple of them wanted to know if they ought to arm themselves. I didn't know what to tell them. They probably couldn't get carry permits, certainly not in a hurry, so that would mean risking an illegal-weapons charge.'

'That's better than getting killed, isn't it?'

'Of course, and these men are respectable establish-ment types; if they wound up defending themselves with an illegal handgun, nobody'd be in a rush to bring charges against them. But suppose some perfectly innocent person asked one of them for a match, or lost his balance and lurched into one of our armed heroes?'

'Bang bang.'

'I told them to call me if anything out of the ordinary happens. They'll keep in touch with each other, too. It's funny.'

'What is?'

'The way it's got them relating to one another. In one way they're closer. Remember, these are fellows who've shared a very intimate association for over thirty years – but only one night a year. They're united by deep and longstanding bonds of brotherhood, but they don't really know each other.'

'And?'

'And now things have changed, and nothing brings you together like the need to defend yourselves against a common enemy. But at the same time, the enemy might be one of them.'

'Didn't Pogo have something to say about that?'

' "We have met the enemy and he is us." The thing is we haven't met the enemy, not head-on. He may be one of us and he may not. So—'

'So they're closely bonded but a little uneasy about it.'

'Something like that. For the first time ever they have to maintain contact with one another. And, also for the first time, they don't dare trust each other. It's like Cannibals and Christians.' She looked bewildered. 'You know, Cannibals and Christians. It's a logic problem, you've got six people trying to cross a river, three cannibals and three Christians, and the boat only holds three people and you can't have one Christian left alone with two cannibals or he'll get eaten.'

'I don't think it's very realistic.'

'For God's sake,' I said, 'it's not supposed to be realistic. It's a logic problem.'

'Well, I'm a Jewish girl,' she said. 'Cannibals, Christians, what's the difference? Who can tell them apart?'

'Not you, evidently.'

'Not me,' she agreed. 'You know what I say? Goyim is goyim. That's what I say.'

We had dinner at an Italian place on the next block. It still hadn't rained, and looked and felt more like it than ever. 'So you met Gerry Billings,' Elaine said. 'I hope you asked him if he could do anything about this weather.'

'God, he must get sick of hearing that.'

'If he doesn't get sick of pointing at the wall and talking about warm fronts and cold fronts, he probably doesn't ever get sick of anything. When you see him pointing at a map or a chart, he's not really, you know.'

'Somebody else is pointing for him?'

'He's pointing at nothing,' she said, 'and the image of him pointing is superimposed on another image of a map or chart. So it comes out looking right, but he's got to stand there and point at a blank wall. That's probably the hardest part of his whole job, remembering what part of the wall is Wyoming.'

We fought over the check. She wanted to pay it because she'd sold one of the paint-by-number paintings for approximately a hundred times what she'd paid for it. I pointed out that that was still only a couple of hundred dollars, while I'd just scooped up a nine-thousand-dollar retainer.

'You still have to buckle down and earn it,' she said. 'The painting, on the other hand, is out of my hands and out of the store. The transaction is completed. Done, *finis, finito*.'

'Too bad,' I said. 'This one's on me.'

Back home, I checked the answering machine. Jim

Shorter hadn't called, and I'd expected that he would. I tried him and he didn't answer. Then I tried my own number across the street, to see if I'd forgotten to engage Call Forwarding, but I got a busy signal, which indicated that I'd remembered.

I tried Alan Watson's widow in Forest Hills. No answer.

'You're restless,' Elaine said. 'Do you feel like a movie? Or do you think you ought to go to a meeting?'

I said, 'I was thinking of taking a cab up to Yorkville.'

'What's there?'

'A meeting.'

'St Paul's is handier. Why go all the way up there? You want to check up on your new sponsee, is that it?'

'He's not my sponsee.'

'Your unofficial sponsee. He didn't call and you're worried about him.'

'I suppose so. What would your friends in Al-Anon say about that?'

'They'd tell me it's none of my business how you work your program.'

'That's not what I meant.'

'I know. You meant what would they tell *you* to do, and if you want to know that you'll have to ask them yourself.'

'I should leave him alone,' I said.

'Think so, huh?'

'I should go to meetings for myself, not for anybody else, and if he gets sober that's fine, and if he goes out and drinks again that's fine, too.'

'So?'

'So I'm afraid he'll drink,' I said, 'and I'm afraid it'll be my fault. But it won't be my fault if he drinks, and it won't be my doing if he stays sober, and anyway he's got his own Higher Power. Right?'

222

'Everything you say is right, master.'

'Oh, boy.'

'So what are you going to do? Grab a cab uptown?'

'Nah, fuck him,' I said. 'Let's go to a movie.'

The movie we saw starred Don Johnson as a homicidal gigolo and Rebecca De Mornay as his attorney. As we left the theater, Elaine said, 'I cannot believe how much she looked like Hillary.' Who was Hillary, I wanted to know, and who looked like her?

'Hillary Clinton,' she said. 'Who else? And De Mornay looked enough like her to fool the president himself. You didn't notice? I can't believe it. Where were you, anyway?'

'Lost in space, I guess. Regretting the past, dreading the future.'

'Business as usual. Just to keep you abreast of things, Don Johnson was the bad guy.'

'I got that much,' I said.

'Well, how much more do you really need to know? I think it's finally going to rain. I just felt a drop, unless it dripped from somebody's air conditioner.'

'No, I felt it, too.'

'Dueling air conditioners? Unlikely, I'd say. What do you want to do now?'

'I don't know. Go home, I guess.'

'Sit around and stare out the window? Make a few phone calls to people who aren't home? Pace the floor?'

'Something like that.'

'I've got a better idea,' she said. 'Walk me home and then go see if Mick wants to make a night of it. Get blitzed on coffee and Perrier. Watch the sun come up. Go to mass, take Holy Reunion.'

'Communion.'

'Whatever.'

'Goyim is goyim, huh?'

'You said it.'

In front of the Parc Vendôme she said, 'It's definitely raining. You want to come upstairs and get an umbrella?'

'It's not raining that hard.'

'Want to see if anybody called? Want to catch the weather report and see what color bow tie your friend Gerry Billings is wearing? Naw, you don't need a weatherman to tell which way the rain is falling.'

'No.'

'Of course not. You just want to get to Grogan's. Give Mick my love, will you? And enjoy yourself.'

TWENTY-TWO

'You just missed him,' Burke said. 'He stepped out not fifteen minutes ago. But he'll be along. He said you might be in.'

'He did?'

'And that you should wait for him as he'll not be long. There's fresh coffee made, if you'll have a cup.'

He poured coffee for me and I carried it to the table where Mick and I usually wound up sitting, over on the side beneath the mirror advertising Tullamore Dew. Someone had left a copy of the *Post* on a nearby table, and I opened it to the sports section to see what the columnists had to say. I wasn't much better at tracking their sentences than I'd been at following the movie. After a while I set the paper aside and thought about trying Jim Shorter again. Was it too late to call him? I was considering the point when the door opened and Mick Ballou entered.

He stood just inside the door, his hair pressed flat against his skull by the rain, his clothes sodden. When he caught sight of me his face lit up. 'By God,' he said, 'didn't I say you'd be in tonight? But what a fucking night you picked for it.'

'It wasn't much more than a fine mist when I came here.'

'I know, for was I not out in it myself? A soft day, the Irish call it. A fucking downpour is what it's turned into.' He rubbed his hands together, stamped his feet on the old tile floor. 'Let me get out of these wet clothes. Catch a cold this time of the year and the fucker's with you till Christmas.'

He went into his office in the back. He sleeps there sometimes on the green leather couch, and keeps several changes of clothing in the oak wardrobe. He has a desk there, too, and a massive old Mosler safe. There's always a lot of cash in the safe, and I can't believe the box would be all that hard to crack. So far no one has ever been fool enough to try.

He emerged from the office after a few minutes with his hair neatly combed and wearing a fresh sports shirt and slacks. He said a few words to one of the darts players, laid a gentle hand on the shoulder of an old man in a cloth cap, and slipped behind the bar to pour himself a drink. He threw down a quick shot to take the chill off, and I could almost feel the warm glow radiating outward from the solar plexus, providing comfort, warming the body and the soul. Then he refilled his glass and brought it to the table along with a fresh cup of coffee for me.

'That's better,' he said, dropping into the seat opposite mine. 'Terrible thing, being called out on business on a night like this.'

'I hope it went well.'

'Ah, 'twas nothing serious,' he said. 'There was this lad who lost a few dollars gambling, and gave a marker for what he owed. Then he decided he'd been cheated, and so he made up his mind that he wasn't going to pay the debt.'

'And?'

'And your man who'd taken his marker offered it for sale.'

'And you bought it.'

'I did,' he said. 'I thought it a decent investment. Like buying a mortgage, and deeply discounted in the bargain.'

'You paid cash for it?'

'I did, and sent Andy Buckley to talk to the lad. And do

you know, he still insisted he'd been cheated, and thus owed nothing, no matter who might be holding his marker. He said there was no point in discussing it, that his mind was made up.'

'So what did you do?'

'I went to see him.'

'And?'

'He changed his mind,' Mick said.

'He's going to pay?'

'He's paid. So you might say it was an excellent investment, offering an attractive return. And it's matured early.'

He is a large man, my friend Mick, tall and heavy, with a head that would not look out of place among the ancient sculptures on Easter Island. There is a primitive and monolithic quality to him. Years ago, a wit at Morrissey's after-hours described Stonehenge as looking like Mick and his brothers standing in a circle.

It may be fitting, then, that he is just about the last of a vanishing breed, the tough Irish criminals who have been drinking and fighting and raising hell in the West Forties and Fifties since before the Civil War. Various gangs and mobs held sway – the Gophers, the Rhodes Gang, the Parlor Mob, the Gorillas. A lot of their leaders were saloon keepers, too, from Mallet Murphy and Paddy the Priest to Owney Madden. They were as cheerfully vicious as any group New York ever saw, and they might have made a more lasting mark on the place if they hadn't had such an all-consuming thirst. According to Mick, God created whiskey to keep the Irish from taking over the world. It had certainly kept the Hell's Kitchen hoodlums from taking over the city.

A few years ago some newspaper reporters started calling the current crop 'the Westies,' and by the time the tag caught on there was hardly anybody left to pin it to. The neighborhood bad guys were mostly gone – dead of drink or violence, doing life sentences somewhere upstate, rotting away in the back wards at Manhattan State Hospital. Or they were married and living somewhere in the Jersey suburbs, getting fat and sluggish, running crooked auto-repair shops, rigging the games in church Las Vegas Night fundraisers, or working all week for their fathers-in-law and drinking themselves sodden on the weekends.

Mick, the son of a woman from County Mayo and a father born in France, not far from Marseilles, was a man who drank whiskey like water, a career criminal, a brutal killer who would costume himself for a night of slaughter in the butcher's apron his father had worn, then wear the same apron to mass at St Bernard's. There was no reason why we should have become friends, and no way to explain our friendship. Nor could I find an explanation for these long nights of ours, when the stories flowed like water or like whiskey. He would drink for both of us, filling his glass time and time again with the twelve-year-old Jameson. I would keep him company with coffee, with Coca-Cola, with soda water.

Maybe, as Jim Faber has suggested, it was a way for me to have the drink without the hangover, to recapture the sweetness of saloon society without risking a seizure or liver damage. Maybe, as Elaine proposed, the two of us had a long karmic history together, and were just renewing the ties that had bonded us in innumerable past lives. Or perhaps, as had sometimes occurred to me, Mick was at once the brother I never had and the road I'd left untaken.

And maybe we're both just men who like a long night in a quiet room, and a good story or two.

★

228

'You recall,' he said, 'when I went to Ireland the year before last.'

His lawyer, Mark Rosenstein, had sent him out of the country to avoid a subpoena. 'I was going to join you,' I reminded him, 'but something came up.'

'Ah, we'd have set the heather blazing, yourself and I. They're a curious people, the Irish. Did I tell you about Paddy Meehan's pub?'

'I don't believe so.'

'Paddy Meehan kept a public house in West Cork,' he said, 'and I believe it was a right hovel, though I never saw it in those days. But your man had an uncle in Boston, and the old fellow died and left a daicent sum, as I heard it called.'

'Left it to Paddy, I suppose.'

'He did, and himself showed a cool head for business for the first time in memory. He invested the whole lot in improvements to his place of business. He had the walls paneled in knotty pine, and he had chandeliers installed and fitted with dimmer switches, and over the door he had a new electric sign hung. A right wonder it was, visible for miles.' He smiled, savoring the memory. 'And he had the wooden floor covered with the finest linoleum, and bought new tables and chairs, and truly spared no expense. But most wonderful of all in this little country pub were the two new doors standing side by side on the back wall, each with a sign on it in the old Ogham script. One door was marked "FIR," the Gaelic for Men, and the other "MNA," for Women. And there were those silhouettes of a man and a woman, such as you'll find on airport rest rooms, for the benefit of tourists who couldn't read the Gaelic.'

'He put in bathrooms.'

'Ah, you would think so, wouldn't you? Quite the fellow was Paddy Meehan. When you walked through either door, FIR or MNA, you found yourself standing in the same five-acre field.'

He told another story about Ireland, and that reminded me of something that had happened years ago at an Emerald Society dinner. The conversation found its own pace, with stretches of silence interspersed. Outside the rain poured down.

'Did I ever tell you,' he wondered, 'about Dennis and the cat?'

'Not that I remember.'

'You would remember,' he said. 'Even if ye drank you'd not likely forget this one. Oh, he was a lad, Dennis was.'

'I remember Dennis.'

'We were raised decently, you know. I was the only one turned out bad. Francis became a priest. Now he's selling automobiles in Oregon. Makes a change, eh? And John's in White Plains, a pillar of the fucking community.'

'A lawyer, isn't he?'

'Law and real estate, and it spoils his breakfast every time there's a story about myself in his morning paper.' His green eyes sparkled at the thought. 'And Dennis,' he said, 'was what you'd call happy-go-lucky. No harm in him, and no darkness, either. Of course he had a liking for the drink.'

'Of course.'

'He liked his few jars. Fresh out of high school he went to work for Railway Express. Midnight to eight five days a week at their central depot, and he never missed a night's work, and he was never without a drink from the moment he punched in until he walked out into the light of dawn. Every one of them drank like that, and when they weren't drinking they were stealing, and when they weren't doing that they were figuring out what to steal next. The company's out of business now, and it doesn't take a genius to tell you why.'

'I guess not.'

'But the finest thing that ever happened there,' he said, 'was when they had the cat. This woman owned a prizewinning cat, a Persian, I believe it was. One of the longhaired sort, at any rate. She'd had a wooden crate specially built for the cat, and brought it to one of the receiving stations for shipment to California.'

'And they stole the cat?'

'They did not. Why would anyone steal a cat? All they did was drop it, crate and all. The fine crate shattered, and the cat stood in the wreckage and looked around at these drunken idjits, and in a flash it was gone. So what do you think they did?'

'What?'

'They reassembled the crate. They got a hammer and nails and put it back together again, and a fine job they did, to hear them tell of it. But when they were done the cat had not reappeared, and who could blame her? Well, they could hardly send an empty crate to San Diego, and so the whole crew of them stalked through the warehouse, calling, "Here, kitty kitty" and making little mewing noises.'

'That must have been something to see.'

'If the cat saw it,' he said, 'it took care not to be seen in return, for never a hair of the creature did any of them ever take sight of again. But they did find another cat, a nasty old tom blind in one eye and missing an ear, and his dirty old coat matted and scabby with mange. He made his home in the warehouse, don't you know, living on rats. And small children, I shouldn't wonder.'

He smiled richly at the memory. 'And it was Dennis who solved the problem,' he said. ' "It says *Contents: One*

Cat and that's all it says," he told them. "She put a cat in the box, she'll take a cat out of the box. What's her problem?" And so they placed the old tom in the crate and sealed him up, and off he went to California.'

'Oh, no.'

'Ah, Jesus,' he said. 'Can ye picture it, man? The poor woman herself opens the crate and out leaps this wee savage with an evil glint in his good eye.'

' "Oh, Fluffy," ' I said, pitching my voice as high as it would go, ' "what have they done to you?" '

' "Ach, Fluffy, I hardly knew ye!" '

' "Was it a hard trip, Fluffy?" '

'Can you see it, man? Oh, you should have heard Dennis tell it. He told it much better than I ever could.' His face darkened, and he took a long drink of whiskey. 'And they called him for Vietnam,' he said, 'and the damned fool went. I'd have got him out of it. I told him I'd get him out of it, there was nothing easier, all I had to do was make a telephone call.'

'He wouldn't let you?'

'I want to go, says he. I want to serve my country, says he. Dennis, says I, let someone else go. Let the fucking niggers serve their fucking country. They've got more to gain and less to lose than yourself. But he wouldn't hear of it. And off he went, and he died there, and they shipped him home in a body bag. Sweet Jesus, what a fucking waste.'

'Why do you suppose he went, Mick?'

'Ah, who can say? He was home on leave before they shipped him overseas. I told him if he wanted to get out now it would take more than a phone call, but 'twould be easy enough to get him out of the country. He could go to Canada, or to Ireland. Mickey, says he, what would I do in Canada? What would I do in Ireland? What did I ever do here? And he gave me this sweet smile, a smile to

232

break your heart. And I knew he was going to die over there, and I knew that he knew it.'

I thought for a moment. I said, 'You think that's why he went?'

'I do.'

' "I have a rendezvous with death," ' I said, quoting the few lines I remembered of the Alan Seeger poem.

'That's it exactly,' he said. 'A rendezvous with death. He had a date and would not break it, the poor lad.'

A little before two, Burke shut down the taps and sent the handful of customers on their way, all but the little old man in the cloth cap. He stayed put on his stool while Burke placed the chairs on top of the tables so they'd be out of the way when the floor was mopped first thing in the morning. When he was through he brought over Mick's bottle and a thermos of coffee, setting them within reach on the next table.

He said, 'I'm off, Mick.'

'Good man.'

'Mr Dougherty's still sittin' there. I'll walk out with him, shall I?'

'Ask him if he'd rather stay until the rain lets up. He's no trouble. Just lock up, and I'll let him out when he's ready.'

But the old fellow didn't want to stay past closing. He followed Burke to the door and they went out together. Mick turned out all the lights but the one over our table, came back and freshened his drink.

'That was Eamonn Dougherty,' he said. 'He never set foot in here, and then in the early spring they closed the Galway Rose on Eleventh Avenue. The building's scheduled for demolition, or maybe they've already taken it down. I haven't been over there to see. Dougherty went every day to the Galway Rose, and now he's here every day. He'll sit for eight hours and drink two pints of beer and never say a word.'

'I don't believe I know him.'

'Why should you? He was killing men fifteen years before you were born.'

'Are you serious?'

'We talked of West Cork,' he said, 'and Paddy Meehan's pub and its improvements. Eamonn Dougherty is from Skibbereen in West Cork. During the Troubles he was with Tom Barry's flying column.' He sang: ' "Oh, but isn't it great to see / The Auxies and the RIC / The Black and Tans turn tail and flee / Away from Barry's coll-yum." Do you know that song?'

'I don't even know what the words mean.'

'The Auxies were the Auxiliaries, the RIC was the Royal Irish Constabulary, and you know who the Black and Tans were. Here's a song you'd understand without a glossary.

> *On the eighteenth day of November*
> *Outside of the town of Macroom*
> *The Tans in their great Crossley tender*
> *Came hurryin' on to their doom*
> *But the boys of the coll-yum were waiting*
> *With rifle and powder and shot*
> *And the Irish Republican Army*
> *Made shit of the whole fuckin' lot.*

'It was a bloody massacre, and trust the fucking Irish to write a song about it. Eamonn Dougherty was in the middle of it. Oh, he did his share of killing, that one. The British had a price on his head, and then the Free State government put a price on his head, and he came here. A relative got him a job unloading trucks in a warehouse, though you wouldn't think he had the size for it. Then he was a taxi dispatcher for many years, and he's long since retired. And drinks his two pints of beer a day, and says not a word, and God alone knows what goes on in his head.'

'When you first started talking about him,' I said, 'I found myself thinking of another little old man. His name was Homer Champney.'

'I don't know him.'

'I never knew him myself,' I said, 'but he started something. Or continued something, it's hard to know for sure. It makes a hell of a story.'

'Ah,' he said. 'Let's hear it.'

TWENTY-THREE

And so I told the story of the club of thirty-one. I talked for a long time. When I was done Mick didn't say anything at first. He filled his glass and held it to the light.

'I remember Cunningham's,' he said. 'They served good beef and the bar would pour you a decent drink. When I think of all the places that are gone, all the people who are gone. I don't understand time. I don't understand it at all.'

'No.'

'Sand through an hourglass. You hold something – anything – for a moment in your hand. And then it's gone.' He sighed. 'When did they have their first meeting? Thirty years ago?'

'Thirty-two.'

'I was twenty-five, and a loutish piece of work I was. They'd never have had me in their club, or any other decent association of men. But that's a club I'd have joined if asked.'

'So would I.'

'And never missed a meeting,' he said. 'Standing together. Bearing witness. Waiting for the man with the broad ax.'

'The man with—?'

'Death,' he said. 'That's how I envision him. A man with his arms and shoulders bare, wearing a black hood and carrying a broad ax.'

'Elaine would say you were put to death in a past life, and the man you just described was the executioner.'

'And who's to say she's wrong?' He shook his big head.

'Sand through an hourglass. Eamonn Dougherty, the fucking Scourge of Skibbereen, sitting on his barstool watching the years slip past him. He outlived the Galway Rose, the murderous little bastard. He'll outlive us all, with his wee cap and his two pints of beer.' He drank. 'A long line of dead men,' he said.

'How's that?'

'Ah, it's a story. Do you know Barney O'Day? He used to come to Morrissey's.'

'I never met him there,' I said, 'but I knew him when I was at the Sixth. He managed a bar on West Thirteenth Street. They had live music, and sometimes he'd get up and sing a song.'

'Had he any sort of a voice?'

'I don't think he was any worse than the paid entertainment. I used to run into him at the Lion's Head, too. What about him?'

'Well, it's a story I heard another man tell at a wake,' he said. 'It seems Barney's old mother was in hospital, and he was at her bedside, and the dear told him that she was ready to die. "I had a good life," says she, "and wrung all the joy I could out of it, and I'm not after havin' machines keepin' me alive, an' tubes stickin' out of me. So give us a kiss, Barney me lad," says she, "as you were always as foine a son as a mother could ask for, an' then tell the doctor to pull the plug an' let me go."

'So your man gives her a kiss and goes off to find the doctor, and tells him straight out what the old woman wants him to do. And the doctor's scarcely more than a boy himself. He hasn't been at it long, and Barney can see he's got no stomach for this sort of thing. He wants to be prolonging life, not cutting it short. He's troubled, and Barney's a gentle soul himself, for all the bluster he puts on, and wants to spare the man some agony.

' "Doctor," says he, "put your mind at ease. It's not

237

such a terrible thing you have to be doin'. Doctor, let me tell you somethin'. We O'Days come from a long line of dead people."'

Outside, the wind blew up and drove rain against the windows. I looked out and saw cars passing, their lights reflected in the wet pavement. 'That's a wonderful story,' I said.

'Ever since it was told to me,' he said, 'I've carried the line around with me. For don't we all come from a long line of dead people?'

'Yes.'

'Your tale of the club put me in mind of it. Thirty-one men, and one by one they go to their graves, and the last man left starts it all over again. A long line of dead men, stretching back through the centuries.'

'All the way to Babylon, rumor has it.'

'All the way to Adam,' he said. 'All the way to the first fish that grew hands and hauled himself ashore. Is some bastard killing these men of yours?'

'It looks that way.'

'Can you tell who it is?'

'No,' I said, 'I can't. It's one of them or it's not, and either way it makes no sense that I can see. One of them gave me some money at the start, and I worked hard for it, but I don't know that I did anything useful. And now they've gone in together to give me more money, and I took it, but I don't know what the hell I'll do to earn it.'

'You'll find him.'

'I don't see how. I don't even know what to do next. I haven't got a clue.'

'Just wait.'

'Wait?'

'How many are left? Fourteen?'

'Fourteen.'

'Bide your time,' he said. 'And when there's but one of them left, arrest him.'

And, a little while later, he said, 'They've a memorial in Washington, a wall with the names of all who died over there. You've seen it?'

'Only in photos.'

'I thought, What the hell do I want to go there for? I know what it looks like. I know his name. I could print it out if I cared to, and hang it on a wall of my own. But something made me go. I can't explain it.

'I rode down on the train. I took a taxi from the station and told the driver I wanted to see the Vietnam Memorial. It wasn't far at all. It's just a wall, you know, with a simple shape to it. But you said you've seen photographs, so you know what it looks like.

'I looked at it and I started reading the names. "A long line of dead men." *That* was a long line of dead men. Thousands of names in no particular order, and only one name among them that meant a thing to me, so why was I reading the others? And how would I ever find his in the midst of them?

'I overheard someone telling someone else where to go to locate a name, and I stopped reading the names and went over to the directory and found out where his name was. I was afraid they might have left it off, but no, it was there, all right. And I found it on the wall. Just his name, Dennis Edward Ballou.

'I looked at that name,' he said, 'and my throat closed up, and I felt an awful fullness in the center of my chest, as if I'd taken a blow there. The letters of his name blurred in front of me, and I had to blink to clear my vision, and I thought I might weep. I haven't done that since I was a boy. I'd taught myself not to weep when my father hit me, and it was a lesson I learned too well. I'd have been glad of a few tears that day, but I'm long past them. They've dried up within me, they've gone and turned to dust.

'But I could not get away from that great fucking monument. I read his name again and again, and then I read the name before his and the one after, and then I walked along and read more names. I was there for hours. How many names did I read? I could not hope to tell you. And from time to time I would go back and find his name again, and look at it.

'I'd thought I would stay the night, see something of the city. I'd booked a room at a hotel across the street from the White House. But I was at the wall until the sun went down, and then I walked until I came to a bar, and I went in and had a drink. Then I went to another bar, and another, and then I bought a bottle and took a taxi back to Union Station.

'I took the first train out, and I left the bottle unopened until the stop at Wilmington, Delaware. Then I broke the seal and had a drink, and by the time we were back in New York the bottle was empty. And I might have been drinking well water for all the effect it had on me. I caught a cab at Penn Station and came right here, and Andy Buckley was waiting to tell me there'd been a phone call from a friend of ours in the Bronx. A fellow we needed to find had been seen going into a certain house off Gun Hill Road.

'So Andy drove, and we went up to Gun Hill Road and found this fellow. And I beat him to death with my hands.'

'Tell me,' he said. 'What was your father like?'

'I'm not sure I know. He was dead before I was grown.'

'Was he a cop himself?'

'Oh, God, no.'

'I thought perhaps it was a family thing.'

'Not at all. He did, oh, different things.'

'Did he drink?'

'That was one of the things he did,' I said. 'He mostly worked for other people, but a couple of times he was in business for himself. The one I remember best was a shoe store. That was up in the Bronx. It was this two-story building, and we lived upstairs of the store.'

'And he sold shoes.'

'Children's shoes, mostly. And work shoes, those steel-toed boots they wear on construction sites. It was a neighborhood store and people would bring their kids in once a year for new shoes, and there was an X-ray machine you stood at and you could see the bones of your feet and tell if you needed new shoes yet.'

'Couldn't you just pinch the shoes and see where the toes reached to?'

'I guess you could, and I guess that's why you don't see those machines anymore, but they were the latest thing when he had the store. I wonder what all those X rays did to your feet. Nobody worried about them at the time, but nobody worried about asbestos then, either.'

'If you live long enough,' he said, 'you find out there's nothing on earth that's good for you. What became of the store?'

'I guess it failed, or maybe he sold it. One day we had to move, and that was the last I saw of the store. I went looking for it years later and the whole street was gone, bulldozed and paved over when they widened the Cross-Bronx Expressway.'

'Is that where you grew up? The Bronx?'

'We moved around a lot,' I said. 'The Bronx, Upper Manhattan, Queens. My grandparents on my mother's side lived in the East New York section of Brooklyn, and

241

a couple of times my parents separated and we wound up living with them. Then they'd get back together again and we'd start over in a new apartment somewhere.'

'How old were you when he died?'

'Fourteen.' I'd switched some time ago from coffee to Perrier, and I picked up my glass and took a good look at the little bubbles. 'He was riding the subway,' I said, 'the Fourteenth Street line, the Double-L train. They just call it the L now, they took one of its letters away. I suppose it's an economy move.

'He was riding between two cars. He'd gone there so he could smoke, and he fell, and the wheels tore him up.'

'Ah, Jesus.'

'It must have been quick,' I said, 'and he would almost have had to be drunk, don't you think? Who but a drunk would think it was a good idea to ride between the cars like that?'

'What did he drink?'

'My dad? Whiskey. He might have a beer with his meals, but if he was going to drink it was whiskey, whiskey and soda. Blended stuff. Three Feathers, Four Roses. Carstair's. I don't even know if those brands still exist, but that's what he drank.'

'Mine drank wine.'

'I never saw wine in the house. For all I know, my old man never had a glass of wine in his life.'

'Mine bought it by the gallon. He bought it from a man who made it, another Frenchman. And he drank marc. Have you ever had that?'

'I'm not even sure I know what it is. Some kind of brandy?'

He nodded. 'After you've made wine, you make a brandy from the spent grapes. The Italians make much the same thing and call it grappa. By either name it's the nastiest thing you could ever have the misfortune to drink. I had some in France, in the town where he was born, and it was all I could do to swallow it and keep it down. It was still another French immigrant he got it from. There were a lot of the French in this part of the city, you know. They worked in the hotels and restaurants, many of them, and some like my father worked in the meat market.' He took a drink. 'Did he hit you, your father? When the drink was on him?'

'Jesus, no. He was the gentlest man who ever lived.'

'Was he then.'

'He was a quiet man,' I said, 'and he was sad. I suppose you could say he was despairing. When he drank he would get happy. He would sing songs and, I don't know, just be silly. Then he would go on drinking and wind up sadder than when he started. But I never saw him get angry and I certainly never knew him to hit anyone.'

'Mine was quiet, too. The bastard never said a word.' He filled his glass. 'His English wasn't good and he had a thick accent. You were hard put to understand the man. But he spoke so rarely it scarcely mattered. He was free with his hands, though.'

'He hit you?'

'He hit all of us. Not her, for I believe he was terrified of her. Like an elephant afraid of a mouse, him a big hulking brute and herself a wee slip of a woman. But she could do more damage with her tongue than he ever did with his fists.' He tilted his head and looked up at the stamped-tin ceiling. 'I got my size from him,' he said, 'and I got it early. He would beat me without a word and I took his beatings without a word, and then one day when I was not quite sixteen it was a time too many, and I didn't even flinch when he slapped me but stood my ground and hit him with my closed fist, hit him right in the mouth. He stood wide-eyed at the wonder of it and I hit him again and knocked him down, and I picked up a wooden chair and held it over my head, and I was going to hit him with it, and I might have killed him that way. It was a heavy fucker of a chair, for all that my anger made it feel as light as balsa wood.

'And he broke out laughing. He was sprawled on the floor with blood running out of his mouth and I was about to break a chair over his head, and he was laughing. I had never heard the man laugh before, and as far as I know he never laughed again, but he laughed that day. It saved his fucking life, and saved me from as black a sin as a man can commit. I put the chair down and took his hand and drew him to his feet, and he clapped me on the back and walked off without a word. And never hit me again.

'A year later I was living in a place of my own, collecting on the waterfront for a couple of Italians and stealing whatever I could. And a year after that he was dead.'

'How did he die?'

'A blood vessel in the brain. It was very sudden, no warning. He was almost twenty years older than my mother, and older when he died than I am now. The man was forty-five years old when I was born, so he'd have been what, sixty-two when he died? He was working when it happened. He'd been to mass that morning, so I suppose he died in a state of grace. I don't know if that truly makes a difference. I know he died with a cleaver in his hand, and wearing a bloody apron. I kept them both, you know, the cleaver and the apron. I wear the apron when I go to mass. And there have been times I've found a use for the cleaver.'

'I know.'

'Indeed you do. He went to mass every morning, and I don't know why he went or what he thought it did for him. I don't know why I go, either, or what I think it does for me.' He was silent for a moment. Then he said, 'Your mother's not alive still, is she?'

'No, she died years ago.'

'So did mine. It was cancer killed her, but I always thought it was Dennis's dying that brought it on. She was never the same after she got the telegram.' He looked at me. 'We're orphans, the two of us,' he said, and waved a hand at the windows, with the rain pelting them. 'Orphans of the storm,' he said, and took a drink.

'The other day,' I said, 'a lawyer I know told me that man is the only animal that knows he'll die someday. And he's also the only animal that drinks.'

'It's an unusual thing for a lawyer to say.'

'He's an unusual lawyer. But do you think there's a connection?'

'I know there is,' he said.

I don't know how we got around to women. He didn't seem to need them as much now, he said, and wasn't sure whether it was the years or the drink that deserved credit for the change.

'Well, I stopped drinking,' I reminded him.

'By God, so you did. And now no woman's safe from Inwood to the Battery.'

'Oh, they're safe,' I said.

'Are you still seeing the other one?'

'Now and then.'

'And does herself know about it?'

'I don't think so,' I said, 'although she gave me a turn the other day. I was trying to get hold of the woman whose husband was stabbed to death in Forest Hills in February. I mentioned to Elaine that I was going to have to go out there and see her. A moment later she told me to enjoy myself with the widow, and I read more into the remark than she'd put in it. I guess I looked startled, but I managed to cover it.'

That reminded him of a story, and he told it, and the conversation meandered like an old river. Then a little later he said, 'The widow in Forest Hills. Why ever would you go to see her?'

'To find out if she knew anything.'

'What could she know?'

'She might have seen something. Her husband might have said something to her.' I told him some of the questions I'd ask, a few of the points I'd try to cover.

'Is that how you do your detecting?'

'That's part of it. Why?'

'Because I've no idea how you do what you do.'

'Most of the time neither do I.'

'Ah, but of course you do. And you try all these different approaches until something works. I'd never have the imagination to devise them all, or the patience to keep at it. When there's something I need to know, there's only one way I have of finding it out.'

'What's that?'

'I go to the man who has the answer,' he said, 'and I do what I have to do to make him tell me. But if I didn't even know who to go to, why, I'd be entirely lost.'

If the rain had let up I might have gone home earlier. I began to flag sometime around four-thirty or five in the morning, and there was a time when the conversation died down and I glanced over at the window. But it was still pouring, and instead of pleading exhaustion and heading for the door I pushed my Perrier aside and poured one more cup of coffee from the thermos. A little later I caught a second wind, and it carried me past dawn and down to St Bernard's for the butchers' mass.

There were fifteen or twenty of us in the little side

chapel, including seven or eight men from the meat market, dressed in white aprons just like Mick's, some of them stained as his was stained. There were several nuns as well, and a couple of housewives and some men dressed for the office. And a few elderly people, men and women, including one who was a dead ringer for the murderous Eamonn Dougherty, right down to the cloth cap.

We left when the mass was over, without having taken Communion. The sky was still overcast but no rain was falling. Mick's Cadillac was where he'd parked it, in the reserved space in front of Twomey's funeral parlor. Twomey was out in front and gave us a wave when he saw us. Mick gave him a smile and a nod.

'It's good days for Twomey,' he said. 'His business is more than twice what it was, now that they're dying of AIDS all around him. It's an ill wind, eh?'

'That's the truth.'

'I'll tell you another,' he said. 'Every wind's an ill wind.'

He dropped me at my door. I went upstairs and tried to make as little noise as possible opening the door, not wanting to wake Elaine if she was still sleeping.

When I opened the door she was standing there, wearing a robe I'd bought for her. The look on her face told me right away that something was wrong.

Before I could ask, she said, 'You don't know, do you? You haven't heard?'

'Heard what?'

She put a hand out, took mine. 'Gerard Billings was killed last night,' she said.

TWENTY-FOUR

For a full twelve years, Gerard Billings had been the weather reporter for an independent New York broadcast channel. While he was officially known as the chief meteorologist, his function was primarily reportorial. His colorful clothing, his irrepressible personality, and his evident willingness to make a fool of himself on camera were more important factors in his rise than his ability to read a weather map.

He was on the air twice a day, at 6:55 P.M., just before the close of the 6:30 news program, and again at 11:15, right in the middle of the late news and before the extended sports summary. Typically, he would arrive at the station at five in the afternoon, work out what he was going to say and get his maps and charts in order, and go out for dinner after the broadcast. Sometimes he would linger over dinner for a couple of hours, then return to the studio. Other nights he'd go home for a nap and a change of clothes, then go back to the studio for his second stint of the day. He'd get there between 10 and 10:30; he didn't need as much time to prepare, because he would be using the same charts and giving essentially the same report.

At seven that Tuesday night he went straight home to the apartment on West Ninety-sixth where he'd lived since his divorce four years previously. He ordered Chinese food from a restaurant on Amsterdam Avenue. Shortly after ten he went downstairs and caught a cab driven by a recent Bengali immigrant named Rakhman Ali. As the cab waited to make a left turn into Columbus

Avenue, it was sideswiped by a car that was attempting to pass it on the right. The driver leaped from his car and got into a loud argument with Rakhman Ali, at the climax of which he drew a handgun, shot Ali three times in the face and upper chest, then yanked open the door of the cab and emptied his gun into Ali's passenger. He then sped away in his own vehicle, which was variously described as anywhere from two to twelve years old. Witnesses seemed to agree that it was a four-door sedan, that it was dark in color, and that it had seen better days.

Elaine, watching the news, knew something was wrong even before they introduced a substitute weatherman to fill in for Billings. There were no jokes about the absent forecaster being under the weather, and all of the reporters in the studio seemed to be keeping a grim secret. It turned out that they had learned of Billings's death moments before they went on the air and decided to hold the story pending notification of kin. This decision was overruled toward the end of the broadcast when they realized they were in danger of getting scooped by their competitors; accordingly, the anchorwoman made the unfortunate announcement right after the sports wrap-up.

'I didn't know what to do,' Elaine said. 'I knew you were at Grogan's and I looked up the number and thought about calling, but what were you going to do in the middle of a rainy night? Besides, for all I knew it was just what it looked like, an argument over a traffic accident that got out of control. It happens all the time, and everybody's got a gun these days, and maybe they'd catch the poor loser who did it within the hour, and why ruin your evening with Mick over that?

'So instead I turned the radio to WINS and stayed up for hours. I had the radio turned down low and I had a book to read, and I heard the same half hour of news over and over, and when they got to the Billings story I would stop reading and turn the volume up, and it would be the same thing as before, word for word. And I wound up falling asleep with the radio on and woke up at seven with it blaring away.

'Should I have called you? I didn't know what to do.'

It was just as well she hadn't called me. There wouldn't have been anything for me to do. There was little enough for me to do now, the morning after the shooting, except field the telephone calls that came in from Ray Gruliow and Lewis Hildebrand and Gordon Walser. I'd have to know more, I told each of them, before I'd know how to proceed.

By early afternoon they'd found the car, a 1988 Ford Crown Victoria with Jersey plates, registered to an ophthalmologist in Teaneck. The vehicle had been located in the pound where it had been towed from a no-parking zone in the midtown theater district. Identification was made on the basis of a partial plate number supplied by a witness, and confirmed by paint scrapings on the car and on Rakhman Ali's yellow cab. The ophthalmologist's wife told police that her husband was in Houston attending a professional conference; he'd flown there Friday from Newark, after having left his car in the long-term parking lot.

There were fingerprints on the steering wheel and the dash, but they turned out to be those of the traffic officer who'd opened the car door and put it in neutral so that it could be towed. There were no prints that could have belonged to the shooter, whom witnesses described as of average height and wearing a baseball cap and a glossy dark blue warm-up jacket with a name embroidered over the breast pocket. None of the witnesses had been close enough to read the name.

The incident looked ordinary enough, newsworthy in that one of the two victims had enjoyed a measure of local celebrity. Someone had stolen a car from an airport parking lot, probably with the intention of using it in the commission of a crime. Maybe he was chemically impaired at the time of the accident. Maybe he was just having a bad day. In any event, he'd reacted badly to an ordinary fender-bender. Instead of exchanging licenses and insurance cards, he'd pulled a gun and started blasting.

It could have happened that way.

Or he could have parked his stolen car where he could keep an eye on the entrance to Billings's building, could have tagged along after the cab that stopped for Billings, could have engineered the collision and its aftermath.

Nothing to it.

I was up all day, drinking too much coffee and fighting off exhaustion. At 8:30 I made myself go over to St Paul's for my regular meeting, but I couldn't make myself pay attention, nor could I keep from leaving at the break. When I walked in the door, Elaine told me to take a hot bath and go to bed.

'Just do it,' she said.

The hot water took away some of the tension, and when I got into bed I fell asleep almost immediately. I must have dreamed about Jim Shorter, because I woke up concerned about him. I said as much to Elaine, and she told me he'd called the night before, while I was at St Paul's.

'He said it wasn't important,' she said, 'and not to call him because he was on his way out. So I didn't mention it.'

I called him. No answer.

I listened to the news and there was nothing about

Billings. I went out and bought the *Times* and all three tabloids and read four versions of the same story. The *Times* article jumped from the front page to the obituary page, where his obituary included a photo and six inches of text. I read the obit, and the half-dozen others. And then I went on to read the half-page of paid death notices. Fully a third of these were for a man who had died the previous week and who had evidently contributed heavily to a wide range of charitable endeavors; each was now taking pains to reward him with a paid announcement of their sorrow at his passing.

I raced through those, but read the others fairly closely, as is my custom these days. My attention slacked off some toward the end, as it generally does. Once I've made it past the *S*'s without finding my own name, my appetite for the pursuit is a little less keen. But I stayed there right through the alphabet, and thus learned of the death on Monday of Helen Stromberg Watson, wife of the late Alan Watson, of Forest Hills.

It took a few calls before I found a cop who would talk to me.

'Accidental drowning,' he said. 'Coulda slipped, hit her head on the tile. Drowned right in her own bathtub. All you gotta do is lose consciousness long enough to fill the lungs with water. Happens all the time.'

'Oh, really?'

'Ask me, they oughta put warning labels on bathtubs. No, see, there's a possibility of suicide. Woman lost her husband earlier this year, despondent over the loss, so on and so on. We found a bottle of J&B on the floor next to the tub. You drink in the tub and pass out, you want to call that suicide? *I* don't, not without a note, not when you got the children's feelings to consider, losing both parents in less'n six months. 'Sides, who knows what's in

252

somebody else's mind? You have a few drinks, and before you know it you pass out and you drown. Or the drinks hit you hard, especially in a hot tub, and you lose your balance and smack your head and that's what knocks you out. Hey, accidents happen.'

'And she died on Monday?'

'That's when they found her. Doc's guess was she was in the water three days by then.'

No wonder she hadn't answered the phone.

'You know what the weather's been like,' he said. 'And maybe you know what a body's like after a couple of days in the water. Put 'em both together, do I have to tell you what they spell?'

'Who discovered the body?'

'A neighbor. One of her kids called next door, concerned because he couldn't reach his mother on the phone. The neighbor had a key and let herself in. Hell of a thing to walk in on.'

I called Jim Shorter. No answer.

I called Elaine at the shop. I said, 'When Shorter called last night did he seem nervous? Did he sound as though he was afraid?'

'No, why?'

'Alan Watson's widow drowned in her bathtub sometime over the weekend. The time of death's hard to pinpoint, but it evidently happened after I went out to Corona and talked to the head of that security firm.'

'I'm not sure I see the connection.'

'There has to be one,' I said. 'I think the killer's tying off loose ends. He must be afraid somebody saw something, or knows something. He killed the widow, and the next logical step is the person who was first on the scene, the guard who discovered Watson's body.'

'Jim Shorter?'

'His phone doesn't answer.'

'He could be anywhere,' she said. 'Maybe he's at a meeting.'

'Or in a bar,' I said. 'Or in his room with a bottle, not picking up the phone.'

'Or having breakfast, or catching the Rothko retrospective at the Whitney, which would be my first choice if I didn't have a business to run. What are you going to do?'

'Look for him. There's something he knows, even if he doesn't know he knows it. I want to find him before it gets him killed.'

'Hold on a second,' she said. She covered the mouthpiece for a moment, then came back and said, 'TJ's here. He wants to know if you want company.'

By the time I got dressed and downstairs, he was waiting for me in front of the building. He was wearing his preppy clothes, the effect slightly compromised by the black Raiders cap. 'We can lose the cap,' he said, 'if I's got to look straighter than straight, Nate.'

'I didn't say anything about the cap.'

'Guess I hearin' things.'

'Or reading minds.' I stepped to the curb, hailed a cab, told the driver Eighty-second and Second. 'Anyway,' I went on, 'I don't think it matters what anybody wears. We're just wasting our time.'

'You don't expect nothing.'

'That's right.'

'Just brung me along so's you'd have company.'

'More or less.'

He rolled his eyes. 'Then what we doin' in a cab, Tab? Man like you take a taxi, be somethin' goin' down.'

'Well,' I said, 'let's hope you're wrong.'

I had him wait in the cab while I climbed a flight of stairs and checked the meeting room at the Eighty-second Street Workshop. That was where I'd brought Jim Friday night, and he'd mentioned going to other meetings there since. There was a meeting going on, and I went in and found a good vantage point beside the coffee urn. When I was sure he wasn't there I went downstairs and got back in the cab. I had the driver go up First Avenue and drop us at the corner of Ninety-fourth.

Our first stop was the Blue Canoe, and if Shorter didn't get drunk and didn't get killed, someday the place might figure in his qualification. 'I met this guy there,' he could say, 'figuring I could con him into buying me a couple of beers, and the next thing I knew I was at an AA meeting. And here I am, and I haven't had a drink since.'

He wasn't at the Blue Canoe now, or at any of the other bars or luncheonettes on First Avenue. TJ and I made the rounds together. It would have been convenient if we could have shared the work, but how would he know Shorter if he saw him?

When we'd finished with a four-block stretch of First Avenue, we walked west on Ninety-fourth to Shorter's rooming house. I'd have rung his bell if I knew which one it was. Instead I rang the bell marked SUPER. When it went unanswered we left and walked to Second Avenue, where we wasted some more time checking more bars and restaurants, from Ninety-second to Ninety-sixth and back to where we'd started. I found a phone that worked and called Shorter's number and it didn't answer.

I was starting to get a bad feeling.

There was no point combing the city for him, I thought, because we weren't going to find him that way. And there was no point dialing his number because he wasn't going to answer the phone.

I walked quickly back to the rooming house, TJ

tagging along beside me. I rang the super's bell, and when there was no answer I poked other buttons at random so that someone could buzz me in. No one did, but after a few minutes a very large woman emerged from one of the first-floor rooms and waddled to the door. She frowned through the glass panel at us, and without opening the door she asked what we wanted.

I said we wanted the super.

'You're wasting your time,' she said. 'He ain't got no vacancies.'

'Where is he?'

'This is a respectable house.' God knows who she thought we were. I took out a business card from Reliable and held it against the glass. She squinted at it and moved her lips as she read it. When she was done her lips settled into a tight narrow line. 'That's him on the stoop across the street,' she said grudgingly. 'His name's Carlos.'

There were three men on the stoop she'd pointed to, two of them playing checkers, the third kibitzing their game. The kibitzer was drinking a can of Miller's. The players were sharing a carton of Tropicana orange juice. I said, 'Carlos?' and they all looked at me.

I held out my card and one of the players took it. He was stocky, with a flattened nose and liquid brown eyes, and I decided he must be Carlos. 'I'm concerned about one of your tenants,' I said. 'I'm afraid he may have had an accident.'

'Who's that?'

'James Shorter.'

'Shorter.'

'Late forties, medium height, dark hair—'

'I know him,' he said. 'You don't have to describe him for me. I know all of them. I just tryin' to think if I seen him today.' He closed his eyes in concentration. 'No,' he said at length. 'I don't see him in a while. You want to leave your card, I call you when I see him.'

'I think we should see if he's all right.'

'You mean open his door?'

'That's what I mean.'

'You ring his bell?'

'I don't know which bell is his.'

'Don't it got his name on it?'

'No.'

He sighed. 'A lot of them,' he said, 'they don't want no name on the bell. I put the name in, they just take it out. Then their friends come, ring the wrong bell, disturb everybody. Or they ring my bell. I tell you, it's a big pain in the ass.'

'Well,' I said.

He got to his feet. 'First thing we do,' he said, 'is we ring his bell. Then we see.'

We rang his bell and got no response. We went inside and climbed three flights of stairs, and the house was about what I'd expected, with a Lysol smell battling the odors of cooking and mice and urine. Carlos led us to what he said was Shorter's door and banged on it with a heavy fist. 'Hey, open up,' he called. 'This gen'man wants to talk to you.'

Nothing.

'Not home,' Carlos said, and shrugged. 'You want to write him a note, put it under the door, an' when he comes home—'

'I think you should open the door,' I said.

'I don't know about that.'

'I'm worried about him,' I said. 'I think he might have had an accident.'

'What kind of accident?'

'A bad one. Open the door.'

'You say that,' he said, 'but I'm the one gets in trouble.'

'I'll take the responsibility.'

'And what do I say, huh? "This guy took the responsibility." It's still my ass inna crack, man.'

'If you don't open it,' I told him, 'I'll kick it in.'

'You serious?' He looked at me and decided I was. 'You think maybe he's sick in there, huh?'

'Or worse than that.'

'What's worse'n sick?' I guess it came to him, because he winced at the thought. 'Shit, I hope not.' He hauled out a ring of keys, found his master passkey, and fitted it in the lock. 'Anyway,' he said, 'you wouldn't have to kick it in, less'n he got the chain on. These locks is nothin', you can slip 'em with a plastic card. But if the chain's on, shit, you still gonna have to kick it in.'

But the chain wasn't on. He turned the lock, paused to knock on the door one final unnecessary time, and pushed the door inward.

The room was empty.

He stood in the doorway. I pushed past him, walked around the little room. It was as neat and bare as a monk's cell. There was an iron bedstead, a chest of drawers, a bedside table. The bed was made.

The drawers were empty. So was the closet. I looked under the bed. There were no personal articles anywhere, just the thrift-shop furniture that had been there when he moved in.

'I guess he moved out,' Carlos said.

The telephone was on the bedside table. I slipped a pencil under the receiver and lifted it enough to get a dial tone, then allowed it to drop back in place.

'He didn't say nothin' to nobody,' Carlos said. 'He pays a week at a time, so he's paid through Sunday. Funny, huh?'

TJ walked over to the bed, picked up the pillow. There was a booklet under it. He took a close look at it and handed it to me.

I already knew what it was.

'It don't make sense,' Carlos said. 'You gonna move out, why you gonna make the bed first? I got to change it anyway before I rent it to somebody else, don't I?'

'Let's hope so.'

'Course I do.' He frowned, puzzled. 'Maybe he's comin' back.'

I looked at the AA meeting book, the one I'd bought him, the only thing he'd left behind.

'No,' I said. 'He's not coming back.'

TWENTY-FIVE

Martin Banszak took off his rimless glasses and fogged the lenses with his breath, then polished each in turn with his handkerchief. When he was satisfied with the results he put them on and turned his sad blue eyes on me.

'You must know the caliber of men we get,' he said. 'Guard work pays just one or two dollars an hour over the minimum wage. It's a job that requires no experience and minimal training. Our best men are retired police officers looking to supplement a city pension, but men like that can usually find something better for themselves.

'We get fellows who are out of work and looking for stopgap employment until something opens up for them. They're often good workers, but they don't stay with us long. And then we get men who work for us because they can't do any better.'

'What kind of checks do you run on them?'

'We do the minimum. I try not to hire convicted felons. After all, this is security work. You don't hire the fox to guard the henhouse, do you? But it's hard to avoid. I can run computer checks, but what good is that when the name's a common one? "Query: Has William Johnson been an inmate in the New York State prison system?" Well, there are probably half a dozen William Johnsons in prison in this state on any given day, so how am I to know? And when a man comes to me and says his name is William Johnson, how can I tell if it's the name he was born with? If a man shows me a Social Security card and a driver's license, what can I do but accept it?'

'Don't you run their prints?'

'No.'

'Why not?'

'It takes too long,' he said. 'By the time I get a response from Washington, two weeks or more have passed. The applicant's found other work in the meantime.'

'Couldn't you hire him provisionally? And let him go if he doesn't check out?'

'Is that how they do it at Reliable? Well, I'm sure you charge more for your services. A Manhattan firm, a fancy address. That's all well and good for the clients who can afford to cover your overhead for you.' He picked up a pencil, tapped its eraser end on the desktop. 'I can't have half my employees checking up on the other half,' he said. 'I'd be out of business in no time.'

I didn't say anything.

'Two years ago,' he said, 'we tried taking fingerprints when we accepted applications for employment. You know what happened?'

'Your applications dropped off.'

'That's exactly right. People didn't want to go through a messy and demeaning process.'

'Especially the ones with outstanding warrants,' I said. 'It would have been particularly messy and demeaning for them.'

He glared at me. 'And the ones who had stopped paying alimony,' he said. 'And the ones running away from bad debts. And, yes, the ones who'd served time for minor narcotics violations and other low-level criminal behavior. It's hard to grow up in certain neighborhoods without getting arrested and fingerprinted along the way. The bulk of those men do just fine in this line of work.'

I nodded. Who was I to judge him, and what did I care how he ran his business? He fired men for drinking because it bothered the clients. But what client was bothered by the fact that the man guarding his warehouse

261

had failed to pay child support, or sold a gram of cocaine to an undercover police officer? Those weren't offenses you could smell on a man's breath, or spot in his walk.

'Let's get back to Shorter,' I said.

Shorter's file contained the application he'd filled out, along with a record of the hours he'd worked and the compensation he'd received. No photograph, and I asked about that. Wasn't it part of the routine to photograph all employees?

'Of course,' he said. 'We need a photo for their ID. We take them right here, in front of that wall. It's a perfect backdrop.' So where was the photo? Laminated to the ID card, I was told, which Shorter would have turned in when they let him go, and which would have been routinely destroyed.

'Did he turn it in?'

'I assume so.'

'And it was destroyed?'

'It must have been.'

'What about the negative?'

He shook his head. 'We use a Polaroid. Everybody does. You want to be able to make up the ID right away, not wait for the film to come back.'

'So there's no negative.'

'No.'

'And you only take the one shot? You don't shoot a backup to have on file?'

'We do, actually,' he said, and shuffled through the file. 'It doesn't seem to be here. It may have been misfiled.'

Or removed from the file by Shorter, I thought. Or not taken in the first place, because Martin Banszak didn't seem to run the tightest ship around.

I took another look at the application. Shorter had had

the same address on East Ninety-fourth Street when he'd applied for the job back in July of '92.

July of '92?

I checked the date with Banszak. Had Shorter actually been working there for seven months by the time Alan Watson was killed?

'Yes, and he was very steady, very reliable,' he said. 'That's why I was inclined to give him a break when he had the first incident.'

'The drinking.'

'Yes. He must have been ashamed, because he didn't even offer an argument in his own defense, just hung his head waiting to be fired. But his record was excellent, and he'd been with us for over seven months, so I gave him that second chance.' He frowned. 'The next time, of course, there was an official complaint called in. I had to let him go.'

Seven months. Waiting, biding his time.

I picked up the application. 'I'll need a copy of this,' I said. 'Is there a place in the neighborhood where I can get it copied?' He said he had a desktop copier and would run it for me. He went into another room, came back with the copy but held on to it for a moment.

He said, 'I'm not sure I understand. If Shorter knows something, if he's disappeared in order to escape from the man who killed Watson' – that was the explanation I'd devised for him – 'shouldn't the police be brought into the picture?'

'If it comes to that,' I said. 'But it looks as though Shorter's been living under an assumed name, and that he might have invented most of what's on that application. If I can spare him the embarrassment of official attention from the police—'

'Yes, of course,' he said. 'By all means.'

★

He didn't exist.

He'd carried a New York State driver's license, and its number was listed on his job application. But the DMV never heard of him, and the license number he'd written down was unassigned. The Social Security number was real, but the account was that of a State Farm insurance agent in Emporia, Kansas, whose name was Bennett Gunnarson, not James Shorter.

It would have made my life easier if Banszak had fingerprinted his employees, even if he'd done nothing with the prints but file them away. Earlier, I'd left TJ on guard at the rooming house and cabbed down to the Flatiron Building and back, borrowing a fingerprint kit from Wally Donn at Reliable. Before I left Shorter's room I had fogged the telephone receiver with my breath the way Banszak had fogged his glasses. I hadn't seen any prints then, but sometimes they show up better when you dust for them. And the telephone wasn't the only surface in the room that would hold a print.

Back on East Ninety-fourth, I dusted the phone, the window, the washbasin, the headboard and footboard, the switchplate, and everything else that looked at all promising. There was nothing, not even smudges.

'He cleaned up,' I told TJ. 'He deliberately wiped every surface in the room.'

'The man be neat.'

'The man's a killer,' I said. 'He killed Alan Watson back in February. A few days ago he killed Helen Watson, and – Jesus.'

'Say what?'

'Helen Watson,' I said. 'One time I was talking to him and he asked me if I'd reached Helen Watson yet. How did he know her first name? He never heard it from me. Jesus, how long was he stalking them?'

★

I had my answer now.

He'd been stalking Alan Watson for a minimum of seven months, from the time he'd started work with Queensboro-Corona to the night he seized his opportunity and stuck a knife in the commodity broker's heart. God knows how many opportunities he must have had in all that time, but he'd been in no hurry, he'd been content to bide his time, waiting, letting the anticipation build.

Then, when he finally struck, he'd allowed himself the extra satisfaction of discovering the body and phoning it in to the police, like a firebug coming back to watch the firemen battle the blaze he'd set. And then, remarkably, he'd stayed on the job another six weeks before he could contrive to get fired.

So I knew that he liked to take his time, and I knew, too, that he could strike quickly if he wanted to. I'd seen him on Friday night, and a day later Watson's widow was dead. A couple of days after that, Gerard Billings was shot to death in the back of a cab.

Oh, he was slick.

But who the hell was he?

I called Ray Gruliow, brought him up to date. 'I feel like a damn fool,' I said. 'I found the son of a bitch and then I lost him.'

'You didn't know what you'd found.'

'No. He knew and I didn't. He was playing with me, the bastard. He was the cat and I was a particularly dimwitted mouse. You want to know what I did? I took the son of a bitch to AA meetings.'

'You didn't.'

'Well, he'd been fired for drinking on the job, and he was leading a shabby life, and he looked for all the world like a drunk getting ready to bottom out. I couldn't see any reason not to talk about the program, and when I did he did a good job of seeming interested but wary. I have to say he's a natural when it comes to the principle of anonymity. He's the most anonymous person I ever met. I still don't know who the hell he is.'

'But you've seen him. You sat across a table and talked to him.'

'Right,' I said. 'I know what he looks like.' I described Shorter in detail. 'Now we both know what he looks like,' I said. 'Does he sound like anybody you know?'

'I'm not very good at recognizing a man from a description.'

'He's forty-eight years old. He listed his place of birth as Klamath Falls, Oregon, but they never heard of anybody by that name, and there's no reason to assume he's ever been within a thousand miles of the place. He moved into his rooming house a week before he turned up on their doorstep at Queensboro-Corona, and it's my guess that James Shorter was born right about that time. I think he slapped together some fake ID, rented himself a room by the week, and went out to look for a job.'

'So that he could stalk Alan.'

'That's right,' I said. 'I think he's a stalker. That's the only way I can begin to make sense out of what he's been doing. I did a little research on the subject, and there are elements here that seem to fit the pattern. The way he structured his whole life to support his pursuit of Alan Watson. And the way he postponed the kill. How many chances do you suppose he had in the six months he worked for Q-C? Twenty? A hundred? But he kept putting it off, and not because he was afraid of getting caught.'

'He was holding back to boost his excitement.'

'Exactly.'

'But with Gerry—'

'I think he started stalking somebody else very shortly after he killed Watson. Probably Billings, but it could have been anybody. Maybe he was keeping tabs on a couple of you. He was still at the same rooming house, still calling himself James Shorter, so I don't think he was anywhere close to the last act of his little drama. But then I turned up, and he realized it was time for James Shorter to disappear, and he wanted to do something dramatic on the way out.'

'He picked a pretty dramatic way to kill Gerry.'

'He would have known where he lived, and his usual schedule. I suppose he had a gun, or knew where to get one. It couldn't have been too hard for him to take a bus to Newark Airport and drive back in a stolen car. Then all he had to do was wait for Billings and pick his opportunity. Engineering a car crash was a nice touch, but he had other options. He could have staged a drive-by shooting, he could have tried running Billings down.'

Or he could have found a way to toss a bomb through Gruliow's high-tech plastic window. That way he could have taken out nine of the fourteen remaining members at once. He'd known about the meeting, because I'd been obliging enough to tell him, and when he'd pumped me a little I'd even said it was in the Village. Gruliow was the only member who lived in the Village. Maybe Shorter had been around Commerce Street Tuesday afternoon, maybe he'd been across the street at the Grange, nursing a beer and watching them file in. Watching me, too.

I said, 'Who the hell is he? Do you have any idea?'

'None.'

'We know he's not a member, but I don't think any of us seriously thought it could be. Who else knows about the club?'

'No one, really. Not in any detail.'

267

'He's forty-eight. In 1961 he would have been what, sixteen? Could he have been somebody's younger brother, transferring a resentment against a sibling to the entire club?'

'God, that strikes me as far-fetched.'

'I don't know that we can expect to find a logical motive,' I said, 'because why should there be a sane explanation for a longstanding pattern of insane behavior? All he needed was a pretext.'

'Wouldn't it have to be a good one to sustain him this long?'

'No,' I said. 'All it had to do was get him started. Once he was in motion his own momentum would sustain him, no matter how frail the original impetus.'

'Because he enjoys what he's doing.'

'He loves it,' I said, 'but I have a feeling it's more than that. It's his whole life.'

I had abbreviated versions of that conversation with as many of the other members as I could get hold of. I described Shorter and asked them if the description seemed to fit anybody who might have picked up a resentment against the group years ago. They all said essentially the same thing – the description fit too many people, and they couldn't think of anyone, of any description, who had any reason, sane or otherwise, to resent the group. Or even to know it existed.

'It's a shame there's no photograph,' more than one of them said. And I explained how his employers in Corona had taken a pair of Polaroids, but nobody could furnish a copy. One was on his ID, which he'd very likely retained; the other had conveniently disappeared from his file.

And when, I wondered, had that happened? Had he been resourceful enough to slip off with the photo before they let him go? Or had he paid an unauthorized visit sometime over the weekend to tidy up after himself? He could have combined it with the trip to Forest Hills to drown Helen Watson in her tub.

'Wouldn't he have had other pictures taken?' Elaine wondered. 'How did he cash his paychecks? I can't believe he had a bank account.'

'He used a check-cashing service. But he had his Queensboro–Corona ID and his driver's license. He wouldn't need anything else.'

'And you sat across a table from him.'

'And took him to a meeting.'

'And you don't get mugged and printed at AA meetings, do you? I guess it would be a violation of the tradition of anonymity, wouldn't it?'

'I'm afraid so.'

'If I'd been along,' she said, 'I could have taken a sneak photo of him, the way we did at Wallbanger's. Remember?'

'Oh, for Christ's sake,' I said.

'What's the matter? Did I say something wrong?'

'No,' I said. 'You said something right. I don't know what the hell's the matter with me, I really don't. Why can't I think straight?'

'What do you mean?'

For answer I pointed to a framed drawing on the wall.

TWENTY-SIX

'I'll tell you something,' Ray Galindez said. 'This is a piece of cake. You got a nice clear picture of the guy in your mind and how long did it take to get it out of your head and onto a piece of paper? Fifteen, twenty minutes?'

'Something like that.'

'Compared to witnesses who don't know how to use their eyes and can't remember what they saw with them, this is a cinch. I had one a week ago, over and over she's telling me I got the eyes wrong. How are they wrong? Too big, too small, too far apart, too close together, what? Are they slanted? Are they almond-shaped? Droopy eyelids? Tell me something, because just saying they're wrong don't cut it. I try this, I try that, I change this, I fix that, all I get is the eyes are wrong. You know what it turns out?'

'What?'

'She never saw his fuckin' eyes. The guy was wearing mirrored sunglasses. It takes her the better part of an hour to remember this, and this is a guy who stood right smack in fucking front of her and held her up at gunpoint. "The eyes are wrong," she said. "I'll never forget those eyes." Except she never saw 'em, so what's she gonna forget?'

'At least she had the sense to sit down with you,' I said. 'I couldn't get past the fact that I didn't have a photograph of him. I was sitting in the same room with one of your sketches and I still didn't get the message.'

'Sometimes it's hard to see what's right in front of you.'

'I guess.'

When I went to pay him he didn't want to take the money. 'I figure I owe you,' he said, 'everything Elaine's done for me. I took my mother to see the gallery and now every word out of her mouth is *mi hijo el artista*. She wasn't this impressed when I got on the job. Speaking of which, it's not the same.'

'The Department?'

'Oh, who's to say, but I'm just talking about my own detail. They want me to use a computer to do what I do.'

'You mean like an Identi-Kit?'

'No, this is different,' he said. 'Much more flexible than the Identi-Kit. You can make minute adjustments to the shape of the mouth, elongate the head, set the eyes deeper, anything you could do with pencil and paper.' He explained how the software worked and what it would do. 'But it's not drawing,' he said. 'It's not art.'

He laughed, and I asked him what was funny.

'Just hearing myself use the word,' he said. 'I would always correct Elaine when she called it art, what I do. I'm beginning to think she's right. I'll tell you one thing, what I been doing with that European woman is different from anything I ever done before. You know about her? Customer of Elaine's, she lost all her family in the Holocaust?'

'Elaine told me. I didn't know you'd started working with her.'

'Two sessions so far, and it's the most exhausting thing I ever did in my life. She doesn't remember what any of the people look like.'

'Then how can you possibly draw them?'

'Oh, the memory's in there. It's a question of reaching in and dragging it out. We started with her father. What did he look like? Well, that doesn't get us anywhere, because she hasn't got an answer. The best she can do is he's tall. Okay, what kind of man is he? He's very gentle, she says. Okay, so I start drawing. He's got a deep voice, she remembers. I draw some more. Sometimes he would lose his temper. Okay, now I'm drawing a tall gentle man with a deep voice who gets angry. Late at night he would sit at the kitchen table adding columns of numbers. Okay, great, let's draw that. And we keep on, and now and then we have to stop because she's crying, or she can't look at the paper anymore, or she's just wiped out. Believe me, time we're done, we're *both* wiped out.'

'And you wound up with a human face?'

'I wound up with a human face,' he said, 'but whose face? Does it look like the man who went to the gas chamber? No way to know. It brought back memories, I know that much, and she's got a picture that means something to her, so what's the difference? Is it as good as a photograph? Well, maybe it's better. Is it art?' He shrugged. 'I have to say I think so.'

'And this?'

'This prick?' He leaned forward, blew some eraser dust from the surface of the sketch. 'This doesn't have to be art. Just so it looks like him.'

I went to a copy shop, ran two dozen copies of the sketch. It seemed to me it was a good likeness. I gave the original to Elaine but told her not to hang it anywhere for the time being. I left a copy with TJ, who raised an eyebrow and announced that Shorter was an ugly-looking dude.

Over the next few days, I got around to most of the men who'd been at the meeting at Gruliow's house, as well as a few who hadn't been able to make it. No one echoed TJ's sentiment, but neither did anyone recognize Shorter as a long-lost cousin.

'He's a pretty ordinary-looking guy,' Bob Berk told me. 'Not a face that would jump out at you in a crowd.'

Several of them said he looked vaguely familiar. Lewis Hildebrand told me he might have seen Shorter before, that it was impossible to say. 'The visual onslaught in this city is overpowering,' he said. 'Walk a few blocks through midtown Manhattan and more people will pass through your field of vision than the average small-town resident will see all year. Walk through Grand Central Station at rush hour and you'll see thousands of people without really seeing any of them. How much of it do we screen out? How much registers, consciously or otherwise?'

In his living room on Commerce Street, Hard-Way Ray Gruliow squinted at the sketch and shook his head. 'He looks familiar,' he said. 'But in a very vague way.'

'That's what I keep hearing.'

'What a crazy thing, huh? Here's somebody who hates us all enough to devote his entire life to killing us. Because he's not a guy who got pissed off one morning and took a gun to the Post Office. This is his life's work.'

'That's right.'

'And we look at him,' he said, 'and all we can say is he looks vaguely familiar. Who could he be? How could he know us?'

'Where could you remember him from?'

'I don't know. The only time we were all together was once a year at dinner. Maybe he was a waiter at Cunningham's. What did we decide he was, sixteen years old? He couldn't have been a waiter. Maybe he was a busboy.'

'And maybe you stiffed him on the tip.'

'No, we wouldn't do a thing like that. We're a generous bunch.'

Local 100 of the Restaurant and Hotel Workers of America maintains offices on Eighth Avenue, just two blocks from Restaurant Row. I talked to a man there named Gus Brann who was amused at the thought of trying to hunt down employees of a restaurant that had gone out of business twenty years ago. 'Restaurant work isn't the trade it once was,' he said. 'Not on the service floor. You used to have waiters who spent their life in the profession. They knew their customers and they knew how to serve. Now do you know what you get? Actors and actresses. "My name is Scott and together we'll enjoy a dining experience." Guess what percentage of the rank and file also holds membership in Actors Equity.'

'I have no idea.'

'Plenty,' he said. 'Take my word for it. You go out for a meal and what you get is an audition.'

'The turnover's not as high in the old-fashioned steak houses, is it?'

'No, you're right about that, but how many of them have we got left? You got Gallagher's, you got the Old Homestead, you got Keens, you got Peter Luger, you got Smith and Whatsisface, Wollensky, you got—'

I said, 'Waiters tend to stay with the same general type of restaurant, don't they?'

'I just told you, they don't even stay with the business.'

'But the old-fashioned type of waiter. If a man was working at Cunningham's and it went out of business, he'd probably look for work at one of the places you just mentioned, don't you think?'

'Unless he had a longing to scoop Rocky Road at a Baskin-Robbins. But yeah, you tend to stay with what you know.'

'So if you wanted to find somebody who used to work at Cunningham's, those would be the first places to look.'

'I suppose.'

'But I myself would hardly know how to begin,' I said. 'And I'd have to spend a couple of days running all over the city, trying to convince people to give me the time of day. Whereas a knowledgeable person like yourself could probably manage the whole thing by just making a few phone calls.'

'Hey,' he said. 'I got a job to do, you know what I mean?'

'I know.'

'I can't sit around making phone calls, bugging people, asking who worked where twenty, thirty years back.'

'You'd be saving me time,' I said, 'and time is money. I wasn't looking to get the information for free.'

'Oh,' he said. 'Well, that puts a different light on it, doesn't it?'

The following day I called Gruliow and told him I'd found not one but two gentlemen who'd spent their lives bringing steak dinners to people with hearty appetites. 'They were both working at Cunningham's when it closed,' I said. 'One of them started there as a busboy over forty years ago.'

'He'd have been there for our first dinner,' he said. 'Christ, he'd have been around for quite a few meetings of the previous chapter.'

'He didn't recognize the sketch, though. Neither did the other fellow, who's actually quite a bit older, although he was only at Cunningham's from 1967 on. He went from there to the Old Homestead, and that's where he was when he retired three years ago last September. They both said the same thing.'

'What's that?'

'They said he looked familiar.'

'Oh, Jesus,' Gruliow said, 'you know what our friend's got? He's got a universally familiar face. Nobody can place it, but everybody thinks he must have seen it somewhere before. You know, Matt, that was just an offhand remark of mine about his having worked at Cunningham's.'

'I know.'

'Yet you followed it up.'

'It was worth checking.'

'How on earth did you find those fellows?'

'I didn't,' I said. 'I found someone who could find them for me. You know, if I were to hand this over to the cops, they'd be able to turn up a dozen men who worked at Cunningham's during the period in question. And one of them might be able to put a name to the face in the sketch.'

'I was talking to some of the others,' he said.

'And?'

'We all intend to be very cautious. We'll keep an eye out for the man in the sketch. But we'd rather not go public with this if we don't have to.'

'If someone else is killed—'

'You said he'd probably lay low for the next six months.'

'That's what I said,' I agreed, 'but what the hell do I know? I can't presume to predict what a madman is going to do next. And so far he hasn't shown any inclination to call me up and let me know.'

That was on a Wednesday afternoon. That night I went to a meeting for the first time all week, and I stopped at the Flame afterward and had a cup of coffee. One of the fellows at the table was a newcomer, and the others were trying to help him, answering his questions and reassuring him that there really was life after sobriety. The new man was in his early thirties and looked nothing like Jim Shorter, but his attitude was very similar to the persona Shorter had adopted for the occasion, mixing guarded hope and cynical skepticism. It made me very uncomfortable to sit at the same table with him. He wasn't doing anything wrong, and I knew he wasn't putting on an act, but I couldn't help feeling as though I was being conned all over again.

I went home and told Elaine about it. She said, 'You'd like to kill him, wouldn't you?'

'The guy tonight? Oh, you mean Shorter.'

'Of course.'

'I guess I'm angry,' I said. 'I don't really feel it, but it must be there. I was trying to help him, the cocksucker, and he was just playing me like a fish on a line. The son of a bitch.'

'Yes,' she said. 'I think you might be the slightest bit angry.' She started to say something else but the phone rang and she got up and answered it. 'Yes,' she said. 'Just one moment, I'll see if he's in.'

She covered the mouthpiece. 'It's him,' she said.

TWENTY-SEVEN

'Jim,' I said. 'I'm glad you called. I was hoping I'd hear from you.'

'Well, I've been busy, Matt.'

'Hey, I know what it's like,' I said. 'I've been running around a lot myself. I tried to reach you a couple of times but I guess you were out.'

'I guess I was.'

'I thought I might run into you at a meeting, but I'm on the other side of town.'

'Whole different world.'

'That's right. How's it going?'

There was a pause. Then he said, 'I know you know, Matt.'

'Oh?'

'Funny thing is I thought you knew from the jump. I thought, shit, they finally figured out what's going on and hired themselves a detective. But you didn't know a thing, did you?'

'No.'

'Getting me to come to an AA meeting. I thought it was a ruse at first. Get me off my guard, take me by surprise. But you weren't suspicious at all, were you? You figured I needed help and you wanted to help me.'

'Something like that.'

'You know,' he said, 'that was very decent of you, Matt. Seriously.'

'If you say so.'

'And the meetings were interesting. I can see how a person with a drinking problem would find a whole new life in the rooms. And I get the feeling some people who aren't alcoholics go for the companionship and the sense that they're getting their lives in order.'

'I don't think you'll find many like that,' I said.

'No? Well, you'd be a better judge of that than I am, Matt. See, I, uh, gave you a false impression. I'm not an alcoholic.'

'Whatever you say.'

He laughed. 'Denial, right? I bet you get to hear it all the time. No, see, I just wanted a neat exit from Queensboro–Corona, and Marty Banszak's a bear when it comes to booze. Son of a bitch eats Valium all day long, he's tranked out like the night of the living dead, but if he smells alcohol on your breath you're history.'

'But he gave you a second chance.'

'Yeah, isn't that a gas? Second time around I figured let's leave nothing to chance.'

'What did you do, call in the complaint yourself?'

'How'd you know? Hey, you're a detective, right? It's your job to figure things out.'

'It is,' I said, 'and I don't seem to be doing too well at it.'

'Hey, I think you're doing fine, Matt.'

'There are things I can't figure, Jim.'

'Like what?'

'Like why you're doing it.'

'Ha. Can't work that out, can you?'

'I thought maybe you'd help me.'

'You mean like give you a hint?'

'Something like that.'

'Nah, I can't do that. Hey, I'll tell you, it hardly matters how I got started on this project. Man starts collecting stamps, pasting 'em in a book, lives in an attic on peanut-butter sandwiches, puts every dime he can into his stamp collection, are you gonna ask him what got him started collecting in the first place? He's a stamp collector. It's what he does.'

'Are you a collector, Jim?'

'Am I collecting the members, is that what you mean? Scooping 'em up in a butterfly net? Can't let up for a minute until the set's complete?' He laughed. 'It's a nice idea, but no, that's not it. Here, I'll tell you this much. I got my reasons.'

'But you won't say what they are.'

'Nope.'

'So I guess they're not rational,' I said. 'Otherwise you wouldn't have a problem putting them on the table.'

'Hey, that's a nice one,' he said appreciatively. 'Make the man prove he's sane. Trouble is, I'd have to be crazy to fall for it.'

'Well, that's one of the things I'm a little worried about, Jim.'

'That I'm crazy?'

'That you're losing control.'

'How do you figure that?'

'The cabdriver.'

'The cabdriver? Oh, the Arab.'

'Bengali, wasn't he?'

'Who gives a fuck? Ali something or other. What about him?'

'Why kill him? He wasn't in the club.'

'He got in the way.'

'You rammed his cab.'

'So? They lie their way through Customs at JFK and ten minutes later they're on the street with a temporary hack license. Can't find Penn Station but they're out there taking a job away from a real American.'

'And that made you angry?'

'Are you kidding? What do I give a fuck? Ali's number

was up and he was in the way. Sayonara, baby. All she wrote.'

'See, that's my point. You sound out of control.'

'You're completely wrong about that,' he said. 'I'm a hundred percent *in* control.'

'You used to limit yourself to members of the club.'

'What about Diana Shipton? She wasn't in the club. I had plenty of chances to take Boyd out when he was alone.'

'Why didn't you?'

'Sometimes you want to make a splash. And that wasn't the only time. What about – no, forget it.'

'What?'

'Never mind. I'm telling you too much.'

'Why'd you go after Helen Watson?'

'Oh, you know about that, huh?'

'Why?'

'You were going to get in touch with her. She might have remembered.'

'What could she remember?'

'Christ, I was fucking her, wasn't I? Think she might remember that?'

'I guess she would.'

'You didn't know about that, did you?'

'No.'

'And now you don't know if you should believe me.'

'I don't even know if you killed her,' I said. 'Maybe she drank too much and drowned.'

'The scotch in the bathroom. I thought you'd like that touch. That was me tipping you a wink, Matt. Saying hello.'

'Like the meeting book under the pillow.'

'Something like that. I appreciated the meeting book, you know. I appreciated your kindness. I'm not used to people going out of their way to do me a good turn.'

'Have people been hard on you, Jim?'

'What's this, Psych 101? "Oh, yes, nurse, people have been hard-hearted and cruel."'

'Just trying to understand, that's all.'

'Trying to crack the code.'

'I suppose so.'

'What's the point? Your buddies can kick back and relax. I'm going into voluntary retirement.'

'Oh?'

'Tell you the truth, I was getting a little tired of Jim Shorter. Tired of that little room on Ninety-fourth Street. You know what I might do? I might leave town.'

'Where would you go?'

'Hey, it's a big world out there. If I'm ever gonna see some of it, I better get my ass in gear. You know how old I am?'

'Forty-eight.'

A pause. 'Yeah, right. Well, I'm not getting any younger.'

'Not too many people are.'

'And some of 'em ain't getting any older, either.' His laughter was harsh, nasty, and it broke off abruptly, as if he'd realized how it must sound. 'Point is,' he said, 'there won't be any more deaths for a while.'

'How long is a while?'

'Why do you want to pin a guy down all the time? No more deaths until the next dinner.'

'And when would that be?'

'What are you, checking me out? First Thursday in May, remember? Until then I'm on the shelf.'

'And I've got your word on that?'

'Absolutely,' he said. 'My word as a gentleman. What do you figure it's worth?'

'I don't know. How did you even learn about the club, Jim?'

'Good question.'

'Why do you hate the members?'

'Who says I hate 'em?'

'I wish you'd explain it so I can understand.'

'I wish you'd quit trying.'

'No you don't.'

'I don't?'

'No, or you wouldn't have called.'

'I called because you were nice to me. I want to be nice back.'

'You called because you want to keep the game going.'

'You think it's a game?'

'*You* think it's a game.'

'Ha! I should hang up right now.'

'Unless you're enjoying this.'

'I am, but why stay too long at the fair? Enough's enough. But you want a hint, don't you?'

'Sure.'

'No, not a hint. You're a detective. What you want is a clue, right?'

'I don't know. I'm not too good at working with clues.'

'Oh, sure you are. Sherlock Holmes.'

'Is that the clue?'

'No, that's what you are. Sherlock fucking Holmes. Rumpelstiltskin. *That's* the clue.'

'Rumpelstiltskin?'

'There's hope for you yet,' he said. 'Bye.'

TWENTY-EIGHT

I arranged to meet Felicia Karp at four o'clock. I got to the house on Stafford Avenue ten minutes early, and at 4:20 I was beginning to worry. Fifteen minutes later I was in the vestibule examining the lock on the door leading up to her second-floor flat and wondering how much trouble it would be to let myself in. The possibility of getting nailed for illegal entry scared me less than the thought of what I might find. She lived, after all, just a fifteen-minute walk from where Helen Watson had drowned in her bath.

I got a flat strip of flexible steel from my wallet and turned to make sure no one was watching me when I took a shot at the door. Across the street, someone was maneuvering a Ford Escort into a tight space. I could have been through the door and up the stairs before the car was parked, but I waited, and Felicia Karp emerged from the car. I put my burglar's tool away and went to meet her.

'I'm sorry,' she said. 'They sprang a meeting on us literally at the last minute and there was no way to reach you.' She gave me her canvas tote bag to hold while she unlocked the door. Inside, she led me to the kitchen and heated two cups of the morning's coffee in the microwave. From the wall, the black cat swung its pendulum tail and rolled its eyes at me.

I showed her Ray Galindez's sketch. She held it at arm's length and asked who it was supposed to be.

'Do you recognize him?'

'He looks familiar. Who is he?'

'He worked as a patrol officer for a private security firm. Back in February he discovered the body of Alan Watson while making his rounds a few blocks the other side of Continental Avenue. Watson had been stabbed, and it wasn't hard for this man to be the first person on the scene.'

'You're implying that he killed him.'

'Yes.'

'Was Alan Watson one of the men my husband had dinner with once a year?' I said that he was. 'And this man? Did he kill my husband?'

'I believe so.'

'My God,' she said, and stared at the sketch, and shuddered. 'I knew Fred Karp would never kill himself,' she said. 'My God.'

I said, 'You say this man looks familiar.'

'I know him.'

'Oh?'

'I know I've seen him. Where did he patrol? We don't have private guards around here, although the neighborhood association has been talking about hiring them. You said the other side of Continental Avenue? I wouldn't have seen him there. It's a nice section, upscale compared to this, but I don't have any reason to go there. Anyway, I know his face, and I wouldn't know it from glimpsing it through the window of a patrol car. Why do I know his face? Help me.'

'Have you seen him in the neighborhood recently?'

'No.'

'Has he come to the house?' She shook her head. 'Have you seen him at the school? He could have posed as a parent.'

'Why would he do that? Am I in danger?'

'It's possible.'

'For God's sake,' she said. She studied the picture. 'He

looks so damn ordinary,' she said. 'To look at him, you'd think he was too much of a nebbish to be a policeman.'

'What could you picture him doing?'

'I don't know. Something menial, something completely pedestrian.'

'Close your eyes. He's doing something. What do you see him doing?'

'What's this, some new guided-imaging technique? It's not going to work. I intellectualize too much, that's my problem.'

'Try it anyway. What's he doing?'

'I can't see him.'

'If you could see him, what would he be doing?'

'I don't—'

'Don't figure it out. Just answer it. What's he doing?'

'Pushing a broom. My God, I don't believe it.'

'What?'

'That's it. He was a janitor in the Kashin Building where Fred had his office. He wore a uniform, matching pants and a shirt in greenish gray. How would I remember that?'

'I don't know.'

'Sometimes I would meet Fred at his office and we would have dinner and go to a play. And one time I saw this man. I think—'

'Yes?'

'I seem to remember that he was in Fred's office when I got there, and they were talking. He was sweeping the floor and he was emptying a wastebasket.'

'What was his name?'

'How would I know?'

'Your husband might have introduced you.'

'I'm afraid . . . John. His name was John!'

'That's very good.'

'Nobody introduced him. It was on his shirt.' She

286

traced a short horizontal line above her left breast. 'Over the pocket, embroidered in white. No! Not white, yellow.' She shook her head. 'It's just amazing the things you remember.'

'And his name was John.'

'Yes. I didn't like him.'

'Why not?'

'There was something about him. I thought he was sly. In fact I almost said something to Fred, but I let it go.'

'What would you have said?'

'I would have warned him.'

'You thought the man was dangerous?'

She shook her head. 'Not physically dangerous. I thought he would steal something. There was a furtive quality about him. Do you know what I mean?'

'Yes.'

'But it wasn't so pronounced that it stayed in my mind. I don't believe I ever gave him another thought from that day to this. And I'm positive I never saw him again.'

'If you ever do—'

'Yes,' she said. 'I'll call you immediately, rest assured.' She frowned at the sketch. 'Definitely yellow. His name, I mean. John, in yellow script, over the left breast pocket.'

The superintendent at the Kashin Building didn't recognize the sketch, and it turned out he hadn't been working there at the time of Fred Karp's death. I went to the management company's office on West Thirty-seventh Street. Nobody there recognized the sketch, either, but a young woman checked personnel records and came up with an employee named John Siebert. He had started work five months before Karp's death and quit three weeks after. Under 'Reason for Leaving,' she told me, it said 'Moving to Florida.'

'I guess he decided to retire,' she said.

Hal Gabriel had been reclusive toward the end of his life, rarely leaving his apartment, ordering in from the Chinese restaurant and the liquor store. There were half a dozen Chinese restaurants within a few blocks of his building at Ninety-second and West End. I didn't know which ones had been in business twelve years ago when Gabriel was found hanged, but I hadn't yet known of a Chinese restaurant that employed Caucasian delivery boys.

I checked the two liquor stores a block east on Broadway. Both had had recent changes of ownership. One had changed hands when the owner retired and moved to Miami. The owner of the other had been killed five years before in a robbery. No one in either store recognized James Shorter from the sketch.

I had TJ along and we worked opposite sides of the street, showing the sketch in coffee shops and pizza parlors. The counterman at Poseidon looked at it and said, 'Haven't seen him in years and years. Two scrambled dry, toasted English no butter.' He grinned at the expression on my face. 'Good memory, huh?'

Almost too good. I complimented him on it and went outside, and TJ reported the dry cleaner across the street had also made Shorter from the sketch, and recalled that his name was Smith.

'Right, Smith,' I said. 'And he didn't want any butter on his English muffin.'

'Huh?'

'Smith? And he happened to remember the guy from twelve years ago?'

'Was a woman,' TJ said. 'An' she remembers him because he never came back for his suit jacket. Lady kept it for him for years, finally gave it to the Goodwill

288

sometime last year. Soon as I showed her the picture, she got scared she's gonna get in trouble. "I kep' it a long time," she said.'

No one in Hal Gabriel's building recognized the sketch, nor did the list of 1981 tenants suggest anything. But there was an SRO hotel around the corner, and an old desk register showed that a Joseph Smith had occupied a room on the fourth floor for several months prior to Gabriel's death. A week after the body was discovered, Mr Smith moved out and left no forwarding address.

Rumpelstiltskin.

I thought of him often, the evil dwarf from the fairy tale. I didn't know what Shorter had meant by the clue, or if it was in fact a clue at all. I followed a lot of very cold trails, looking for further traces of his presence near the scene of other deaths.

It didn't matter. Nothing led anywhere.

I have been detecting one way or another for so long that certain parts of the process have become virtually automatic for me. Now and then in recent years I have looked around for some other way to make a living, and invariably I have realized that this is what I do, that I am reasonably good at it, and that my experience and talent equip me for nothing else.

And yet I don't begin to understand it.

Sometimes it's reasonably straightforward. You go up one side of the street and down the other, you knock on every door, figuratively and literally, and each new piece of data clicks into place and points you toward a new street, with new doors to knock on. Finally you've walked down enough streets and knocked on enough doors, and the final door opens and there's your answer. It's not easy and it's rarely simple, but there is a logic to the way it unfolds.

But it's not always like that.

Sometimes it's like a jigsaw puzzle. You separate all the straight-edged pieces and get the outside hooked together, and then you sort by color, and you try this and try that until you've made a little progress. And you're looking for a certain piece, and it's not there. It's got to be missing, and you want to write the manufacturer and complain, and then you pick up a piece you've already tried in that particular spot three or four times already, and you know it's not the one you're looking for, but this time it fits.

It's not always like that, either.

Jim Shorter, aka Joseph Smith, aka John Siebert. Aka Rumpelstiltskin?

'Maybe he stole some monogrammed luggage,' Elaine suggested, 'and he can't bear to part with it.'

'The places he lives,' I said, 'you'd be conspicuous if you moved in with shopping bags from a good store. He does like to hold on to those initials, though. What does JS stand for?'

'Joan Scherman.'

'Who's Joan Scherman?'

'A photo stylist. She showed up at the shop yesterday and wanted to rent that little Biedermeier chair as a prop for a magazine ad. I had it tagged three-fifty and I would have taken three hundred for it, and she's paying a hundred dollars to rent it for two days. Isn't that great?'

'It is if you get the chair back.'

'Oh, she gave me a damage deposit and everything. It's a nice way to make money, don't you think? But that's not helping you.'

'No.'

'JS, JS, JS. Just Shopping. Jonas Salk. Jesus Saves. Jelly Sandwich. I'm sorry, I'm no help at all.'

'That's okay.'

She struck a pose. 'I've got it,' she said. 'Jewish Sexpot. What do you think?'

'I think it's bedtime,' I said.

And so I went to bed and forgot all about James Shorter and his several aliases, and the next morning, shaving, it came to me.

I put on a suit and tie, drank a cup of coffee, and took a cab to Penn Station.

Sixteen hours later I emerged from Penn Station. It was past midnight. There was a man I wanted to talk to, but it was too late to call him. It would have to wait until morning.

It was cool for a change, and although I'd been on my feet a lot earlier in the day, I'd spent the past several hours sitting on the train. I felt like stretching my legs, and I wound up stretching them all the way to the corner of Tenth Avenue and Fiftieth Street.

'I thought of you today,' I told Mick Ballou. 'I was in Washington, and I went to have a look at the Vietnam Memorial.'

'Did you now.'

'I saw your brother's name.'

'Ah,' he said. 'Then no one's gone and rubbed it out.'

'No.'

'I hadn't thought they would,' he said, 'but you never know what someone might do.'

'You don't.'

'It's quite a sight, isn't it? The Memorial. The shape of it, and all of those names. Name after name after name.'

'It's a long line of dead men,' I said. 'You were right about that.'

'You couldn't have gone just to look at Dennis's name. You scarcely knew him.'

'That's true.'

'You knew Eddie Dunphy, and Eddie knew Dennis, but beyond that—'

'I knew him by sight, but no, I didn't really know him.'

'So you must have had other business in Washington, and just thought you'd have a look at the Memorial while you were there.'

'No,' I said. 'As a matter of fact I went there just to look at the Memorial.'

'Did you then.'

'I used the directory,' I said, 'and I managed to find Dennis's name, and the names of a few other men I'd known who died over there. The brother of a girl I knew in high school. Fellows who'd gotten killed over there twenty or twenty-five years ago, and I thought of them for the first time in years and looked for their names and there they were.'

'Ah.'

'And then I found myself doing what you mentioned having done, just walking along and reading names more or less at random. It was very moving. I'm glad I went, if just for that.'

'But you didn't go just for that.'

'No,' I said, 'I didn't. There was another name that I went to look for.'

'And was it there?'

'No, it wasn't.'

'So you went all the way there for nothing?'

'No,' I said. 'I found what I was looking for.'

TWENTY-NINE

I met Ray Gruliow in a bar called Dirty Mary's a block from City Hall. They do a brisk lunch business there, the crowd running to lawyers and bureaucrats, the specialty of the house a shepherd's pie topped with cheddar and browned under the broiler, but we were an hour too early for lunch and the place was empty except for a couple of old lags at the bar who might have been left over from the night before.

Hard-Way Ray looked as though he, too, could have been left over from the night before. His face was drawn and he had dark circles under his eyes. He was in a booth with a cup of coffee when I got there, and I told the waiter I'd have the same.

'No he won't,' Gruliow said. 'He'll have an ordinary cup of coffee. Black, right?'

'Black,' I agreed.

'And I'll have another the hard way,' he said. That, he explained when the waiter had withdrawn, was with a shot in it. I told him I'd figured that out.

'Well, you're a fast study,' he said. 'I don't usually start the day this way, but I had a hell of a night last night. Anyway, I've been up for hours. I had to be across the way there when the gavel came down at nine o'clock. I got a postponement, but I had to show up and ask for it.' He sipped his fortified coffee. 'I like drinking out of coffee cups,' he said. 'Gives you an idea what Prohibition must have been like. And I like a shot of booze in a cup of coffee. It keeps the caffeine from making you too edgy.'

'Tell me about it.'

'You used to drink it that way?'

'Oh, once in a while,' I said. I took out a copy of the sketch and handed it to him. He unfolded it, got a look at it, shook his head, and started to refold it. I put out a hand to interrupt the process.

'God,' he said. 'I've looked at this guy's ugly face until I can see it in my dreams. And I find myself expecting to see him everywhere, do you know what I mean? In the cab coming down here this morning I kept sneaking peeks at the driver, trying to see if it could be him. I took a second look at the waiter before.'

'Just take a look at the sketch for now,' I suggested.

'What am I going to see that I haven't already seen?'

'You used to know this man,' I said.

'I already told you he looks familiar, but—'

'You haven't seen him in thirty years. He was in his middle twenties when you knew him.'

He ran the numbers, frowned. 'He's forty-eight now, isn't he? Thirty years ago he would have been—'

'He lied about his age, either to be consistent with his fake ID or because he didn't want to be considered too old for the security-guard job. He must have taken eight or nine years off his real age. It's not the biggest lie he ever told.'

'God, I know him,' he said. 'I can picture his face, I can see him talking, I can almost hear the voice. Help me out, will you?'

'You know his name. It's part of your annual litany.'

'Part of our—'

'For years now,' I said, 'you all thought he was dead.'

'My God,' he said. 'It's him, isn't it?'

'You tell me, Ray.'

'It is,' he said. 'It's Severance.'

★

294

'I made a couple of stops on my way here,' I told him. 'I went over to Lew Hildebrand's apartment and caught him before he left for work. I saw Avery Davis at his office. They were both able to identify the sketch as James Severance. In fact Davis said he had already been struck by the killer's resemblance to Severance, and would have mentioned something except that he knew Severance was dead. Everybody knew it, and how could you possibly forget it? You've been reading his name all those years.'

'And he's not dead?'

'I went down to Washington yesterday,' I said. 'I went to see if his name was engraved on the Memorial down there.'

'And it wasn't?'

'No.'

'I'm not sure if that proves anything, Matt. Their accuracy's a long way from a hundred percent. People have been left off the Memorial, and guys who survived the war have found their names carved in stone. He could be carried on the books as MIA, he could have been overlooked in any number of ways—'

'He never served,' I said.

'He was never in Vietnam?'

'He was never in the service, period. I went to the Veterans Administration and I found somebody who knew somebody at the Pentagon. They did a pretty comprehensive check of the service records. He was never in any branch of the service. I don't know if he was ever called up, or if he even bothered to register for the draft. That would be harder to check, and I'm not sure there's any point to it. What's relevant is he didn't die in Vietnam, and he doesn't seem to have died anywhere else, either. Because he's still alive.'

'It seems impossible.'

'Avery Davis said it's like finding out at age thirty that you were adopted.'

'I know what he meant. I barely knew Severance. He never said much. I saw him once a year for a couple of years, and then he missed a dinner because he was in the army, and then the following year or the year after Homer read his name. And I've heard it read once a year ever since.'

'How did he get chosen for the club?'

'I don't know. Either he was somebody's friend or Homer found him all by himself. Did Lew or Avery—'

I shook my head. 'They met him for the first time at Cunningham's. And they didn't know how he got there. I wonder how he faked his death. How did you learn of it?'

'Let me think.' He took a sip of his hard-way coffee. 'God, it was a long time ago. I seem to remember Homer reading a letter from him, explaining that his heart was with us even though his body was wearing a uniform. And he hoped to be with us soon, and if anything happened to him he'd made arrangements for us to be notified.'

'He was setting you up.'

'I guess so. It must have been a year later that Homer read his name along with Phil Kalish's and explained that he'd received a telegram a couple of months before.'

'From whom?'

'I don't think he said. I suppose I assumed it was either from the army or from a relative of Severance's. Obviously it wasn't from either, no matter how it may have been signed. Severance sent it himself.'

'Yes.'

'Was he already planning to kill us?'

'Hard to say.'

'And why, for God's sake? What did we ever do to him?'

296

'I don't know,' I said. 'You know, I met him a few times. I sat across a table from him.'

'So you've said.'

'And I've met the surviving members, most of them, anyway. And it's hard to imagine him sitting down to dinner with the rest of you. I'll grant you that you've all worked hard and created successful lives for yourselves while he's been living in cheap hotels and eating in diners and holding subsistence jobs when he's worked at all. The different paths you've taken for the past thirty years would account for some of the difference, but I think he must have been different to start with.'

'Well, hell,' he said. 'I didn't like to say it when I regarded him as one of our honored dead, but I can say it now, can't I? He came across as a loser.'

'A loser.'

'A nobody, a nebbish. A guy who wasn't going to make the cut. You're right, he wasn't in our league. He didn't belong at the same table with the rest of us.'

'Maybe he realized that himself,' I said. 'Maybe it pissed him off.'

He wanted to speculate on Severance's motives, and what might have gone through his mind. Earlier, he said, before he had any idea who the killer was or what might be motivating him, it had struck him that the whole affair was a sort of collective form of erotomania, where a disturbed individual becomes fixated on someone, often a celebrity. 'Like that woman who kept breaking into David Letterman's house,' he said. 'Or the lunatic who killed John Lennon.'

'Afterward,' I said, 'there will be plenty of time to figure out what makes him tick.'

'Afterward?'

'After he's locked up,' I said. 'And I think it's time to

make sure that happens as soon as possible. I'm afraid I've gone about as far as I can go with this, Ray. I'm ready to turn it over to the professionals.'

'I never thought of you as an amateur.'

'I am when it comes to mounting an all-out manhunt. That's the way to catch him fast. Between the cops and the tabloids and *America's Most Wanted*, there's no way he'll be able to stay hidden.'

He looked at me. 'And what about us?'

'The club's story will come out,' I said. 'If that's what you mean. But there's no way to avoid that.'

'No?'

'I don't see how.'

He cupped his chin in his hand. 'Let's assume he's in New York,' he said. 'Do you think you could find him?'

'Without the police?'

'Without the police or the press.'

'I don't have their resources.'

'No, but you have other resources at your disposal. We could give you a substantial operating budget. And you could offer a reward.'

'It's not impossible,' I said. 'But you'd just be postponing the inevitable. The story would have to come out when he went to trial, and it would be every bit as sensational and get just as much of a play.'

'When he went to trial.'

'That's right.'

'And what do you suppose would happen at that trial? And afterward?'

'I'm not sure I follow you.'

'What would happen? What would be the outcome of the trial?'

'I suppose he'd get convicted of murder,' I said. 'Unless he had Hard-Way Ray for a lawyer.'

He laughed. 'No, I'm afraid he'd have to get along

without my services. But are you all that certain he'd be found guilty? Which killing do you suppose he'd stand trial for?'

'Billings is the most recent one.'

'And what's the evidence? Can you put him on the scene? Can you tie him to the car? Can you produce a murder weapon, let alone prove it was in his hand?'

'Once the police go to work on it—'

'They might have an eyewitness or two who can pick him out of a lineup,' he said, 'but I wouldn't count on it, and I don't have to tell you how little most eyewitness testimony is worth in a courtroom. Who else has he killed? Watson's widow? Watson himself? Can you prove any of that? We know he was on the scene, he discovered Alan's body, but where's your evidence?'

'What's your point?'

'My point is that a conviction is by no means a foregone conclusion. You can throw out the early cases entirely. He killed Boyd and Diana Shipton, he went down to Atlanta and shot Ned Bayliss, he hanged Hal Gabriel with his belt, God knows what else he did, and you can forget all of that because there's not going to be any way to prove it. And I seriously doubt you can convince a jury he killed anybody else, either.'

I recalled something Joe Durkin had said. 'It's a wonder anybody ever goes to jail for anything,' I said.

'I don't know about that,' he said. 'I think the system is generally pretty good at locking people up. Too good, sometimes. But that doesn't mean you can make a tight enough case against Severance to put him away. Hell, if you had the goods on him, he could probably plead insanity and make it stand up. He's devoted his life to a career of senseless systematic serial murder. You want to try to sell him to a jury as a model of mental health?'

'I can't even buy that myself.'

'Neither can I. I figure the bastard's nuts. I also figure he's done enough harm for one lifetime.'

I had an idea where this was going. I didn't much want to go there. I got the waiter's attention and had him refill my coffee cup.

Gruliow said, 'Say I'm wrong. He stands trial, they find him guilty on all counts, and he goes to prison.'

'Sounds good to me.'

'Does it? Obviously, it makes the club and all of its members the focus of a lot of unwelcomed publicity, but there's no avoiding that, is there? Maybe we'd survive as an institution. For my own part, I can't imagine ceasing to get together every May. But I hate to think how all that media attention would change things.'

'That's unfortunate, but—'

'But we're talking life and death here, and our desire to stay out of the spotlight is comparatively inconsequential. I can't argue with that. But let's take this a little further. What happens to Severance?'

'He stays in some maximum-security joint upstate for the rest of his life.'

'Think so?'

'I thought we were supposing he'd be found guilty. I don't think the court's going to slap his wrist and let him off with time served and five years' probation.'

'Let's assume he gets a life sentence. How much time would he serve?'

'That depends.'

'Seven years?'

'It could be a lot more than that.'

'Don't you think he could behave himself in prison? Don't you think he could convince the parole board that he's a changed man? Matt, the man's the most patient son of a bitch on God's earth. He's spent thirty years killing us and he's only a little more than halfway through. You think he won't be content to bide his time? They'll have him stamping out license plates and it'll just be another menial job, like working as a rent-a-cop in Queens. They'll stick him in a cell and it'll just be another in a long string of furnished rooms. What does he care how long he has to sit on his ass? He's been sitting on his ass for thirty years. Sooner or later they'll have to let him out, and do you think for one moment that he'll be magically rehabilitated?'

I looked at him.

'Well? Do you?'

'No, of course not.'

'He'll start in where he left off. By the time he gets out, Mother Nature will have done some of his work for him. There'll have been some thinning of the ranks. But some of us will be left, and what do you bet he comes after us? What do you bet he tries to pick us off one by one?'

I opened my mouth, then closed it without saying anything.

'You know I'm right,' he said.

'I know you've always opposed capital punishment.'

'Absolutely,' he said. 'Unequivocally.'

'That's not how you sound this morning.'

'I think it's regrettable that a man like Severance could ever be released from prison. That doesn't mean I think the state should go into the business of official murder.'

'I didn't think we were talking about the state.'

'Oh?'

'You want to apprehend him without involving the media or the police. I get the feeling you'd like to see sentence passed and carried out in much the same manner.'

'In other words?'

'You want me to find him and kill him for you,' I said. 'I won't do it.'

'I wouldn't ask you to.'

'I don't want to find him so you can kill him yourself, either. How would you do it? Draw straws to see who pulls the duty? Or string him up and have everybody pull on the rope?'

'What would you do?'

'Me?'

'In our position.'

'I was in your position once,' I said. 'There was a man named . . . well, never mind what his name was. The point is that he had sworn to kill me. He'd already killed a lot of other people. I don't know if I could have got him sent to prison, but I know they wouldn't have kept him there forever. Sooner or later they'd have had to let him out.'

'What did you do?'

'I did what I had to do.'

'You killed him?'

'I did what I had to do.'

'Do you regret it?'

'No.'

'Do you feel guilty?'

'No.'

'Would you do it again?'

'I suppose I would,' I said. 'If I had to.'

'So would I,' he said, 'if *I* had to. But that's not what I have in mind. I don't really believe in capital punishment whether it's the state or an individual who imposes the sentence.'

'I'm lost,' I said. 'You'll have to explain.'

'I intend to.' He drank some coffee. 'I've given this some thought,' he said, 'and I've talked to several of the others. How does this sound to you?'

I heard him out. I had a lot of questions and raised a lot of objections, but he had prepared well. I had no choice but to give him the verdict he wanted.

'It sounds crazy,' I said at length, 'and the cost—'

'That's not a problem.'

'Well, I don't have any moral objection to it,' I said. 'And it might work.'

THIRTY

The first week in August I got a call around one in the afternoon. Joe Durkin said, 'Matt, I'd like to talk to you. Why don't you come around the station house?'

'I'd be happy to,' I said. 'What would be a good time?'

'Now would be a good time,' he said.

I went straight over there, stopping en route for a couple of containers of coffee. I gave one to Joe and he lifted the lid and sniffed the steam. 'This'll spoil me,' he said. 'I've been getting used to squad-room coffee. What's this, French roast?'

'I don't know.'

'It smells great, whatever it is.'

He set it down, opened a drawer, took out one of the palm cards that had been circulating around town for a couple of weeks. It was on postcard stock and about the size of a standard postcard. One side was blank. The other showed James Severance as sketched by Ray Galindez. Beneath the sketch was a seven-digit telephone number.

'What's this?' he said, and flipped it across the desk to me.

'Looks like a postcard,' I said. I turned it over. 'Blank on the back. I guess you would write your message here and put the address over here on the right. The stamp would go in the corner.'

'That's your phone number under the picture.'

'So it is,' I said. 'But if the picture's supposed to be me, I'd have to say it's a lousy likeness.'

He reached to take the card from me, looked at me,

looked at it, looked at me again. 'Somehow,' he said, 'I don't think it's you.'

'Neither do I.'

'Whoever it is,' he said, 'I got a snitch tells me the guy's picture's all over the street. Nobody knows who he is or why somebody's looking for him. So I figured I'd call the number and ask.'

'And?'

'And I'm asking.'

'Well,' I said, 'it's in connection with a case I'm working on.'

'No kidding.'

'And the subject of the sketch might be an important witness.'

'Witness to what?'

'I can't say.'

'What did you do, take holy orders? You're bound by the seal of the confessional?'

'I was hired by an attorney,' I said, 'and what was told to me comes under the umbrella of attorney-client privilege.'

'Who hired you?'

'Raymond Gruliow.'

'Raymond Gruliow.'

'That's right.'

'Hard-Way Ray.'

'I've heard him called that, come to think of it.'

He took another look at the sketch. 'Guy looks familiar,' he said.

'That's what everybody says.'

'What's his name? That can't be confidential.'

'If we knew his name,' I said, 'he'd be a lot easier to find.'

'A witness saw him and sat down with an artist, and that's where the sketch came from.'

'Something like that.'

'I understand there's a reward.'

I looked at the palm card. 'Funny,' I said. 'It doesn't say anything here about a reward.'

'I heard ten grand.'

'That's a lot of money.'

'It seems like a lot to me,' he said, 'when I think of what I've done for the price of a hat. What's funny is you never brought the sketch around here.'

'I didn't think you'd recognize him. You don't, do you?'

'No.'

'So there wouldn't have been much point in showing you the sketch.'

He gave me a long look. He said, 'When there's that much of a reward for somebody, it's generally somebody who doesn't want to be found.'

'Oh, I don't know,' I said. 'What about that little boy who disappeared in SoHo? There were reward posters all over the place.'

'That's a point. There aren't any posters with this fellow, are there?'

'I haven't seen any.'

'Just cards you can tuck away out of sight. Nothing on the lampposts or mailboxes, nothing tacked up on bulletin boards. Just a lot of cards circulating quietly around the neighborhoods.'

'It's a low-budget operation, Joe.'

'With a five-figure reward.'

'If you say so,' I said, 'but I still don't see anything here about a reward.'

'No, neither do I. This is good coffee.'

'I'm glad you like it.'

'Last time we talked,' he said, 'you were looking into all these old cases. That painter and his wife, that gay guy

306

who got more than he bargained for, that cabbie who picked up the wrong fare. Remember?'

'As if it were yesterday.'

'I'll bet. This guy here tied in with them?'

'How could he be?'

'Why do you always answer a question with a question?'

'Do I have to have a reason?'

'Fucking smartass. What's the status of those old cases, anyway?'

'As far as I can tell,' I said, 'they're all still dead.'

The waiting was hard to take.

We got the word out on the street a good ten days before I heard from Joe Durkin. I started with a few people like Danny Boy Bell who are professionally adept at spreading and gathering information, and I gave each of them a sheaf of palm cards bearing Severance's likeness and my phone number. TJ went to work on Forty-second Street, spreading the word among the people he knew on and around the Deuce and working the cheap hotels and SRO rooming houses in the neighborhood. Gruliow made a few phone calls and sent me off to see various criminals and political outcasts he'd defended over the years. Of one he said, 'This one hugged me after the trial and said to call him if I ever wanted somebody killed. I've been tempted a few times, believe me. It's a good thing I don't believe in capital punishment, not even for ex-wives.'

I was pretty sure he'd go to ground in Manhattan. If he'd ever lived outside the borough, I didn't know about it. In all the months he'd stalked Alan Watson, patrolling his streets in a Queensboro-Corona uniform, even (if he was telling the truth) having an affair with Watson's wife, he'd chosen to live in Manhattan. He could have found a cheaper and more comfortable room a few blocks from the Q-C offices, or within easy walking distance of Watson's Forest Hills home. But he'd moved instead to East Ninety-fourth Street. He'd have had to take two trains to get to work, and two more to get home.

So I centered the manhunt in Manhattan, and I put the most energy into those parts of town where someone like Severance wouldn't stick out like a white thumb. I hit the places that called themselves hotels or rooming houses, and I went to lunch counters and drugstores and asked if they knew where I could find a room for rent, because every neighborhood has some SRO hotels that don't hang out a sign.

And we left palm cards in delis and bodegas, too, and in shoeshine parlors and ginmills and numbers drops. And then it was time to sit back and wait, time to be home in case the phone rang, and that's when it got difficult.

Because it's easier when you're doing something. Sitting in my room at the Northwestern, watching a ball game or a newscast, reading a book or a newspaper, staring out the window, I couldn't avoid the thought that it was all misplaced effort, all a waste of time.

He didn't have to be in Manhattan. He could be lying on a beach in California, biding his time, waiting for the New York heat to die down. He could be in Jersey or Connecticut, stalking one of the club's suburban members. While I sat here, waiting for the phone to ring, he'd be sighting his target and making his kill.

The day after I spoke to Durkin, I picked up the phone and called Lisa Holtzmann.

I didn't even think about it. I had the phone in my hand and was dialing her number without having made any conscious decision. The phone rang four times and her machine picked up. I rang off without leaving a message.

The following afternoon I called her. 'I was thinking of you,' I told her, but I don't even know if that was true. She told me to come over, and I went.

Two days later I went to the 8:30 meeting at St Paul's. I left on the break and called her from a pay phone on the corner. No, she said, she wasn't busy. Yes, she felt like company.

In her bed that night, she lay beside me and told me that she was still seeing the art director for the airline magazine. 'I've been to bed with him,' she said.

'He's a lucky man.'

'I don't know why I bother planning conversations in my head. You never say what I expect you to say. Do you really think he's a lucky man? Because I don't.'

'Why not?'

'Because I'm such a whore. I saw him the night before last. You came over during the afternoon, and then I went out to dinner with him that night. And brought him home and fucked him. I was still sore from the afternoon but I went ahead and fucked him anyway.'

I didn't say anything and neither did she. Through her window I could see New Jersey all lit up like a Christmas tree. After a long moment I reached out and touched her. At first I could feel her trying to hold herself in check, but then she let go and allowed herself to respond, and I went on touching her until she cried out and clung to me.

Afterward I said, 'Am I screwing up your life, Lisa? Tell me and I'll stop.'

'Ha.'

'I mean it.'

'I know you do. And no, you're not. I'm screwing up my own life. Like everybody else.'

'I guess.'

'Someday you'll stop calling me. Or someday you'll call and I'll tell you no, I don't want you to come over.' She took my hand, placed it on her breast. 'But not yet,' she said.

The days came and went and the summer slipped away. Elaine and I got out to a few movies and listened to some jazz. I went to meetings and, a day at a time, I didn't pick up a drink.

Wally called, but I told him I couldn't take on any per diem work, not until I cleared the case I was working on.

On Sundays I had dinner with my sponsor. Now and then I dropped in at Grogan's, usually after a midnight AA meeting. I would sit for an hour or so with Mick, and we always managed to find things to talk about. But we never made a long night of it, and I was always home well before sunrise.

A friend of Elaine's invited us out to East Hampton for the weekend, and I didn't feel I could afford to put myself a couple of hours away from the city. I told her to go by herself, and she thought it over and went. Perversely, I didn't call Lisa at all that weekend. I did go out for dinner with Ray Gruliow, to a seafood restaurant he liked. They didn't have his brand of Irish whiskey, but he made do with something less exotic, and drank a hell of a lot of it in the course of the evening.

I wound up telling him about Lisa. I'm not sure why. He said, 'Well, what do you know? The guy's human.'

'Was the issue in doubt?'

'No,' he said, 'not really. But I thought people quit doing that sort of thing when they joined AA.'

'So did I.'

'So we were both wrong. Well, that's good to hear. And good for you, my friend. You know the four things a man needs to sustain life, don't you?' I didn't. 'Food, shelter, and pussy.' That was only three, I said. 'And strange pussy,' he said. 'That's four.'

He was good company until the booze took him over the line, and then he started telling me the same story over and over again. It was a pretty good story, but I didn't need to hear it more than once. I put him in a cab and went home.

The Yankees were making it interesting in the American League East, winning a lot of games but having trouble gaining ground on the Blue Jays. In the other league, the Mets had last place pretty well sewn up. We stayed in the city for Labor Day, and Elaine kept the shop open the whole weekend.

On a Thursday afternoon in the middle of September, I was sitting in my hotel room watching it rain. The phone rang.

A woman said, 'Is this the man looking for the man in the picture?'

There had been calls from time to time. Who was the man in the picture? What did I want with him? Was it true about the reward?

'Yes,' I said. 'I'm the man.'

'You really gonna pay me that money?'

I held my breath.

''Cause I seen him,' she said. 'I know right where he's at.'

THIRTY-ONE

Two hours later I was in a Laundromat on the corner of Manhattan Avenue and 117th Street, next door to a Haitian storefront church. I had TJ with me, dressed in khakis and a light green polo shirt and carrying his clipboard. The manager was a short, squat woman in her sixties with unconvincing yellow hair and a European accent. It was she who had called me, and I had a hard time convincing her that she would indeed get ten thousand dollars when we had the man on the palm card in custody, but nothing if he gave us the slip. She wanted more than a promise before she parted with her information, and I could see her point. I gave her two hundred dollars up front and made her sign a receipt for it, and I think it was the receipt that convinced her, because why would I want anything on paper if I planned to stiff her? She took four fifties from me, folded them together, tucked them in a pocket of her apron and secured them there with a safety pin. Then she took me to the window and pointed diagonally across the street.

The building she indicated was a seven-story apartment house built sometime before the First World War. The façade was in good repair, and there were plants hanging in some of the windows. It didn't look like any SRO I'd ever seen.

But she was sure that was where he lived. He had come in at least once before, and afterward she had remembered the card someone had given her and found it in a drawer, and sure enough, it was him. So she almost called the number, but what was she going to say? She didn't know his name or where he lived. And if she said anything to anybody, how could she be sure she was the one who wound up with the reward?

So she'd said nothing, electing to wait for him to return. Laundry, after all, was not a one-time occurrence. You washed your clothes, sooner or later you would have to wash them again. Every day she looked at the sketch on the card to make sure she would know him if she saw him again. She was starting to think maybe it wasn't really him, and then today he'd come in with a laundry bag and a box of Tide, and it was him, all right. No question. He looked just like his picture.

She almost made the call while his clothes were spinning around, first in the washing machine, then in the dryer. But how could she make sure she was the one who collected the reward? So she'd let him sit there, his face buried in the newspaper, until his wash was done. When he left, she slipped out the door and followed him. She left the Laundromat unattended, risking her job in the process. Suppose the owner stopped in while she was gone? Suppose there was an incident in her absence?

But she wasn't gone long. She followed her quarry a block and a half uptown and waited across the street while he stopped in a deli. He came out moments later carrying a shopping bag in addition to his sack of clean clothes, and he turned back in the direction he'd come from, and wound up entering the apartment house diagonally across the street from her Laundromat.

From the doorway of the apartment house, she watched him get on the elevator, watched the doors close behind him. There was a panel of numbers above the elevator that lit up when the car was moving to show you what floor it was on. She couldn't make it out from the entrance, but when the elevator had finished its ascent she walked through the unattended lobby and pressed the button to summon it. The 5 lit up right away.

'So he's on the fifth floor,' she said. 'I don't know which apartment.'

And she thought he was there now. She couldn't swear to it, because she had a job to do, making change for people, washing and drying and folding clothes for customers who paid extra to drop their laundry with her and pick it up later. So she'd been unable to spend every moment watching the entrance of his building, but she'd watched it as much as she could, and she hadn't seen him leave.

I stayed in the Laundromat, not wanting to risk running into him in the lobby or being spotted from a fifth-floor window, while TJ checked the bells and mailboxes. He came back with a list of the fifth-floor tenants. There were twelve apartments on the fifth floor, and there was a nameplate in every doorbell and mailbox slot. None of the surnames began with an *S*.

I slipped out the door with my face averted, walked to the corner of 116th Street, then crossed the street and walked back to the building where Severance had been spotted. I rang the super's bell, and a voice came over the static-ridden intercom. I said, 'Investigation. Like to talk to you.' He told me to come to the basement and buzzed me through the door.

I rode down on the elevator, walked past a padlock door marked LAUNDRY and another marked STORAGE. At the end of the corridor was an open door. Inside a white-haired man was watching television and drinking coffee. His hands were arthritic, their backs dark with liver spots. I showed him the sketch and he didn't recognize it at first. I said I believed the gentleman was living on the fifth floor. 'Oh,' he said, and got out a pair of reading glasses and took another look.

'I didn't place him at first,' he said. 'It's Silverman.'

'Silverman?'

'Five-K. Subletting from the Tierneys.'

Kevin Tierney was on the faculty at Columbia, his wife a teacher at a private school in the West Eighties. The two had the summer off and were spending it in Greece and Turkey. Shortly before they left, they had introduced Joel Silverman as a friend who would be staying in their apartment.

'But he wasn't no friend of theirs,' he said. 'All that month they were bringing people in, showing the place. They didn't want to notify the landlord and sublet formally, so as soon as somebody took the place he becomes their friend, if you take my meaning. Tierney gave me a couple bucks to look the other way, which was decent of him, no question, but it shows you where he's coming from, don't it?'

And what kind of tenant was Silverman?

'I never see him. That's why I didn't recognize him right off, not until you said fifth floor. No complaints from him, no complaints about him. Be okay with me if they were all like him.'

If I'd been a cop, with a warrant and some backup and a Kevlar vest, I would have gone right in. I'd have put a man on the fire escape and others on the exits, and gone through the door with a gun in my hand.

Instead we waited across the street at the Laundromat. TJ and I took turns keeping an eye on the entrance across the street, and on the one set of 5-K's windows that were visible from our vantage point. TJ kept coming up with stratagems for gaining access to the apartment. He could pose as a delivery boy, as a student of Professor Tierney's, as an exterminator come to spray for roaches. I told him we'd just wait.

Shortly before sunset a light came on in Severance's window. I was on the phone when it happened, and TJ pointed it out to me. Now we knew that he was still in there, that he hadn't slipped out before we reached the scene, or while we were looking the other way.

TJ went around the corner and brought back pizza and a couple of Cokes. I made another telephone call. The light went out across the street.

TJ said, 'What's that mean? He goin' to sleep?'

'Too early.'

Five minutes later he was standing in front of his building, wearing a T-shirt and a pair of army fatigues. His hair was cut shorter than the last time I'd seen him, but it was unmistakably him.

'Go,' I told TJ.

'You got the beeper?'

'I've got everything. Try to keep him in sight, but I'd rather have you lose him than let him spot you. If you do lose him, beep me and let me know. You know the code.'

'Got it all writ down.'

'After you beep me, come back here where you can watch the entrance. Beep me again when you see him come home. It's no big deal if you lose him, but try not to let him spot you.'

He grinned. He said, 'Hey, don't worry, Murray. Nobody spots the Shadow.'

I'd acquired a set of keys from the super, easing his conscience with cash. One of them let me into the building. The other two opened the dead-bolt locks on the door of apartment 5-K. I let myself into the darkened apartment, drew the door shut, and refastened the locks.

Without turning on any lights, I moved around the apartment, getting a feel of the place. There was a good-sized living room, a small bedroom, a windowed kitchen, and an office in what must originally have been a smaller second bedroom.

I sat down and waited.

The time would have passed faster if I could have read a book from the Tierneys' enormous library, but I didn't want to risk a light in the window. I left the television set off for the same reason. The boredom was part of the territory, but fatigue was a problem. My mind drifted, and my eyes kept wanting to close. I went into the kitchen, looking for something that might keep me awake, and found a half-full sack of unground coffee beans in the refrigerator. I stuck a handful in my pocket, chewing one from time to time. I don't know what did more for me, the caffeine or the bitter taste, but one way or another my eyes stayed open.

Some forty-five minutes after I got there, TJ's beeper sounded. We'd worked out a whole system of two-digit signals, but he'd punched in a whole seven-digit number. I picked up the phone and dialed it.

He answered the instant it rang. His voice pitched low, he said, 'We in the movies. I followed him over to Broadway an' down. You know how people keep lookin' over their shoulders, seein' if they bein' followed? He didn't do that.'

'It's probably a good thing.'

''Cept I thought maybe he's bein' slick. Maybe he just goin' to duck into the movies and then slip out a side exit. Minute he bought the large-size popcorn I knew I didn't have to worry. Man's in for the duration, Jason.'

'You're in the theater?'

'Phone in the lobby. I went in, saw where he's sittin'. Soon's I hang up I'll go back where I can keep an eye on

317

him. Won't be keepin' no eye on the screen, tell you that. You know what he had to see?'

'What?'

'*Jurassic Park.*'

'You already saw that, didn't you?'

'Seen it twice. Man, I so sick of dinosaurs. They wasn't extinct, I'd go out an' kill 'em myself.'

The show was scheduled to break at 10:15, and we added a new signal to our battery of codes. At twenty after ten the beeper sounded and I saw that he'd punched in 5–6, indicating that they had left the theater. In the course of the next hour he beeped me three times, each time with the same code, 2–4, indicating he was still in contact with Severance. Another beep came at ten to twelve, and the 1–1 meant Severance was entering the building.

I switched off the beeper. I didn't want it making any sounds. I moved to a chair to the left of the doorway.

I got out the gun, the one I'd been carrying since I got the first call that afternoon. I turned it over in my hands, trying to get accustomed to the feel of it.

I put it in my lap and sat there, waiting.

I was listening carefully but I didn't hear any footsteps. The hallway was carpeted and I guess that must have muffled them, because the first warning I had of his presence was the sound of his key in the lock. He opened one lock, and then there was a long pause, just long enough for me to wonder if he'd somehow sensed something. Then I heard his key again and he opened the second lock. I watched the doorknob turn, watched as the door opened inward.

He came in, reached automatically to switch on the overhead light, turned automatically to lock the door behind him.

I said, 'Severance!'

He spun toward the sound of my voice. I had the gun raised, and as he came around to face me I aimed it at his middle and gave the trigger a squeeze. It made the sound of a small twig snapping.

He looked at me, then down at his chest. A three-inch dart hung from his T-shirt. His hand groped for it in slow motion. The fingers would not quite close on the dart. He tried, God how he tried, but he couldn't do it.

Then his eyes glazed over and he fell.

I got another dart from the case, loaded the pistol. I stood watching him for a few minutes, then bent over him to check his pulse and respiration. I had brought two sets of handcuffs and I used them both, cuffing his hands together behind his back, cuffing his feet together with the chain looped around a table leg.

I went over and picked up the phone.

THIRTY-TWO

When he woke up I was the first thing he saw. I was sitting on a folding metal chair. He was lying on a mattress atop a low plywood platform. His hands and one leg were free, but there was a thick steel cuff fastened around one ankle. A chain was attached to it, its other end anchored to a plate in the floor.

'Matt,' he said. 'How'd you find me?'

'You weren't that hard to find.'

'I spend two hours watching dinosaurs, I walk in the door, and whammo! What did you get me with, a tranquilizer dart?'

'That's right.'

'Jesus, how long was I out? Couple of hours, it must have been.'

'Longer than that, Jim.'

' "Jim." That's not what you called me just before you shot me.'

'No.'

'You called me another name.'

'I called you Severance.'

'Any point in pretending I don't know what you're talking about?'

'Not really.'

'Of course if there's a tape recorder running—'

'There's not.'

'Because I don't remember anybody reading me my rights.'

'Nobody did.'

'Maybe you ought to, huh?'

'Why? You're not under arrest. You haven't been charged with anything.'

'No? What are you waiting for?'

'There's not going to be a trial.'

'I get it. You son of a bitch, why didn't you use a real gun? Why not get it over with?' He sat up, or started to, and noticed the chain on his leg. With the discovery came the realization that he wasn't still lying on an Oriental carpet in the Tierneys' apartment in Morning-side Heights.

He said, 'What's this, fucking leg irons? Where the hell am I?'

'Red Hawk Island.'

'Red Hook's no island. It's just a bad part of town.'

'Red Hawk, not Hook. It's a small island in Georgian Bay.'

'Where the fuck is Georgian Bay?'

'In Canada,' I said. 'It's an arm of Lake Huron. We're a couple of hundred miles due north of Cleveland.'

'You're telling me a story, right?'

'Sit up, Jim. Look out the window.'

He swung his legs over the side of the bed, sat up, got to his feet. 'Whew,' he said, sitting down again. 'Little groggy.'

'That's the drugs.'

He stood again, and this time he stayed on his feet. Dragging the chain, he walked over to the room's single window. 'Pine trees,' he said. 'There's a fucking forest out there.'

'Well, it's not Central Park.'

He turned to face me. 'What the hell is this? How'd we get here?'

'A couple of men carried you out of the Tierney apartment on a stretcher. They loaded you into the backseat of a limousine. You were driven to a private airport in Westchester County, where they transferred you to a private plane. There's a small landing strip here on Red Hawk Island, and that's where we touched down. That was around noon when we got here, twelve hours or so after you came home from the movie. It's almost five in the afternoon now. You've been kept unconscious with injections while we got everything ready for you.'

'And what's this? A cabin?'

I nodded. 'There's a main house and several out-buildings. This is one of the outbuildings. The floor's poured concrete, in case you were wondering, and the metal plate you're chained to is anchored solidly in it. In case you were wondering.'

'Message: I ain't going nowhere.'

'Something like that.'

He went back to the bed and sat down on it. 'Lot to go through to kill a guy,' he said.

'Look who's talking.'

'Huh?'

'Look at all you went through,' I said, 'to kill all those men. Why, Jim?'

He was silent for a moment. Then he said, 'You called me Jim all along. That's the name you met me under, Jim Shorter. It's funny, 'cause that was the one name I stayed away from. For years I'd pick different names, always the same initials, but never Jim, never James. I used Joe a few times, John, Jack. I was Jeremy on one occasion. And Jeffrey, I was Jeffrey when I got Carl Uhl. "Oh, God, Jeff, what are you doing!" He begged for his life, that cocksucker.' His grin was quick and nasty. 'All sorts of different names. But I didn't use the name I was born with once in all that time. Then finally I figured why not, what's it gonna hurt? So the name you met me under, it turned out to be my real name. The first name, anyway.'

322

'What got you started?'

'Why the hell should I tell you a fucking thing?'

'It's been a lot of years,' I said. 'Isn't it about time you told somebody?'

'A lot of years. I got a bunch of 'em, didn't I?'

'Yes, you did.'

'I shoulda just disappeared, you know? Time I met you, I already had this place rented.'

'This place?'

'Can you believe it? I think I'm still back on Manhattan Avenue. I already had it arranged to sublet Tierney's apartment. I was just waiting for them to get on the plane. Soon as that happened, goodbye Jim Shorter, hello Joel Silverman. He's a nice Jewish boy, Joel is. You know you can trust him to water your plants and not piss on your carpet.' He laughed. 'Then you turned up. I couldn't disappear right away, not the way I'd planned. I had to wait for you to lose interest. But instead of shining you on and getting rid of you, I let you take me to a fucking AA meeting. Can you believe that?'

'And one meeting changed your life.'

'Yeah, right, just like those lamebrains telling their stories. All of a sudden you're calling me on the phone, I'm calling you on the phone, and how do I get you off my back and quit being Jim Shorter? First I went and did Helen in Forest Hills, because that wasn't a load of shit about having an affair with her. Widows are pretty easy targets, you know. She's not the first I got next to after I did the husband. There was a guy named Bayliss you wouldn't even know was one of mine—'

'In a hotel room in Atlanta.'

'Yeah, well, I looked up the wife afterward. Same thing with Helen, such a shock discovering your husband's body, blah blah blah, next thing you know she's got her knees up and I'm slippin' her the salami. I don't know if I can explain what a pleasure it was. It's like killing the husband a second time.'

'And then you killed Helen.'

'I thought I could keep you from finding out. You were talking about going out to see her, so I figured I'd better see her first. Then afterward I thought, shit, even a good accident's suspicious. You got to know I'm good at doing accidents. I realized I had to pull the plug on Jim Shorter and disappear, and the hell with whether or not you figured it out. So I thought let's go out with a bang, let's be dramatic, and I got that fucking clown of a weatherman.'

'Gerry Billings.'

'Asshole. Chirpy little fucker with his bow ties and his million-dollar smile. The look on his face when I shot him. He bought the scene, you know. Thought it was a traffic accident and he was an innocent bystander who was getting shot for no reason at all. I was praying he'd recognize me and go out knowing, but I didn't have time to waste so I just shot him and got it the fuck over with.'

'Why kill them, Jim?'

'You think I need a reason?'

'I think you've got one.'

'Why should I tell you?'

'I don't know,' I said, 'but I think you probably will.'

He hated them from the start.

Bunch of self-satisfied bastards. Eating and drinking and running their mouths, and he sat there among them and wondered what he was doing there. Whose idea had it been to invite him? What made anybody think he fit in?

Crazy, too. Bunch of grown men sitting around and waiting to die. The whole idea of dying made him sick to

324

his stomach. He didn't like to think about it. Everybody died, death was out there waiting for everyone, but did that mean he had to think about it?

He was shaking when he left Cunningham's that first night back in 1961. If there was one thing he was clear on, it was that he was done with this group of fruitcakes. They could meet next year without him. He was done. Let 'em read his name or burn his name, whatever the fuck they wanted, because he was through with the whole deal. Luckily they hadn't made him sign his name in blood, or swear an oath on the head of his mother, or any of the usual secret-society mumbo jumbo. They had let him in, God knows why, and he could let himself out. And don't bother to show me to the door, thank you very much, but I can find my own way out.

But he went back the next year. He hadn't planned on it, but when the time came something made him go.

It was just as bad. Most of the talk concerned the progress they'd made since the last dinner — the promotions, the raises, the goddamn successes all over the place. The following year was more of the same, and he decided that was it, he was finished.

Then Phil Kalish died and excitement went through him like an electrical charge. I beat you, he thought. You were smarter and taller and better-looking, you were making good money, you had a wife and a family, and where did it get you? Because you're dead and I'm alive, you son of a bitch.

And wasn't that the point of it, staying alive? Wasn't that what they got together to celebrate? That they were alive and the ones who weren't there were dead?

So he went to the dinner in 1964 and heard Phil Kalish's name read. And he looked around the room and wondered who would be next.

That's when he started planning. He wasn't sure he

was going to do anything, but in the meantime he could set the stage.

The first thing to do was die. He thought of a lot of ways to do it, most of them involving killing somebody and planting his identification on the corpse. But Vietnam was starting to heat up, and that was easy. He called Homer Champney and explained that his reserve unit had been called up and he couldn't make it back to the city for the dinner. He wasn't in the reserves, he'd never been in the army or the National Guard, a psychiatric evaluation had kept him out, which showed what they knew, the idiots, because he had turned out to be a far better killer than the people they took in. He phoned again, the week before the dinner, to report that he was being sent overseas.

By the following year he'd died in combat. The night of the dinner he went to a movie on Forty-second Street and thought how they'd be reading his name along with Kalish's, and they'd all say nice mournful things about him, and every one of the cocksuckers'd be glad it was him and not them.

A lot they knew.

He took plenty of time setting up the first one. He took his time with each of them, wondering how many of them he could do before they started to get suspicious. Well, they were down to fourteen men before anybody suspected a thing. More than half of them gone, although not all of them were his doing, not by any means.

But most of them were. And each time, all through the planning and the preliminary steps, he felt really alive, really in charge of his life. And then when he did it, well, actually doing it was pretty exciting, because it was dangerous and you had to be careful nothing went wrong.

Once it was done, though, it was sort of sad.

Not that he mourned for them. Fuck 'em, they deserved what they got. And it was wonderfully satisfying, because each time it was one more down and he was still standing, and he'd beaten another of the bastards.

No, what was sad was that it was over. A cat probably felt the same way when the mouse she was playing with finally gave up the ghost and died. You got to eat your dinner, but the game was over. Kind of bittersweet, you could call it.

That's why he was stretching it out. That's why he'd taken so many years instead of knocking them off at the rate of one a month. He'd kept them from finding out for a long time, and now they knew, and in a way that made it even better, because what could they do about it? Gerard Billings had known, and what good did it do him?

They wore the best clothes, and they ate at the best restaurants, and they got their names in the paper. Expensive dentists kept their teeth white and expensive doctors kept them feeling fit, and they got their suntans on expensive beaches. And this was their game, not his, and he was beating them at it. Because someday they'd all be dead, and he'd be alive.

'Except I guess I lose,' he said. 'You're gonna kill me.'

'No.'

'Then someone else'll do it for you. What's the matter, you don't want to get your hands dirty? That's why they hired you, 'cause I know those fucks wouldn't get *their* hands dirty, but what's your problem that you got to pass the buck? I'm ashamed of you, Matt. I thought you had more to you than that.'

'Nobody's going to kill you, Jim.'

'You expect me to believe that?'

'Believe what you want,' I said. 'In an hour or so I'm getting back on the plane with the other fellows.'

'And?'

'And you're staying here.'

'What are you trying to say?'

'You haven't been arrested,' I said, 'and you haven't been charged, and there won't be a trial. But sentence has been passed, and it's a life sentence with no possibility of parole. I hope you like this room, Jim. You're going to spend the rest of your life in it.'

'You're just going to leave me here?'

'That's right.'

'Shackled like this? I'll fucking starve.'

I shook my head. 'You'll have food and water. Red Hawk Island is the property of Avery Davis. He comes here once a year to fish for smallmouth bass. The rest of the time there's nobody here except for the family of Cree Indians who live here and maintain the place. One of them will bring your meals to you.'

'What about keeping myself clean? What about using the toilet, for Christ's sake?'

'Behind you,' I said. 'A toilet and a washbasin. I'm afraid you'll be limited to sponge baths, and you won't be changing your clothes much. There's another jumpsuit like the one you're wearing and that's the extent of your wardrobe. See the snaps along the inseam? That's so you can get the suit on and off without unfastening the ankle cuff.'

'Great.'

I watched his eyes. I said, 'I don't think it'll work, Jim.'

'What are you talking about?'

'You think you'll be able to get out. I don't think you will.'

'Whatever you say, Matt.'

'The Cree family has worked for Davis for twenty

328

years. I don't think you're going to be able to bribe them or con them. You can't slip the shackle or open it, and you can't get the metal plate out of the concrete slab.'

'Then I guess I'm stuck here.'

'I guess you are. You can vandalize your cell, but it won't do you any good. If you break the glass out of the window, it won't be replaced – and it can get pretty cold here. If you wreck the toilet you'll get to smell your own waste. If you find a way to start a fire, well, Davis has instructed his employees to let the place burn down around you. No one's greatly concerned about saving your life.'

'Why not kill me?'

'Your fellow club members don't want your blood on their hands. But they don't want any more of their blood on your hands, either. There's no appeal from this sentence, Jim. No time off for good behavior. You stay here until you die. Then you'll wind up in an unmarked grave, and they'll start reading your name again at the annual dinners.'

'You son of a bitch,' he said.

I didn't say anything.

'You can't keep me caged like an animal,' he said. 'I'll get out.'

'Maybe you will.'

'Or I'll kill myself. It shouldn't be too hard to figure out a way.'

'It won't be hard at all,' I said. I took a matchbox from my pocket, tossed it to him. He picked it up from the bed and looked at it, puzzled. I told him to open it. He picked up the contents, held it between his thumb and fore-finger.

'What's this?'

'A capsule,' I said. 'Courtesy of Dr Kendall McGarry. He had it made up for you. It's cyanide.'

'What am I supposed to do with it?'

'Just bite down on it and your troubles are over. Or if that doesn't appeal to you—'

I pointed to a corner of the room. He didn't see it at first. 'Higher,' I said, and he raised his eyes and saw the noose dangling from the ceiling.

'If you drag a chair over there and stand on it,' I said, 'it ought to be just the right height. Then kick the chair out of the way. It should do for you as well as the belt in the closet door did for Hal Gabriel.'

'You bastard,' he said.

I stood up. 'There's no way out,' I said. 'That's the bottom line, and it's the only thing you really have to know. Sooner or later you'll probably try to trick the Cree guard, figuring you can knock him out or over-power him. But that won't do you any good. You can't force him to release you because he couldn't manage it if his life depended on it. He doesn't have a key. There is no key. The cuff's not locked around your ankle, it's welded. You'd need a torch or a laser to get through it, and there's no such thing on the island.'

'There has to be a way.'

'Well, you could chew your foot off,' I said. 'That's what a fox or a wolverine would do, but I don't know how well it works for them, or how far they get before they bleed to death. I don't think you've got the teeth for it. Failing that, you can try the rope or the capsule.'

'I wouldn't give you the satisfaction.'

'I wonder. Personally, I think you'll kill yourself. I don't think you'll be able to stay like this for too long, not with a quick exit that close to hand. But maybe I'm wrong. Hell, maybe you'll get what you've wanted all along. Maybe you'll outlive everybody. Maybe you'll be the last one left alive.'

★

When I got back to the main house, Davis and Gruliow were having a drink. I looked at the bottle and the two glasses of amber whiskey and it seemed like a perfectly wonderful idea. It was a thought I chose not to entertain. The pilot was drinking coffee, and I poured myself a cup.

Well before sunset we were on the plane and in the air. I closed my eyes for a minute, and the next thing I knew Ray Gruliow was shaking me awake and we were on the ground again in Westchester.

THIRTY-THREE

When the dust had settled I took Elaine to a high-style vegetarian restaurant on Ninth Avenue in Chelsea. The room was comfortable and the service thoughtful, and, remarkably enough, it was possible to spend a hundred dollars on dinner for two without having anything that ever crept or swam or flew.

Afterward we walked down to the Village and had espresso at a sidewalk café. I said, 'I figured a few things out. I'm fifty-five years old. I don't have to knock myself out trying to be the next Allan Pinkerton. I'll go ahead and get my PI license, but I'm not going to rent an office and hire people to work for me. I've been getting by for the past twenty years doing it my way. I don't want to change it.'

'If it ain't broke—'

'Well, *I've* been broke,' I said, 'from time to time. But something always turns up.'

'And always will.'

'Let's hope so. Here's something else I decided. I don't want to put off the things I really want to do. You've been to Europe what, three times?'

'Four.'

'Well, I've never been, and I'd like to get over there before I have to use a walker. I want to go to London and Paris.'

'I think that's a great idea.'

'They gave me a nice bonus,' I said. 'So as soon as the check cleared I went to a travel agent and booked a trip. I figured I'd better spend the money right away.'

'Otherwise you might piss it away on necessities.'

'That was my thinking. Our flight leaves JFK a week from Monday. We'll be gone for fifteen days. That gives us a week in each city. It'll mean closing the shop, but—'

'Oh, screw the shop. It's my shop. I ought to be able to decide when to close up. God, this is exciting! I promise I won't pack too much. We'll travel light.'

'Yeah, sure.'

'You've heard that song before, huh? I'll *try* to travel light. How's that?'

'Pack all you want,' I said. 'It's your honeymoon, so why shouldn't you have whatever you want with you?'

She looked at me.

'We keep saying we're going to get married,' I said, 'and we keep not quite getting around to it. Trying to figure out where to have the wedding and who to invite and every other damn thing. Here's what I want to do, if it's okay with you. I want to go down to City Hall Monday morning and have the standard three-minute ceremony. Twenty-four hours later we'll be landing at Heathrow.'

'You're full of surprises, aren't you?'

'What do you say?'

She put her hand on mine. 'In the words of Gary Gilmore,' she said, ' "Let's do it." '

In Paris, drinking the same kind of coffee at the same sort of café on the Rive Gauche, I found myself talking about James Severance. 'I keep seeing him sitting there,' I said. 'Sitting on the edge of his bed with a chain on his leg, and over his shoulder I could see the noose dangling from a hook in the ceiling beam.'

'Rumpelstiltskin,' she said. 'The evil dwarf. What did that mean, anyway? Did he tell you?'

'He probably would have, if I'd thought to ask him. I

forgot. But I think I know what he meant. In the story, the dwarf told the girl he'd let her off the hook if she guessed his name. In other words, if you know my name then you have the power. If I looked at all the names he used over the years I'd see the pattern of the initials, and then I'd know who he was.'

'But you got there backwards, didn't you? First you learned who he was, and then you figured out what the clue meant. Some clue.'

'I don't think it was supposed to lead me anywhere.'

'Why do you think he gave it to you?'

'To feel powerful. The man in control, handing out clues like alms, and feeling superior to the beggars standing around with their hands out.'

'I suppose,' she said. 'What do you think he'll do?'

'I don't know. Kill himself, I guess. How long can you stay there before you stick your neck in the noose and step off into the air?'

'It seems so cruel,' she said.

'I know, and if there'd been a more humane alternative I would have argued for it. The noose was my idea, that and the cyanide capsule. If you're going to lock a man up for life, it seems to me he should have the option of shortening that life. I've never been able to understand why they have suicide watches on death row. Why stop a condemned man from killing himself? Hasn't he got the right?'

'I guess so.'

'Gruliow's completely opposed to capital punishment. I can't say I agree with him. That doesn't mean I want to lead parades in favor of it.'

'It's like my position on abortion,' she said. 'Strictly middle-of-the-road. I don't believe it should be illegal, but I don't believe it should be compulsory, either.'

'You're a moderate.'

'You bet.' She gave me what I believe they call a sidelong glance. I don't know what the French call it, but I'm sure they've got a word for it. 'All this talk about death,' she said. 'You wouldn't want to go back to the hotel for an affirmation of life, would you?'

A while later she said, 'Wow. You really, uh, made me see *les étoiles*. That means stars.'

'No kidding.'

'You old bear. God, what you did to me.'

'Well, when in France—'

'That's right, they invented that particular activity, didn't they? Or at least they get the credit. You want to hear something ridiculous?'

'It wouldn't be the first time.'

'I was afraid it might not be as good after we were married.'

'And here we are, acting like a couple of newlyweds.'

'Newlyweds, at our age. Who'da thought?' Her fingers moved to toy with the hair on my chest. She said, 'I like being married.'

'So do I.'

'But it's really just a piece of paper. It doesn't have to change anything.'

'What do you mean?'

'I mean our life works. We don't have to fool with it just because we're wearing wedding rings. They're on our fingers, not in our noses. We can have just as much space in our lives as we had before. I think you should keep your hotel room across the street.'

'Think so?'

'Definitely. Even if all you do is go there when you feel like watching a ball game and staring out the window. That doesn't have to change.' Her hand found mine, squeezed. 'Nothing has to change. We can still go to Marilyn's Chamber once in a while. I can still wear leather and look dangerous.'

'And I can wear my guayabera and look ridiculous.'

'Nothing has to change,' she said. 'Do you hear what I'm saying?'

'I think so.'

'Your private life is your business. Just don't stop loving me.'

'I never have,' I said. 'I never will.'

'You're my bear and I love you,' she said. 'And nothing has to change.'

Early in December I had lunch with Lewis Hildebrand at the Addison Club. Our conversation ranged far and wide in the course of the meal, and over coffee he said, 'I have something to propose to you, and I'm not quite sure how to begin. As you know, our little club has a member who's no longer able to attend meetings. In point of fact, he resigned his membership years ago, but we were under the impression that he had died. Is he still a member? Shall we resume reading his name when he does in fact pass on?'

'Those are interesting questions.'

'And there's no need to answer them now. But in addition to having this member who's not a member, we also have for the first time in our history a nonmember who is intimately acquainted with the club. You've met most of our members, you know our history. As a matter of fact, you've been a part of our history. Some of us were discussing the rather special status you enjoy, and someone suggested that perhaps you ought to be a member.'

I didn't know what to say.

'We have never taken in a new member before,' he said, 'and we've never replaced members who have died, because that would be contrary to our whole design. But this would be a case of replacing a member who has *not* died, and it seems curiously appropriate. Obviously a step of this nature would require the unanimous endorsement of the entire membership.'

'I would think so, yes.'

'And it has received it. Matt, I've been authorized to invite you to take up membership in the club of thirty-one.'

I took a breath. 'I'm honored,' I said.

'And?'

'And I accept.'

This year the first Thursday in May fell on the fifth. I was there in the upstairs banquet room at Keens with the other thirteen surviving members. I listened as Raymond Gruliow, our chapter's senior member, read the names of the deceased members, starting with Philip Kalish and ending with Gerard Billings. He did not read James Severance's name, but the omission did not require a policy decision. Severance is still alive, still chained to the floor of the cabin on Red Hawk Island.

Maybe he'll outlive us all.

Three weeks and a day after our annual dinner, Ray Gruliow called me. 'You'd know this,' he said. 'Do they still have AA meetings at the little storefront on Perry Street?'

'They do indeed,' I said. 'Six or seven times a day.'

'The times I went, the room was so smoky you couldn't see from one end of it to the other.'

'It's smoke-free these days,' I said.

'Well, that's something,' he said. 'I was thinking I might see what the place looks like these days. How'd you like to keep me company?'

I met him at his house and we walked over there

together. He said, 'I feel a little funny about this. I'm sort of a controversial character. And I haven't exactly kept a low profile over the years. I'm in the media all the time.'

'You've even got a sandwich named after you.'

'I told you about that, huh?'

'Listen, if some deli owner made a sandwich and called it the Matt Scudder, I'd tell the whole world. But what's your biggest fear, Ray? That people at Perry Street will recognize you? Or that they won't?'

He stopped in midstride, looked at me, and let out a bark of laughter. 'Jesus,' he said, 'it really is all ego, isn't it?'

'Pretty much.'

'My wife left. That's three marriages down the toilet. Last week I was hung over during jury selection and made a really bad call. And my liver's swollen, and I woke up the day before yesterday and couldn't remember how I got home. And just before I called you I was thinking about Severance and it struck me that it wouldn't be that bad to stick my neck in a noose and kick the chair away. You know something? I don't give a shit who recognizes me and who doesn't. Something's got to change while I can still recognize myself.'

'It sounds as though you're ready.'

'Jesus,' he said, 'I hope you're right.'

'So do I,' I said. 'The last time I took a guy to a meeting, it didn't work out too well.'

also available from

THE ORION PUBLISHING GROUP

☐ **A Dance at the Slaughterhouse**
£5.99
LAWRENCE BLOCK
0 75272 746 4

☐ **The Devil Knows You're Dead**
£5.99
LAWRENCE BLOCK
0 75282 747 2

☐ **Eight Million Ways to Die** £5.99
LAWRENCE BLOCK
1 85799 725 5

☐ **Even the Wicked** £5.99
LAWRENCE BLOCK
0 75380 218 x

☐ **Everybody Dies** £5.99
LAWRENCE BLOCK
0 75282 683 2

☐ **In the Midst of Death** £5.99
LAWRENCE BLOCK
1 85799 415 9

☐ **Hit Man** £5.99
LAWRENCE BLOCK
0 75282 592 5

☐ **Out on the Cutting Edge** £5.99
LAWRENCE BLOCK
1 85799 304 7

☐ **The Sins of the Fathers** £5.99
LAWRENCE BLOCK
1 85799 413 2

☐ **A Stab in the Dark** £5.99
LAWRENCE BLOCK
1 85799 726 3

☐ **A Ticket to the Boneyard** £5.99
LAWRENCE BLOCK
1 85799 312 8

☐ **Time to Murder and Create**
£5.99
LAWRENCE BLOCK
0 75282 749 9

☐ **A Walk Among the Tombstones**
£5.99
LAWRENCE BLOCK
1 85799 302 0

☐ **When the Sacred Ginmill Closes**
£5.99
LAWRENCE BLOCK
1 85799 724 7

All Orion/Phoenix titles are available at your local bookshop or from the following address:

Littlehampton Book Services
Cash Sales Department L
14 Eldon Way, Lineside Industrial Estate
Littlehampton
West Sussex BN17 7HE

telephone 01903 721596, *facsimile* 01903 730914

Payment can either be made by credit card (Visa and Mastercard accepted) or by sending a cheque or postal order made payable to *Littlehampton Book Services*.
DO NOT SEND CASH OR CURRENCY.

Please add the following to cover postage and packing

UK and BFPO:
£1.50 for the first book, and 50P for each additional book to a maximum of £3.50

Overseas and Eire:
£2.50 for the first book plus £1.00 for the second book and 50p for each additional book ordered

----

BLOCK CAPITALS PLEASE

name of cardholder ....

address of cardholder ....

....

....

postcode ....

delivery address
(if different from cardholder)

....

....

....

postcode ....

☐ I enclose my remittance for £................................

☐ please debit my Mastercard/Visa (delete as appropriate)

card number ⬚⬚⬚⬚⬚⬚⬚⬚⬚⬚⬚⬚⬚⬚⬚⬚

expiry date ⬚⬚⬚⬚

signature ....

prices and availability are subject to change without notice

For Kim—my partner in crimes of passion

—NM

EXTINCTION

Many species have become extinct because of human destruction of their natural environments. Indeed, current rates of human-induced extinctions are estimated to be about 1,000 times greater than past natural rates of extinction, leading some scientists to call modern times the sixth mass extinction.

—*Encyclopedia Britannica*

TOY

A material object for children or others to play with (often an imitation of some familiar object); a plaything; also, something contrived for amusement rather than for practical use.

— *The Oxford English Dictionary*

Prologue

7-4 DAY

I WILL NOT forget this moment for as long as I live, which, in truth, might not be that long anyway. I pop the ominous disc labeled "7-4 Day" into the player and sit back on the dusty, thread-bare couch in my parents' cluttered fallout shelter at our beloved lake house in the north country.

I figure that something titled "7-4 Day" can't be good news.

And it isn't.

Wham!—no slow reveal, no fade-in. There are just bodies everywhere. Human beings are slumped in car seats, collapsed on sidewalks, lying on the floor in front of the counter at a once popular fast-food restaurant called McDonald's.

Next comes a classroom in which high school

students and their teacher are just lying, pale and bloated, at their desks.

A construction worker is dead in a cherry-picker, and it is possible that his eyes have actually popped from his face.

A postman is sprawled on a porch, the mail still held dutifully in his hands.

A towheaded girl is dead on her bicycle at the bottom of a roadside culvert—and this finally brings tears to my eyes.

It's as if some master switch has been thrown, turning off their hearts and brains just as they went about their daily lives.

Not everyone's dead though.

In one indelible scene, elevator doors are pried open and a screaming, traumatized business-woman emerges—at least seven corpses of business types are visible behind her.

There is some hope at least.

A few hundred survivors are gathered at mid-field in a baseball stadium, possibly in New Chicago. The camera pans around. *Horrible!* The pitcher is dead on the mound, his face buried in dust. There are uniformed bodies at the bases, in the outfield, in the dugouts. The stands are filled with fifty thousand forever-silent fans.

I'm light-headed and ill as I sit on my parents' couch and watch all this. I've been forgetting to breathe, actually; my skin is clammy and cold.

Now I view a snapped-off flagpole displayed against an urban skyline—a skyline of blackened, broken, and smoking buildings. They're like teeth in a jawbone that somebody has pulled from a funeral pyre.

I'm beginning to suspect that this footage *must* have been staged—but who could have made such a clever and horrifying film? How had they been able to pull off this hoax with such authenticity? And for what possible reason?

Now there's street-level, hand-shot footage showing thousands of people coursing over bridges and along highways. They're carrying coolers, water bottles, blankets, small children, the infirm. There are furtive close-ups of military patrol vehicles at intervals along the way. Checkpoints. Tall, broad-shouldered government soldiers with mirror-faced helmets and automatic weapons attempt to bring order to this incomprehensible chaos.

The film's final scenes are of earthmoving machines and the enormous trenches they've made. These trenches are as wide and deep as strip mines. Bulldozers are standing by to help refill them, their scoops loaded with the uncountable dead.

The video ends and I sit in the dark, lost in shock, horror, and total confusion.

Is it some sick joke? A staged holocaust? Am I supposed to believe that some hideous plague has been hidden from history? When did it happen? Why have I never seen anything like it before? Why has *no one* ever seen or heard about this?

There are no answers to my questions. How could there be? What I have just witnessed simply isn't possible.

Suddenly there are hands on my shoulder, and I leap up from the couch, fists clenched, crashing into an end table and knocking a coffee cup to the concrete floor. There is the sound of breaking glass, and my heart nearly explodes.

"Hays! It's just me. Dad. Hays, *it's me!* Down, boy."

Of course, it was just my father putting his hands on my shoulders, meaning to comfort me. Still, I can't quite give him a pass for this. It is his shelter, and his damned film, and his hands.

6

"*What*—what was that?" I demand to know. "Tell me. Please? Explain it."

"That film?" he says. "That, Hays, is the truth. That's what really happened on 7-4 Day. They almost killed off the entire human race. What you learned in grade school, everything you read at university, is just a cruel hoax."

Book One

FALL FROM GRACE

Chapter 1

FORTY-EIGHT HOURS EARLIER—a mere two days before I watched the 7-4 Day film at my parents' house.

When I arrived at President Hughes Jacklin's inauguration party that night in the year 2061, I was flying high, happier and more self-satisfied than I had ever been. I couldn't have dreamed I would end up losing everything I cared about— my home, my job, my two darling daughters, Chloe and April, and my beautiful wife, Lizbeth, who was there by my side.

In the catastrophic whirlwind of those next horrible days, it would seem as if my world had been turned upside down and any part of my personality that wasn't securely bolted in place had fallen into the void. And what was left was what I guess you'd call the essential Hays Baker—well, if you brought the old me and the new me to a party, I guarantee nobody would accuse us of a family resemblance.

Lizbeth and I arrived at the presidential estate at around eight thirty, delivered in high style by our artificially intelligent Daimler SX-5500 limo. This wasn't our usual car, of course.

A cheery, top-of-the-line iJeeves butler helped us out onto the resplendent, putting-green-short grass of the front lawn. We promptly began to gawk at our surroundings—like a couple of tourists, I suppose. Hell, like lowly *humans* given an unlikely glimpse of the good life.

Even now, I remember that the warm night air was sweet with the fragrance of thousands of roses, gardenias, and other genetically enhanced flowering plants in the president's gardens, all programmed to bloom tonight. What a botanical miracle it was, though a bit show-offy, I'd say.

"This is absolutely incredible, Hays. Dazzling, *inspiring*," Lizbeth gushed, her gorgeous eyes shining with excitement. "We really do run the world, don't we?"

By "we," Lizbeth wasn't talking about just herself and me. She was speaking of our broader identity as ruling Elites, the upper echelon of civilized society for the past two decades.

Most Elites were attractive, of course, but Lizbeth, with her violet hair set off by ivory skin and an almost decadent silver silk gown, well, she sparkled like a diamond dropped into a pile of wood chips.

"You're going to knock them dead, Jinxie," I said, winking. "As always."

"Flattery," she said, winking back, "will get you everywhere."

Jinxie was my favorite nickname for her. It stemmed from the fact that she'd come into this world on a Friday the thirteenth, but there wasn't a single thing unlucky about her—or our life together, for that matter.

I took her tastefully bejeweled hand in mine, inwardly thrilled that she was my wife. God, how I loved this woman. How lucky I was to be with her, as husband, as father to our two daughters.

Every head turned as we walked into the huge, high-ceilinged ballroom, and you'd have thought we were music or film stars from the bygone human era.

But not everybody in the high-society Elite crowd was pleased to see Lizbeth and me.

Well, hey, you can't make everyone happy. Isn't that the sanest way to view the world? Of course it is.